Also by WILLIAM BERNHARDT

CAPITOL CONSPIRACY

CAPITOL
CONSPIRACY

A NOVEL

WILLIAM
BERNHARDT

BALLANTINE BOOKS • NEW YORK

Copyright © 2008 by William Bernhardt

Published in the United States by Ballantine Books, an imprint of The Random House Publishing Group, a division of Random House, Inc., New York.

BALLANTINE and colophon are registered trademarks of Random House, Inc.

Library of Congress Cataloging-in-Publication Data
Bernhardt, William.
Capitol conspiracy : a novel / William Bernhardt.
p. cm.
ISBN 978-0-345-48756-8 (alk. paper)
1. Kincaid, Ben (Fictitious character)—Fiction.   2. Legislators—United States—Fiction.
3. National Security—United States—Fiction.   4. War on terrorism, 2001—Fiction.
5. Washington (D.C.)—Fiction.   6. Political fiction.   I. Title.
PS3552.E73147C35   2008
813'.54—dc22   2007028570

Printed in the United States of America on acid-free paper

www.ballantinebooks.com

2 4 6 8 9 7 5 3 1

First Edition

For Karis, my sister
mother, doctor, darling

Constitutions are merely the lengthened shadows of men. They are invented by men to protect themselves from one another. When they fail to do that, when the fate of human society is at stake, more drastic measures must be taken for society's own sake.

—Ralph Waldo Emerson

CAPITOL CONSPIRACY

Prologue

Abandoned warehouse
Georgetown, Washington, D.C.

*Y*ou're a proud man, Marshall told himself when he regained
consciousness, *and a proud man doesn't scream. No matter
what they do to him.* He was a former marine. He was trained to resist. So when they first began hitting him, he almost wanted to
laugh. Did they seriously believe he would betray his country because of that? They would never get anything out of him. This became his mantra. It was a form of self-hypnosis; he would immunize
himself against the pain.

It worked—for the first four minutes. Then he screamed with
such ferocity that he could not stop long enough to breathe.

They did not relent. They hit him again and again.

He was securely tied to a chair; there was nothing he could do
to stop them. They took turns, one after the other, which made the
blows rain down on his battered body all the more quickly. The one
called the General worked on his abdomen while his sadistic underling kicked him repeatedly, at the base of his spine, his groin, the

front of his kneecaps. He kicked and kicked over and over again on the same tender knee until Marshall felt something break. He realized to his disgust and despair that despite the unbearable new shock wave of misery that coursed through his body, it was not physically possible for him to scream any louder than he was already screaming.

"You will give me the code name," the General said, and then he hit Marshall again, without even waiting for a reply. Marshall couldn't make him out: he wasn't sure if the man was dark-skinned or merely shrouded in darkness. The room was nearly black but he sensed a window behind him that permitted the faintest moonlight into his utterly barren surroundings. It didn't help for long. Nothing was visible to Marshall now, because his eyes were swollen shut.

"Can't . . . ," Marshall mumbled in a broken voice that sounded nothing like his own.

"You mean you won't," the General said, and he drove his fist into Marshall's putty face with such blinding speed that it burst his nose like a balloon. Blood and cartilage flew through the air.

The General grinned, wiped the mess away with a rag, flipped it back into Marshall's face, and repeated himself. "Give me the code name."

Marshall could taste his own blood and flesh. He wanted to wipe it away, wanted to feel himself to see what was left of his face, but his hands were bound fast. "I . . . can't."

"Won't."

"I can't."

"Won't."

"*Can't!*"

"Will."

His scream was silent, as Marshall felt the second kneecap shatter, because he had no more air left in his lungs. But the sound in his head was more intense than anything he had heard in his entire forty-seven years. And then, mercifully, he succumbed to unconsciousness.

They woke him.

And when he still refused to talk, they cut him. They put a

bowie knife at the base of his receding hairline and skinned him, scalp and hair and all. They sliced off an ear. They ruined his face, cutting around his eyes and down his cheeks, always careful not to inflict a fatal wound, avoiding the eye sockets and the carotid artery, but skillfully inflicting the maximum pain possible. Nothing bled like a head wound, he knew, and soon his face was bathed in his own blood. And still they would not stop cutting.

Every nerve was on fire, sending electrical ribbons of pain radiating through him. As unconsciousness clamped its cold black shroud around him once more, he was gripped with terror—but not because of the pain.

He realized, when they ruined his face, that there was no chance they could ever let him go.

The next time Marshall woke, at least the next time he remembered, he had been stripped naked and strung from the ceiling, hanging by his outstretched arms like raw beef in a meat locker, his useless legs dangling tantalizingly close to the floor without touching it. He did not know how long he had been hanging, but he knew they had been working on him the whole time, even while he was unconscious. Hours. Days. Every muscle and tendon was stretched beyond capacity. His arms felt as if they had been ripped from their sockets. Perhaps they had been; surely the pain could be no worse.

"I can make this end," the General growled. "All you must do is give me the name. Then it will be over."

"You'll . . . never . . . let me live," Marshall mumbled, his tongue thick and numb.

"Nor did I claim I would. But I can make your suffering end."

"Can't."

"Don't be a fool."

"Can't . . . *aaaahhh*!"

Marshall thought he had been skewered like a bull polished off by a matador, like a dumb animal in a slaughterhouse. He wanted to curl up in a fetal ball, but he couldn't—couldn't move at all. He could only dangle like a piñata, unable to help himself, unable to do anything but wait for the next blow to arrive.

If they were less . . . effective, Marshall was certain he could resist indefinitely. If they went too far and killed him, it would be over. But he knew they would not do that. And he realized now that even he, with all his strength and training, could not resist forever.

"Give me the name!"

"It's . . . it's . . ." Marshall tried to catch his breath, tried to enunciate despite his missing teeth. ". . . Hawkman."

Even though he was blind, Marshall sensed the slight change, the tiny play of the General's expression. He was considering.

The wait seemed eternal. The beating briefly subsided. Marshall could feel his heart pounding fiercely as he waited for the verdict.

"No," the General said finally. "You are lying."

"No," Marshall choked. "I'm not!"

"You are. The valiant always attempt a lie at first, until they learn that it will hurt them, not help them. I am not a man who likes to be lied to. You have made your situation much worse."

Worse? Could it possibly be worse?

"A man such as Blake would never accept such a code name. It is too . . . politically suggestive. You're lying."

Marshall braced himself for the excruciating agony he knew would follow—but it did not come. Somehow that was even more frightening.

He heard a faint click of rubber-heeled boots receding, then returning. A moment later, he heard a splashing noise.

"I wish for you to recall," the General said, as the splashing continued, "that you have no one to blame for this but yourself. I have given you every possible opportunity. But it will soon be daylight. I must have this information."

Marshall knew his thinking was muddled; all the blows to the head had probably given him a concussion, maybe brain damage. What was coming next?

And then, despite the extreme damage to his nose, Marshall detected the acrid noxious fumes that fired every broken capillary in his nostrils.

Gasoline fumes.

After the General had splattered the floor in a circle around his dangling victim, he doused Marshall himself. Marshall felt the fuel enter his mouth, his eyes, the open wounds and festering sores that covered his body.

"Please . . . don't," he managed, his voice rasping.

"Give me the name."

"Please don't do this."

"The name!"

"I have a wife. Three girls—"

"Give me the name or I will burn you all to hell!"

Marshall's jaw dangled open. He had resisted so long, had endured so much. But who could possibly have the strength to let this sadist burn him alive?

"Samson," he whispered, weeping, tears somehow managing to seep out of his swollen and bloodied eyes.

"Samson," the General repeated, and again Marshall could sense him running the possibility through his head. "Yes, that I can believe. It would flatter his ego." The General pressed himself close to Marshall's broken face. "And the other?"

"The . . . other?"

"Do not play games with me. You know what I want. Samson and—what? What is the other name?"

"Delilah. I—isn't it—" He found it impossible to catch his breath, the pungent scent of gasoline was so pervasive. "Isn't it . . . obvious?"

"Ah." Again, the General considered. "Yes, it is obvious." Another pause. "Much too obvious."

Marshall heard a flicking noise, then felt heat on his cheek. Even with his eyes sealed shut, he knew his torturer had just ignited a lighter.

"Juliet!" Marshall shouted. "Samson and Juliet!"

The General emitted a soft chuckle of appreciation. "Clever." And then he dropped the lighter.

Flames encircled Marshall. He could feel fire licking the hair on his broken legs.

"But—but you said—"

"Now you will give me the defense formation," the General said calmly. "Every detail you know."

"But—I can't!"

"Must we go through all that again? Your feet are already black. You are burning like a chicken on a rotisserie spit. Is that not enough? Fine." Marshall heard a sudden splashing noise that told him the bastard was adding more gasoline to the flames.

He heard a sudden whooshing sound that signaled the floor erupting with fire.

"Nooooo!" Marshall screamed as he felt his own flesh peeling away. His feet were already dead, gone, and the flames were working their way up his legs.

"You will be dead in seconds," the General said, "if I do not douse the flames."

"And . . . you'll never get . . . what you want . . ."

In one rapid movement, the General brandished the knife used to mutilate Marshall's face and cut free the ropes that held Marshall's arms to the ceiling hook. Marshall tumbled into the inferno. He cried out and gagged as his lungs filled with smoke and his flesh began to swell and bloat. His assailant was right—he would be dead in seconds. And he was glad.

To his great disappointment, the General hauled him out of the flames. "Tell me what I wish to know!" he bellowed.

Marshall wanted to laugh. He knew he would be gone soon. What more could the man do to him? "Never."

The dark man pressed both thumbs into the most tender and seared part of his thigh. The pain was like nothing Marshall had ever experienced, not even throughout this entire unbearable ordeal. It was as if his body had been turned inside out and a branding iron had been thrust into his heart.

"I do not have time for this!" the General bellowed. *"Tell me!"*

"It—won't help. I'll be missed—"

"We know about your meeting with the senator. Arrangements have been made." He pressed several fingers deep down in the same open festering third-degree burn. "Tell me!"

"No!"

Marshall felt himself being hauled by the neck, his exposed scalp and one remaining ear dragged bleeding across the floor. He sensed he was moving closer to the window. But his attacker did not bother to open it. He hoisted Marshall's broken body into the air and heaved him through it.

Marshall felt himself falling—then jerked to a sudden stop.

The General held him by one charred foot dangling limply from a shattered kneecap. "You are forty-five feet in the air. After you fall, I will take what is left of you and feed it to your wife. And then I will do to her everything I have done to you. Except more slowly."

"No. God, no," Marshall cried, whimpering.

"Then tell me!" the General shouted.

And then the information spilled out, one detail after another, everything Marshall had. He knew he was betraying his country and so many who trusted and relied upon him. He could not help himself.

"And the defense formation?"

"Domino Bravo! It's . . . Domino Bravo!"

The General slowly drew in his breath. "At last. I was beginning to think—well, I've never done this before."

Through his clouded brain, Marshall tried to understand. "Never . . . tortured?"

He heard a soft chuckle. "Never tortured the director of Homeland Security." And then he released Marshall's foot and listened to his final screams as he plummeted to the concrete embankment that would shatter each of the few bones in his body that remained intact.

U.S. CAPITOL BUILDING
WASHINGTON, D.C.

"Still no word from Marshall?" Senator Robert Hammond, D-Iowa, asked his secretary of thirty-two years.

"No," Marjorie replied, pushing her wide-rimmed translucent pink eyeglasses up the bridge of her nose. "But he's only ten minutes late."

"The man has never been late for a meeting in his life, Marjorie. He's a former marine, you know."

"I think you could give him five minutes before you call out the search and rescue dogs."

"Are you suggesting that I'm overreacting?" Hammond replied, with mock irritation, tugging at his vest. Hammond was perhaps the only senator left who still wore three-piece suits every day he went to work. He felt they worked better with the bow tie.

"As I recall, when Bill Clinton was ten minutes late for a meeting, you were on the phone to the Secret Service."

Hammond grinned. "And as it turned out, they didn't know where he was, either. Should've called his intern."

"When former President Bush was late, you called the secretary of defense, suspecting some dastardly plot. What was it again?"

"Decided to jog another lap around the Rose Garden with Barney. His dog."

"And if I'm not mistaken, when they first allowed female pages in the Senate, you predicted the end of the world."

"You've made your point, Marjorie." Hammond gazed out the window of his premium office in the Rayburn Building. As Senate minority leader and the official liaison with Homeland Security, he was entitled to a perk like this view of the smooth green expanse of the Capitol lawn with the Supreme Court building in the background. Beyond that he could just barely make out the Potomac as it flowed from Georgetown on the west all the way to Anacostia on the east.

There were other more tangible privileges for a man in his position. Twice as many hideaways as any other senator. The best illegal Cuban cigars, the first-cut Kentucky bourbon . . . and a few other perks that kept him very warm at night. He'd had a good career and he didn't plan to see it end any time soon, thank you. Many had tried to bring him down—from LBJ to Ben Kincaid. But guess what? He was still here.

That last conversation with Marshall had troubled him, though. And now with this on top of everything else . . .

He ran a hand through his silver pomaded hair. "I'm still concerned, Marjorie. Particularly given—" He turned back to face her. "Call his cell phone."

"As you wish. Oh—have you seen this?"

"Seen what?"

She handed a sealed letter to him. "Something from Marshall. Courier brought it over early this morning. Probably explains why he's not here."

"Hmmph. Couldn't the man just pick up the phone?"

"He probably could, but I don't think you'd be allowed to talk unless you knew the password. And with your memory . . ."

"Ha-ha." He placed a wrinkled finger under the envelope flap, but before he had it half open, a white powder spilled onto his hands.

"What the—?" Marjorie was about to speak, but before she could, the elderly senator moved it closer to his face to get a better look—and immediately regretted it.

"Oh my God. Oh my God."

"Robert? What is it?"

"Get out of here, Marjorie."

"But what—"

"I said, Get out of here! Leave!" He already felt his knees buckling. His stomach knotted and his digestive tract began to cramp. "Get everyone out. The whole staff. Lock the door behind you. Seal it. And don't let anyone in until the Capitol Police arrive."

"But—"

"Marjorie! Do it!" His body began to shake. He realized he was going into shock. Bad memory or not, he remembered the briefing they had all been given when the white powder was found in Senator Frist's mailroom. "Damn. *Damn!*"

Marjorie fled the office. Senator Hammond crumpled to the floor. Barely thirty seconds had passed, but his organs were already beginning to liquefy. Blood seeped from his ears and his eye sockets.

Damn it, this was not how he wanted to go out. He still had work to do!

To his credit, his last thought was not of himself. He thought of Marshall, of what must have happened to him. He realized the only possible reason someone would want to kill him, here, now. He was helpless, paralyzed, as every cell in his body was systematically attacked and destroyed. He heard the pounding of heavy-booted footsteps out in the corridor, but he knew the Capitol Police would not get to him in time.

"Oklahoma City," he whispered to the lead police officer, with his final breath. Then he closed his eyes and passed from being the most powerful Democratic senator in the country to being a helpless puddle on the carpet.

Part One

To Ensure Domestic Tranquility

1

THE OKLAHOMA CITY NATIONAL MEMORIAL
OKLAHOMA CITY, OKLAHOMA

Ben Kincaid stood at the corner of Lincoln Boulevard, still unable to believe he was really about to meet the President of the United States. In his short time as a replacement senator he had viewed President Blake from a distance, even attended ceremonies at the White House—but an actual face-to-face meeting was something else again. Was it only yesterday he was a small-time attorney with a struggling, profitless practice and a shoddy office in downtown Tulsa? It seemed that way. The whirlwind of events that had put him in the Washington limelight still seemed unreal. And the most unreal part was that his meteoric rise to the U.S. Senate was not the most amazing, unbelievable, life-shattering thing that had happened to him recently.

He stared at the gold band on the ring finger of his left hand, incredulous.

Ben Kincaid was a married man.

Major Mike Morelli, standing just beside him, leaned toward Ben's ear. "Still can't believe it, huh?"

"No. I was convinced I'd be a bachelor my entire life."

Mike did a double take. "Ben—I was talking about shaking hands with the leader of the free world."

"Oh."

"This is a major event."

"Getting married is a major event."

"Ah, the lover. 'Sighing like furnace, with a woeful ballad / Made to his mistress's eyebrow.' "

"If you're going to start with the poetry, I'm disinviting you," Ben said. "It's just a big life change, that's all. After you've been single so long."

"Poor boy. 'So we'll go no more a-roving / So late into the night . . .' "

"I think I'm hearing poetry again."

"You need to relax, Ben. People get married all the time. In fact, some people get married several times. But there's only one president."

Ben shrugged. "I didn't vote for him."

"You didn't vote at all!"

"I voted for Christina. Till death us do part."

Mike rolled his eyes. "You are too sappy for words."

"I recall a time—" Ben stopped short. He remembered when Mike was in the flush of new love—with Ben's younger sister, Julia. He and Ben had been college roommates, Mike an English major, Ben studying music, when Mike met Julia. After a whirlwind courtship, they were married, but the union didn't last long. Julia fled to somewhere on the East Coast and neither of them had seen her in years. Happily, despite this trauma and the deep scars it left, he and Mike had remained best friends throughout the intervening years, as Ben established his law practice and Mike rose to become a senior homicide investigator with the Tulsa Police Department.

Mike glanced at him, a small sad smile flickering on his face. They'd known each other long enough that Ben didn't have to finish the sentence.

As if he sensed the need for a mood change, Mike's expression suddenly shifted to a broad and rather naughty grin. "Speaking of your new bride—is she still pissed?"

Ben's neck stiffened. "I wouldn't put it quite like that."

"I'll bet. 'Hell hath no fury . . .' "

"She's just . . ." Ben drew in his breath, then slowly released it. ". . . Grumpy."

"Imagine. And all you did was cancel her honeymoon."

"There were extenuating circumstances. President Blake personally requested that I be here when he visited my home state."

"But that didn't satisfy Christina?"

"You know how . . . forceful she can be. Plus, she's wanted to see France all her life." He paused. "Plus, the man is a Republican."

Mike smirked. "Which I guess explains why she's not standing beside you playing the loyal wife."

Ben shuffled his feet. "Well, someone had to stay in the gallery with my mother."

"Senator Kincaid?"

Ben felt a light tap on his shoulder. The man standing behind him was young, perhaps early thirties, sandy-haired. He was wearing a midnight-blue suit, thin tie, and sunglasses, which Ben knew meant he must be one of the dozens of Secret Service agents stationed around the Oklahoma City National Memorial. "Yes?"

"I'm Agent Max Zimmer. I'm here to escort you to the reception position, where the cameras and crowd can see the president emerge from Cadillac One"—he smiled—"from a safe distance."

But of course. It wasn't as if the president had asked him here because of his deep personal affection. After that business over the nomination of Justice Roush to the Supreme Court, it was a miracle the man would speak to Ben at all. What he wanted was to be seen at an important Oklahoma event with a newly minted senator with unaccountably high approval ratings.

Ben heard what sounded like the buzz of a bumblebee coming from Zimmer's coat sleeve. The agent casually raised the sleeve to his mouth, listened for a moment, then spoke into it. "Understood. Samson in five." He looked up. "Come along, Senator. Time for you and your guest to move."

Ben and Mike followed the agent to the street just behind the

Oklahoma City National Memorial, erected on the site of the former Alfred P. Murrah Federal Building, the office complex that was blown to bits by Timothy McVeigh's fertilizer bomb on this very date, several years before. It was a catastrophic event no Oklahoman would ever forget. Memorial services were held here on this date annually, and this year, the sitting president was in attendance to offer his condolences and help the healing.

And, Ben supposed, the fact that Oklahoma was a borderline red/blue state whose electoral votes were currently uncertain had nothing to do with it.

It was a magnificent memorial, the largest of its kind in the United States, designed to honor the fallen, the survivors, the rescuers, and everyone else whose life had been indelibly changed by the tragedy. Enormous twin bronze gates framed the 3.3-acre expanse within. Because the explosion occurred at 9:02 a.m., the eastern gate was engraved with the time 9:01—the last minute of peace—and the western gate was engraved with 9:03—the first moment of the ensuing horror. A reflecting pool stretched across the center of the memorial between the two gates, a thin layer of water over polished black marble. On one side of the pool was the Field of Empty Chairs: 168 chairs of bronze, glass, and stone, one for each of the people who died in the explosion.

As they walked, Ben saw a face he recognized.

"Brad Tidwell. My senatorial comrade." Ben held out his hand. "Good to see you."

The tall, lanky man in the blue suit took Ben's hand cordially. "Kincaid, you are the worst liar I have ever met."

Ben's face colored.

"Seriously. Worst liar in the history of humanity. Which explains why you'll never make it in politics."

"Or," Mike grumbled, "explains why his approval rating is so much higher than yours."

Tidwell responded with a thin smile that, were Ben in a less charitable mood, he might have called a sneer. "Senator Kincaid has never had the pleasure of conducting an actual campaign. Believe me, if he ever does, his numbers will drop."

Tidwell was a two-term senator based in Oklahoma City. After

Senator Todd Glancy resigned, he had become the state's senior senator, with Ben as his very junior partner. Since they represented different parties, they had spent much of the past few months canceling out each other's votes.

"Since you're a newbie, I wanted to make sure we were clear on protocol: when the president approaches us, I shake his hand first."

Ben caught Mike rolling his eyes.

"Maybe I'm crazy," Ben said, "but shouldn't we let the president decide who he wants to greet first?"

"And he will. He knows how the game is played. You're the one I'm worried about. No grandstand plays for the cameras and the folks back home. Don't lunge for the man's hand."

"If he were stupid enough to lunge for the president's hand," Mike noted, "he would probably be tackled by a dozen Secret Service agents."

"Another good point. See, Kincaid—I'm just looking out for your best interests. Brother senators should be friends."

Riiiight, Ben thought. *And with a friend like you . . .*

They stopped walking as Agent Zimmer approached with another similarly garbed older man. "Senator Kincaid, this is Agent Gatwick, my immediate superior. Everything in place, Tom?"

"Right on schedule."

"Snipers?"

"In place."

"Agents?"

"As planned. Domino Bravo."

"Excellent." Zimmer turned toward the north end of the street. "Here he comes."

Ben followed his gaze and saw a large black sedan followed by what appeared to be an endless stream of black sedans flanked by motorcycle cops. "How many cars are in the presidential motorcade?"

"Twenty-two."

Ben's eyes bulged. "Are you joking? Who's in all of those cars?"

"Secret Service in several. Homeland Security in a few. Local police. Press vans. One car carrying the president's doctor and several refrigerated pints of the president's blood. Various important dignitaries, not important enough for a personal meet-and-greet like you, but important enough to walk to the dais in the president's wake. A counterassault team, to deal with potential attacks. The 'bomb sweep'—that's the first police car. It has the unpleasant and danger-ous job of clearing the way for the motorcade. Another eight or so vehicles—the 'secure package'—will split off from the motorcade and take the president somewhere safe in the event of an emer-gency."

Ben continued to stare. "Is that the president's car?"

"Nah. The Beast will be packed somewhere in the middle."

"The Beast?"

Agent Gatwick nodded. "That's what we call the president's car. Cadillac One."

"Why 'The Beast'?"

"Because it's a monster. A real leviathan. A Caddy DTS stretch sedan with satellite GPS and communication equipment. He could call an astronaut on the moon from that car. Carries its own air sup-ply in case someone gasses the outside air. Totally bulletproof—the body is constructed of antiballistic steel paneling and the windows are made from inch-thick polycarbonate glass. In the event of a puncture, the tires can heal themselves."

"It's the Batmobile."

"Basically, yeah. Without the tail fins."

"What's a car like that cost?"

"Last I heard, about twelve million."

Ben whistled.

"And for all that—it gets lousy gas mileage." Behind the sun-glasses, Ben sensed a twinkle in Zimmer's eye. "But it has a hell of a sound system."

Far above the motorcade, in a grandstand recon office tem-porarily constructed on the roof of the adjoining Oklahoma City Memorial Museum, three sets of eyes were trained on the activities below.

"So she made it in time," the oldest of the three, an extremely tall black man, commented.

"Just barely," said the other man in the group. "But from what I hear, they had a little snuggle on Air Force One."

"Never underestimate a woman," said the only female of the three. "She can do anything she wants to."

"I don't doubt it," the younger of the two men replied. "The question was whether she wanted to."

"Don't be absurd. If this is a marriage of political convenience, then it would be pretty stupid to miss a television spot that more than forty million people are expected to view live."

"You seem to have some real insight here. Maybe you should go into politics."

"Tempting. But I would hate campaigning. Can't keep my mouth shut long enough. And I have a few skeletons in my closet."

"Who doesn't?"

"Nerds are the only people who can run for political office in this country these days. To get elected, you have to be one of three possible things: old, homely—or male." She smiled. "I'm none of the above. Also, I enjoy a healthy, unmarried sex life. I'm unelectable."

"But if the reports and rumors I'm getting about the first lady are true—"

"She's here, isn't she?"

"But the scuttlebutt—"

"And she's always there when he needs her, right?"

"But—"

"Don't be so easily misled," the woman said, pointing a finger so close, it almost touched his nose. "All the sex in the world can't compete with the thrill of receiving the applause of millions of potential voters. Remember what Kissinger said."

"And that would be?"

Her upper lip curled in a distinctively naughty manner. "Power is the greatest aphrodisiac."

Joel Salter felt a shiver creep up his spine. Bad enough he had to be the only Feeb in the outpost without that woman here making him supremely uncomfortable. He could still recall a time when this would've been an FBI operation and the Secret Service agents, nominally under the direction of the secretary of treasury, would've been managed by the deputy director of the FBI. Ever since the Secret Service had been transferred to Homeland Security, though, he hated these assignments. He was worse than a third wheel; he wouldn't be useful even in the event of a flat tire. Unless he had some intel to provide, they didn't want any part of the FBI. The general attitude seemed to be that if the FBI had been doing its job, Homeland Security would never have come into existence. People like Carl Lehman and Nichole Muldoon didn't want him tainting their operation.

Muldoon was watching through high-powered binoculars that allowed her to peer through the green-tinted windows of Cadillac One. "My God," she said, "they're not even sitting on the same side. I guess absence does not make the heart grow fonder."

Salter cleared his throat. "My understanding is that she sits facing him so that when the rear door is opened, spectators and cameras will only see the president. An unshared spotlight. A generous gesture, really."

Muldoon snorted. "More likely she wants a minute to pull up her pantyhose." She lowered the glasses and gave Salter another one of those looks. "You might know that, Joel. If you'd ever seen a woman's pantyhose."

He smiled faintly, trying to be a good sport. Truth was, Nichole Muldoon was no worse than most of the women he'd met in his law enforcement career, and was better than some. Certainly smarter than most. But something about her made him feel awkward. And ancient. At forty-six, he was only about a decade older than she. He'd worked hard to get his position in the FBI, as opposed to her meteoric rise in Homeland Security. He had years of experience where she had brains. But all of this was beside the point. At the end of the day, he knew it wasn't her brains that were intimidating him.

The woman was knock-down-drop-dead-heart-stoppingly-pulse-poundingly-oh-my-God beautiful. She didn't even have to try. Didn't need makeup. She could stand there in a beige business suit with a little gold-buttoned jacket and it looked like a floor-length ruby red ball gown with a slit up the side and cleavage down to her navel. Nichole Muldoon had the look—the Look—that forced you to fantasize about what it would be like to have sex with her, even though you knew there wasn't the slightest chance of it ever happening.

He couldn't even have the pleasure of blaming her for the effect she had on him, suggesting she was using sex appeal to get ahead. As far as he knew, she was totally oblivious to the impact she was having on his libido. Sure, she made remarks about the first lady's sex life and the size of the president's equipment, but who didn't? That was SOP in the sheltered world of Protect-the-President. That was just being one of the boys. If anything, that behavior should make him forget she was a beautiful woman. But he didn't. Not ever. Not for one second. All she had to do was toss that shoulder-length blond hair back and he was orbiting Jupiter.

"Did you hear what I said, Joel?"

He jerked to attention. "I'm sorry. I was . . . surveying the crowd."

Carl Lehman frowned down at him. *Great. Make the deputy director of Homeland Security think you're an idiot. That'll push you up the ranks.* "I told you we still haven't located Marshall."

"Really?" He had to seem surprised, even though he wasn't. "Did someone call his wife?"

"Yeah. She's clueless."

"Didn't he disappear once before?"

"Yeah." Lehman ran his hand over the top of his head as if he had hair, although there hadn't been any for many years. But since he was so much taller than anyone else in the room, who could notice? "We weren't on duty that day. Samson wasn't out amongst the Philistines."

"Any cause for concern?"

Muldoon jabbed him in the side. "You know Carl. The rising of the sun in the morning is cause for concern."

"But your people know what to do, right?" Salter asked. "They don't need Marshall breathing over their shoulders."

"True enough," Lehman agreed. "But it's still strange. Damn strange." He drew in his breath, then slowly released it. "I suppose I'm just an old man worrying about nothing. Look," he said, pointing toward the tableau below. "Samson is getting out of The Beast."

. . .

The first six cars in the motorcade passed by, but the seventh slowed precisely opposite where Ben and the others were standing. Two police motorcycles swirled around the car, sirens blaring. Ben felt a tingle course through his body. Even though the windows were tinted, he knew who was sitting in the backseat of that car. It would be hard to miss. The presidential seals were emblazoned on the rear doors; an American flag flew proudly from the bumper.

Zimmer talked into his sleeve again. "Roger. Samson has arrived." He leaned closer to Ben. "See the presidential standard raised from the left front fender? That tells us that the commander in chief is inside the vehicle."

Zimmer stepped forward and pressed the security release button under the handle that allowed the door to be opened from the outside. Ben felt a sharp intake of breath. At first, all he could see was the interior of the car—blue leather upholstery with wood veneer accents. He spotted a fold-out desk being returned to its upright position. A long leg in a blue suit emerged. Behind the dark, green-tinted window, Ben saw the outline of a familiar female face.

Beside him, Ben sensed Senator Tidwell inch ever so subtly forward.

Zimmer helped President Franklin M. Blake from the car while Gatwick positioned himself behind. A dotted circle of agents surrounded the car, some of them scanning the horizon, some of them scanning the sky.

Behind the rope line, a huge swell of shouting and applause erupted. The president waved, smiled, then turned his attention to the phalanx of people waiting to greet him.

The president spotted Senator Tidwell and nodded, spotted Ben and nodded . . .

Then he walked directly up to Mike and shook his hand.

"A pleasure to meet you, Major Morelli. A real pleasure."

Mike was obviously stunned. His usual savoir faire had utterly abandoned him. "A . . . p-pleasure to—to meet you, too, Mr. President."

"I was very pleased when I heard Senator Kincaid had invited you. Always glad to meet a true public servant, someone who puts himself on the line for the common good. If there could be any benefit emerging from 9/11, it's that we've all come to realize just how important the work you and your brethren do really is."

Mike was still shaking his hand. "I—I don't know what to say."

"You don't have to say anything," the president replied, gently using his left hand to extract his right. His mostly gray hair shone in the morning sun. "Your work says it all for you. I'm a fan."

Mike's lips parted, a blank expression on his face. "You're—a fan—of mine?"

"Absolutely. That work you did on the Kindergarten Killer case—outstanding. Showed up the Feds on that one, didn't you?" he added, winking collegially. "No telling how many lives you saved. Made the world a better place, that's for sure."

"But—" Mike stammered. He still couldn't think clearly. "How do you know about that case?"

President Blake took a step to the right. "Because I read this man's book." He extended his hand again. "How are you, Senator Kincaid?"

Ben felt startled and confused. "You read my book?"

"Both of them, actually. Excellent pieces of work, though I preferred the first." He winked again. "Have to. I'm a law and order candidate."

Ben struggled to work his head through this revelation, without success.

"Meant to tell you," the president continued. "Appreciated the hard work you did to get Justice Roush on the Supreme Court."

It was Ben's turn to arch an eyebrow. The president may have nominated Justice Roush, but he and his party abandoned him when it was revealed that Roush was gay. "You did?"

"First rule of politics, Senator—don't jump to any conclusions. I did what my party required. We can't afford to lose the support of the religious right. But Thaddeus Roush was a fine man when I nominated him and he remains one today."

"Yes, sir. Thank you, sir."

As if he were passing through butter, President Blake eased on down the line. "Senator Tidwell. Good to see you."

Ben didn't have to be a mind reader to know that Tidwell was fuming. Ben could almost sympathize. Tidwell was the only member of the president's party in the reception line and he was the last to be received.

"And you, Mr. President."

As if to give the last man a special bonus, the president leaned forward slightly and placed his hand on Tidwell's shoulder. "I've seen that energy bill you co-sponsored. I like it."

"Thank you," Tidwell said. Ben noticed that even this two-term senator was stammering a bit. "Does that mean we can count on you to sign the bill after it's passed?"

The president smiled the sort of wide, friendly, earnest-looking grin that could get a man elected to the highest office in the land. "I said I liked it, Brad. Signing is a whole different thing. You can't marry every woman you like." He pivoted. "Which reminds me of a woman I like very much."

As he turned, the first lady, Emily Blake, stepped from the limo. If anything, the chorus of hooting and hollering that followed exceeded the reception that had been given the president. Emily Blake was younger than her husband, but not by so much as to attract discussion. She was medium-sized, dark-haired, and dressed in a tasteful but sensible manner that reflected her tasteful but sensible demeanor. Ben knew she was extremely popular, especially in the Southwest.

The president took her hand, helped her off the curb, then raised both their hands into the air. The crowd went wild.

"Listen to that," Tidwell murmured in Ben's ear. "Her approval ratings are considerably higher than his and he knows it. He's milking her for everything she's got."

"Isn't that a bit cynical?" Ben said, as he watched the First Couple bathe in the limelight. "It's hardly unusual for a man to bring his wife to a major event."

Tidwell made a snorting noise. "He didn't bring her. She flew in from Tucson. They met at the OKC airport down the road."

Ben nodded. Oklahoma City's Will Rogers World Airport was one of only three very special airports named for men who died in a plane crash. "She probably had a fund-raising event. It's that time again."

Tidwell shook his head. "It's a marriage in name only, contrived purely for political purposes. They don't do anything together. They don't share anything. Not even the First Bedroom."

Ben reared his head back, appalled. "How could you possibly know that?"

Tidwell shrugged in a nonchalant manner that Ben found extremely off-putting. "Word gets around. If you travel in the higher circles."

Which, Ben knew Tidwell was implying, he didn't. But of course—Tidwell was right. Ben didn't know what to make of Tidwell's gratuitous scuttlebutting of his party's leader. Was he ticked off because the president greeted him last? Or was there something more going on?

The Secret Service agent closest to the president lightly touched his sleeve, which Ben knew was the signal for him to move on. Even with all this security, they never liked the president to stay in one place for too long until he had arrived at his destination.

As the First Couple turned toward the dais, the first lady stopped. "Senator Kincaid!"

Ben stood at attention. "Yes, ma'am?"

She smiled, exuding warmth. "Where's that pretty little wife of yours?"

Ben fumbled for words. "She's . . . in the audience. With my mother."

Emily Blake's eyes narrowed. "Is there a reason for that?"

"Well . . ."

"Tell that lovely redhead I'm inviting her to the White House for tea. We need to have a heart-to-heart."

The president took his wife gently by the arm. "Now, Emily. We don't harass a man about his wife. Even if he is a Democrat."

"But, Frank—they're newlyweds."

"That's right. It slipped my mind." He gave Ben another wink. "So what the hell are you doing here, son?"

Secret Service agents Zimmer and Gatwick flanked the president and slowly escorted him toward the dais from which he would speak. All around them, Ben saw agents scurrying into position, watching all possible angles, talking into their sleeves. Ben knew there were at least as many, possibly more, agents working undercover, filtering quietly through the crowd looking for signs of trouble, as well as numerous sniper nests covering not only the ground but the surrounding downtown skyscrapers.

Ben and his group took the stage several steps behind the First Couple and were escorted to their seats. Risers had been erected opposite the reflecting pool to create a presidential platform with seats for important dignitaries behind and to each side. A podium bearing the presidential seal stood in the center. Just beyond the podium, a dense crowd of reporters hovered with mikes and minicams.

Ben marveled at all the activity, all the work that went on behind the scenes of a relatively simple presidential appearance. But he was cheered by the realization that, after so much work, caution, and preparation, nothing could possibly go wrong.

2

At the rear of the stage, Agent Zimmer made a slow circuit from stage right to stage center. He tugged at the hem of his suit jacket. All the agents got their suits a little big in the chest to disguise the fact that they were carrying weapons, currently .357 SIGs. Personally, Zimmer had preferred the previous nine-millimeter version, but oddly enough, the director of Homeland Security hadn't asked for his opinion when the decision was made.

He met Agent Gatwick in the rear center.

"You getting the same reports I'm getting?" Gatwick asked, not looking at him. With the dark sunglasses, it would be impossible for a spectator to know exactly where he was looking.

"About Marshall?"

"Yeah."

"You worried?"

Gatwick scanned the Oklahoma City skyline surrounding the

memorial complex. "I don't think it's worrisome. Weird. But not worrisome."

"He's always played point man for presidential appearances in the past."

"Because he wants to, not because he has to. He knows he can trust us."

Zimmer subtly stepped forward, adjusting his gaze ever so slightly to examine a Middle Eastern–looking woman wearing an overcoat about three people deep behind the rope. An overcoat on a warm Oklahoma City spring day? That was more than enough to raise his suspicion. He whispered into his sleeve, sending three agents to check her out. "So you think that's it? He's decided he can let the little birds fly free?"

Gatwick shrugged. "Who the hell knows? Maybe he got tied up in some Senate meeting. It's happened before."

"Congressional oversight of Homeland Security was a big mistake."

"You're preaching to the choir, bro."

Beyond the rope, Zimmer saw his agents approach the woman in the overcoat and quietly search her and run a metal detector over her body. Through his sleeve receiver, he heard the result. She was clean. Claimed she had some weird disease that lowered her body temperature. Like some kind of human lizard—she was cold even when the sun was shining. Still, Zimmer told them to take down her name and address.

Returning his attention to his partner, he noticed that Gatwick was scrutinizing the first lady.

"I don't like where we've got her," Gatwick said flatly.

"Who? Juliet?"

"Right. Too close to Samson."

"She's to the right and two feet back. Exactly where Samson likes her. So when the cameras shoot him from their assigned station, she can be seen in the background beaming at him with adoring eyes."

The tiniest of smiles cracked Gatwick's stoic facade. "I'm moving her."

"What? Why?"

He tucked his head forward in a quick and almost imperceptible nod. "Only skyscrapers in range are to the south. She doesn't need to be in the potential line of fire."

"Don't we have snipers up there?"

"Yeah. But still—I'm moving her."

Agent Zimmer's brow creased. "I thought it was agreed—Domino Bravo."

"I'm making a slight alteration."

"Don't you think you should get approval first?"

"From who? Marshall's out."

"Then Deputy Director Lehman."

Gatwick bristled. "I'm in charge, at least on site." He whispered a few terse commands into his sleeve. "I'm just moving her to the other side of the stage. What difference can it make?"

Zimmer exhaled slowly. "I suppose it can't hurt anything."

"Course not." At the front of the stage, two agents carried out their new instructions. "This is Oklahoma City, for God's sake. What could happen?"

Ben was pleased to see the first lady move to his side of the stage. He was a good deal more comfortable around her than her husband. He knew in his heart that the only difference between the two was one of methodology, not purpose. Still, when she smiled at him, he couldn't help but feel she was sincere, even when his brain told him not to be so naïve.

She leaned back toward Ben, smiling. "So where did you two go on your honeymoon?"

Mike covered his mouth.

"Uh . . . here."

The first lady gave him a long look. "Your bride must love you very much."

Ben fingered his collar uncomfortably. "Something like that."

The governor of the state of Oklahoma, the same man who had appointed Ben to replace Senator Glancy, was the first to speak. He made several gracious remarks, commented on how lovely the first lady looked, then toned down his smile to establish the appropriate gravitas for the commemorative service to follow. "As Oklahomans, we are a proud and stubborn lot, Boomers and Sooners and settlers and farmers and Native Americans. We will move ever forward, and this gleaming monument is a memorial to our indomitable spirit. But we will never forget."

The governor singled out a few individuals in the crowd, people who had lost husbands, wives, children. He recognized some of the rescue workers who had displayed such valor on that most horrific of days. And when his predetermined five minutes was completed, he said, "Ladies and gentlemen, it is my very great privilege to introduce to you . . . the president of the United States!"

Thunderous applause greeted President Blake as he made his way to the podium. Ben marveled at the ease with which he moved, despite the fact that so many eyes were bearing down upon him. What a burden—to try to think of something to say on such an occasion. Nothing could ever truly comfort the survivors. Words were simply not enough.

As he watched the president approach the podium, he heard Agent Zimmer, standing just behind him on the left, talking into his sleeve again. "What do you mean? In the Senate building? How is that possible?"

The applause began to ebb. On the opposite end of the raised platform, Ben saw Agent Gatwick talking into his sleeve as well. Several of the agents in the rear were signaling one another.

"No, I don't understand," Zimmer whispered. "What has Senator Hammond got to do with Marshall?" There was a pause. All around him, Ben noticed Secret Service agents in motion. "He said what? What does it mean?"

Ben noticed that Mike, sitting beside him, was also observing the sudden increase in activity. "What's going on?"

"I don't know," Mike whispered back. "But something's come up."

Ben saw Agent Zimmer advance toward the podium. Before he could get close, however, the president began his speech.

"My fellow Americans," President Blake said, gripping each side of the podium. Although he had recently hit sixty, he looked older. Like all the presidents before him, he had been aged prematurely by the job. His hair was more gray than black; the tiny creases across his forehead had become pronounced; the folds of flesh around his eyes were so intense, his eyes almost seemed sunken. And yet, for all that, he was still a handsome man. His gaze was steady and the timbre of his voice was rich and forceful.

"How appropriate it is that as we stand here today, we can gaze upon the golden gates and read the words so appropriate to the communal spirit we all share." The president recited the words as many in the audience quietly read with him:

We come here to remember those who were killed,
Those who survived and those changed forever.
May all who leave here know the impact of violence.
May this memorial offer comfort, strength, peace, hope, and serenity.

"I ask you," President Blake said, dabbing his eyes, "were truer words ever written? We know we live in violent times. And yet despite the horrors that sometimes confront us, there is hope, and there is courage. There is the resilience of the American people. There is the nobility that comes from living in a land in which individual rights are our most precious commodities, more so than gold or silver or . . ."

Only days later did Ben realize that the sound he heard next was not the popping of a lightbulb or the backfire of a passing automobile. The president paused. Had he forgotten his speech? Ben wondered. Impossible—he was reading it off the translucent TelePrompTer before and beneath his podium. Then Ben heard another series of popping noises, as if someone had ignited an entire package of Black Cat firecrackers. Only a microsecond later, when he saw two Secret Service agents diving toward the stage, did he realize what was happening.

"We have fire!" he heard Agent Gatwick shout somewhere behind him. "Emergency response mode—now! I repeat: We have fire!"

"Get down! Get out of the way!"

From that point forward, Ben felt as if time went into slow motion. He had been taught in school that time was relative, and for the first time, he believed it. From the shots to the time he was inside Cadillac One, he later realized that barely thirty seconds had elapsed. But it seemed an eternity.

The president had stopped speaking and there were at least half a dozen men racing toward the podium. Ben knew they were running as fast as possible but to him it seemed as if they were moving unbearably slowly, like on *The Six Million Dollar Man*.

The Secret Service agents finally reached the presidential podium. Two of them tackled the president and quite literally knocked him to the ground.

When the leader of the free world hit the floor, panic ensued. The people at the front of the rope line surged forward, pushed against their will by the teeming mass behind them. The police officers guarding the line attempted to hold them back—but there were a lot more people in the crowd than there were police officers. People buried in the middle tried to race off to the sides and break free, creating even more turmoil and confusion.

The shots continued, faster and louder.

"Get down!" Ben heard Agent Zimmer shout, lunging toward him. He thought the man was protecting him, but of course he was actually guarding the first lady. He grabbed her and pulled her to her feet, careful to position his body between Emily Blake and the line of fire. He placed his hands under her arms and lifted her off the ground. As he carried her toward the back of the raised platform, her face showed that she knew she was in danger, but to her credit, she remained quiet and cooperative.

"Tell me about Samson!" Zimmer barked into his sleeve, even as he carried the first lady away. "Is Samson down?"

Ben waited for an answer, but before he heard one, two plainclothesmen approached and began herding his group to the side of the stage.

"Man down!" he heard someone shout, but he didn't know whom they were talking about. One of the Secret Service agents standing by the presidential podium dropped, obviously wounded. Blood saturated his neck and shirt with astonishing speed. *Aren't they wearing Kevlar?* Ben wondered. Another agent to his right fell. *How many shooters are there? How many bullets? How many people are dead already?*

The remaining Secret Service agents formed a circle and pulled the president to his feet, careful to keep him surrounded at all times. Another round of shots rang out and another agent dropped. The remaining four instantly closed the circle, keeping the president covered. Another line of agents went down on one knee, aiming their weapons into the distance.

Pop! Pop! Pop pop pop!

Even from the side of the stage, Ben could see a war was taking place. Four more Secret Service agents crouched on the sides of the stage, weapons out, pointed above the heads of the crowd. He knew the problem. They couldn't find the target.

"Nest One!" the agent standing in front of him shouted. "Where is Nest One? Come in, Nest One!"

Ten more agents came out of nowhere and formed a protective perimeter. The four circling the president moved backward as quickly as possible.

Agent Gatwick raced by, shouting, "Cadillac One. Now!"

The agent in charge of herding Ben's group nodded and steered Ben, Mike, and Tidwell in the same general direction that the president was moving.

"Cadillac One?" Ben whispered under his breath.

He heard Mike grunt a reply, talking as he moved. "Right now, it's probably the safest place in the city."

Before they reached the steps at the rear of the stage, Ben saw three more Secret Service agents drop to the ground. The two men moving his entourage forward continued to plow ahead as if oblivious to the death and carnage.

Outside the stage, the crowd had advanced from panicked to frenzied. The police tried to restrain them, without success. People were climbing walls, splashing through the reflecting pool, climbing the Survivor Tree—anything to get out of the line of fire. Parents were torn between trying to keep their children covered and trying to move them as quickly as possible. Terror had seized the assemblage. The screams were heartrending. A woman near the front was holding a small child in her arms. The child was not moving.

"How can it happen again?" the woman wailed, her voice a piercing, aching cry that cut through the turmoil like a knife. "How can it happen here again?"

The raised platform that had served as a stage began to buckle. Too many people were pressing up against it, trying to escape. Ben just prayed no one had crawled beneath it. The metal supports creaked and groaned and then it all came tumbling down, buckling under the collective pressure of hundreds of desperate people.

As he approached the parked motorcade, Ben for the first time heard shots echoing far above them from different locations. Federal snipers, he guessed, or hoped, and only prayed they would find their target. Was he out of range yet? A Secret Service agent standing next to the rear door of Cadillac One suddenly dropped to the ground, horrifically answering Ben's question.

And then he heard the shriek. In the days to come, Ben would try to explain how he knew it had come from the first lady. Was there something unique about her voice? He could never answer their questions convincingly. But he knew. He knew it with unshakable certainty.

It took his own injury to snap Ben out of his trance. All at once, he felt a stinging sensation race across his cheek, as if someone had tried to strike a match on the side of his face.

I've been shot! Ben thought, lightly touching the side of his cheek. Blood trickled onto his hand. His entire body began to tremble.

Dear God. I've been shot!

Four Secret Service agents positioned themselves around the car, guns drawn and at the ready. On a signal, the two men in front began firing, laying down a blanket of cover fire as the president's four remaining bodyguards literally shoved him into the backseat of the car. No one was more surprised than Ben when his protectors pushed him in behind the president. Mike and Senator Tidwell were the next to enter the bulletproof sanctuary of the automobile.

"Does anyone know what's going on?" he heard a Secret Service agent outside the car cry out. "What happened to Nest One? Why wasn't Juliet where she was supposed to be?"

Agent Gatwick ran up to the car, shoved the doors closed, and slapped the windshield. "Go!"

"What about Emily?" President Blake shouted back at him.

Gatwick simply shook his head and pointed at the driver. "Go!"

The driver, who had never left the car, nodded.

"*Go!*" Gatwick shouted again.

The driver held up his hands helplessly. The panicked crowd blocked his path. There was nowhere he could go without mowing down a dozen people.

"Damnation!" President Blake swore. His face was scraped and his mouth was bleeding, but he seemed essentially intact. There was a wildness in his eyes that Ben suspected could come only from realizing that someone, perhaps many people, had tried very hard to kill him. And he wasn't in the clear yet. What a change—ten minutes ago Ben had been stammering in the presence of this man; now he had been thrown practically on top of him and barely noticed. "At least we're safe in here. Bastards can't hurt us as long as we stay inside."

Mike nodded. His ears were starting to recover from the constant sound of bullets whizzing by much too close to his face. Thank God they'd made it here. This had to be the safest place in the city right now.

So why didn't he feel relieved?

It was a comfort knowing that Cadillac One was bulletproof, but in truth that was not being tested because the bullets weren't coming this way. Why not?

There were ony two possible explanations. Either the president was not the primary target . . .

Or the sniper had him exactly where he wanted him.

Mike whispered into Ben's ear. "Do you see that?"

"What?"

Mike was staring out the window. "It's a reflection. On the chrome of that officer's motorcycle. And it's . . . changing." His eyes widened. "We have to get out of this car."

"Are you insane?" President Blake said. "There's a killer out there! Maybe a whole terrorist cell!"

"You don't understand," Mike said insistently. "There's a bomb. We have to get out of this car."

The president protested, but Mike didn't wait to hear any more. He lunged forward, grabbing the door handle and flinging it open.

The Secret Service men outside had their attention trained away from the car on the potential assailants, so they were taken by surprise when the rear door suddenly burst open. Mike grabbed Ben by the coat lapels and tossed him out of the car.

"What the—"

Mike didn't hesitate a second. He hoisted the president up and out. Several agents immediately formed a protective perimeter around him.

And Gatwick and the rest of the agents had their guns trained on Mike.

"Stand down! What do you think you're doing?"

"There's a bomb in this car," Mike answered, not moving. "It could blow any second."

Gatwick stared at him. "On Cadillac One?"

"I tell you, there's a bomb! I saw the clock. We only have seconds—"

Agent Colbert, who had done time with a bomb squad unit, ran to the far side of the limo. "My God, he's right. Get Samson out of here."

Two agents grabbed the president and carried him away much as Ben had seen the first lady carried earlier.

"Go!" Mike shouted as he tried to clamber out of the car. Tidwell had the opposite door open and was making his escape in the other direction.

Ben suspected there would be no personal escort for him, so he didn't wait for help. He scrambled to his feet and ran.

The force of the explosion knocked Ben to the ground, chin first into the pavement. The sonic boom shattered his ears. Car parts flew all around him, like a hideous metallic rainfall.

Cadillac One had become a fireball.

In the midst of the thick, billowing smoke, Ben pulled himself to his feet, his face bleeding in a dozen places, his eyes watering from the fumes. He knew he had been shot at least once, maybe more. He wasn't sure the president had moved far enough quickly enough to be protected from the explosion. But none of that was uppermost in his mind.

"Mike!" he shouted to no avail, desperately trying to locate his best friend. "Mike? Where are you?"

Stumbling backward, crying, coughing, lost in the sudden cloud of smoke, he was so confused and distraught he crashed into the EMTs who were moving a female body from the stage to someplace away from the fray.

They were moving Emily Blake. Not that there was anything they could do for her now.

The first lady was dead.

3

U.S. SENATE, RUSSELL BUILDING,
OFFICE S-212-D
WASHINGTON, D.C.

Christina McCall pulled at her long strawberry blond locks so hard, she feared she might pull them out by the roots. "Where is he?"

Jones looked at her sympathetically. "Where do you think." It was a statement, not a question.

"I'm about to go nuts, *mon ami*." She was wearing a red body stocking with a fur collar, a short red skirt with a scalloped hem, black and white striped tights, and boots—which for her was a fairly conservative look. Her hair was pulled forward in Bettie Page bangs. "I've been dealing with calls from constituents, demands for action, expressions of sympathy, all very difficult and demanding, and all of it directed toward the only surviving senator from the great state of Oklahoma. Except—guess what? I'm not the senator!"

Jones laid a hand on her shoulder, trying to quiet her. "I'm sure he'll turn up soon. You know how the Boss gets sometimes."

"I certainly do. And *pardonnez-moi,* but that's no excuse." She slumped into the nearest available chair and stared out the window. Her normally chipper, freckled face was drawn and haggard. The crow's-feet around her eyes were more pronounced than their sparkling blue color. "Did I mention that I'm supposed to be on my honeymoon?"

Jones felt a tug at his heart. Even his normally acerbic exterior was melting. "You didn't have to."

"I'm supposed to be sipping French wine in a Parisian café, having a tête-à-tête with my *grande passion.* Not dealing with the worst security crisis on American soil since 9/11." Her shoulders sagged. "I'm tired of talking on the phone."

Jones sat beside her and placed his hand on her shoulder. "I'll take your calls."

"And I'm tired of trying to explain why Senator Kincaid isn't in his office."

"I'll make up a story."

"And I'm sexually frustrated."

Jones removed his hand. "That you're going to have to handle on your own." Christina's head drooped even lower. "Did I mention that I was tired?"

"I'm pretty sure you did."

"I can't do this by myself. I mean, I appreciate your help, Jones. You're the best aide-de-camp in the building, as far as I'm concerned. But it's too impossible. Loving is still off with that Trudy woman, right?"

Jones coughed into his hand. "Loving is still with, um, Trudy, yes."

"And Ben hasn't been in the office since the attack. He has to take control of this situation. He has to decide if he's going to run for reelection. He has—" Her voice choked. "He has to take me on my honeymoon, damn it."

"I'm so sorry, sweetie."

Jones squeezed her hand, then returned to his station where his phone was ringing off the hook, while Christina continued to stare blankly at the office around her. She had put a lot of effort into improving the decor here during the past few months. Even though the name on the door and the desk read BENJAMIN J. KINCAID, she knew she couldn't leave the interior decoration to him. The office would end up resembling a monk's cell: two chairs and a dead plant. At best, it would be a reproduction of his office back in Tulsa, and that was not a work space that deserved the opportunity to reproduce. So despite the budgetary restrictions that accompanied working for an unelected senator with no war chest and a law practice that had not practiced for months, she tried to improve the joint. On weekends, she frequented flea markets—there were dozens of them in the Washington, D.C., area—looking for salvageable furniture and knickknacks. She nurtured plants at her apartment until she thought they were strong enough to survive Ben's negative botanic energy. Christina even replaced some of the fixtures, which apparently hadn't had any attention since before the first World War. Her efforts had turned a sterile government office into a cozy workplace.

Today it seemed colder than a tomb.

She knew the specifications of the building all too well; she heard a tour guide leading a group of citizens down the corridor or around the rotunda almost every day. She knew this capitol building covered 153,112 square feet, which worked out to about three and a half acres. Somehow, though, it managed to have a floor area of more than fourteen acres. And 435 rooms, 554 doors, 679 windows.

Didn't matter. It was still a tomb. The first lady was dead, along with eight Secret Service agents and four civilians, one a little girl of three. Two U.S. senators. And Mike . . .

She closed her eyes tight. She couldn't allow herself to wallow in the misery that had blanketed the country. Someone had to keep this office together.

But who was going to keep her together?

"We just got a memo," Jones said, back at his desk by the front door. "Want to hear the latest?"

"You tell me, Jones. Do I?"

He made it succinct. "DEFCON Three."

There it was. Just as she had feared. The Strategic Air Command

and the associated military alerts had been ratcheted up another notch. Christina knew that had happened only three times since the DEFCON system had been devised: first during the Cuban Missile Crisis, then after 9/11, and now.

The attack on the president, the slaying of the first lady, not to mention so many Secret Service agents and civilians, had sent shock waves rippling through the nation. Homeland Security had issued its first-ever Red Alert. The Dow Jones had gone into a free fall; airports shut down; most retail businesses had closed and remained closed. There was no point in being open. Few people were leaving their homes if it was not absolutely necessary. Even if it wasn't entirely rational—there was no sign that anyone other than the president had been or would be targeted—the horrific incident had left such an imprint on the country that most people just felt more secure staying home.

The upward spiral in hate crimes against Americans of Middle Eastern descent—or in some cases, dark-skinned souls some redneck thought were Middle Eastern—was equally frightening. All across the country, people were lashing out, venting their fear in the form of violence. International tensions were at a fever pitch; the hostility between the United States and the Arab world never seemed so ominous. Many foreign leaders had spoken out, demanding reprisals, asking for the president to make a public statement.

So far, the president had remained silent.

The entire United States intelligence community was making a concerted effort to work together and discover who was behind the heinous attack. The FBI, CIA, NSA, and Homeland Security were acting as one, sharing information on a daily basis at Pentagon and White House rendezvous, wiretapping and spying and making the most of their international allies. Diplomatic inquiries were being made wherever possible, though no one had much hope that they would be useful, because no one really believed the attack had been orchestrated as a formally sanctioned act of a foreign power. The military top brass were engaged in major saber rattling. The Pentagon was requesting permission to employ new high-tech weapons and eavesdropping equipment. On CNN, analysts were saying that it wasn't a question of whether America would go to war—only when. Public support was clearly there; so in all likelihood the politicians would accommodate once the identities of the perpetrators were known. Pundits predicted that the U.S. military readiness standard could go all the way to DEFCON 1 inside of a week, depending on the temperament and inclination of the president.

And still the president remained silent. He had not been seen or heard publicly since the tragedy occurred. At a time when the nation needed leadership most, he was providing least. While the nation worried about its future—the president grieved for his wife.

No one knew what would happen next—least of all Christina. But she knew some action would be taken soon.

And that worried her.

She remembered the White House study back in 2006 that revealed that the war in Iraq had actually increased global terrorism rather than squelching it, due to the wave of reprisals that followed with ever-increasing gusto and fervor.

After a tragedy of this magnitude—what might happen next?

Near the front of the office, Christina heard someone clearing his throat.

With no small degree of regret, she opened her eyes.

"Jimmy?" She rose as she was approached by James Claire, the Senate Information officer who had been assigned to this wing of the Russell Building. "More news?"

"Or the lack thereof," he said, adjusting his collar. He was new in this position, and Christina knew he was not altogether comfortable with it yet. Only last week he had been the lowest ranked clerk in Senator Dawkins's office. After the tragedy of three days before, he had been recruited by the Information Office to help fill the huge surge in demand for news about the tragedy. "At any rate, I've been instructed to provide updates to all my offices twice a day now, so here I am. Is Senator Kincaid around?"

"Uh, no. He's still . . . sick. But I'll pass along any information you have."

"I know. It's just that I've been told to speak directly to the senators."

"Jimmy." Christina placed her hand on his shoulder reassuringly. There were not many people who worked in this building who were younger than she, but happily, he was one of them. "You're talking to the senator's chief of staff, not to mention his wife. Isn't that good enough?"

He smiled a lopsided, somewhat goofy twenty-something smile. "I suppose."

Christina guided him to the nearest chair in the lobby. She did not mince words. "Have they caught the bastards who did this?"

Jimmy sighed. "That's always the first question. No, they haven't caught anyone."

"Do they know who's behind it?"

"Several groups have taken credit—more than a dozen, in fact. It's hard to know who to believe."

"Surely it must be terrorists. Maybe al-Qaeda?"

"We don't think so. The intelligence community is investigating several other satellite Middle Eastern groups, especially one called Saifullah."

"I don't think I've heard of it."

"Who has? The name is a religious reference, naturally. Means 'sword of God' in Arabic."

"And the Feds think they were behind the attack?"

"They sent the President's Office an e-mail that provided a lot of details about the attack. It's possible they're just good guesses, but the intelligence community is taking their claim seriously. And they've made a list of demands."

"Like what?"

"Oh, everything you would expect. Complete withdrawal of U.S. and UN troops from the Middle East, including Iraq and Afghanistan. Shutting down all U.S. military bases in the region, including those in Saudi Arabia. Turning over all oil operations, including pipelines, to native businesses. Promising not to invade sovereign nations unless we're attacked first or demonstrably threatened. Allocating funds to needy Middle Eastern nations matching those provided to Egypt and Israel. Publicly declaring that Islam is a great and sacred religion."

"Pretty standard stuff."

"Exactly."

"Every Middle Eastern terror cell known to man has been making the same demands for decades. Do they ask for anything specific? Release of a prisoner, maybe?"

"No. We're not aware that we have any members of Saifullah in captivity. But frankly, we barely knew anything about the group."

"That seems incredible."

"Bear in mind, we didn't know that much about al-Qaeda while their members were buying box cutters and taking flying lessons in Florida. Took 9/11 to put them in the public consciousness."

"So maybe that was the real point of the attack. To put themselves on the geopolitical map? To make them players?"

"It's not impossible."

Christina laid her head back against the sofa cushion. "High school kids want attention—they spray-paint a bathroom wall. Terrorists want attention—they kill the first lady."

"The first lady was collateral damage. But still—" Jimmy lowered his head. "Yeah. Same mentality."

"Surely the Feds have found some useful forensic evidence," Christina said. In the past, she had worked with Ben on any number of cases where eyewitness testimony proved dubious, but carefully analyzed forensic evidence solved the case.

"Not that I've heard."

"Computer facial recognition? DNA? Eyewitness? Fingerprints?"

"Not so far."

"The combined force of the entire United States intelligence community has come up with nothing?"

"As of my last briefing."

"Not even a weapon?"

"After he took out Nest One, he used their weapon."

"He?"

Jimmy stopped, as if he had reached a piece of information so horrible, he could barely transmit it.

"What? What is it?"

He took a deep breath. "I know the press is talking as if there must have been a fleet of assassins. Dozens of them. But the sad fact is—both the FBI and Homeland Security agree it's entirely possible there was only one."

"*What?*"

"Granted, there must have been more people involved in the operation. They obviously employed sophisticated military reconnaissance of the staging area, not to mention advanced planning and intelligence gathering. Capturing Director Marshall just in time to extract the information they needed—but not so early we would become suspicious and alter our plans. Simultaneously killing Senator Hammond to delay the recognition that Marshall was MIA. But as far as actual assassins—there's just no evidence of more than one shooter. And given the totally clean getaway, one seems more likely than twenty."

"How is that possible?"

Jimmy's eyes lowered. "What I'm about to say next . . . is not for public consumption. It's only speculation. Homeland Security doesn't want to hear it on *Meet the Press.*"

"Get to the point. How could one person find, much less take out, the sniper nest?"

"You might as well ask how he got a bomb under Cadillac One. How could he have so much information about the president's plans? How was he able to so brilliantly penetrate the Secret Service defense formation?" Jimmy sighed again. "Even assuming they were able to extract information from Director Marshall, there's only one possible answer to all those questions."

Christina looked at him levelly. "They had someone on the inside."

"You said it, not me. But . . ."

"But it's the only possible explanation."

Jimmy drew himself up. "Christina, you know how many cases of Secret Service traitors there have been in the history of the Service? None. You know how many FBI agents have gone rogue? Exactly the same number. It just doesn't happen."

"Until it does," Christina said quietly. "Until someone gets so fed up with our foreign policy, they can't stand it anymore. Or someone gets to them, or gets to their family. Forces them to do something they would normally never do."

Jimmy looked back at her solemnly. "Our intelligence forces are investigating all those possibilities. And there's one other you haven't considered yet."

That caught Christina's attention. She was relatively sure she had considered every possibility, even some that a conspiracy buff like their investigator Loving would find preposterous. "What would that be?"

"Remember, the ricin that poisoned Senator Hammond was delivered via a letter he received here in the Senate. In this very office building. We're recommending that no one touch any mail without wearing gloves. Perhaps even a face mask."

"I assume the Capitol Police have instituted some increased security measures in the mailroom."

"That's just the thing, Chris. They've been doing that for years."

"How did that tainted letter get into Senator Hammond's inbox if it didn't go through the mailroom?" Her eyes widened suddenly as the answer came to her, as she realized where Jimmy had been steering her. "Someone hand-delivered it."

Jimmy nodded solemnly. "Exactly. Not an outsider. Not a Middle Eastern demagogue. One of us."

Christina escorted Jimmy to the door.

"Chris, much as I enjoy talking to you . . . I think my bosses would be happier if I could tell them I was giving my reports personally to Senator Kincaid. No offense, but—"

"None taken." She thought for a moment. "When will you be around next?"

"Tomorrow morning, I assume."

She nodded. "I'll have him here."

"That would be good. No one has seen him since the attack. But I kept telling them—she's married to him, for Pete's sake. She must know where he is. He probably checks in with her constantly."

Christina chose not to mention that she hadn't seen him since the attack, either.

"I'll make sure he's here for your briefing, Jimmy."

"Great. So . . . you do know where he is?"

Christina tried to put on a brave face. "Yeah. I have a pretty good idea."

4

Ben Kincaid sat, eyes closed, in the same chair he had occupied for so many days, it felt like a formfitting new pair of pants. It was almost embarrassing to stand; the cheap green vinyl retained the impression of his rear end long after he had risen. So he stayed in the chair, his head resting against the metal guardrail of the hospital bed.

There was not much to think about. The hospital room was not furnished at all, unless you counted the television mounted on the wall. Foliage filled the empty spaces. Ben had never seen so many plants in his entire life, outside of a nursery. All tokens of affection and concern. Funny, wasn't it—you would send flowers to an ailing female, but never a male. Manly men got plants. As if it really mattered.

He opened his eyes and stared ahead, but he saw nothing, heard nothing of consequence. The only sound was the hum of the air conditioner, already forced to do double-time by the hot Oklahoma weather.

Mike's eyes were closed, just as they had been every second since they pulled him from the wreckage. He did not move, not even a twitch.

For the first few days, Ben had read him poetry. Started at the front of *The Oxford Book of English Verse* and worked his way to the end, all the way from John Gower to Seamus Heaney. Bored Ben to tears, truth be told, but he knew Mike liked that stuff. The English major to the end. So there was at least a chance he might get some pleasure out of this marathon reading. There was a theory, still unproved, that patients in a deep coma, even those teetering on the very brink of life and death, could still hear and understand. Some said that the sense of hearing was the last to go and the first to recover. And so Ben read and read and read, waiting for some indication that he was being heard.

He never received any.

After a few days, his voice grew hoarse and he gave up the reading. But he remained in the chair, waiting for a sign, praying for the recovery the doctors said was unlikely, and wishing he had not been so stupid as to draw his best friend into the line of fire.

He blamed himself entirely. The attack had been a nightmare. A national nightmare, true, but one he had experienced firsthand and up close. His cheek still stung where the bullet had grazed him. But that was the least haunting memory plaguing him. All those men— dropping right before his eyes. He'd seen death before, even witnessed it—but not like that. Never like that. And the director of Homeland Security—gone. He couldn't cry many tears about Senator Hammond. If the rest of the world knew what Ben knew about the former Senate minority leader, they would understand. But all those other people. All those public servants, all those innocent bystanders, children. And—

And after all the times Mike had stood by him, all the times he had pulled Ben's fat out of the fire—

Ben repaid the debt by putting him in the intensive care unit, his right leg and arms broken, his flesh rent in more than a dozen places, his head so concussed that even if he did recover . . . the doctors were not sure it would be such a good thing.

A Hispanic nurse entered to take Mike's vitals. She was on the short side, brisk, and efficient. No-nonsense but still friendly. As Ben well knew, her name was Beatrice.

"Get any sleep last night, Senator?"

Was it morning? Ben instinctively clutched his jaw and felt a wealth of stubble. He must look a wreck.

"Not much," Ben mumbled.

"Still having those dreams?"

Had he told her about the dreams? Why? Must've been so brain-dead he didn't realize what he was saying.

"I . . . don't remember."

"You know," she said, as she wrapped the blood pressure monitor around Mike's upper arm, "you might consider talking to someone about that. Not that it's any of my business. But if I'd been through what you've been through . . ." She shook her head. "I'd want to talk to someone. I'd need to get something off my chest."

"Like what?"

"I dunno." She finished with the blood pressure and started the tricky task of trying to take an unconscious man's temperature. Ben knew wires hooked up all over Mike's body were monitoring his heartbeat and brain activity and other vital signs, but apparently Beatrice preferred to do some things the old-fashioned way. "The lingering fear that accompanies being in a horrific event. Anxiety. Grief." She paused ever so slightly. "Guilt."

"I don't want to talk to anyone," Ben said with more than a little crust. "I don't like . . . talking. Especially not about myself."

"Suit yourself." She finished her work and gave Mike's sheets a little tuck. "Sir, you're welcome to stay here as long as you like. But you know—we'll call you if there's any change."

"I know."

"So . . ."

"I'll stay. As long as I can."

"As you wish." She started out the door, then stopped. "Oh. Major Morelli has a visitor. I asked her to wait until I finished my business. Do you mind if I send her in now?"

"No, I don't mind."

"Very good, sir. Umm . . . could I bring you something to eat?"

"I'm fine."

Beatrice nodded, then left the room.

When was the last time he had eaten? Ben wondered. He couldn't recall. Perhaps that was why he felt so . . . feeble. Perhaps that was part of it, anyway.

He stared into Mike's expressionless face. *Come back,* he thought, as if his mental urging might somehow make the difference. *Come back to us.*

"Ben?"

Ben looked up, startled. It took him a moment to focus and make the proper mental connections. "Sergeant Baxter?"

"Would you call me Kate already?" The woman was tall and almost wiry thin. She had dark hair and eyes and, Ben knew from experience, was just as tough as she looked. She had been Mike's partner.

He mentally corrected himself. She still was Mike's partner, damn it.

"Kate," Ben said, rubbing his hands against his face, trying to bring himself back into the world of the living. "How are you?"

"How am *I*?"

"Right. Stupid question."

They both stared down at Mike, lying quiet and still on his bed.

"You know," Kate said, "I've been telling him he needed to get more rest. But this is ridiculous."

Ben tried to laugh, but it just wasn't in him.

"Sorry I haven't been here more often. But you know, it's such a long drive from Tulsa. The Turner Turnpike is so boring."

Ben didn't say anything.

"Okay, I'm lying through my teeth. I just . . . I don't know." She pressed her wrist against her mouth, obviously trying to stop her emotions from spilling out. "I guess I don't like seeing him like this."

Ben nodded slowly. "It just isn't him, is it?"

"No! Mike is always so full of life and energy and—" She

caught herself. "I mean, he's a sexist pig and I hate working with him and I only do so under protest but . . ." She let out a long sigh that said more than any number of words might have done.

After a long silent moment, she changed the subject. "Any word from the ex?"

"No." Hell of a thing, wasn't it? When you couldn't track down your own sister. "I don't know where Julia is. I don't know if she knows Mike has been wounded. And I don't really even know if she would care."

"That's harsh, surely."

Ben said nothing. He was much too tired to argue. But he'd been dealing with his younger sister all his life. She had reclaimed her infant son—the one Ben had been raising for her—in a sudden frenzy several years ago, run off with some doctor, and he hadn't heard from her since. Neither had his mother.

"So is that how you met Mike?" Kate asked. "When he married your sister?"

"Oh, no. I knew him first. We were college roommates at OU. Even played in a band together. I played piano and keyboards and sang badly. He played guitar and sang slightly less badly. Wrote some of our songs himself."

"Really! Good stuff?"

Ben shrugged. "Very poetic."

They shared a small smile.

"We were distant for a while, after the divorce. Very messy. But we managed to reclaim our friendship after I moved to Tulsa and started practicing law. We've been close ever since. My best friend, really." He paused. "Best male friend, for sure. He's saved me a hundred times over."

"From bad guys?"

Ben stared at the floor. "From myself, mostly."

Kate was carrying a paper bag. She set it on a table and withdrew a thermos. "I think you need a pick-me-up." She began unscrewing the lid.

"Thanks, but I don't really drink coffee. Upsets my stomach."

By the time she had the lid off, Ben recognized his mistake.

"Chocolate milk?"

Kate grinned broadly. "My favorite."

He gave her a long look. "I don't believe you've ever drunk chocolate milk. Even when you were five, I'll bet you were too tough to drink chocolate milk."

"Well . . ."

"You've been talking to Christina, haven't you?"

Kate started to protest.

"Don't bother denying it. I know."

She passed him a cup. "You can hardly blame a woman for looking after her husband. Especially a newlywed."

Ben held up his hands. "I don't care for any. I—"

Kate looked at him harshly. "Drink it!"

Ben took the cup obediently and drank.

"I brought you some coneys, too."

Ben didn't argue this time; he just took the food as she offered it. "Bet they aren't as good as Carl's in Tulsa."

"They'll be much better. My own secret recipe."

Ben blinked. "They're hot dogs. You stuck a wiener inside a bun."

"Hey, I'm a working girl. What do you expect? For me, that's a secret recipe."

"I'm not sure I can eat anything."

"You have to. You look pathetic."

"Thank you so much. But I—"

"Look, you want to stay in that chair and wallow in sorrow, that's your business. Waste away to nothing, I don't care. But you've got a brand-new wife, buster. And she does care, you get what I'm saying? So eat already!"

Ben took a bite. Not half bad, actually.

"I talked to the docs out in the hallway," she continued. "No change, right?"

Ben nodded and took another nibble.

"Prognosis?"

Ben wiped his mouth, then spoke. "Poor."

"That's what I thought." She looked down at her stricken partner again, then pointed to the green vinyl chair next to the one Ben was sitting in. "That chair empty?"

"Uh, yeah."

She plopped into it. "You know, Ben—this is not your fault. No one could have foreseen—"

"Stop."

"I'm just saying—"

"Stop."

"But you can't go on—"

"Would you please just stop!"

This time, it was Kate who fell silent.

For a moment. "You're wounded."

"Please don't get all psychological on me."

"I'm being literal." She touched the side of his cheek.

"Oh. Right. Bullet grazed me. Docs say it will heal. Won't leave a scar."

"I've seen bullet creases before. I think the doctors are wrong."

"Whatever. Who cares? By all rights, it should've taken my head off. I was lucky. Unlike—"

He didn't finish.

She decided to change the subject. Slightly.

"Saw the first lady's funeral on television. A horrible thing."

Ben agreed. "Saw the start. Couldn't stand it any longer."

"Good to see the president back on his feet, though. He looked strong. Grief-stricken, sure. But he still had it together. Some of the rumors going around—" She paused. "Well, it was good to see him back in action, even under these circumstances. I'm glad he's going to speak to the nation. I think it's the right thing to do. What everyone needs. A feeling of unity. Strength. Resilience. What do you think he's going to say?"

Ben shrugged.

"Ben, you *are* going back to Washington, aren't you? The president is addressing a joint session. I'm no political expert, but I'm pretty sure that means the U.S. senators are supposed to be there."

"I'm not a real senator."

"Ben—at the moment, you're the only senator this state has got."

It was too sad, too true. With Tidwell killed in the explosion, and the governor hesitant to name a successor so soon after the tragedy, Ben was Oklahoma's only rep in the Senate.

Kate gently laid her hand over Ben's. "We need you in Washington, Ben. You go back and do your job. I'll stay here with Mike."

He turned slowly. "That's why Christina sent you, isn't it? To take my place. So I'd go to Washington."

Kate's eyes told him all he needed to know.

Ben waited until Kate had closed the door behind her; then he leaned forward, his eyes on Mike. "I remember when our roles were reversed, pal. After I took that spill at the refinery and ended up in the hospital, out for days. You stayed by me. I may not have known it at the time . . . but then again, somehow I think I did. And I like to think you know I'm here now."

He drew in his breath. "I have to go now. But I'll still be thinking of you. I will not forget—anything. I especially won't forget that you tossed my butt out of that car before you saved your own. If it had gone the other way around, you'd still be hale and hearty. You took that explosion for me, and the president. You did what you always do. Took care of others better than you take care of yourself. And I won't forget it—ever."

He steadied himself with the metal guardrail.

"I will do everything in my power to make sure that this does not happen again. Not to anyone else. Not ever. That's what you would do, if you were here. So since you can't—I'll do it for you."

He opened the door and handed Kate *The Oxford Book of English Verse*. "He's all yours now."

As he rose, he gave Mike one last look.

Come back to us, Mike. Please.

5

CHAMBER OF THE HOUSE OF REPRESENTATIVES
WASHINGTON, D.C.

"Where's the script?" Christina kept asking. "Don't we get advance copies? We always get advance copies."

"I asked Jimmy twice," Ben said, as they took their designated seats in the chamber. "There are no copies."

"But—that's just not done. The President of the United States does not address a joint session without providing advance copies."

"This isn't the State of the Union address."

"No, this will probably be about a thousand times more important than the State of the Union address. People will actually be watching."

"I hear what you're saying," Ben replied, as the throng of senators and representatives and staff began taking their seats. "But the fact remains. There are no advance copies."

"Did Jimmy give a reason?"

Ben hesitated. "He did, but . . . well, it almost seems too incredible to believe, much less repeat."

"Don't hold out on me, hubby. What did the man say?"

"Jimmy said . . ." Ben took a deep breath. "He said the president wasn't quite sure yet exactly what he was going to say."

Christina looked at him with eyes wide as Frisbees. "The president has requested an invitation to address a special joint session—but he hasn't decided yet what he's going to say?"

"I know. Difficult to imagine."

Christina shook her head sadly. "I suppose anything is possible. The man just lost his wife in a horrible, violent manner. He must be more shaken up than we realized."

As Ben gazed around the huge and historic chamber, he saw that most of the key players had taken their designated seats, just as they would if this were the State of the Union address. Near the front of the chamber, the joint chiefs of staff sat in a row, next to the nine members of the Supreme Court and the president's cabinet. Ben did a quick count and realized that one of the cabinet members was missing—the secretary of commerce, if he wasn't mistaken. He was the designated survivor, the man who would ensure continuity in government in the event that some tragedy should take out everyone above him in the constitutional line of succession. Ever since 9/11, Ben knew a few members of Congress also were quietly asked to view the proceedings from another location by closed-circuit monitor, for exactly the same reason.

"Virtually everyone we know in Washington is here," Ben commented.

"Yes, and about a thousand people we don't know," Christina said wryly. "It's a veritable 'Who's That' of politics."

"Well, if the list had been more exclusive, we wouldn't be here."

Behind him, Ben saw the sergeant at arms making his way down the central carpeted aisle to perform his ceremonial function. Traditionally, since the president was not a member of Congress, he was not allowed to enter the chamber, much less address it, without requesting permission. In response to the request, the Speaker of the House issues a formal invitation.

The sergeant at arms stopped midway down the aisle and spoke in his deepest stentorian tones, "Mr. Speaker, the President of the United States."

Behind him, President Blake entered, a somber, if not grave expression on his face. Everyone in the room rose instantly to their feet and delivered a spontaneous standing ovation. Ben knew it was traditional, during the State of the Union addresses, for the president's walk down the carpet to take several minutes, as he stopped to glad-hand and exchange smiles with a select and predetermined few members of his own party. There was none of that today, however. The applause was strong, but also respectful. Everyone was cognizant that they had been assembled in the face of a national tragedy, at the request of a man who was not only the leader of the free world, but who had just lost his wife.

President Blake reached the front of the gallery without interruption and proceeded directly to the podium. Ben spotted creased foreheads on the faces of several of the bigwigs sitting up front. Traditionally, the president would present written copies of his speech to both the vice-president, fulfilling his constitutional role as president of the Senate, and the Speaker of the House. It was a token of respect; in exchange for the invitation to speak in their house, he let them hold the text in their hands. Today, however, no scripts were provided.

"This is very strange," Christina whispered into Ben's ear, just above the continued tumult. "Does this mean he still doesn't know what he's going to say?"

"Or perhaps," Ben suggested, "he doesn't want anyone to know what he's going to say until he says it."

After a few more moments, the applause faded and those in attendance reclaimed their seats. The Speaker of the House pounded his gavel and announced, "Members of Congress, I have the high privilege and distinct honor of presenting to you the President of the United States."

Once again the crowd rose and applauded. This, too, was a long-standing tradition, but Ben noted that the applause faded much more quickly than it would during a typical presidential address. Perhaps that was out of respect for the solemnity of the occasion, but Ben suspected it was more because everyone was increasingly anxious to hear what the man had to tell them.

The president squared himself behind the rostrum. "Members of Congress, staff, cabinet members, members of the Supreme Court, and honored guests. Thank you for joining me tonight."

Ben craned his neck to check out the two transparent Tele-PrompTers that were traditionally located just below the president's eye level to the left and right of the podium, so he could look into either camera and still give the home television audience the illusion that he was talking, not reading. Neither of them was turned on. Now this was genuinely unprecedented, and it meant that the president, not generally considered a great master of the English language, would be speaking without a safety net. Was this address so top secret he wasn't even willing to give a copy to the people who operated the TelePrompTers?

"There is much to be said tonight," President Blake began. Ben observed carefully the lines etched in his face. Had he opted to go on without stopping in the makeup room? He looked as if he had aged a decade in the past week. "But before I proceed, I would like to ask you all to join me in a moment of silence in remembrance of the first lady of the United States, my dear wife, Emily Blake."

Heads bowed. The president probably felt he could not actually call for a prayer, even in a chamber that opened each day's business with a prayer, but he came as close as was constitutionally possible. Every head in the room lowered, and Ben heard considerable sniffling and choking. It was a supremely moving moment.

When the president raised his head again, Ben saw that his eyes were moist, almost limpid. He steadied himself and continued. "Emily loved this country. She loved everything about it. She didn't care that much about politics, but she cared about people. Good people. Like all married folk, we had our . . . difficulties. But my ardent admiration, and my undying love, remained just as constant as her devotion and support to me and my work. Emily was indeed a unique, gifted, and very special individual. For those fortunate enough to call her friend, she was the best friend they could ever have. For the one man fortunate enough to call her his wife, she was a loyal and tireless companion, and quite simply the best woman—no, the best person—I have ever known."

Someone in the rear began clapping, not thunderously, but in a strong steady rhythm, soon joined by many others. It was not so much a round of applause as a token of remembrance, like tossing dirt onto a casket.

The president cleared his throat, brushed away another tear, and continued. "But we must not let our grief over the loss of the first lady lead us to forget the many others who fell in service of their country during this cowardly terrorist attack. Eight Secret Service agents also fell, men and women who gave their lives in defense of the country, to ensure that our leaders are chosen by the people, not terrorists. Four civilians, including a"—hard as he tried to stop it, his voice cracked—"a little girl age three named Pauline." He paused. "Her family called her Poppy, and she liked to skip rope, and to color pictures of flowers, and she was kind to her little brother, Kevin." He inhaled, and once again Ben felt certain the man's voice would break. "Now poor Kevin is an only child, unable to understand what has happened to the big sister he loved so much."

The president turned his head to one side, blinking rapidly. A quick survey told Ben that he was far from the only person in the gallery fighting back tears.

"Major Mike Morelli, the man who in all probability saved my life, as well as others, remains in critical condition."

Ben felt a clutching in his chest. Christina reached across and squeezed his hand tightly.

"We also lost two august members of Congress—Senator Tidwell of Oklahoma, killed during the attack, and Robert Hammond, the minority leader and longest-serving member of the Senate, in an equally cowardly poisoning. We have now learned that . . ."

The president paused again, gritting his teeth. What more could there be?

"We have discovered the remains of Lucas Marshall, Director of Homeland Security, who was killed in advance of the Oklahoma City attack. It appears that Director Marshall was killed in an effort to obtain critical security information that would allow the killers to do their dirty work. I don't want to shock any sensitive ears . . ." He paused, as if allowing parents watching at home a moment to get their children out of the room. "It appears that he was tortured, slowly, then killed by . . . well, in the most painful and horrific manner that could possibly be imagined."

This time there was no sound from the gallery, only a numbed silence.

"Members of Congress, if this could happen to the director of Homeland Security, the man in charge of ensuring the domestic security of this nation, it could happen to anyone. We have done much in recent years to tighten our security, but it is now self-evident that we have not done enough. The people of this great nation depend upon us to protect and defend them against threats to their security, whether from home or abroad. And on April nineteenth, ladies and gentlemen—we failed them."

More silence. Harsh words, especially coming from the President of the United States. But difficult to deny.

"We have two choices: We can admit defeat, and leave ourselves open to attack by any demented individual or group with an axe to grind, or we can take action. I do not believe the people elected me to do nothing in the face of a clear and present danger. Therefore, we will take action."

The president reached inside his jacket and withdrew what appeared to be a proposed bill, with the traditional blue backing.

"Some members of the press have suggested that I have spent the past week wallowing in grief. I can assure you that is not the case. To the contrary, I have been closeted with my closest and most trusted advisors, not only in my cabinet but in the FBI, CIA, NSA, and Homeland Security, for the purpose of drafting emergency legislation. Members of Congress, when you return to your offices, you will find a copy of my proposed bill on your desks. But I will tell you now what I am proposing. I propose that we stiffen our anticrime and antiterrorism laws to protect us from the enemy that lurks both outside and within our borders. I am not talking about another Patriot Act, something with a fixed term that will periodically need to be renewed. Until America's enemies expire, we cannot allow our defenses to expire. Therefore, members of Congress, I am proposing a permanent law, an amendment to the Constitution."

"I get why he wants it to be permanent," Christina whispered. "But why does it need to be part of the Constitution?"

"So it can't be declared unconstitutional," Ben said quietly. "No matter what it contains."

"I'm sure there will be some who will oppose this new amendment," the president continued. "To them, I can only say: if it had been your wife, or your brother, or your little girl who was taken by an act of unreasoning violence on April nineteenth, you would feel differently. I continue to stand firmly in support of our basic American civil rights—but not at the cost of our most essential freedom, the right to live unmolested by acts of terrorism and violence. Therefore, I ask Congress to move this bill to the top of their agenda and to pass it in both houses before the end of the month. After that, it can be ratified by the states and the new law could conceivably come into effect in a matter of weeks. Some may argue that this is undue speed, that we should be more deliberate. To them I simply say: every day this nation continues without the protection of these new rigid security measures, we risk another 9/11, another April nineteenth. So for once, Congress, in the memory of Emily Blake and all the others who fell on that tragic day, I ask you to reach across the aisle and join me in a bipartisan effort to make this nation a safer place. There is no room for delay. Time is of the essence. Members of Congress—this nation is depending on you."

The president fell silent, and after a moment, the crowd realized that he had said all he intended to say. The applause began slowly, then gained speed and force with almost breathtaking alacrity. Ben noted that the support came from both sides of the aisle, both parties. Even at the front of the room, people were rising to their feet, some even cheering. Traditionally the joint chiefs did not applaud statements relating to domestic policy, since the military was theoretically supposed to be uninvolved in matters not relating to military or foreign policy. But in truth, no one was sure what this bill was, domestic or foreign, military or not. They simply knew that the nation had been bruised, wounded, and something needed to be done to begin the healing. Traditionally, the nine members of the Supreme Court did not applaud at all during the delivery of the president's speeches, since they were also supposed to be impartial and nonpartisan. Nonetheless, Ben spotted several members of the Court rising to their feet, applauding enthusiastically.

"My God," Christina said, shouting to be heard over the growing tumult, "is that possible? Could he really get a new amendment to the Constitution passed in a few weeks?"

Ben carefully viewed the faces of the people standing all around him. "In this climate? Anything is possible."

"Is that a good thing?"

Ben took a deep breath, then slowly released it. "Let's go read the bill."

6

U.S. SENATE, RUSSELL BUILDING,
OFFICE S-212-D
WASHINGTON, D.C.

"Can you believe this?" Christina exclaimed. "He wants to repeal the Bill of Rights!"

"Not all of it," Ben said quietly. "Just the inconvenient parts."

"But isn't that the whole point of the Bill of Rights? The Founding Fathers added it to make sure that no law could ever remove them."

"You know what the president's response to that suggestion will be. The Founding Fathers thought the worst threat imaginable was Hessian mercenaries with muskets that took a minute and a half to load and fire. They never envisioned snipers with MI-50s. Or ricin-laced letters. Or entire regions of the world wielding weapons of mass destruction aimed within our borders."

"But this is the Bill of Rights! When I took Constitutional Law from Professor Tepker, he taught us that the Bill of Rights was inviolable."

"It has been, in theory. But you know as well as I do that in reality, we restrict those rights all the time." Ben dropped his copy of the bill on top of his desk. "There are many restrictions on the freedom of speech—you can't shout 'Fire!' in a crowded theater. You can't post bills on private property. We have gun legislation that restricts the right to bear arms. There are more restrictions on the right of assembly than I can count."

"Yes, there have been reasonable, commonsense abridgements of rights here and there. But not wholesale suspensions." She pointed at the bill that lay between them. "This is something else entirely."

"Yes," he agreed solemnly. "This is something else entirely."

He quickly scanned the bill one more time, just to make sure he understood it properly:

RESOLVED by the Senate and the House of Representatives of the United States of America, two-thirds of each House proposing that an amendment to the Constitution of the United States be adopted which shall become law and a full and effective part of the Constitution of the United States when said proposed amendment is ratified by three-fourths of the state legislatures of the fifty states.

The proposed amendment shall read as follows:

Section 1. Effective immediately, upon the declaration by the president of the United States that a clear and present danger to the safety of the United States and the peoples therein exists, an Emergency Security Council, headed by the director of Homeland Security and consisting of the leaders of the Federal Bureau of Investigation, the Central Intelligence Agency, the National Security Agency, and three other members appointed by the President of the United States, shall be convened.

Section 2. After due and deliberate consideration, if the Emergency Security Council declares that a state of national emergency exists, the council may assume any and all necessary plenipotentiary powers.

Section 3. These plenipotentiary powers assumed by the

Emergency Security Council include the power to supersede the First, Second, Third, Fourth, Fifth, Sixth, and Eighth Amendments to the Constitution, overriding said constitutional authority.

Section 4. These plenipotentiary powers shall exist only until such time as the Council declares that the state of national emergency no longer exists. At the time of said proclamation, the suspension of the enumerated amendments shall cease, and they shall regain all prior full force and effect.

Section 5. During any such period of national emergency, all other rights and privileges of the citizens of the United States not specifically suspended herein shall remain in full force and effect.

"I think it's frightening," Christina said. "This Emergency Security Council could wipe away every important civil right on the books."

"In times of national crisis," Ben noted.

"As defined by the president and his Emergency Council."

"Would you rather leave it to Congress? Then it would never happen. We could have bombs dropping like snowflakes and they'd still be arguing over parliamentary procedure."

"I'm surprised the president even bothered with Congress. He obviously wants to ram this right down the throats of the states."

"He didn't have any choice." Ben pulled out a copy of the Constitution he always kept in the top drawer of his desk. "Technically, the president has no power to propose amendments—only Congress does. The Constitution also allows state legislatures to propose amendments, but it has never been done that way. Congress must propose the amendment by resolution. The resolution then goes to the Rules Committee in the House and the Judiciary Committee in the Senate. If they pass it, the amendment goes to the floor for a vote by the full membership of both bodies. If they both pass it, then copies are sent to the governors of each state, who then pass it along to the state legislatures for consideration. It takes three-fourths of them—thirty-eight of the fifty." Ben sighed. "It's a complicated process. The Founding Fathers meant it to be. They recognized there might be need for change in the future. But they wanted it to be well-considered and deliberate—not something that could be accomplished easily in a rash reactionary moment."

"Which is exactly what the president is doing here. Why do you think he urged everyone to move so quickly? He knows he needs momentum to keep this thing alive. If it gets bogged down anywhere along the way, the chances of passage will drop significantly. He's trying to steamroller this through before people have a chance to think clearly about it. Exactly what the prudent Founding Fathers didn't want."

"You know," Ben said, "the Founding Fathers were not a bunch of old fogey conservatives. They were basically young wild-eyed radicals who overthrew one government and created another."

"And we need to stop President Blake before he does the same thing. He's trying to use a tragedy to sweep away our civil rights. Surely no one—not even the most conservative of the conservatives—will be that foolhardy. Right?" She swiveled Ben's chair around so that he faced her. "Right?"

Ben pursed his lips, then said quietly, "Let's read it over one more time."

7

J. EDGAR HOOVER BUILDING
BALLISTICS RANGE
FBI HEADQUARTERS, WASHINGTON, D.C.

Deputy Director Joel Salter walked down to the second-level basement of the J. Edgar Hoover Building with no small amount of dread. He hated this assignment. Ever since the disaster of April 19, he had been made permanent liaison to the new director of Homeland Security. And ever since Lucas Marshall was discovered dead, burned and mutilated almost beyond recognition, the director of Homeland Security had been former deputy director Carl Lehman. And he always seemed to be accompanied by his new deputy director, Nichole Muldoon, the only woman he'd ever known capable of giving him both a hard-on and chills simultaneously.

He found Lehman and Muldoon leaving the ballistics range.

"Did you see that?" Lehman said, bubbling with enthusiasm like a kid at Christmas. "Did you see how high I scored?"

Even though the question was directed at Salter, Nichole Muldoon took it upon herself to answer. "I did. You scored quite well. Almost as well as I did."

He waved her away. "Ah—you have younger eyes." He showed Salter the target he had hand-pumped two rounds into. "Sweet, huh?"

Salter resisted the temptation to roll his eyes. *Amateurs. You pull people who haven't had the proper training out of nowhere and suddenly make them more important than the FBI, and this is what you get. They think the ballistics range is a toy shop.* "I understand you wanted to tour the labs?"

Lehman and Muldoon exchanged a look. "Well . . ."

"The FBI crime labs were established by J. Edgar Hoover in 1932. They were the first of their kind, and they are still the best forensic laboratories in the world. What would you like to see first? The DNA lab? Hair and Fiber unit? Blood works, maybe? Luminol is always fun to play with."

Lehman and Muldoon did not indicate any interest.

"Okay, there's the spectrograph—great for paint analysis. Chemistry? Can probably find the boys doing an autopsy or boiling human organs. Serology? Explosives? Firearms and Toolmarks? Investigative Computer Training? Physical Training? Practical Applications? Forensic Science Research?"

"To tell you the truth," Muldoon said, stepping forward slightly, "we'd like to meet with you privately."

She was still flushed and sweaty from the firing rage. Salter could feel the heat radiating off her. Could it be accidental? Or did she know what effect the words "meet with you privately" would have on him, coming from her?

"Follow me." He escorted them into a nearby interrogation room and locked the door behind them. It was a standard room— table and two chairs, with a one-way mirror so interrogations could be observed. Salter offered Muldoon a chair but, of course, she didn't take it.

"Can we just cut straight to the point, Salter?" Lehman said, direct as ever, now that he'd been removed from his playthings. "I'd like to know how the Feebs feel about this bill the president has proposed."

"I don't think there's a consensus on that."

"But you must have some idea what people are thinking."

He shrugged. "Mixed bag. Some think it's a dangerous precedent. Others think it's the only chance we have to protect ourselves in the modern world."

"And what about your boss? What does he think?"

Salter considered for a moment, but in the end, he couldn't think of any reason not to be honest. "He's against it."

"Really? Hanging Bob Banner? Worried about civil rights?"

Salter offered a weak grin. "I think he's more pissed off because the bill makes you the chairman of the Emergency Security Council instead of him."

Lehman let loose a belly laugh that could probably be heard in the next room. "I like that. At least it's honest."

Muldoon arched an eyebrow. "Engaging in a little schadenfreude?"

Lehman stared back at her with a look that suggested he thought she might've just said something dirty. "I just like to see Hanging Bob get his comeuppance. See who the president really trusts and who he doesn't."

"The director doesn't think it has anything to do with trust," Salter said. In for a penny, in for a pound. "Or competence. Or talent. He thinks it has to do with the fact that you play golf with the president every other Tuesday. And that you made a big contribution to his campaign fund."

Lehman laughed all the louder. "Sounds like sour grapes to me."

Privately, Salter tended to agree, but he certainly wasn't going to say that. "I gather then that you and your department are all for this thing."

"It was my idea, son. We need it, if we're going to survive. You think all those Middle East maniacs care about civil rights? Hell, no. They just want to blow us off the map. Destroy our way of life."

Salter addressed Muldoon, not quite looking her in the eye. "And that goes for you, too, I guess. Faithful follower and all that?"

"Actually, no."

Lines creased Lehman's forehead. Salter got the impression he wasn't accustomed to being disagreed with—especially not by his second in command.

"I think it's crazy," Muldoon continued. "One horrible incident and we decide to eradicate our fundamental freedoms?"

"There's no freedom if we're all dead," Lehman countered.

"Masterfully argued," Muldoon said, and for once, Salter liked her a little, especially as he watched Lehman try to figure out if he'd been complimented or insulted.

"You think this is the first time something like this has happened?" Lehman asked. "I can assure you it isn't. I've been around a long time, and I'm a student of history, too. The real history, not what they teach you in sixth-grade civics class. Remember the Alien and Sedition Acts? Clear violation of freedom of speech, but that didn't stop John Adams from pushing for it when he started getting scared. During the Civil War, our beloved Abe Lincoln suspended habeas corpus and replaced civil trials with military trials. He didn't have any constitutional amendment backing him up, either. He just did it. President Wilson gave us the infamous 'Red Scare' and Palmer raids during and after World War One. During World War Two, FDR signed Executive Order 9066 that put 3,500 Japanese Americans who had not even been *accused* of crimes into concentration camps. Nixon's Organized Crime Control Act suspended search and seizure laws and most of the accused's Fifth Amendment rights."

"Yes," Muldoon said, "and if all those violations could occur with the Bill of Rights in place, imagine what might happen if someone got the right to suspend the Bill of Rights for an indefinite period."

"It's only a temporary measure."

"Yeah, it was only a temporary measure that suspended the Bill of Rights in India in 1962. A national emergency was declared and an emergency council was convened, and the Bill of Rights was held in abeyance. For six years. Then they suspended them again not ten years later, in 1975. How do we know that won't happen here? Every time some worrisome little Orange Alert occurs, our fundamental liberties could fly out the window."

"Are you suggesting I might abuse my power?"

"I'm suggesting," Muldoon replied, not backing down in the least, "that the whole amendment is a very bad idea."

Exasperated, Lehman blew air through his teeth. He turned his attention to Salter. "I gather you share your boss's sentiments?"

Salter took a deep breath. "I have concerns about giving so much authority to a relatively new governmental department. I think the director of the FBI would've been a better choice."

"I'm just one member on a committee of six."

"I know how these things work. The chairman will wield a huge amount of authority and influence. Especially in the face of a crisis."

"You Feebs just don't get the picture," Lehman said, and this time there was a touch of a growl in his voice. "Your day is done. When the president decided to move the Secret Service—the men protecting his butt on a daily basis—out of Treasury, did he give them to you? Hell, no. He gave them to Homeland Security. We're today, not yesterday. We've got 184,000 employees. We're the third largest cabinet department—only the Department of Defense and the Department of Veterans Affairs are larger. You Feebs are pipsqueaks compared to us. We're not sitting around stroking ourselves because we caught Dillinger two hundred years ago. We're making things happen today."

"Yes," Salter said dryly. "I thought the color-coded alert chart was a brilliant innovation. Changed the face of the nation."

Lehman's anger was not disguised. "You laugh all you want, but those alerts gave a lot of comfort to a lot of people."

"Who are you kidding? All they ever did was scare people to death." Salter drew in his breath. "You know as well as I do that ever since 9/11, the FBI's number one priority has been counterterrorism. We've used the powers the Patriot Act gave us to stop numerous terrorist plots."

Lehman leaned forward for a counteroffensive, but Muldoon held him back with a light touch of her hand on his chest. "It's okay, Carl," she said quietly. "We got what we came for."

Salter watched carefully as her hand lingered on his chest, scrutinized the subtle expression on her face. Was she doing him? Was that how she rose so fast? Why he never went anywhere without her?

"I'm sorry to hear you're not on board with this bill," Lehman said, obviously wrapping up the conversation. "I'd hoped we could all be on the same page with this."

Salter eyed Muldoon. "Sounds like you're not on the same page in your own department."

"Yeah, but I can handle my own department. You Feebs are sneaky. I worry about you."

"It's in the hands of Congress, not the FBI."

"Right. Decision-making by the clueless. It's the American way. Come on, Muldoon. Let's get out of here."

She followed her master's bidding and left the conference room, but as she passed by Salter, she mouthed, "Let's talk."

Salter felt his blood pressure rising as the door closed behind her. Was it what she said, or just those full lips, that ruby red lipstick? She was so damn sexy.

He hated working with her. Them.

Or maybe he just hated himself. Or maybe it amounted to the same thing.

8

DEPARTMENT OF HOMELAND SECURITY
NEBRASKA AVENUE NAVAL COMPLEX
WASHINGTON, D.C.

He knew he shouldn't be sitting around in the dark, especially if he was trying to read. But the fluorescent lights that filled his tiny office were much too intense, too glaring. Too much at odds with his current mood. And the reading . . . well, his attention drifted so often, he wasn't sure whether he was absorbing it anyway. Or whether he really cared.

Agent Max Zimmer heard a sound outside his closed door. Through the window he could see two men outside talking. He made a silent prayer that he wouldn't be bothered. He did not want to be bothered. Especially not by the man he saw in the window.

No such luck. A few moments later, the doorknob turned, and Agent Thomas Gatwick stepped into the office.

"How're you doing, partner?" Gatwick said, affecting a breezy cheerfulness that was not remotely convincing. He turned on the overhead light.

Zimmer winced. Bad enough the man had to intrude on his privacy. "I'm okay. Not bad for a guy who probably needs serious psychiatric counseling."

Gatwick's neck stiffened. "Ouch. Were we talking that loudly?"

"No. I'm just psychic." In truth, Zimmer was an excellent lip-reader. His younger sister had been born deaf, and he had gone to all the classes with her to learn to read lips. As a result, he'd been able to eavesdrop on a conversation he could see but couldn't hear. But he wasn't going to tell Gatwick that. Let the man think he was some sort of wizard. A little mystery couldn't hurt his reputation.

"I didn't mean anything by it. It's just . . . standard procedure. You know. By the books."

"There's a book that says that when an agent starts sitting around in his office in the dark all day he needs psychiatric counseling?"

"Well, I don't really need a book to figure that one out." Gatwick took a deep breath. "Look, Max. It's not like I haven't seen this before. I've been in the Service a long time. Longer than you."

"Your point being?"

"You've been through a traumatic event."

"We all were. Every one of us in Oklahoma City that day."

"Yes, but you had it worse than most."

"I'd say the eight agents who died probably had it worse than most."

"Max. You know what I mean."

Yes, unfortunately, Zimmer did know what he meant. He meant that he was suffering more posttraumatic stress than the others—because he was protecting the first lady when she was killed.

"You did everything according to protocol, Max. Right down the line. You went straight to her, carried her off the dais. You did everything you could. There just wasn't enough time."

"Or agents."

Gatwick stared at the carpet. "You and I both know that, whether we like it or not, the President of the United States is our first priority. That's why most of the agents in the immediate area raced to protect him."

"If there had been more agents around the first lady, she might still be alive."

"Yes, and the president might be dead! Would that be better?"

Zimmer threw his book down on the table and pushed away from the desk. "I don't know, Tom. I just . . . I don't know anything anymore."

"That's why you need to talk to someone. Someone professional."

"But what you said . . ." Zimmer paused, trying to think just exactly how to say it. "It isn't true."

Gatwick's eyebrows knitted together. "What isn't true?"

"What you said about how I followed protocol. I didn't. *We* didn't."

"What are you talking about?"

"I think you know. The defense formation we agreed upon was Domino Bravo. But you changed that at the last minute. You moved the first lady."

"Are you suggesting her death was my fault?"

"The only thing I'm suggesting is that you broke protocol."

"And it's a damn good thing I did. The killers obviously knew our defense plan as well as we did. They knew exactly how to hit us the hardest. They were probably monitoring our communications— which is supposed to be impossible. They knew where the agents would be located. Altering the preplanned defense formation was probably the best thing I could have possibly done."

Zimmer looked at him stonily. "You moved her."

"I took her out of a potential line of fire. Which turned out not to be potential at all, but very real."

"If she had been closer to the president, it might've been easier for the Secret Service agents on hand to protect her. To protect them both."

Gatwick leaned across Zimmer's desk, his face rippling with suppressed anger. "Are you sure you're not suggesting that the first lady's death was my fault?"

They stared each other down for a long moment.

"No, of course not," Zimmer said finally. "I'm just saying . . . we have a lot to account for. We made mistakes. And we paid dearly for them."

Gatwick balled his fists. "I am . . . outraged by the suggestion that my actions killed the first lady. I knew Emily Blake. I knew her personally."

Zimmer's face remained stoic. "That's what I've heard."

"I don't know what you've heard, but we were friends. Good friends. Known each other since college. She specially requested that I be assigned to any security detail that involved her."

"So you would always be wherever she was."

"Yes, so—" Gatwick stopped short. "What the hell are you saying?"

Zimmer waved his hand in the air. "The only thing I'm saying is that we screwed up. That's the truth. We need to admit it and accept it."

"Is that what you're worried about? Sharing the blame? Max— I will not let them scapegoat you. I was in charge on site. I take full responsibility for everything."

"Sounds good. But when the hellhounds need a sacrifice, it won't be you."

"There aren't going to be any scapegoats. No one wants one. All the polls show the people don't see this as a failing on the part of the government. They see an evil enemy who will be unstoppable unless we make serious changes in current law enforcement procedures."

Zimmer fingered the Secret Service pin on the lapel of his midnight-blue suit. He had been so proud the day he received it. Now it seemed like a horrible reminder of his greatest failure, a millstone weighing him down so heavily, he could barely walk. "I've seen those polls. The president's proposed amendment is barely a day old and already the majority of the population favors its passage."

"And thank God for that. We need it, Max."

"Do we?"

"If we're going to do our job, yes. If we're going to prevent Oklahoma City from ever happening again. Those terrorists are bastards. They don't care about civil rights. We have to fight fire with fire."

Zimmer's mind wandered even as Gatwick continued his rant on the need for stronger crime-fighting laws. He'd heard it all before. Ever since the Service had been transferred to Homeland Security in 2003, they had been obsessed with stopping terrorism. That wasn't their job. Ironically, the Service had first been created in 1865 to suppress counterfeit currency, which is why it was part of the Treasury Department. After the assassination of President McKinley in 1901, they added the protection of the president to their list of duties, and over the years that became their primary focus. When Zimmer first joined the Service only a few years ago, their job description had been pretty simple. They protected the president, the first lady, their family, all their transportation vehicles, the White House and other presidential offices, the vice-president and his family, presidential candidates, and the occasional foreign dignitary. But with 9/11, it all changed. Now they were inextricably linked with Homeland Security and the orange alerts and all the other counter-terrorism efforts enacted with more fear than thought in the aftermath of that great tragedy.

Could he fault the American people for the direction public opinion was taking? The fact is, the Secret Service had more than 5,000 employees, including 2,100 special agents. But they still hadn't been able to prevent the April 19 massacre.

And he hadn't been able to save the first lady.

Zimmer suddenly realized that Gatwick had stopped talking. He was probably waiting for some kind of response, but Zimmer had no idea what that might be.

"I take it from your silence," Gatwick said, "that you actually oppose the president's proposed amendment?"

Zimmer tilted his head silently.

"Let me guess. Secretly a card-carrying ACLU member? Bill of Rights freak?"

"Is it freaky to think the Bill of Rights important?"

Gatwick rolled his eyes. "If you knew how many convictions we've lost because some damn lawyer made a constitutional argument based on those ten amendments—"

"But how many people have avoided false conviction because they were in place?"

"For a guy supposedly torn up about the act of an unknown terrorist or terrorist cell, you're pretty damn generous about making sure they have their rights."

"The Bill of Rights is not just about guaranteeing rights to accused criminals." Zimmer picked up the book he had tossed onto his desk. "I've been doing a little reading. Something I found in the library. Do you know why the Bill of Rights exists?"

"Well . . ."

"It exists because the people demanded it. Not the Founding Fathers—they thought the Constitution was a sufficient guarantee of rights in and of itself. But the people wanted more. Even after the Constitution was ratified, there was a strong feeling that the rights of states and individuals should be given greater protection. So at the very first session of Congress, back in 1791, they began drafting a Bill of Rights. Patrick Henry wanted twenty amendments; James Madison fought for twelve. But the Massachusetts delegation wanted the ten we have today, and they were influential enough to get their way. Not all the states adopted them immediately, though. In fact, three of the original thirteen states didn't ratify the Bill of Rights until 1939."

"This is all very fascinating, but—"

"Since that time, the Constitution has been amended only twenty-seven times in more than two hundred years. But there have been more than six thousand proposed amendments. Everything you can imagine. Abolish the electoral college. Limit private income to ten million dollars. Replace the presidency with a three-person council. Change the name of the country to the United States of Earth."

"I'm amazed that one didn't go through," Gatwick said drolly. "So what's your point, assuming you actually have one?"

"There are two things I've gathered from my research. One: the people, when they are thinking rationally, want a Bill of Rights. And two: we need a slow and deliberate process to prevent wacky amendments from becoming law."

"Aw, hell. It'll probably take forever. That ERA thing was tossed about for years."

"But it never made it into the Constitution. Three states short. The timing wasn't right. It was too soon."

"So if this drags on for years—"

"The Twenty-sixth Amendment, on the other hand, became national law only three months and seven days after it came out of

Congress. That was the one that gave eighteen-year-olds the right to vote. Of course, the Vietnam War was raging. If eighteen-year-old boys could be shipped overseas to be napalmed to death, shouldn't they have a say in the government that was sending them? It was the right idea at the right time. The amendment was adopted practically overnight."

"And your big worry?"

Zimmer looked up from his book. "This is clearly the right time for this amendment. Couldn't ever be a better one. But what if it's the right time—but the wrong law?"

Gatwick waved him away. "I think you worry too much. Because you're depressed about what happened. Give it a week or so—you'll see the light."

Zimmer's eyes seemed far away. "Perhaps."

"Anyway, the states will never vote on it if it doesn't get out of Congress. And how can it, with flaming liberals in the Senate like that kid from Oklahoma?"

9

U.S. SENATE, RUSSELL BUILDING,
OFFICE S-212-D
WASHINGTON, D.C.

"You see what he's trying to do, don't you?" Christina asked. "The president is using the tragedy to promote his own agenda. After the Kennedy assassination, LBJ could get almost anything passed in Kennedy's memory. This is the same thing. President Blake is using his wife's memory to promote his own conservative goals. To get rid of those pesky civil rights once and for all."

Ben stared down at the blue-backed bill resting on his desk. "I think that's a bit extreme."

"It's a pretty extreme bill." Christina paced back and forth across the length of Ben's office. "Okay, here's what we do. First, I'll line up all the chiefs of staff and take the pulse of their bosses. *Tout de suite.* I think we can assume the president will get the votes of all or most of his fellow Republicans, but he's going to need more than that to get this passed. He'll pull his strings with the religious right and the wealthiest political donors. He'll try to make it a matter of patriotism. He'll suggest that people who oppose the amendment don't care about the safety of the nation. They'll be trotting out relatives of the victims, trying to make it an emotional issue. This amendment is already being met with cheers and applause in the red states and at least half of the blue. He may have sufficient support in thirty-eight states, and that's all he needs to make this thing law—if it gets out of Congress. So we have to make sure that never happens."

She grabbed her husband squarely by the shoulders. "You'll have to be at the forefront of the fight, Ben. Whether you like it or not, you have a reputation for being one of the most liberal senators in Congress. How many other senators do you think we can count on to oppose this?"

She paused, waiting for an answer. "Ben?"

He looked up, his eyes dark and tiny.

"I asked, 'How many senators do you think we can count on to oppose this?'"

Ben tossed his head to one side. "I . . . really don't know."

She leaned across the desk. "Why are you mumbling?"

"I didn't realize I was."

"Trust me. I've known you a long time." Her eyebrows knitted together. "Why am I getting the feeling you're not hearing what I've been saying?"

Ben looked down again. "I heard you. Every word."

"And you understand why it's important to move quickly?"

No response.

"And we're going to fight this thing, right?" She waited an uncomfortably long time. "Right?"

Ben picked up the bill. "You know, Christina . . . these are tough times."

She stared at him, her eyes wide. *"No."*

"You haven't spent most of the past week watching your best friend vegetate in a coma he may never recover from."

"But that's not the point—"

"I think it is," Ben said, his voice rising.

She gaped at him, incredulous. "What are you saying, Ben?" Pause. *"Ben?"*

He gazed down at the bill now clenched tightly between his fingers. "I think maybe this isn't such a bad idea."

10

Belinda DeMouy walked briskly through the dark underground parking garage. This was no place for a lady, much less a senator's wife. It would have been smarter to park in one of the areas patrolled by the Capitol Police, but sometimes even a blue-blooded daughter of the American Revolution from Martha's Vineyard didn't make the smartest choice. Actually, she reflected, some might argue that her entire life had been a case study in not making the smartest choice. But it had worked out all right. She had her health, she had her weight back down into the double digits, and she was very popular with the other senators' wives—even though most of them were considerably older than she was. She gave great tea. Even when she wasn't smart, she was always proper.

Where exactly had she parked? If she got close enough to her car, she could use her keyless lock to flash the lights and make a beeping sound. Problem was, you had to practically be at the car before the keyless would work. Her Jag was equipped with a GPS so she wouldn't get lost while driving. What a joke. She needed a GPS in her purse so she could find the car. Or she could leave it and take a taxi home. But no. That would not be proper.

Her mother's favorite word. Proper.

She had been raised to do everything just so. There was a right way and a wrong way, and the Bradford girls did things the right way. Tasteful, fashionable clothes, matched and accessorized to perfection. Makeup. Hair styled and dyed and tone-matched to your complexion. Appearance. Presentation. Bradford girls must always be on their best behavior. Napkin in lap. The right fork. Appropriate dinner conversation. Dating only those boys deemed suitable for a Bradford girl. And even then—well, she was twenty-five before she let anyone get past first base.

Her marriage, to a politician twenty-two years her senior, had been calculated, strategized, and arranged. It was a good marriage, at least as judged by the society page. The engagement party, the bridal shower where she made the rehearsed speech telling all the guests how important they were to her, the wedding at Washington National Cathedral, and her elegant Vera Wang bridal gown. She had proved a great asset to her husband in his senate work, not to mention on the campaign trail. If nothing else, she ended the constant rumors and speculation that haunted every unmarried politico—the suspicion of gayness. And now they were saying Jeff would become the next Senate majority leader in the wake of Senator Hammond's death. Amazing. In many respects, it would be the apex of his career—at least, so far. Much as he denied it, she knew he wanted to make a run for the presidency. This "apex" might well be the stepping-stone he planned to convert into a much bigger move. She knew something was in the offing. Jeff had always been busy, but these days she wasn't even sure he slept. It wasn't just the amendment debate, either, although he was doing a lot of wheeling and dealing on that. He was constantly over at Homeland Security, taking closed-door meetings at strange hours. Had been for months. What were they hatching?

She'd spent the evening being introduced to so many people, she couldn't count them. She'd given up on trying to remember names after the first fifty or so. Of course, she always behaved properly at these little soirees—but that didn't mean she had to remember all the guests' names and the names of their children, and which was the scholar and which was the drug addict, and all the other biographical minutiae. Her husband's chief of staff, Jason Simic, always took care of her. He was very good at what he did.

She turned the corner in the parking garage and saw the cobalt blue nose of her XJS poking out. Very chic. She and Jeff had never had children, so she was spared the whole minivan thing. This was much more to her liking. Sporty and elegant. Much like she herself. They went together like—

Did she hear something? She stopped for a moment to listen. Nothing. And for that matter, if she did hear something, stopping to listen would probably be about the most stupid thing she could possibly do. Better just to keep walking . . .

There it was again. Footsteps, and not hers. Of course, that was no cause for concern, even at this time of night. There were other cars in here. She didn't expect a lot of traffic this late, but it was certainly possible.

Belinda resumed walking. The footsteps returned. Okay, that was a little creepy. She walked faster. At this point, the smartest thing she could do was get inside her car and get the doors locked. It was ridiculous to be scared, wasn't it? She was a senator's wife. She wasn't that far from the Senate. Even in a city with a skyrocketing crime rate like D.C., it was absurd to think that anything could happen. She was perfectly safe. She was letting the lateness of the hour and the darkness and her imagination get to her. She was as safe as a pearl in an oyster.

She was still thinking that when she felt the hand clamp down on her mouth.

"Don't scream!" a male voice barked into her ear. She tried to resist, but he had both arms wrapped around her, holding her immobile.

When she gave up trying to struggle, he spun her around. He was tall, thin, younger than she was. Dark, in his eyes and his hair and his . . . manner.

He pulled a knife from a sheath and pressed it flat against her neck. She shuddered, involuntarily recoiling from the cold blade. It was a large curved knife with a jagged edge—a bowie knife, she thought.

"I could skin you alive," he whispered. "And I will unless you give me everything I want. Without hesitation."

She started to speak, but he pressed the knife down harder. She felt the tip prick her neck. "Whisper," he commanded.

She complied. "What—what do you want?" As she spoke she tried to look and listen for signs of other people. There were none. As far as she could tell, they were totally alone. "What are you going to do to me?"

"It's not what I'm going to do to you, at least not at first. It's what you're going to do to me."

"Look, my name is Belinda DeMouy. My husband is a senator. Senate Majority leader, in fact."

"I know."

"Are—are you some kind of terrorist?"

A thin smile curled on his lips. "Not in the way that you mean." He removed the knife and took a step back, looking her up and down, letting his eyes linger where they would.

He poked the knife toward her blouse. "Take that off."

"Here? I can't do that."

"You take it off or I'll cut it off," he growled.

Belinda's throat went dry. "Look—I've got money. Lots of it. Plastic, if you want it. More in the car."

"That's not what I'm after."

"If you've got some kind of . . . habit . . . I can get you what you need. Drugs, booze, anything."

"That's not what I want."

Desperation crept into her voice. "What do you want?"

All at once, he grabbed the back of her hair and pulled her head back harshly. He pressed his lips against her ear. "I want your clothes off. I want your panties in my teeth. I want inside you."

Oh, God. Oh, God God God God God.

"Now take off the damn blouse."

Belinda trembled. His eyes were fierce and unrelenting. She knew she had no choice.

Her hands shook as she pulled the black silk blouse over her head.

"Are they real?" he asked, none too subtly.

She tried to cover her breasts with her hands. "I've . . . had some work done."

"Thought they were pretty damn perky. Not that I mind. Take off the bra."

"Please, no. Don't make me."

"Take off the bra, woman. Now!"

"No. God, God, no."

"Then I'll do it for you." He pulled her hands away and then slid the tip of the knife under the right shoulder strap and cut it. He cut the other strap, letting his hand linger, pressed against her. He leered at her, then sliced the rear strap and watched the pink brassiere tumble to the concrete floor.

She tried to cover herself. He slapped her hands away.

"Are you—are you going to hurt me?"

"Depends on what you mean," he said, pulling back her head by the hair again and burying his face under her chin, biting her and sucking on her skin. "I like it rough."

"Oh, Goddddd . . ."

A second later, his hand was up her skirt. He shoved her down onto the hood of her car. He ripped her panties off in one quick violent motion.

He pressed himself on top of her. "Are you ready for it, lady? 'Cause that's what's going to happen now. I'm going to take you again and again, long and hard. I'm going to pound you and pound you until you just can't stand it any longer, because it hurts but it feels good, too, 'cause you've never had anyone like me and you love it and you want more. You'll beg me for it. You'll beg me for more."

"Oh, Goddddd . . ."

"Are you ready, lady?" With the tip of the knife, he drew a line up her exposed torso, drawing circles around both breasts, then moving upward and toying with her face, her lips. "Are you ready to find out what it means to have a real man?"

She was breathing so hard and heavily, she could barely speak. "Goddddd . . ."

"I'm going to take you now. You're going to do everything I tell you to do, everything I want. And then next time . . ."

"Yes? Yes?"

"Next time," he whispered in her ear, "next time remember to tell me where you parked before you leave the office. It took me ten minutes to find you."

"Oh, God, yes. Oh yes. Oh, God, yes yes yes yes yes! . . ."

Her eyes rolled back into her head and she surrendered herself to him. She was going to come; she could feel it already building up inside her, with such speed that it frightened her. And felt so damn good.

"God, yes, Jason. God, yes. Don't stop. Don't stop. . . ."

Her husband's chief of staff, Jason Simic, always took care of her. He was very good at what he did.

11

*P*resident Franklin M. Blake sat in the Oval Office, his head resting on the historic Resolute desk, feeling nothing so much as exhaustion. The past few days had been filled with grief, coupled with a profound need to take action. The rest of the world thought he was secluded in mourning, but this office had been the site of frenzied activity, many heads working together to produce a proposed constitutional amendment in less than a week. He had been driven, and not only by the need to fulfill his duty to serve and protect this nation.

He gazed down at the framed photograph still clenched in his right hand. It was an AP shot of the two of them on the stage at Springfield the night he was elected by a sweeping majority, their outward arms raised in triumph, their inward arms wrapped around each other.

He and Emily.

What had happened since that glorious day? Of course he had

been busy—he was the leader of the free world, for God's sake. She had been busy, too. A first lady's agenda is almost as busy as a president's, and in many ways more demanding—or perhaps, demanding in different ways. She had to be feminine without appearing weak, strong without appearing masculine, valuable without becoming political. It was an almost impossible balancing act. He couldn't have done it—he knew that. But Emily could. She was something special, and her innate talent had made her one of the most popular first ladies in the history of the nation. Her approval ratings far surpassed his; by all indications, her popularity spilled over and improved his on a regular basis. She did incredible work.

And most of the time, she did it alone. No, not alone. Without him.

Was it any wonder . . . ?

His staff had been concerned for some time. Much babbling about Caesar's wife and all that rot. He didn't believe it, not a word of it.

Not until it was impossible to ignore. Or deny.

Even now as he looked at the picture, as he gazed at those lovely blue-green eyes, he knew he was deeply in love with her, a love founded on respect and admiration. He had loved her since the day they met and the affection had never waned, not in the face of all the rumors, and not now, in the face of death itself.

And yet, so many times in the preceding months, he had found himself recalling the famous words of Henry II, frustrated by Thomas Becket, the man he had loved and once called friend: Who will rid me of this meddlesome priest?

My God, he thought, his head almost pounding the desk. *What happened? What have I done?*

He stared at the green leather blotter built into the top center of the Resolute desk, so called because it had been made from the timbers of the British frigate HMS *Resolute,* discovered by American whalers after being caught in the ice and abandoned. The ship had been repaired by the U.S. Navy and returned to England as a goodwill gesture. This desk, Blake knew, had been a reciprocal gift from Queen Victoria to President Rutherford B. Hayes, many years ago.

Numerous great men had sat here pondering some of the most dire crises the nation had faced, confronting each challenge with courage and intelligence. Some had been brilliant; some had been crooks.

But no one had done what he had done. Not one of them.

He heard a knock on the northeast door. Who the hell's idea was it, anyway, to make the president's office oval-shaped? Made his head spin, some mornings. Imagine an office with four doors! The northeast door led to his secretary's office; the northwest door led to the main corridor of the West Wing; the west door led to a small study and a dining room, and the east door led directly to the Rose Garden. The president could never tell what problem was going to confront him next unless his hearing was accurate enough to trace the source of the knocking. Assuming the problem was courteous enough to knock.

Only two people came in by the northeast door, and he was relatively certain this wasn't his secretary, Emmylou.

He straightened himself, adjusted his tie, and made it look as if he had been working. "Come in, Tracy."

Tracy Sobel entered with her usual alacrity. Even walking down a West Wing corridor, she moved as though she were running a footrace. "We need to talk, Frank."

He leaned back in his chair. "What's up, Tracy?"

"Got the intel you wanted. On the amendment." She positioned herself in front of the fireplace at the north end of the room. The only three windows in the Oval Office were all south-facing and positioned behind the president's desk. In her usual station by the fireplace, she was directly in front of him. Unavoidable. Just understanding that told you everything you needed to know about Tracy Sobel. Appointing a female chief of staff had seemed a brilliant idea when he did it, and to her credit, Sobel had performed efficiently and given him no cause for complaint. But he was never entirely comfortable around her and he suspected he never would be. It wasn't that she was female. It was that she was Tracy. "I'd have to say it's going down even better than you expected. But there are still hitches."

"There always are," Blake said amiably, trying to erase every trace of the grief and doubt he had been wallowing in only moments before. "That's life in politics."

"Your military advisors are all in favor of the amendment. For whatever it's worth, I think you can count on one hundred percent support from the Pentagon."

"No big surprise there."

"No. And that generally goes for the federal and state law enforcement communities. Lots of talk about protecting the rights of the people, not the rights of criminals and terrorists. You know, the usual cant people use when they want to disregard the Constitution."

Blake raised an eyebrow. That was telling. "What's the word at Homeland Security?"

"Oh, Carl Lehman thinks this is the greatest idea since wheeled luggage."

"He would. Started with a memo he sent, you know."

Sobel batted her pencil against her clipboard. "Was it also his idea that he be designated chairman of the Emergency Security Council?"

"Well . . ." The president grinned. "He suggested it as a possibility. Makes a certain sense. They are supposed to be our first line of defense against domestic terrorism."

"But it didn't make the amendment popular with the director of the FBI. Or the CIA."

"I thought about both of those possibilities. I even considered some sort of three-man tribunal. But you know that would only lead to chaos. There needed to be one person in charge. Someone who could set the agenda, make sure things got done."

"I understand your reasoning, sir. But if the director of the FBI comes out publicly against this amendment—"

"He won't. What could he say, other than he's jealous because ever since Homeland Security was created, his agency has seemed less important? How could he explain to the law enforcement world why he objects to them acquiring additional powers in a time of great need? He's not that stupid."

"With all due respect, sir, it's hard to gauge just how stupid a man can be when he's really pissed off."

Again Blake raised an eyebrow. The always professional Ms.

Sobel did not often go in for profanity, even something as mild as that. Despite her measured and professional demeanor, he definitely detected an edge about her today.

"If the FBI had made any progress catching the assassin," Blake responded, "I might be more sympathetic. Have they got any leads at all?"

"They've got hundreds of leads, Mr. President. And they're following up on them. They've assigned all available manpower and then some to the case."

"But so far—nothing."

"They're very interested in that Middle Eastern group that's taken credit for the attack. Saifullah."

"Because they have evidence indicating these people were behind the shooting? Or because they're an easy and readily available target?"

Sobel paused before answering. "Because they're investigating all possibilities. With great vigor."

"Tell them I don't give a damn about their vigor. I want to know who killed my wife."

"Understood, sir. But if it is a Middle Eastern group—it may not be within the FBI's jurisdiction."

"I don't give a damn about jurisdiction, either. Haven't I made it clear I want everyone working together on this?"

"Yes, sir. You have."

"This isn't about who gets to take credit. This is about catching the bastards and making them pay for what they've done."

"Yes, sir. Understood, sir." Sobel brushed a strand of her yellow-blond hair off her forehead. Every lock perfectly in place.

"What about Congress? Do you have a feel for what's going on there? I've been on the phone most of the morning, but I can't get any straight answers."

"I think we can count on early passage in the House," she replied. "We still have a large majority there. Polls show most people favor the amendment. They're not going to go against party lines and public sentiment. The Senate is a little more difficult to call."

"And why is that, Tracy? I thought you had the inside track to everyone worth knowing."

"Probably an accurate assessment, sir," she said, without the slightest hint of irony. "But there's still a certain amount of chaos in the wake of the Oklahoma City tragedy. Two Democratic senators gone. The new minority leader barely has his head on straight."

"Some of those Democrats like to rattle on about constitutional rights, although sometimes I suspect the men have never actually read the document." He pushed away from his desk and paced a moment, walking closer to Sobel, pausing at the north end of the room just beside the portrait of George Washington. "What about you, Tracy? What are your thoughts about the amendment?"

"My job is to make your policy reality, sir."

"Yes, but that wasn't the question." He was standing close to her now, close enough that she was forced to look directly into his eyes. He prided himself on his ability to communicate, on his ability to talk to people and make them feel as if they were the only sentient beings in his universe while they talked. That, perhaps more than any other, was the attribute necessary for success in politics, at least in his opinion. He was giving Tracy that look now, and she was probably familiar enough with it to know that he wasn't going to let her slip away. "I asked you what you thought of this amendment. You, personally."

"Does it matter?"

"It does to me."

She stared at him a moment, blinked a few times, then answered, "Well, sir, since you asked, I think it's a very bad idea."

"And why is that?"

"I believe the Bill of Rights exists for a reason. To protect the people from the state. If we allow those rights to be taken away under any circumstance, we risk losing them forever."

"Those rights have been suspended many times before when our security was threatened. Lincoln suspended habeas corpus. The NSA wiretapped private citizens—"

"Yes, but that was blatantly illegal and unconstitutional, even if they got away with it. It wasn't done under the color of law. This amendment would change that. It would effectively repeal the Bill of Rights during a time of crisis. If we allow those rights to be taken away in this manner—we may never get them back."

"I think you're being a bit melodramatic."

"Sir, the Founding Fathers—"

"They killed my wife, Tracy!" He took a step back, his elbow resting on the Spanish ivy atop the mantel. His voice dropped to a whisper. "The bastards killed my wife."

Sobel's eyes dropped to her clipboard. "I know, sir."

Blake took a moment, wiped his forehead, pulled himself together. "Sorry. I just got—"

"No need to apologize, Mr. President. None at all."

"So," he said, wiping his eyes, "I guess the question is whether you're going to be able to work for me effectively on a bill you don't support."

"Of course I will, sir. No question about it. That's my job."

"Even if you oppose my policy?"

"With respect, sir—are you assuming this is the first time I've opposed one of your policies?"

Now that took him by surprise. Maybe this woman had hidden depths he'd never imagined. "All right then, Tracy. You're my master architect. Tell me how I get this amendment through the Senate. As quickly as possible."

"It won't be easy, sir. It might be impossible."

"Yes, yes, cut through all the 'impossible odds' chatter. I already know you're a miracle worker, and I already know you have a plan. Spill."

Sobel tapped her clipboard a few times before answering. "You are aware, I assume, that"—she drew in her breath—"Major Morelli has not come out of his coma. In fact, he's still in ICU. Critical condition."

"Yes, I read the update this morning. Your point?"

"He was—is—Senator Kincaid's best friend. Has been for many years."

"Isn't Kincaid pretty liberal?"

"What I hear is that he's very shaken up about his friend. Has spent days in the man's hospital room."

"Kincaid's the most junior senator the Democrats have. At least until the governors appoint replacements for Tidwell and Hammond. How influential can he be?"

"How influential was he during the confirmation hearings for Justice Roush?"

The president pursed his lips. "Mmm. Good point. So you're suggesting . . . ?"

"I think you know what I'm suggesting, sir. And as it happens, I have the phone number right here."

12

U.S. Senate, Russell Building,
Office S-212-D
Washington, D.C.

Christina rushed into the office, her arms brimming over with files, folders, and large saddle-stitched reports. Somehow, in an act seemingly defiant of gravity, she also managed to carry a briefcase, although in the mass of paperwork obscuring the upper half of her body and most of her strawberry blond hair, the briefcase seemed to be floating along on its own powers of levitation.

As she passed by his station, Jones eyed her with his usual stoic expression. "Got anything going on, Chris? Or are you just goofing off again?"

As if in response, or perhaps in revenge, she dumped the entire mass of papers on his desk, knowing full well the effect it would have on Jones's neat-freak temperament.

When the screaming stopped, she smiled and said succinctly, "File that, would you?"

Jones's eyes narrowed to tiny slits. If heat vision had been among his powers, Christina would have been charbroiled. "May I ask what this is?"

"Everything I've been able to drum up relating to the new proposed constitutional amendment. Polling data, both of the public and the Congress. Judicial and historical precedents. A formal copy of the evil amendment itself as submitted to the appropriate committees in both houses. And a lot of other crap acquired from virtually every other senator's office."

"Were you able to get an idea which way Congress leans on this?"

"The problem is that every other chief of staff in every other office is doing exactly the same thing."

"Ah, but they don't all have your gift for setting tongues a-wagging."

"Well, I like to think I have a certain panache," she said, lightly buffing the bob of her hair. "But they do their best. At any rate, I was able to learn what the consensus opinion is on who's leaning where. Whether that reflects actual reality I can't be certain."

"So don't keep me in suspense."

Christina picked up one of the file folders she had dumped on Jones's desk and flipped it open. "Everyone seems to think the House is a done deal. The Republicans have a significant majority; the president basically has them in his back pocket."

"But he'll need two-thirds."

"And everyone seems to think he'll get it, given the massive public support for the bill. Have you seen today's polls?" Jones nodded. "They show that the voting public favor passage by a huge margin. Apparently a lot of people have always thought civil rights favored criminals more than good honest God-fearing folk. But even some who generally consider themselves civil libertarians are supporting the bill. The attack in Oklahoma City dramatically changed the way some people think."

"It—was a rather horrific event," Jones said. "You can see where people might feel the need for greater protection."

"I can see that people are running scared," Christina replied. "And when people are scared, they don't think clearly. Somehow, we have to slow down this process. Give the reasoning public a chance for some sober second thoughts." She did a quick scan of the office. "So where's our dear senator Benjamin?"

Jones hedged. "Well . . ."

Loving, their huge barrel-chested investigator, sauntered down the hallway, grinning from ear to ear. "I think the correct answer to that question is: Deep in hiding."

Christina couldn't help returning the smile. "Good to see you again, Loving. How was the vacation?"

"It . . . had some interestin' moments. But I came back soon as I heard about the amendment."

"Appreciate that. So Ben is hiding from the press?"

Loving chuckled. "Actually, I think he's mostly hiding from you."

"Damn well he should. First the man cancels my honeymoon, then he says he thinks this fascist amendment might not be a bad idea. Ever since the attack, I've barely seen him. He always manages to come back to the apartment after I'm sound asleep. I don't even remember the last time we—"

"Whoa, whoa, whoa!" Loving held out his hands. "Too much information alert."

"Moving right along," Jones said, nervously shuffling his papers. "You do remember that Ben is supposed to represent his home state, don't you? He should implement the will of his people, not the, um, will of his wife."

Christina gave him a look that could stop traffic.

"Support for this bill in Oklahoma is even higher than the national average. The word on the street—"

"Is this the word on the street?" Christina said sharply, "or the word in the library?" Jones's wife, Paula, was a librarian for the Tulsa City/County Library system.

"I have talked to Paula, since you ask, in your rather pointed I'm-an-underdog-and-crusader-for-justice-so-I-can-be-as-rude-as-I-want way. She says she doesn't know anyone who doesn't support the amendment. And she travels with a pretty highbrow crowd."

"I hear the same thing from my people," Loving added.

Christina suspected that "his people" were mostly found in honky-tonks and strip bars, but still, they were giving her an interesting cross section of public opinion.

"Just because it's popular doesn't make it right."

"No," Jones replied, "but bear in mind that Ben is not only Oklahoma's U.S. senator, he's currently Oklahoma's *only* U.S. senator. Doesn't he have an obligation to vote the will of the people?"

"Absolutely not," Christina said firmly. "He has an obligation to do what he thinks is right. Public opinion is no excuse for betraying your conscience. If the people don't like what he does, they can vote him out next election."

"Well, technically, they never voted him in."

"Nonetheless, while he's in office, his job is to do what's best for the nation. Which is not necessarily appeasing a reactionary public opinion."

"But what if he wants to run for reelection?" Loving asked. "Goin' against a huge majority favorin' the amendment could tank him."

"Have you heard him say he's running for reelection? Last I heard he was still dithering about, avoiding a commitment. As usual."

"This amendment's gonna be a big deal, Chris. If he comes out on the wrong side—it's good-bye Washington."

Christina grabbed her phone messages—there were more than thirty—and marched back to the main corridor. "This speculation is all well and good, but I think I'd like to talk to the senator myself. There's a remote chance he may have made up his mind what he wants to do. I'll—"

The phone rang, cutting her off.

"Just a minute, Chris," Jones said, clicking the button that activated his phone earpiece. "It's probably for you."

He waited a moment, listening to the voice on the other end of the line. His jaw slowly dropped. "Or . . . maybe not."

He continued listening. Christina and Loving moved in closer.

"Oh, right. Like he makes his own phone calls. Is this you, Morgan? Because if it is, let me tell you that this is not funny in—"

Another abrupt pause. "Really?" Jones's shoulders sagged. His forehead creased. "Really? Well, I don't know exactly where he is, sir, but I can find him. Yes. As soon as possible."

Christina gave him a long look. "Who's calling?" she whispered.

Jones cleared his throat again. "That would be the, um, President of the United States," he said, his voice warbling. "And he wants to see Ben. Immediately."

13

DOVE AVENUE
ROCKVILLE, MARYLAND

Shohreh's hands trembled even as she completed her *salat,* but it was not due to her fear of God. It was due to her fear of what she had to do next.

Like every good Muslim, she recited her morning prayers, but on this particular morning, she did so with a sense of both conviction and desire that exceeded the norm. She needed God's help. She would never be able to do this alone. But it had to be done. She had sworn an oath to God, and she had made a promise to Djamila. So she performed the usual ritual cleansing, removed her shoes, draped her head, and placed herself on her prayer rug, standing, then sitting, then bowing and prostrating herself as she performed the invocations of faith.

"*La ilaha illa'Llah,*" she recited. There is no god but God. That was the *shahada,* the fundamental statement of her religion. She recited from memory the opening *sura* from the Qur'an. As always, she recited silently, moving her lips but not speaking aloud. These words were for God and no one else, and He did not need to hear the words to know they were being said. When at last she finished, she changed her clothes and left the shabby apartment to do what had to be done.

She hated this neighborhood. She had left as soon as she extracted herself from the cell and promised never to return. Rockville was actually one of the better suburbs in the D.C. area: population of only about sixty thousand, good schools, clean streets. The pride of Montgomery County, favored by many politicians, staff members, and even lobbyists—the people with the real money. But like every other town in this dramatically divided country, there was a dark underbelly, the slum neighborhood that provided housing affordable to low-income workers who made it possible for the rest of the town to live in the manner that they did. Even given her circumstances, she knew she could do better.

And she had not been gone a week when she received that fateful call, the one she should never have answered. The one that took her to Oklahoma City.

Damn Yaseen. The General, as he was so fond of being called. He knew she would not be able to say no. He had been a Shiite general, back before he was forced to leave Iraq. He knew how to lead. And he knew how to manipulate. He knew how to make sure she would not be able to refuse.

She had gone to Oklahoma City, done as he asked, and regretted it ever since. Before, she had been almost invisible. Now she lived in fear of discovery, a discovery that would not only end her own short life, but make it impossible to honor her commitment to Djamila. She knew that every law enforcement official in the country was poring over the footage that had been taken by the media in Oklahoma City. It didn't matter that she had disguised herself, changed her name, traveled under false papers. Eventually someone would remember seeing her there. They would link her to the cell. And given the current sentiment in the country, she would be lucky if she were not lynched in the street.

Americans were so easily led. She remembered the first Oklahoma City incident, the bombing that cost so many lives. In the immediate aftermath, all the experts and commentators attributed the attack to Middle Eastern terrorists. Several of her friends were beaten mercilessly that night by rednecks for no reason other than the color of their skin. And the next day the truth was revealed. The bombing had nothing to do with Middle Eastern terrorists. It was a homegrown crazy, an antigovernment zealot just as white as the stars on the American flag.

And now, once again, most people had no idea what had really happened a little over a week ago in Oklahoma City. But she did, at least somewhat. That information alone made her a keenly sought target by both American law enforcement and the members of her former cell. One wanted to question her; the other to kill her.

Shohreh was five foot three, petite, barely a hundred pounds. What chance did she have, a woman alone against powers so great? But what chance had she ever had? What choice did she ever have?

None. None at all.

Her identity papers said she was Saudi Arabian, a deceit practiced so commonly in the aftermath of President Bush's invasion of her homeland that it was barely worth the trouble. In truth, she was Iraqi, a Sunni Muslim. Globally, more than eighty percent of all Muslims were Sunnis. Only in Iraq were they in the minority. The division was almost as old as Islam itself, dating back to the seventh century. The Shiites believed that Muhammad had selected his son-in-law and cousin, Ali ibn Abi Talib to be his successor prophet. Shiites traditionally performed a hajj to the Blue Mosque in Mazar-i-Sharif where Ali was buried. Sunnis believed that Muhammad had not chosen a successor so the church leaders, the caliphates, should guide the church. The differences were trivial compared to the doctrinal distinctions that divided the hundreds of Christian denominations. But the differences had proved great enough to produce incalculable bloodshed, leading to the loss of millions of lives. Sunnis and Shiites were impossible to distinguish by appearance, but their names were often a clear indicator to the knowledgeable elite, and all Iraqis were required to carry a national identification card. Omar, Marwan, and Othman were popular Sunni given names; Ali,

Abbas, and Hussein were equally popular among Shiites. So those in the minority often changed their birth names, even though to do so was considered shameful and abhorrent—but not enough so as to inspire many to reveal a name that in the wrong circle could be an instant death sentence. During the Gulf War, when Iraqi civilians were often stopped at military checkpoints or even randomly on the streets, a name or hometown suggesting affiliation with the rival sect could lead to summary execution. Identification forgery became a boom business.

Shohreh was a "Saudi Arabian" name she adopted when she came to America, although her associates knew her only as 355. She resisted both changes. What was wrong with her original name?

A good deal, as it turned out.

She heard something move behind her and froze. She hated these streets. She might as well be walking through a war zone in her home country, waiting for another American bomb dropped from thirty thousand feet to kill anonymous targets.

Someone was moving back there. She was certain of it.

A cold sweat broke out all over her body. She felt paralyzed, afraid or unable to move. She was breathing fast and shallow, making noise at just the moment she knew she most needed to remain silent. The people looking for her were trained to kill instantly, efficiently, in so many ways that there was always some means available. They could kill with a pencil, a matchstick, a spoon. They could kill with their bare hands and it would take only slightly longer. They were the deadliest people on the face of the earth.

Had they found her at last?

Her knees trembling, she turned slowly to face whatever lurked in the darkness.

A cat jumped off a trash can and scampered away.

She would've laughed if she hadn't been so terrified. This was only a temporary reprieve, not a release. The General had said he would come alone, but she knew better. He would not come at all. He would send someone else; he would take no risks, not even with a tiny woman with no friends or resources. Not even with a former ally.

Shohreh had lived a privileged life, once upon a time, far from the cliché American view of life for a woman in the Middle East. In Iraq, even while Saddam Hussein ruled, Shohreh's mother could drive a car, she could vote, she could leave home without a note from her husband, and she didn't have to be completely covered from head to foot—unlike Saudi women. Shohreh had been well educated. She wore clothes she chose herself. She welcomed the American invasion.

And then one day she came back and found her entire affluent neighborhood was gone. Flattened by an off-target American air strike. It was the last day she saw her parents.

It was the last day she saw Djamila.

She initially lived with relatives in Tikrit, thought to be much safer than Baghdad. They died in a car bombing. She found work as a servant in Mosul, demeaning for a person of her background, but still, a way of living. But the war followed her there, too. All at once, this privileged well-educated woman was homeless, caught in the crossfire between the rapidly growing army of the insurgents and the Americans. What was she to do?

The General had the answers she sought. And she would regret that every day thereafter.

General Yaseen Daraji hated the Americans for, he claimed, philosophical and political reasons. They cared nothing about human rights for Iraqis, or freedom or self-governance. They didn't even care about the supposed weapons of mass destruction or catching the perpetrators of 9/11. All they cared about was oil, he preached. This was a war of aggression carried out not by political ideologues, but by businessmen.

As she would later realize to her great dismay, the General was a businessman, too. In the most horrible business imaginable.

As all good Muslims knew, the greater jihad was the internal struggle to obey the teachings of Muhammad. In time, thanks to the General, she was allowed to join the lesser jihad, the holy war, the struggle against the invaders who had divided her country. She should have known better—but what choice did she have, really?

She arrived at the appointed rendezvous and, although it went against her every instinct, she turned down the alley that bisected the Dove Avenue and Second Street block and plunged in. If it had been dark before, it was black now, an absolute Stygian nothingness. The stench was tremendous. Even without vision, she knew she was plunging into a sea of mud and grime and human waste.

She could not see anything. She did not hear anything. And she knew they were there. Three of them.

She slid on her glasses and waited for them to make the first move.

"355?" one of them said, in their native tongue.

"I'm here, Ahmed." She recognized his voice. They had been associates, companions. They had worked together on many occasions. "Where is the General?"

"He has unfortunately been detained. And please do not use my other name. You know how this is done."

"Sorry, 111. The General said he would come alone."

"He thought it unwise to leave the safe house. Given the current state of national security."

"I'm sure the current state of affairs has not prevented him from conducting his business. I was not anxious to leave safety, either." She could sense that the two men behind her were moving closer. "And yet I came."

A long pause ensued. She waited. Even at this point, she held out hope that she would be honored by those with whom she had worked so long and done so much.

"Please follow me," the one she called 111 instructed.

The other two silent men inched even closer. They were near enough now that she had a sense of them. They were huge men, bulky, both at least a foot taller than she. And she knew from experience how formidable Ahmed was.

"Please, 355. Follow me."

Again the two associates stepped closer. She did not move at all.

"If you planned to take me to the General," she said, her voice calm and even, "you would blindfold me. You have not come to escort me. You have come to kill me."

Ahmed was silent; then he gave a quick gesture to his companions that they heard more than saw. "I told the General you would be wary."

"But he did not really care, since he was planning to have you kill me anyway."

Ahmed did not bother to respond. "You are a woman, vastly outnumbered. Our strength far exceeds yours. It would be better if you did not struggle."

"Better for you, at any rate," Shohreh said, and a moment later, she felt one of the men behind her wrap his arms around her body while the other crept toward her from the front, his arms outstretched to strangle her.

She knew she must act in seconds, or she would lose the opportunity forever. She recognized the Thai clinch; she knew how to break it and she knew how to make it work to her favor. Bracing her arms back against the man holding her, she used him as a fulcrum and flung both feet forward in a frontal teep, or foot jab. She caught the man in front of her just under the chin, knocking him backward. Before the other man could react, she rammed her elbow back with a diagonal thrust. Because he was so much taller, she caught him in the side of his rib cage, but that was enough to loosen his grip. She swung around and delivered an uppercut elbow to his eyebrow. The blow ripped open the skin and the wound bled profusely, blinding him almost instantaneously. He fell to his knees, clutching his face and crying out.

Shohreh whirled around. The other attacker had recovered and was almost upon her. She knew he, too, was trained in the Muay Thai, and given his greater strength, it would be a mistake to let him get close again. She might surprise him once, but this time he would be more careful. She would use the *kao loi;* it was the only maneuver that would give her a chance in such close quarters. While he was still several feet away, she sprang forward, leaped off one knee, but while in midair switched to the other knee and smashed the side of his head. Before he could recover, she followed with a roundhouse kick, slamming her shin into his neck. Like all trained in the Muay Thai, she knew the foot had many bones and was fragile, the knee was easily broken, but a trained and muscled shin was almost invulnerable. She delivered another blow with her other shin and he fell to the pavement, motionless.

The man behind her was still struggling to stand and see. She used a simple *kao tone* to the chin to finish him. He reeled backward, writhing in pain.

Ahmed was still out there, somewhere in the darkness. She executed a 360-degree turn, her hands raised in the traditional "wall of defense" that prepared her for any attack from any direction. Nothing came.

"Will you not fight, Ahmed?" she shouted into the black emptiness. "Or are you so weak now, you leave that only to your clumsy assistants?"

He was, at first, understandably reluctant to speak. Then, finally: "Night-vision goggles?"

"It seemed a prudent precaution."

"It would appear that since your retirement from our cause, 355, you have acquired some new skills."

"Or perhaps I had them all along, and you and your masters were too ignorant to realize it."

"You have lost none of your skill for self-preservation."

"It would be foolish to do so, while men such as you still walk the face of the earth."

"You cannot win, Shohreh."

"I do not wish to win anything. Tell the General I want him to abandon his filthy enterprise. For Djamila's sake. Tell him that unless he gives me what I want, I will expose him."

"That would be very foolish of you."

"But I will do it, just the same. Tell him."

Out of the corner of her eye, Shohreh saw two figures at the end of the alley. Police? No, they were younger. But they were watching, apparently not so frightened as entertained. That was life here on Dove Avenue. Only a thin line separated entertainment from near death. But then, that had been the case for her for so long, for as long as she could remember.

She could not afford to remain there any longer. "This is not over, Ahmed. Tell your master to give me what I want. Or I will come and take it from him!"

She ran down the other end of the alley, staying clear of Ahmed's approximate position, disappearing into the darkness.

Her fears had been justified. The General had not come. Perhaps she had accomplished nothing. But she had to try. She owed Djamila that much. And this debt would be paid. No matter what they tried to do to her. No matter what the consequences—and she knew they would be great, if she were linked to the horror of Oklahoma City. But that did not matter.

She would have her satisfaction. They would pay in blood. Just as Djamila had done for them.

14

THE WHITE HOUSE
WASHINGTON, D.C.

*B*en had been to the White House before, sort of. He'd attended the announcement of the nomination of Supreme Court Justice Roush in the Rose Garden. He'd been through a receiving line in the eastern and oldest section of the building. So he knew, for instance, what a hassle it was to get there, even when you were being personally transported by a chauffeured limo driven by a member of the Secret Service. Ever since the 1995 bombing of the Murrah building in Oklahoma City, the Secret Service had closed off Pennsylvania Avenue from the eastern perimeter of Lafayette Park to 15th Street—the entire passage in front of the White House and then some. Now the sidewalk between the White House and the Treasury building, where the public used to line up for White House tours, was also closed. After 9/11, tours had been sharply curtailed. Now they were available only on a limited basis for groups that had made arrangements through their congressional representatives, and even then all participants had to submit to background checks. Various civic groups had opposed the street closings, but given the current security climate, Ben thought it highly unlikely any of those challenges would ever succeed. The security of the president came first— now more than ever.

Ben had never been inside the Oval Office. He knew many senators with far more years of experience than he had also never been inside this most famous of workplaces. He could barely believe he was going himself as the designated agents led him down the corridors of the West Wing.

A Secret Service agent, who had never seen the necessity of identifying himself, knocked on the east door.

"Enter."

Ben did. Standing in the northeast corner of the room, leaning against an antique grandfather clock, was the President of the United States.

Ben tried to suppress the nervous tingle that surged through his body, including the knees that were becoming increasingly wobbly. He had met the president before, of course, but not since April 19. Not since the first lady was killed. And not in the Oval Office—this was an entirely different kind of meeting.

He tried to pull himself together and act in a manner somewhat appropriate for a U.S. senator. He shuddered, trying to think how to break the ice. He wasn't sure what to say.

As they clasped hands, Ben managed, "Mr. President . . . I'm so sorry for your loss."

"And I for yours, son. I know Major Morelli is still listed in critical condition. Is there any news from the doctors?"

Ben shook his head. "I call in several times a day, but they never have anything new for me. He suffered extensive internal injuries from the explosion. He's healing, but the damage was profound. And he still hasn't come out of the coma, so even if he does recover, he might suffer—" Ben stopped himself. "But what am I talking about? My loss can't begin to compare with—"

"Every loss is felt profoundly by the persons who loved them," President Blake said, his eyes focused firmly on Ben, making him feel as if he were the only person in the room, the only person in the universe. "All hearts are equally capable of grieving. I'm sure, in your own way, you feel your loss just as much as I feel the loss of my wife."

"The whole nation feels the loss of your wife, sir," Ben replied. "I only met her once, but I thought she was an extraordinary person. Very kind."

"Thank you, son." He ran his fingers through his silver locks. "Thank you very much. I appreciate your kind words."

He turned slowly, breaking the eye contact lock. "Ben, have you met Tracy Sobel?"

An attractive woman in her fifties approached Ben with a direct and efficient manner. "Haven't had the pleasure." They shook hands. Her hands were cold.

"She's my chief of staff," the president explained, although Ben of course already knew that. "Keeps me in line," he added, winking, as if they had just shared a private joke, even though everyone in the room had heard it. "And I also want you to meet the new director of Homeland Security. Carl Lehman."

Ben nodded toward the large black man sitting on one of the sofas in front of the fireplace. Even seated, Ben could see the man was well over six feet tall.

"Would you have a seat, please, Ben?" President Blake gestured toward two high-backed Martha Washington–style lolling chairs in front of the fireplace. Ben took the seat on the right. He had noticed from various media appearances that the president always sat on the left. He wasn't sure why, but given how every move the president made these days was carefully calculated and orchestrated in advance, he was sure there was a reason.

"Comfy, huh?" The president smiled a little, probably as much as could be permitted from a man who had only recently lost his wife. "One of the perks of the presidency. You get to redecorate the Oval Office." He stopped, sighed. "Emily picked out the carpet, the drapery, the paintings, most of the furniture. Had the old carpet shipped off to my predecessor's presidential library. The only thing I chose myself are these two chairs. Had them special made by an old college buddy. Told him I wanted a chair I could sit on for hours without getting anything worse than a leg cramp. Did a pretty good job, don't you think?"

Ben had to admit his chair was exceedingly comfortable.

"Course I had to consult with the media experts on the color. When George W. Bush first took office, he put in some nice little melon-colored chairs. But after his first appearance, the press described them as 'pink.'" Blake chuckled quietly. "Those chairs disappeared in a hurry. Tough macho presidents from the great state of Texas can't be seen sitting in anything pink."

Ben laughed with him, but he also noticed that the chairs currently in place were a very deep and manly shade of tan.

"I like the Remingtons," Ben said, gesturing toward the bronze sculptures on the coffee table before them. "We have a great collection in Tulsa, at the Gilcrease Museum. Best collection of Western art in the world."

"I've been to Gilcrease," the president said. "Spent a happy afternoon there a few years back. Peaceful. No one recognized me all day."

Tracy Sobel cleared her throat. "Sir," she said, tapping her wristwatch.

"Oh, right, right." He looked over at Ben. "See what I told you? The woman keeps me in line."

"I have a chief of staff who performs a similar function," Ben answered. "Whether I like it or not."

"I don't want to rush, but as you can imagine, I have a heavy schedule today, what with the amendment going before the two congressional committees and all. But I carved out time for this meeting, Ben." He paused. "Because I really wanted to talk to you."

"May I ask why?"

"Oh, I bet you can guess that, Senator," Director Lehman said. His gaze was almost as fixed and intense as the president's, but it didn't exude nearly as much warmth.

"I'm assuming it has something to do with your proposed amendment."

"You're right about that," the president confirmed.

"I imagine you want to take my temperature. See if you can count on my vote."

"Now that's where you're mistaken."

Ben sat up straight. "I am?"

The president looked at him with all apparent sincerity. "If I may be so bold, Ben, I know how close you were to Mike Morelli. So despite the technical fact that you are a member of the opposition party, I feel I already know where you must stand on this bill."

"To tell you the truth, Mr. President," Ben said, "I haven't made up my mind yet."

"That so," the president said quietly. He exchanged a glance with Sobel, then with Lehman. "That so."

"May I ask what your concerns are?" Lehman asked, jumping in. "Surely you don't want to see another tragedy like what happened in Oklahoma City."

"No, of course not. But I do have concerns about the long-term consequences of this amendment to our civil liberties."

"Do you think I don't?" Lehman said, with such alacrity that it took Ben by surprise. "I've wrestled with this thing for days myself."

"And he's the one who first suggested it," the president added. "And the one who would wield the most power if and when an Emergency Security Council were ever convened."

"But the bottom line is," Lehman continued, "we have to do something. Whether it's domestic terrorism like the first Oklahoma City attack, or foreign terrorism like 9/11, or whatever the hell this most recent attack turns out to be, the nation can't tolerate this any longer. It's more than demoralizing. It's the sort of event that brings a nation to its knees."

"Surely that's an exaggeration."

"Ever read Gibbon's *Decline and Fall of the Roman Empire*, son?" Ben shook his head. "Let me tell you—there are strong parallels. Once the barbarians gain a foothold, it becomes very hard to fight them back."

"We have to take action," the president said firmly. "And we have to do so quickly."

"Before the people come to their senses and public opinion changes?"

The president ignored the implication. "No. Because we need to show whoever was behind this—and anyone else who might be planning an attack—that we are not a nation in decline. That we will fight for our liberty with whatever means are available and necessary."

"So you want me to lend your amendment my support?"

"More than that, Ben. I want you to lead the charge."

Ben's eyes ballooned. *"What?"*

"You heard me. I need help in the Senate."

"There are a lot of senators far more influential than I am."

"Maybe. But I need a Democrat—someone willing to break party lines to support an amendment whose time has come. Plus, you're from the state where the tragedy occurred. You were intimately involved in the attack. Your best friend was seriously wounded. If you start speaking out in favor of the amendment, people are going to listen."

"I'm the most junior senator in Congress. I wasn't even elected."

"All of which I see as a plus. You don't have political enemies—people who will oppose something you support just out of spite for some past grievance. You can't be accused of being beholden to special interests, since you've never collected a penny in campaign funds."

"Right or wrong, you're still perceived as being outside politics," Sobel added. "And even though I know you consider yourself a centrist . . ." She paused, as if choosing her words very carefully. "Well, there are many who see you as tilting somewhat toward the liberal side of the fence."

"Exactly," the president rejoined. "So if you came out in support of this amendment, it would demonstrate once and for all that this has nothing to do with politics. It is simply about doing what is best and right for the security of the nation."

"I don't know," Ben said. "I thought I heard Senator DeMouy was leading the charge on this one."

"He is, technically. But he's a Republican. I need someone from the other side of the fence if I'm going to get the votes I need."

"There is one additional consideration," Sobel added. This time, Ben noted, she was staring off somewhere in the space between them, not quite looking him in the eye. "I don't know if you've decided yet whether to run for reelection, but the word on the street is that you are at the least giving it serious consideration.

If so, this leadership role we're offering you could be exactly what you need—to attract the kind of media attention necessary to win an election. Forget the state election—you could come out of this with national name recognition, even more than you got when you appeared on television during the Roush hearings. You couldn't buy this kind of publicity, not if you had a trillion-dollar war chest. This could be the opportunity of a lifetime."

"Assuming I want to run for reelection," Ben added.

"Or," the president said, "assuming you want to do something to protect the citizens of this nation. Good people. Like Major Michelangelo Morelli."

The room felt silent. Ben knew it was incumbent upon him at this point to say something, but he didn't know where to begin.

He saw Sobel once again tapping her wristwatch.

"I'm afraid this offer has totally taken me by surprise. I don't know what to tell you. Can I have some time to think about it?"

Blake and Sobel exchanged a quick glance. "We don't have much time, son. We have to move on this fast."

"Give me till tomorrow morning."

"Midnight," Sobel replied. "Call us by midnight. Don't worry—I'll be up."

No doubt, Ben thought. He wondered if she ever slept at all.

"I'll get back to you as soon as possible," Ben said, rising.

"You do that, son." The president rose and walked Ben toward the east door. "I don't mean to scare you. But we've already gotten wind of at least three other terrorist plots against this nation. Against me and several other important governmental figures. Some random attacks against the general population. Anything to demoralize and terrify the people. Evil, cowardly plots."

He put his hand firmly on Ben's shoulder. "I don't know how much more bluntly I can put it, son. We must act quickly, before it's too late. And I don't think I'm overstating things when I say the fate of this great nation may well rest upon your shoulders."

15

Ben felt ridiculous creeping through the back stairwell that led to the rear door of his Senate office. He had discovered this private passageway when he was working on Senator Glancy's defense—the murder had been committed there—but he had never expected to use it himself. He was a U.S. senator, for Pete's sake. However junior or unelected he might be, he shouldn't have to sneak into his own office. But he knew what would happen if he came through the front entrance in his usual manner, and he was in no mood to be ambushed by Christina. He needed some time to be alone. He needed to think.

He tiptoed through the rear door as quietly as possible and gently closed it.

"Got a hangover, champ?"

Ben froze.

"I can only assume your head was throbbing, given the way

you're tiptoeing around. Guess you and the leader of the free world hit the bourbon bottle too hard."

Ben slithered into the chair behind his desk. Busted.

"So you know I met with the president?"

"That's not the sort of thing you can keep quiet," Christina said, hovering over his desk like a vulture scrutinizing its prey. "This whole wing of the Russell Building knows you met with the president. A minute ago, I heard it on CNN."

"Hardly seems that newsworthy . . ."

"The President of the United States invites in a junior senator, a political opponent, the other politician who survived the April nineteenth attack, just after proposing a sweeping constitutional amendment that would dramatically alter the status of civil rights in America. You're right—nothing newsworthy about that."

Ben didn't have to look up to know she was wearing her sarcastic face, which he knew many in these hallowed halls referred to as her "How stupid are you?" face. "I guess I'm not used to having people tracking my movements."

"Well, you'd better get used to it, if you're going to be hanging out with the president. Or running for reelection. What did he offer you?"

"Offer me?"

"In exchange for your support of his Nazi amendment. Some pork barrel project for the state of Oklahoma? Or maybe something you'd find even harder to resist. More money for education. Support for some version of your antipoverty bill. Maybe he even said he'd throw his weight behind the Protection of the Alaskan Wilderness legislation."

"Wouldn't you like that?"

"Depends on what it costs," Christina said curtly. As if by sleight of hand, a report suddenly appeared in her hands. "I've been talking to Barry Koehler. You know who he is?"

Ben racked his brain. "Some sort of lobbyist . . ."

"Close. Works for the ACLU. Possibly the leading expert on American privacy—or the lack thereof."

Ben clenched his eyes shut. *Here we go. . . .*

"Did you know that the government has reconnaissance satellites that can take pictures all over the globe—pictures with a resolution rating of ten centimeters, which is good enough to read the title on the spine of a book?"

"I assume that's for foreign intelligence gathering."

"You'd think. But it's becoming increasingly clear that the spy satellites are also being used to track the activities of U.S. citizens. There's a little-known federal agency called the National Imagery and Mapping Agency that collects, analyzes, and saves images taken by these satellites all over the world."

"Isn't that good for law enforcement?"

"Sometimes. The FBI and CIA use them to monitor security when various dignitaries are making public appearances. They were used at the Winter Olympics for the same reason several years ago. But why are they being used to observe the activities of ordinary Americans?"

"It's probably just a temporary thing. . . ."

She continued unabated. "Another hush-hush operation called Future Imagery Architecture recently launched another dozen spy satellites. They're ramping up, not down. We're looking at the possibility of constant, real-time surveillance of the entire planet."

"They'd need a warrant to take pictures of private citizens."

"You're supposed to need a warrant to wiretap private citizens. But with a new intelligence program called Echelon, the NSA is now capable of intercepting three billion communications a day. Think about it. What are the odds that any given call you make might be recorded by the NSA? Pretty darn good, as it turns out."

"Christina . . ."

"Needless to say, the government is monitoring Internet traffic in a big way. The FBI has a program called Carnivore that targets an ISP and scans all the information that passes through it—e-mail, Web surfing, anything they want. Carnivore can analyze and, if desired, record millions of messages per second."

"Anybody who expects privacy on the Internet is delusional."

Christina leaned in closer, the lines of her face tightening. "The Treasury Department has a program called the Financial Crimes Enforcement Network."

Ben folded his arms across his chest. "Good. Financial crimes are bad. Wreck people's lives."

"Don't kid yourself. This is an excuse to collect and save financial data on private citizens, possibly matched with the digitized pictures taken by spy satellites and recordings of their telephone and Internet conversations. FinCEN requires banks to provide them information on private citizens whenever the Treasury Department issues a suspicious activity report—which they can do anytime they want."

"I'm sure the bank would notify its customer."

"To the contrary, banks are forbidden by law from notifying their customers. The whole process is totally invisible to the people being spied upon."

"Well, that doesn't seem quite kosher. . . ."

"Did you know the government now has something called Forward Looking infrared cameras that can literally look through walls and take pictures? Did you know they can digitize your face, record it, and store it in a computerized database?"

"What could they possibly do with that?"

"The Pentagon initiated a fifty-million-dollar effort to develop what they call 'Human ID at a Distance.' In theory, they use these digitized databases to protect government installations from terrorists. As a practical matter, they could use them to track the movements of anyone they want. The reality is, Ben, that each new boost in computer memory has proportionately diminished American privacy. The more the government improves its holographic storage capacities, the better they can coordinate their various means of collecting intelligence on private citizens. A recent Wisconsin report discovered more than two thousand databases recording information on private citizens—in Wisconsin. Imagine how many there must be at the federal level, or nationwide. Soon they'll be able to find out virtually anything they want about anyone they want anytime they want."

"Well . . . if you haven't done anything wrong, why do you care who's watching?"

"Yeah, that's what Hitler said when he started rolling back the rights of his citizens in 1933. And pretty soon, they had no rights at all."

"I know there are congressional oversight committees monitoring NSA activities."

"And yet, look what happens. People in government will always grasp for more power, Ben. And sometimes, even with the Bill of Rights in place, our rights will be violated. But at least with the Bill of Rights, American citizens have some means of recourse. They can go to the press. They can go to court. If you take that away, there will be no way of stopping these invasions of our constitutional rights—at a time when the government has greater capacity to invade those rights than it has ever had in the history of this nation."

"And our enemies have a greater capacity to destroy than they have ever had before."

Christina laid her hands flat on his desk. She slid one more slim stapled packet of paper across to Ben. "This is a Supreme Court opinion in the case that ruled that police couldn't use thermal imaging to observe the heat signatures of people inside their homes without a warrant. This was written by Justice Scalia—probably the most conservative Supreme on the bench. And yet even though the Constitution obviously doesn't say anything about thermal imaging, he wrote that it was an unconstitutional invasion of privacy. See the part I underlined? He said the use of this technology"—she traced her fingers along the words for Ben as she read—" 'would leave the homeowner at the mercy of advancing technology.' Toward the end, he says that in the home, 'all details are intimate details, because the entire area is held safe from prying government eyes.' "

Ben pushed himself away from his desk—and from her. He was getting upset. He needed distance. "I hear what you're saying, Christina. And I agree, to some extent. But there are other issues that have to be considered."

"What you need to understand, Ben, is that this is important— maybe critical to determining what kind of country this is going to be in the future. A future that seems to be increasingly resting upon your scrawny shoulders."

"*What you need to understand*—" He realized he had snapped and stopped himself. *What's happening?* He wasn't sure he had ever shouted at Christina—certainly not since they had been married. "What you need to understand, Christina, is that . . . this is a very hard thing for me. And I need some . . . time. To process information. To think about what I've been told. To listen."

"Don't just listen to those bozos at the White House," Christina said, matching his tone, "or even just to me. Listen to your heart."

"Christina . . ."

She laid her hand softly on his cheek. "You have a good heart, Ben. I know you do. That's why I married you. And that's why, ultimately, I know you'll do the right thing." She paused a moment, and Ben could see that her lovely blue eyes were beginning to water. "I'll see you at home. I hope."

She turned and quietly left the office.

The clock on the office wall told Ben it was half an hour till midnight. Tracy Sobel would be waiting for his call. And he still didn't know what to tell her.

What a night. He'd been thinking so much, so hard, his head throbbed. He needed some relief. He opened the bottom drawer of his desk, removed a flask, and chugged.

Ahh. The cool liquid felt good going down. The calm it induced, however artificial, spread through his body like a flannel blanket.

Amazing what a thermos of chocolate milk could do for a man.

He dialed the number just as he had done so many times before this week. He knew it by heart now.

"Hello, this is Senator Ben Kincaid and I was—"

"I'm afraid there's been no change, sir." The attending nurse, who by this time knew Ben quite well, understood why he was calling. "The night doc making rounds just checked him a few minutes ago. He hasn't come out of the coma. His respiratory system has stabilized somewhat, but not enough to move him out of ICU."

"Still . . . stabilized. . . . That sounds good."

"I hope so, sir."

"That means he'll recover, eventually."

A long pause. "We just don't know yet, sir."

Ben had heard it many times before. No matter how hard he pressed, they weren't going to give him any false hope. As long as his future remained uncertain, the prognosis would be equally discouraging.

"Is Sergeant Baxter still with him?"

"Night and day. I understand she's taken an authorized leave of absence from work so she can be here."

"She still reading to him?"

There was a moment of silence. "Yes . . ."

"Got sick of the poetry, didn't she?"

"My understanding is that she's now reading him something by Mickey Spillane."

"Well, he'll like that, too."

If he can hear it, Ben thought, as he hung up the receiver. *If he can hear it.*

When the phone rang, Ben practically jumped out of his chair. Good grief—had he fallen asleep? What a stupid thing to do, when so many people were waiting to hear from him. This would be Tracy Sobel, pressing him for an answer. Or perhaps Christina, wanting to know if and when he was coming home.

He punched the appropriate red button and picked up the phone. "Hello?"

"Ben, is that you?"

Ben felt a sudden clutching at his chest. He didn't need help recognizing that voice, even if he hadn't heard it for years. He'd grown up hearing it.

"Ben? It's Julia."

Which he already knew. His sister, so long gone. After all these years.

"Ben, you don't know how hard it was to get through to you. I had to pass through like a thousand security clearances and operators. No one would believe I was your sister. They said they'd never heard anything about Senator Kincaid having a sister."

And for a reason. For all intents and purposes, he didn't.

"I can't believe I just said that. *Senator* Kincaid? How the hell did that happen?"

"It's a long story. . . ."

"I remember when you were so shy, you couldn't speak aloud in class without stuttering. And now you're this big-shot attorney. And a U.S. senator!"

"Life is a funny thing."

"I guess. It's been pretty funny for me, too."

After so much time, he hardly knew which question to go with first. "How's Joey?" he asked, referring to her son, his nephew, who he had helped raise for a time.

"Oh, gosh. More than I can handle. And he's ruining my chances with this cute guy. He's nice, but the thought of linking up with someone with a child terrifies him."

"So you're not still—that doctor—"

"That ended a long time ago. He said he wanted to help raise Joey. That's why I took him back, remember? But it turns out . . . well, we think Joey has some special problems. He's not doing well in school. He may have Asperger's, or something in the autistic spectrum. He may be dyslexic and dysgraphic. Some mornings, I just think . . ." Her voice drifted. "But this isn't why I called. I heard that Mike got hurt! In that horrible attack on the president in Oklahoma City?"

"Yes." She was being purposefully detached, and yet Ben couldn't help but be touched. Maybe she still cared for her ex-husband, at least a little. "He was being the hero, as always. Saved the president's bacon. Mine, too. But didn't get himself out in time."

"Ohmigod. That's so horrible. Poor Mike. Poor Mike." He heard a little gasping sound escape from her voice. "I called the hospital, but they wouldn't tell me anything. Apparently ex-wife doesn't count as a relative in their books."

"No," Ben said quietly. "I suppose not."

"So how is he?"

"Well, he's still in ICU, but they told me tonight that he's . . . stabilizing."

"Don't bullshit me, Ben. I grew up with a doctor daddy, too, remember? What's the prognosis?"

"They just don't know."

"That doesn't sound good."

"No," Ben said simply. "He was severely wounded when that bomb exploded. Internal organs were messed up. Respiratory system went into shock. Broke several bones. He's been in a coma ever since."

"Do they think he'll come out of it?"

"Julia . . ." Ben didn't have the words. "There's no way of telling."

All at once, Ben realized that Julia was crying, and a moment later he realized that he was, too. Crying for the first time since April 19.

"My God, Ben . . . how did this happen?"

"I don't know."

"I remember when we were all in college. We were the best of friends, the three of us. Mike and I were so in love. Dad was still alive. We were happy and together and . . ." Her voice choked. "What went wrong, Ben?"

"I . . . don't know."

"What's happened to the world? What the hell is wrong when . . . when things like this go on?"

"I don't have any answers for you, Julia, but—"

"You have to do something about this, Ben. You're a big shot now. You have to . . . you have to . . . see that something like this can never happen again. For Mike's sake. And mine."

His voice was so tremulous, he could barely speak. "I will, Julia. I'll do what I can."

A long stretch passed, silent except for the crying on both sides of the line.

"You know, Ben . . . we should get together sometime."

"I'd—I'd like that."

"Maybe if"—she drew in her breath and corrected herself—"maybe when Mike gets better."

"I know he'd like that, too."

"Okay. Um . . . you'll call me if there's any change?"

"Of course." He took down her number. "It's been . . . very good talking to you, Julia. Very good. You know, I . . . I—"

"I know, Ben. Let's talk again soon. Best to Mother."

She rang off.

Ben wiped the tears from his eyes. He tried to think clearly, but it wasn't possible. His chest was heaving. He had released a great deal that had been waiting a long time to get out.

Tears trickled into the wound on his cheek and it stung.

His eye caught the clock on the wall. Five minutes till midnight.

Without even thinking about it, his hand moved toward the telephone.

"Ms. Sobel? Yes, it's Ben Kincaid. Yes, sorry. I know it's late. But not too late, right?"

He waited for her assurances.

"As a matter of fact, I have. You may tell the president on my behalf that the answer is yes. I'll do it. Whatever he needs me to do."

They talked a moment longer, then hung up. Ben slowly lowered his head to the desk.

It was a good thing this chair was so comfortable, because he suspected he would be sleeping in it for a long time. He knew he was not going back to the apartment tonight. He needed rest, and he needed it now.

Tomorrow, everything was going to change. Permanently.

Part Two

The Politics of Fear

16

U.S. Senate, Russell Building,
Office S-212-D
Washington, D.C.

Christina tried not to let it show, but she was worried. If she had
learned anything in her short time in Washington, it was the
truth of that old maxim about never letting them see you sweat. It
was political suicide. No matter what the circumstances. But she
was still worried.

"Hey, Christina," Loving said, as he ambled into the office.
"How's it hangin'?"

"Oh, fine. Just fine."

"How's Ben?"

"Oh, he's . . . he's . . ." Damn it, she wasn't going to let it
show. But she already had.

Loving laid his hand gently on her shoulder. "What's wrong,
Chrissy?"

She shrugged, trying to fight back the tears. "He didn't come
home last night."

"Like that's never happened before. He probably fell asleep in his office again. I'll go—"

"I already looked. He's not there."

A thin line traced a course across Loving's forehead. "Well, that's different. You called his cell?"

She nodded.

"Still, I'm sure he's around somewhere. He's always got a hundred balls in the air at once. You shouldn't worry."

She was embarrassed at herself for letting down her defenses—so quickly and so thoroughly. It was unprofessional. But she couldn't help herself. "I was pretty hard on him last night. Really laid into him about this proposed amendment."

A small light of comprehension glowed behind Loving's eyes. "Oh. Spat."

"I'm just afraid. . . ."

"That he didn't come home because he's mad at you or somethin'? Chrissy, listen to me." He took her by the shoulders and turned her so she faced him. "That kid loves you to pieces. I know he doesn't say much about it. He ain't good with words like me. But I know he loves you. All you have to do is see the way he looks at you to know that."

"But . . . sometimes love isn't enough."

"Says who? Look, I know this absolutely: No matter what he's up to this time, he would never deliberately do anythin' to hurt you. He would never leave you. He needs you. And he knows it."

Christina sniffed, wiped the dampness from her eyes. "I hope you're right. I just worry that—"

"Hey, guys! Look at this!"

It was Jones, shouting at them from his station near the outer door.

"What is it?" Christina asked.

"Fox News."

"Oh, joy."

"The president's giving a press conference. From the Rose Garden. Looks lovely this time of year."

"Only on television," Christina remarked. "In person, you notice the snipers on the roof and the Secret Service swarming everywhere and the bomb-sniffing dogs eyeing your purse and the manhole covers that have been sealed shut with acetylene torches. And the security line is incredibly slow. By the time you're actually inside, you've forgotten what a rose looks like."

"Killjoy. Look—the president is about to speak!"

"I'm sure he will be just as enlightening as ever." She grabbed her briefcase. "I'll be in the office if—"

"Ben is right behind him."

"*What?*" Christina was shoulder-to-shoulder staring at the television before another second passed.

The president was striding toward the podium bearing the presidential seal with his usual display of calm confidence. A band somewhere off camera was playing "Hail to the Chief." She'd had greater appreciation for the song before that literature geek Mike explained that the words came from a poem by Sir Walter Scott that actually depicted the death of a Scottish chieftain executed by the British king. Apparently President Polk's wife Sarah was irritated when her tiny husband entered a room and no one noticed, so she started ordering the band to play the blaring march whenever he made an entrance. The tradition stuck.

Ben was keeping pace, walking somewhat less forcefully—but then, he always did. Beside him was Senator Jeffrey DeMouy, the man who led the Republican senatorial delegation. The two stood at attention while the president spoke.

". . . and so for the safety of this great nation, it is not only important that we move with all deliberate speed, but that we have the finest people the Senate has to offer leading the charge. It is my great pleasure to announce that I have chosen a truly representative cross-section of Congress to take this important leadership role: a Republican and a Democrat, representing both viewpoints and the bipartisan need for tightened security—one of the Senate's most senior senators and one of the most junior, giving us both the wisdom of age and the enthusiasm of youth. Most important, they are fine men whom I admire and respect, men I trust to make this urgently needed constitutional amendment a reality—Senator Jeffrey DeMouy of Louisiana and Senator Benjamin Kincaid of Oklahoma."

Christina's voice dropped to its lowest tone. "No."

After a spattering of applause, Senator DeMouy began speaking. Christina didn't catch most of it. It was the same predictable twaddle she would expect from a presidential flunky with White House ambitions of his own. Her attention was focused on the smaller figure standing just to his side. The one she had recently married on the front steps of the U.S. Supreme Court building.

What did Ben think he was doing? And how could he possibly consider doing it without telling her first?

". . . in these dire days, we must move quickly to tell the enemies of freedom that we will not be cowed by their cowardly attacks. This is a nation forged in fire. We have always been strong. We will remain strong. Quick action on this amendment will send a message saying that no matter what you do, we will fight back, and we will win. We will be resolute in our . . ."

His Cajun-flavored voice was like a droning buzz in Christina's head. *Enough with the claptrap already. Get to Ben!*

Only a moment later, he did. After being introduced, Ben approached the podium. His lack of experience with press conferences was immediately apparent, but in a strange way, that lent what he said a genuineness that the other politicians lacked.

"As you know," Ben said in careful, measured tones, "I was present during the April nineteenth attack. My wife and mother were put in jeopardy; my best friend, a law enforcement officer who has put his life on the line time and again for the betterment of the commonwealth, is still in critical condition, and we simply don't know if there's any chance that he will recover—or if he does, if he will resemble the man he once was."

Ben turned, a pivot Christina recognized as shifting from Camera Two to Camera One, though Ben might've done it just because he was too nervous to stand still. "I have always been a firm believer that the rights of the people take precedent over everything else, that the increasing intrusion of government into our lives is a threat to our privacy, that the least government is the best government. But if the attack on April nineteenth brought anything home to me, it was that there are many dangerous threats to the American way of life, and those who make those threats are not playing by the same rules that we do. I would never support any measure that abolished the Bill of Rights or threatened to do so. But those rights have been suspended in the past when the need was great, and today we must face the reality that temporary suspensions of those rights may be necessary in the future."

A flurry of hands rose in the audience, but Ben was apparently not yet ready to take questions. "This amendment is simply a temporary measure suspending some rights in times of great urgency—the rights most likely to shield and protect criminals and terrorists and those who present the greatest threat to our national security. The decision whether to implement this suspension, and the exercise of powers pursuant to any such suspension, appears to me to be placed by this amendment in the most competent, capable, and knowledgeable hands. Therefore, for the sake of all Americans, and in a concerted effort to make sure that nothing like 9/11 or April nineteenth ever happens again, I lend my full support to this measure, and I urge others to do the same."

Christina stared at the television screen, her jaw agape. "I don't believe it. I just don't believe it."

Loving laid a hand on her shoulder. "Take it easy, Christina. He's only doin' what he thinks is right."

"But he's wrong."

"But he thinks he's right."

"He's not thinking at all. He's so torn up about Mike, he can't see straight."

"Are you sure? Maybe we need to be tougher on criminals."

"You think we need to be tougher on illegal aliens. The ones who come from outer space."

"I've been out on the streets tryin' to catch bad guys, and lemme tell you, it's no picnic."

"This won't make things better."

"You don't know that. There are two sides to this issue."

"Yes, and Ben has just taken the wrong one."

Loving took a deep breath. "Chrissy—are you mad at Ben because he's supportin' the amendment—or because just for once, he disagrees with you about somethin'?"

She turned slowly to face Loving, her eyes blazing. Her lips parted—then froze. *No,* she thought. *Don't kill the messenger. You may need him.*

"I'm mad because he did this without even telling me."

"Well . . . ," Loving allowed, "he probably could've handled it better."

On the television screen, Ben was fielding questions.

"Have you discussed this with the Democratic leadership in the Senate? Do they support your position?" asked a salt-and-pepper-bearded reporter from *The Washington Post.*

"No," Ben said, "I haven't discussed it with anyone. I'm taking a position that seems to me necessary—even essential—in these difficult days. But I do know that there are others in the Democratic Party who feel the same way I do."

"Enough to get the amendment passed?"

"I don't know," Ben said quietly. "I hope so."

"I understand that you want to make the American people safe," said the brunette reporter from *The New York Times,* "but isn't there a danger that the price tag for that security is our fundamental American freedom?"

"We're talking about fighting terrorists. Maybe it's Saifullah, maybe it's someone else. Domestic or foreign—it doesn't really matter. The men who wrote the Bill of Rights could never have conceived of a threat of this nature. If they had, I shouldn't wonder that they might've written an emergency clause like this one into the Bill of Rights themselves."

The questioning continued, but Christina couldn't stand it any longer. She snapped the television off.

"We have to do something," she said, arms folded across her chest.

Loving gazed at her, puzzled. "Not sure what you mean, Chrissy."

"I'm talking about someone doing some serious legwork. To be more specific—you."

"Me? What're you talkin' about?"

"You are the office investigator, aren't you?"

"I just got back from vacation!"

"But you are the office investigator, aren't you?"

"Well, yeah, but—"

"So as of now, I'm giving you an assignment. Start investigating. The attack on April nineteenth."

"What?"

"You heard me. I want to know what happened. What *really* happened. Who was behind it." She glared at the television screen, even though it was dark. "All these people keep babbling about terrorists, but the truth is, we have no idea who orchestrated this crime. I want you to find out."

"Me?" He looked at her as if she had asked him to find the Lost Ark of the Covenant. "Isn't more or less the entire U.S. government tryin' to find out who was behind the attack? And comin' up with nothin'?"

"Yes," Christina said, staring directly into his eyes. "But I know something the entire U.S. government does not."

"You've got a killer clue? A smokin' gun?"

"Something even better," she said, motioning him toward her office. "Good gossip."

17

"Have you been a bad girl?"

"I've been a bad girl. I've been a very, very bad girl."

"Have you been naughty?"

"Very naughty."

"What happens to naughty girls?"

"They should be . . . punished."

"I agree. Pull down your knickers."

Underneath her clothing, Belinda DeMouy was wearing a pink bustier with a garter strap linking it to matching pink fishnet hose. Her pumps were pink and silver with little fluff balls over the toe.

She slithered over the side of the bed, rubbing up against the covers like a kitten. "You won't hurt me very bad, will you?"

"I'm sorry, but you've been naughty, and naughty girls must be seriously punished."

"Are you going to take your great big hand and spank me?"

"No. I think this calls for something that will make more of an impression." Jason Simic reached under the bed and withdrew a long mahogany paddle with a small hole drilled through the center.

Belinda shuddered when she saw the menacing implement. "Oh, God," she murmured. "Oh, Goddddddd . . ."

"Pull down your panties, dear."

Belinda complied.

He pulled her across his lap. "I just hope you remember this the next time you think about being bad." He swung the paddle five times in rapid succession.

She screamed with an ecstasy born of some potent combination of pain and pleasure. He spanked her again and again and she gasped and screamed. Soon he established a rhythm, pounding at her with an increasingly accelerated pace, as if Ravel's *Bolero* were playing somewhere in his mind.

"Oh," she screamed out. "Oh! Oh! Oh!" But she did not ask him to stop.

When her bottom was properly pinked, Jason pulled her upright. "Now go stand in the corner. With your panties dangling around your ankles."

"Yes, sir."

"If you're going to be a naughty girl, then I'll have to punish you like a naughty girl."

Her breasts heaved. Her lips parted.

"Now get in that corner before I start paddling you again!"

She obeyed.

He left her there for a good ten minutes, her panties around her ankles, her flaming buttocks lit like a Christmas ornament. Finally, he led her back to the bed, laid her down, and snapped the cuffs around her wrists.

"Oh my God, they're so tight," she said breathlessly. "So tight."

"It's going to hurt," he informed her. "But a naughty girl has no right to complain."

"I know."

"I'm going to spank you some more, then I'm going to take you, very fast and very hard."

"Oh, Goddddd . . ."

"I'm going to use you for my own personal pleasure."

"Oh, use me. Use me!"

"You won't get any pleasure out of this, and frankly I don't care. A naughty girl doesn't get to choose what she wants."

"Yes . . . yes . . ."

"You're a naughty girl, and I'm going to punish you with my brush hog."

"Oh, Goddddd . . ."

"But first I want that ass of yours nice and hot."

"Oh, yes. God, yes."

He spanked her until he could see bruised blood vessels appear on her buttocks; then he flipped her around and went about his business. He pounded away at her, judging his rhythm by the frequency of her cries of tortured delight.

"I've been bad," she cried out, rocking her hips back and forth, gasping with passion. "Punish me, master. Punish me!"

Despite what he said about her not getting any pleasure out it, she climaxed before he did.

Half an hour later, Jason and Belinda lay in a heap on the brass bed, their feet intertwined, her face glowing. He was reading some work materials; she was gazing at him with watery eyes.

"God, you really get into the subjugation/domination stuff, don't you?" she asked.

Jason did not look up from the papers he was reading. "Uhh, I'm pretty sure that was you."

She shoved his shoulder. "Don't give me that. You loved it."

"I love making use of your body."

"You sweet-talker."

"But the corporal punishment fetish is all yours."

She curled up closer and purred. "You're indulging your naughty girl?"

"I'm doing what needs to be done so I can screw her brains out. Several times a night."

"You're so romantic."

What would her mother think about this? Belinda wondered. Her mother had always taught her to be proper. To behave with decorum. This was about as far from proper as it was possible to get. Bad enough to be having an affair. But she was having an extremely kinky affair, and with her husband's chief of staff, no less.

And loving every minute of it.

Could she help herself? It's not as if she had ever been in love with the great and distinguished Senator Jeffrey DeMouy. She married him because everyone thought she should. Seemed like a good idea at the time. But it wasn't. It was an empty marriage. Not that it was loveless, exactly. She knew he loved her, in his own dry perfunctory missionary-position way. But where was the passion? He was so much older than she; he was well into his forties when they married. He didn't have the stamina for much. If it weren't for those magic little blue pills, they might not have had a sex life at all.

It would be better if he were around more. If he were one of those doting spouses who was always buying her flowers or giving her presents or other tokens of his affection. She could live with knowing he'd lost interest in sex, but she couldn't live with knowing he'd lost interest in her. She was a tool to him and she always had been, the hostess with the mostest, never anything more. She increased his electability, increased his visibility, made him more socially desirable. She wasn't a wife; she was an asset. At least—as long as she remained proper.

The hell with Mother. Who cared what she might or might not think? Belinda had been proper all her life. She was ready for something different. She wanted to be loved passionately, to be taken forcibly in parking garages and chained down with handcuffs and taken from behind. She had never once had an orgasm with Jeffrey. Never once. At some point, Belinda had decided she just wasn't a very sexual person, that whatever gene it was that caused people to be swept away in paroxysms of passion wasn't included in her DNA strand.

Then she met Jason.

The whole thing had started at an office Christmas party, trite but true. They'd both had too much eggnog, and since Jeffrey was planning to stay at the office all night, the dutiful chief of staff offered to walk her to her car and somehow he went from opening her car door to squeezing her right breast, and the next thing she knew they were humping like rabbits in the backseat of the Jaguar. She had an orgasm that night, the first time in her life. It was so explosive, so unaccustomed, at first she thought she'd had some sort of stroke. Jason laughed at her, and then, just to prove what had really happened—he made it happen again. Two O's in half an hour, in the backseat of a small foreign car. She was hooked. It wasn't at all proper. But she liked it.

Tonight, when he took her forcefully after making her stand in the corner, she had her forty-second orgasm. Yes, she counted. And it was quite possibly the best one yet. She didn't care about social functions or politics or visiting the White House. She just wanted to have sex with Jason, over and over again. She wanted this to go on forever.

"It could, you know."

She looked up at his handsome face. "Excuse me?"

"Go on forever."

Had she actually said that out loud? "I don't know what you mean."

"Sure you do." Jason put down his papers. "We have a terrific sex life. And I like to think we love each other, but as long as the sex is so hot, who really cares? The problem is"—he glanced at his watch—"in about fifteen minutes, I'm going to have to leave. And tonight, your husband is going to lie down right where I am now. And he'll be naked and hairy and even if he can't actually have intercourse, he'll fumble and grope and paw you until you want to vomit."

Belinda shuddered. "Don't. You know I cringe every time that man touches me. Every time I even think about him touching me."

"You could divorce him."

"And live how?"

"Family money?"

"You know there isn't any."

"Property settlement?"

"All the loot is in trusts. Plus, I signed a prenup. I won't get a penny."

"Well, if it's not too radical a notion . . . you could work."

"No, thank you. Tried it once. Didn't care for it."

Jason reached across and cradled her in his arms. "Well, then. That makes it more complicated."

"Try impossible."

"Oh, nothing is impossible. If you're sufficiently creative. And . . . adventurous."

She arched an eyebrow. "What exactly is that supposed to mean?"

He smiled. "See all these papers in my lap?"

"I do. And just for the record, I don't think bringing your work to my bed is sexy. Especially when you work for my husband. And we're fornicating in his bed."

Jason ignored her. "All these papers relate to the various contingency plans being tossed around in the event of further attacks like the one in Oklahoma City or the one on Senator Hammond. Everyone expects another attack—it's a question of *when,* not *if.* That's why we're still at DEFCON-Three."

"It's so sexy when you talk politics."

"Make fun if you want. But I think this presents us with a perfect opportunity."

"I'm not following you."

"Then let me spell it out for you." He reached over and slid his finger under the cup of her bustier, pulling it away from her breast. "Someone already killed the Senate minority leader. Would it really be unusual if the majority leader got offed, too?"

Belinda stared at him. "I'm—not sure what you're saying."

"Oh, I think you are. Doesn't matter how it happens. Anyone important dies in the next few weeks, people are going to assume it was terrorists." He leaned over and began slowly stroking her nipple with his tongue. She closed her eyes and moaned.

"You can't divorce him, darling, and sadly, he's in excellent health."

"Yes. Ohhhh, yesssss . . ."

He reached inside her panties and went to work. "So what do you say? Let's kill the son of a bitch."

18

Ben stumbled home as tired as he ever remembered being in his entire life. Since five a.m., he'd been with the president's advisors, preplanning every aspect of the press conference. They considered the proper tone to strike, the common themes, what Ben and DeMouy would say so they didn't contradict each other. For that matter, they considered tie colors, makeup, and who would walk forward in which order. The president's media experts left nothing to chance. And in the end, the entire conference had taken less than twenty minutes.

But it was viewed, he had been informed afterward, by more than twenty million Americans, despite the fact that it aired in the middle of the morning. Millions more would see excerpts on the evening news or the 24/7 cable news outlets and the Internet. Ben wondered which excerpts would prove most popular. He hoped it wasn't his lame invocation of "the American way." He always claimed he wasn't really a politician—where had that come from?

Some vestigial memory of the Nixon administration? Or maybe *The Adventures of Superman* with George Reeves? He had no idea. Somehow, when the klieg lights went on and the reporters started slinging questions at you, your mind traveled to a different dimension, one where everything you had planned to say was forgotten and weird stuff like "the American way" came out of nowhere.

And to think that, once upon a time, he had thought speaking in a courtroom was difficult.

At any rate, he had survived that round of questioning. Would he survive the next? The one that was bound to begin the moment he opened the door?

Christina was already home—he saw her coat on the hook. Fine. Gird the loins, take a deep breath, and try not to pass out. Christina made that woman from *The New York Times* look like a lightweight.

He heard water running. Apparently Christina was in the bathroom, probably showering. He took a few tentative steps forward.

"Christina?"

All at once, the water stopped.

"Christina? It's Ben."

"I should hope so," said the voice, reverberating with a bathroom echo. "If it were anyone else, I'd be dialing 911."

"Christina, I think we should talk. I did something—"

All at once, the bathroom door opened. Christina stood there, a towel wrapped just under her arms, her hair still wet. She looked lovely.

"Christina," he said, licking his lips, "I did something today. I wanted to tell you about it. I—"

"Don't bother. I saw you on television."

"Oh." Well, that simplified matters. Maybe. "I just wanted to explain—"

"Don't bother."

"But I wanted to tell—"

"Frankly, Ben, at the moment, I don't care to hear anything you have to say."

"But I wanted to explain—"

"Then you should've done it before you told the rest of the

Western world on national television!" And with that, the door slammed between them.

Ben dropped his briefcase, his shoulders sagging. He had thought a moment ago that he felt more tired than he could ever possibly feel. He had been wrong.

They had never even taken a honeymoon. But now he had a distinct feeling that the honeymoon was over.

19

DEPARTMENT OF HOMELAND SECURITY
NEBRASKA AVENUE NAVAL COMPLEX
WASHINGTON, D.C.

Agent Max Zimmer stared at the framed photograph in the hallway, hoping he might draw some strength from it before he proceeded with the extremely unpleasant task that lay before him. The photo was of Leslie Coffelt, the only member of the Secret Service (at the time, it was called the White House Police Force) to die while protecting the president. In 1950, President Truman was living in Blair House, because the White House was being renovated. Two Puerto Rican nationalists opened fire on the temporary residence. Even though he had taken three shots to his chest, Coffelt returned fire, killing one of the assassins and wounding the other. As a result, they did not penetrate the perimeter and the president was saved, but Coffelt subsequently died of his wounds. He was, some believed, the greatest hero in the history of the Service.

And who am I, Zimmer wondered, *compared to a man like Coffelt? I'm the screwup who let the first lady be killed.*

He would never be a hero. The name Zimmer would never be remembered in that way, and his photo was not likely to ever be hanging on this wall. Not after the way he'd bungled that job.

But at least he'd gotten himself out of that darkened office. He knew there was only one way he could in any tiny measure make up for what had happened. And that was to get to the bottom of the matter. To understand what had really happened, and why.

And then do something about it.

This would probably cost him his job, he realized, and maybe more than that. But it was something he had to do.

He turned the doorknob and entered Gatwick's office.

He had expected to find the senior agent poring over reports, trying to uncover the magical lead that might finally give them some confirmation about whether Saifullah was behind the April 19 attack—or if not, who was. That's what virtually every other available agent in the department was doing. Instead, he was sitting at what appeared to Zimmer to be a miraculously neat desk polishing his weapon—what the other agents commonly referred to as "masturbating." Zimmer was familiar with the common association made by Freudian analysts about a man's gun, but he thought that was carrying it a bit too far.

Gatwick looked up at Zimmer, nodded, then returned to his work. "Good to see you up and about, buddy. Guess Dr. Dobson does better work than I realized."

"It wasn't the shrink who got me out of my funk," Zimmer said defensively, although privately, he knew those sessions had helped. She told him he needed to confront his guilt, rather than wallow in it. She had been right.

"What was it then?"

"My own self," he said, considering for a moment how exactly to put it. "My personal need to see a job to its completion."

Gatwick continued polishing. "I assume that means you're going to join the task force trying to track down the perpetrators. We need all the help we can get."

"That—isn't exactly what I meant," Zimmer explained slowly, "when I said I needed to see this job to its completion."

Gatwick finished polishing and carefully slapped the ammunition magazine back into the handle of the gun. "What did you mean?"

Zimmer licked his lips, trying to remain steady. "I've been reviewing the videotape of the attack. Media stuff."

"Yeah. The team downstairs has confiscated and reviewed every piece of tape known to exist."

"But they aren't looking at the same parts I reviewed," Zimmer said. "I was looking at some outtake shots, stuff that never aired." He took a deep breath. "I was looking at footage taken before the shooting began."

The creases at the corners of Gatwick's eyes evinced his puzzlement. "And you find that useful in some way?"

"I find it interesting. Specifically, the arrangement of the chairs."

Gatwick laid down his gun. "Zimmer, you're talking in circles, and frankly it's making my head hurt. What is it you're trying to say?"

"What I'm trying to understand," he said carefully, "is why a chair had been placed on the left side of the stage for the first lady . . . before you announced your decision to move her there."

"I'm not following."

"I've reviewed a lot of tape, Tom. I saw the way the stage was originally arranged—with the first lady's chair on the right where it usually is for Domino Bravo. Then I saw you step to the stage and move it." Zimmer rested one hand on the desk. "You knew you were going to move her, Tom. Long before you did it. Or at least, long before you announced it. You had already decided to deviate from Domino Bravo."

Gatwick appeared nonplussed. "Yeah, you're right. I saw the moment I took the stage that the arrangement wasn't the most advantageous, so I adjusted it to make it better. That's my job."

"Not exactly. We didn't know yet that Marshall was out of the picture. So why would you override his authority? Unless you . . . knew something."

Gatwick leaned forward slowly in his chair. "What exactly are you suggesting, Max?"

"I'm attempting to gather information. I'm not suggesting anything."

"Are you sure? Because it really sounds a hell of a lot like you're suggesting that I somehow knew that Marshall had been kidnapped and tortured at a time when I couldn't possibly know it." He paused, staring at Zimmer with steely eyes. "Unless I was in on it."

Zimmer stared right back at him, not saying a word.

"And coming at a time when we're all wondering if the assassin had inside assistance," Gatwick continued, "this is a particularly disturbing accusation."

"I haven't made an accusation."

"Then what the hell would you call it?" Gatwick's teeth clenched tightly together. "Do you know how many years I've been with the Service? Do you know what I've sacrificed? My whole life, practically. My family. My ex-wife."

"Is that why you lost your wife? Or was it something else?"

Gatwick's eyes widened like fiery coins. "You filthy little— I will not be tried and hanged based on locker room rumors."

"I haven't done anything like that," Zimmer said, although he knew that wasn't entirely true. "I'm just trying to understand why you took authority that was not, at that time, yours to command. Why you violated protocol and moved the first lady."

"I was trying to protect her!"

"Domino Bravo would've protected her. Your changes killed her."

"Are you sure that's what it was, Max?" Gatwick said, rising slowly to his feet. "Or was it maybe your own incompetence?"

"You son of a—"

"All I know is you were supposed to protect her while the rest of us covered the president. And you let her get killed."

"*Let her!*" Zimmer felt his fists clenching so tightly, his knuckles turned white. "I did my best."

"You should've taken the bullet."

"I tried. I didn't know where the shots were coming from."

"Everyone else did. There probably was only one shooter. Were you confused because you panicked? Or because you are just fundamentally incompetent?"

Zimmer tried his best to swallow the bile and rage rising in his throat. He knew what Gatwick was doing. Trying to deflect Zimmer's inquiries by creating phantom issues of his own. He had done everything he could to save Emily Blake. But he still felt guilty about what had happened to her and Gatwick knew it. He was exploiting the younger agent's guilt to the best of his very great ability.

"I'm a good agent," Zimmer said as calmly as he could manage. "You know that. I've been decorated twice. That's why I'm on the presidential detail."

"Your medals didn't help the first lady."

"Neither did you moving her into the sniper's direct line of fire."

"What the hell do you want from me?" Gatwick shouted. Whatever cool he had been maintaining was gone now. "The sniper was after the president. The first lady was collateral damage."

"That's what we've all assumed. But we don't really know, do we?"

"Even if she were a target, we had no way of knowing the move would put her in the sniper's path."

"Well, certainly *I* had no idea."

"You bastard," Gatwick spat out.

"You're getting very excited for a man who has nothing to hide. All I've done is state facts. If Emily Blake had not been moved, she would still be alive today."

"Do you think I wanted her to die?" Gatwick screamed, totally out of control. "I've known her since I was in college. *I loved her!*" His face froze the instant the words escaped. He moved his lips again, but nothing emerged. Some words could never be retracted, no matter how much you tried to explain.

Zimmer couldn't help but notice that Gatwick was still holding his gun. Standard protocol was to unload while cleaning, but he'd seen Gatwick load it. Gatwick held the gun limply, but that could change in less than a half second.

"So it's true," Zimmer said quietly.

"Don't—don't misunderstand me," Gatwick said, stumbling to assemble an explanation. "I'm not saying that anything . . . inappropriate occurred. I'm just saying I loved her. Hell, the whole country loved her."

"Tom . . ."

"And don't go spreading what I said all around the office. You know what will happen if that hits the rumor mill. Everyone will be talking."

"They already are. Tom—I think we need to have a talk with Director Lehman."

"I'm telling you, there was no unprofessional contact between the first lady and me."

"Then you have nothing to fear from talking to Director Lehman."

"I do if you try to twist this into something it isn't."

"Tom, you have to come clean about this. If there's any chance—"

"If I were having an affair with Emily," Gatwick shouted, "do you think I would want her to die?"

Zimmer paused.

"I mean, does that make any sense?" Gatwick crumbled back into his seat. "When you hold someone so . . . dear. So special. Do you think I would want her to come to harm? Do you think I would want her to be killed by a sniper's bullet?" His head fell onto the desk. "I was trying to protect her. And I failed." He drew in his breath. "It wasn't you that failed, Max. It was me. You think I don't know that?" His voice became barely more than a whisper. "It was me."

Zimmer let himself out of the office quietly, unsure what to do. Should he report this to Director Lehman? Was there anything to report? Even if an affair did occur, it proved nothing. The fact that Gatwick moved the first lady proved nothing.

There had never been a turncoat, never a traitor, never once in the history of the Secret Service.

Was it possible he had just left the office of the first?

Zimmer stopped for a cup of coffee on his way back to his office, hoping a caffeine jolt would clear his head. One thing was certain: before he said anything to anyone, he needed more information. So he would find it.

20

Shohreh had not emerged from her safe room once since the brutal incident with Ahmed and his underwhelming associates. Her dedication to her cause had not weakened, but she knew that Ahmed would be seeking revenge and the General would be seeking her death. Ultimately, the only way to keep safe in a safe room was to never leave. So she remained inside, but she still worked her contacts. Through the magic of the Internet, anyone—even the General—could reach her, if he had anything to say.

As it turned out, he did. This time, he claimed, he would meet her in person, no substitutes, no intermediaries, and presumably, no attempts on her life.

She would have to be a fool to believe this. Shohreh was many things, some good, some not. But she was not now, nor had she ever been, a fool. All that had changed was that the General now understood that she could defend herself, a little secret she had managed to keep to herself while they worked together. He would still try to kill her. He just would not let anyone get close enough that she could use her Muay Thai skills against them.

What chance was left to little Shohreh, the tiny woman with no home, no connections, not even a real name?

She held out one small hope: that no matter what protection he brought with him, he would come himself, if only because she had no incentive to show herself unless he did. He knew what she wanted. Only he could provide it to her.

If he came, she would get to him. Didn't matter how many thugs he brought along, didn't matter what martial arts training they had, what weaponry, what black magic. If he appeared, she would get to him. She would find a way.

So when she got the e-mail inviting her to this most desolate section of Capitol Hill, using the encryption they had developed back when they all worked together, she left her safe room.

The wrought-iron sign on the door told her that the Congressional Cemetery, established in 1807, was the United States' oldest national cemetery—but then, it was a very young country, wasn't it? Tucked away in the darkness behind Christ Church, many congressmen and other notables were interred here—America's Westminster Abbey. So why was it so desolate? Or was that just her imagination? Was the iconography of death that now surrounded her too foreboding?

She slipped on her night-vision goggles and slowly, one cautious step at a time, passed down the rows of virtually identical cenotaphs commemorating congressmen in office from 1807 to 1877. It was a huge expanse—thirty acres, according to the sign. Too many places to hide a trained killer. A crazed zealot. Or General Yaseen himself.

She saw a large marble tomb that looked more like a park bench which marked the final resting place of someone named John Philip Sousa—apparently a musician. She found another stone marking the grave of Matthew Brady, a photographer. How nice that these Americans would honor artists along with their political leaders— that would be unlikely back in her homeland.

A full moon was out tonight, and Shohreh was grateful, because there was no other illumination for miles around. It reminded her all too much of the bleak nights on the deserts of Afghanistan, one of many places she had gone after being forced to flee Iraq. After she left Djamila behind forever. Everything changed in Afghanistan—her status, her lifestyle, her soul. For the first time, she wore the burka, all but hiding her face. Afghan men kept their women in the burka, even after the Taliban was gone, because it obscured their peripheral vision: If a woman wanted to look at something not directly in front her, she must turn her entire head. Insecure husbands would always know if their wives' attention had strayed. Of course, it also kept other men from seeing their wives and daughters to any appreciable degree. The burka was primarily a symbol; the Afghan men controlled their women's lives in every possible respect. The freedoms she once had enjoyed had been sacrificed in the name of survival.

Until she met General Yaseen. At the time, she believed him to be her savior. But then, she did not yet know how he financed his operations. She only knew that he wanted her, had a place for her. He could give her a way to live. She had given him her childhood.

And then, when she was old enough, he had allowed her to join his cell. Normally, women would never be allowed to participate in terrorist cells. Among other reasons, the strict religious and tribal restrictions against the mingling of unrelated men and women made it impossible. She could thank the Americans for changing that. After 9/11, all Muslim men came under much greater scrutiny by American intelligence forces, while women were largely ignored. To survive, the General began to recruit women into his operations.

The indoctrination began immediately. The General and his minions did everything possible to eliminate any favorable impressions of America. They taught her that America and everything about it was decadent, evil. They taught her that the American way of life was an abomination, in complete opposition to Muslim teachings. Moreover, they told her to look beyond the veil of deceit that American politicians spewed. They would not be content with the removal of all the Arabic oil, although they certainly wanted that. Their ultimate goal was the complete obliteration of the Islamic nation.

She had met a man there, in the cell, the first she had ever known in that way. Abbas. Lovely, dear, honey-sweet Abbas. So strong, and yet so fragile. They were companions, and then they were more than companions. He taught her the ways of Muay Thai, the kickboxing martial art that he, ironically enough, had learned from a former member of the Massad. He taught her and they worked out together, until at last they found other ways to satisfy their frustrations.

Marriage was impossible. It was not true, as many believed, that Muslim women are forced to marry. It is a contract entered into between families, mutually agreed upon by all parties. But she had no family, nothing to attract even the poorest man. And her history—

No. It was hopeless. And he was troubled. In their brightest moments, a dark shroud, a pervasive melancholy enveloped him. He was a true member of the cause. Contrary to what many Americans believed, the Qur'an does not require sacrifice to obtain eternal life. Anyone who has led a righteous life and has been faithful to God will ascend to paradise. But the only way to be certain—to be absolutely guaranteed eternal life regardless of what you might have done previously—was to martyr yourself in a holy war.

She did not know what Abbas had done in his past that made him so sure he needed redemption of the utmost form. She could not believe it was his relationship with her, although they had transgressed against many tribal laws. But there was something burning inside him, something he needed to purge. And he did so, just as the mullahs said that he should, to the great benefit of people like the General.

The General sent Abbas to his death in a suicide run against a minor American installation. No Americans even died.

But Abbas was gone to her forever. She had lost Djamila. She had lost Abbas. She had nothing to live for.

She was ready to die.

General Yaseen took advantage of her grief, as he took advantage of everything. He was planning to relocate his operation to America, a move he had planned for years. Another strike was being planned, something potentially greater than even 9/11. He wanted her to be a part of it.

She had never had any taste for killing, and she had lost whatever fervor she had once possessed for the cause. But she needed a life. So she let him create a new identity for her. She became Shohreh, an émigré from Saudi Arabia, the nation Americans laughingly called their ally. And she let him take her to America, the land of unmitigated evil.

Problem was, when she arrived—the country did not seem that evil. The people were much like other people she had known: some good, some bad, all flawed. But not evil. Certainly the lifestyle was different from what she had known, especially in Afghanistan. The Americans had nice clothes and big cars that they drove without regard for the cost or scarcity of fuel. They ate too much. They shopped for amusement. Women revealed themselves in a manner that shocked even her. They kissed in public. But she could not see them as the Great Satan. She knew not what was in the hearts of the political leaders, but when she talked to ordinary people, she got no indication that anyone wanted the obliteration of Islam. To the contrary, what she most often heard was a desire for the conflict between America and the Middle East to be over, for the world to learn to live in peace.

It was her friends, her coworkers, the other members of her cell, who wanted to kill—the greater the number, the better. They became a part of an operation so immense, so twisted, that she found herself shocked at their brutality, at their utter lack of remorse. She had studied the Qur'an. She had read all 114 *suras*. She knew that although believers were told to defend themselves and their faith, Islam was a peaceful, tolerant religion. Even in the midst of holy war, the Hadith forbade the killing of children.

It would not countenance the death of innocent children, mere bystanders. And it would certainly not approve the death of the first lady.

Shohreh withdrew from the cell, even though she was totally dependent upon the General for her livelihood. She knew the risks she took. She expected to die. But she could not go on living as she had. She found work as a receptionist, then as a telemarketer, then more housecleaning, anything so she could eat without knowing her bread came from the death of innocents.

To her surprise, the General left her alone, let her get a taste of freedom, freedom from fear and guilt and danger. She was surprised but pleased. She should have known there was a trick. He was only letting her learn to love her new life—so she would do anything to maintain it.

When at last he contacted her and asked for one final favor, one little gesture that would buy her freedom forever, of course she listened.

Thus she had traveled to Oklahoma City. She had done what he asked.

It was the final betrayal. She would not be used again. That was why—

Her head jerked, ears pricked by the tiniest alteration in the soundscape. That was something else Addas had taught her. You could learn every Muay Thai move in the world; you would still be safer if you could avoid combat altogether.

She heard it again, above her, and at least a hundred yards to the north. A clicking noise.

The General had sent a sniper. Naturally. If he had no fighters who stood a chance against her, he would send someone who did not need to get near her to kill her.

She dove forward, hands over head, just as the bullet ricocheted against the cenotaph she'd been crouching behind. She doubled over and rolled, kept moving in a serpentine pattern, until she was crouched behind another in the low row of memorials.

If he'd had a bead on her before, he must be to her north; he would have to move again before he could see her. To wait for him to do so would be suicide. They could go on all night, he adjusting his position and she trying to anticipate it and stay out of range. But eventually he would get her. She would have to—

The first bullet shattered against the facing wall of the cenotaph, spraying dirt and sandstone into her eyes. The next one came even closer, scraping the exposed edge of her thigh.

It seemed her opponent was able to move even more quickly than she had imagined. And he seemed to have some height.

She dove again, this time moving back to her first position, which she hoped would be the last move he would expect. Her body collided on hard cobblestone, and the tremendous pain in her leg reminded her that even a creasing wound from a bullet will hurt and bleed. She could steel herself, using the powers of combat concentration Abbas had taught her. But eventually the leg would weaken. The killer would catch her.

While she still could, she sprang from behind the stone tomb and ran. Navigation was difficult in the darkness, even with her glasses, but she had little choice. If he was above her, perhaps poised on a high tomb, then she must get closer and below him. It was the only place she would be safe.

As soon as she emerged, the rain of automatic bullets cut a trail behind her, bouncing off stone surfaces all around. But she knew he had not had a chance to change his position. So long as she remained to his left, it would be difficult for him to get her. He was trying to frighten her, or slow her down, to buy himself time.

The bullets stopped. She heard footsteps above her, not far in the distance.

He was atop a redbrick tomb, large enough to be a small house or garage. She had noticed it on her way into the cemetery. Greek Revival style, if she wasn't mistaken. She ran for it, hoping to her God that the darkness would hinder the killer just as much as it did her.

Bullets rang out. She kept on running. Another bullet hit her arm, this time a much more solid hit. She kept on running. When she approached the tomb, she did not stop. She executed a quick series of *kao moi* steps and moved vertically up the side of the building, faster than gravity could restrain her. She flung herself on top of the tomb, her hands grasping for purchase.

What she found was a boot. The sniper's boot.

"May I help you up, 355?"

"You may burn in the land of the damned," she shot back. She struggled to pull herself all the way up, but he held her back. "Where is the General?"

"Did you really think he would come? Then you are more stupid than everyone says."

"I told him I would not appear unless I saw him first."

"But I found you, didn't I? Stupid woman." He grabbed her long black hair and yanked her onto the roof, scraping her face on the surface. She started to rise to her hands and knees, but he jabbed the barrel of his rifle against her face. "Unclean harlot. I spit on you." And he did.

"Throw away your rifle and we will see who is weak," she snarled.

He sideswiped her across the face with the butt of his gun. Blood spilled from her lips. "You do not cover yourself. You have no husband. You do not follow the ways of the Qur'an."

"The Qur'an does not require marriage and it only says that both men and women should dress modestly. Perhaps if you had read it, you would know more about its teachings."

He hit her again, this time even harder. "Eliminating you will buy my ticket into heaven."

"Murder will only make you the pawn of a man who has destroyed lives many times over."

"You know nothing!" he shouted. A cruel smile spread across his face. "Perhaps I will take my advantage before I kill you. There can be no crime in taking pleasure from one already so soiled."

"If you touch me, I swear that I will kill you."

He moved forward, pointing his rifle. "I will cripple you like a pig. I will shoot you in both legs. You will not be able to resist me as I take what I want." He put his eye to the sight and aimed at her right leg. "I don't know which will give me more pleasure—hurting you or having you. I shall do both, many times."

His finger moved toward the trigger.

Shohreh closed her eyes.

A moment later, he was on top of her. But he was not moving.

She opened her eyes and pushed his heavy body away. A broad-shouldered white man stood behind him holding a large stone in his hands.

"Yeah, it's crude, I know," he said, smiling. "But I had to do the best I could with what was handy."

She stared at the man, dazed, uncertain what to say or do. "Have—have you also come to kill me?"

"Nah. I just wanna chat a little."

"You—don't work for the General?"

"No, I work for the senator. Ben Kincaid. Well, technically, at the moment, I'm workin' for his wife." He extended his hand. "Name's Loving. Why don't we get your wounds taken care of? Then maybe we can jawbone a little. You got no idea how long I've been lookin' for you."

21

J. Edgar Hoover Building
FBI Headquarters

Joel Salter never ceased to be amazed by the high-tech labora-
tory the Bureau called the Computer Investigations and Infra-
structure Threat Assessment Center (CIITAC). The transparent
acrylic dividers, the countless blue-flickering computer screens, the
constant clickety-click of printers recording data: all seemed like
something out of a Steven Spielberg movie, not anything that could
relate to real-life law enforcement. But it did. CIITAC superficially
had many domestic purposes relating to Internet activity, such as
protecting the Net from viruses, worms, and other invasive pro-
grams that could cause havoc with American computer networks.
But inside the hallowed halls of this building, no one had any doubt
about the true reason Congress had authorized the tens of millions
of dollars necessary to put this sci-fi dream together.

Terrorism. After 9/11, the FBI, which supposedly focused on domestic federal crime prevention, was all about the international

threat. The Bureau's number one priority was counterterrorism—the detection and prevention of crimes of large-scale violence. Its number two priority was the gathering of counterintelligence, once the sole province of the CIA and NSA. But those days were long past. Today most people cared far less about kidnappings and bank robberies and far more about airport security, the water supply, and the white powder that might spill out of the morning mail.

Salter had not been happy about watching his job at the Bureau mutate from what he signed up for to something that, in his opinion, he had no business doing, didn't do well, and left other important duties neglected. He knew he wasn't the only one who lamented the transformation of FBI agents from door-kicking G-men to intelligence analysts. The CIA did spies; the FBI caught crooks. At least, that was the way it was supposed to be. But the Joint Terrorism Task Forces, an initiative that allowed the FBI to work with state and local law enforcement agencies, had expanded from thirty-five to 101 offices—and more were likely forthcoming in the future.

The Patriot Act had granted the FBI greatly enhanced powers, in particular the ability to wiretap with more leniency and to monitor private Internet activity. Salter knew this was a slippery slope, and sure enough, it was almost no time at all before the FBI was using the "sneak and peek" provision of the Patriot Act to search houses while residents were absent without giving prior notice, or snooping into individuals' library records. CIITAC was used to keep the FBI abreast of the ever-advancing telecommunications industry and the various ways to invade it, including all forms of electronic surveillance. Just as the fear of communism in the 1960s had resulted in FBI surveillance of Martin Luther King, Jr., and John Lennon, so the current fear of terrorists could lead to even greater abuses.

Fabulous powers to have in a crisis, Salter acknowledged. And dangerous powers in the wrong hands, a fact he was constantly reminded of as he watched the newly appointed director of Homeland Security's eyes light up like a cocaine addict's as he explained what all these computer gizmos could do. For someone who had such contempt for the FBI, he sure did like its toys.

"So let me see if I understand this correctly," Lehman said, rubbing his hands together gleefully. "You have the ability to eavesdrop on Internet communications as they are made?"

"That's about the size of it," Salter acknowledged. "Of course, that would be unconstitutional absent a warrant, even under the Patriot Act."

"And the NSA can tap into virtually any telephone conversation," added Nichole Muldoon, Lehman's ready right hand, looking fabulous as always. She was wearing a gray suit jacket with no apparent blouse beneath. He tried not to stare, but he thought she had already caught him several times. Or maybe not. Maybe she was just so damn good-looking, she knew he was staring at her whether she saw it or not. "It's a wonder anyone can heist a liquor store these days."

"It only happens because we're soft," Lehman said firmly. "Because Congress and the courts have kept us working with one hand tied behind our backs. Sometimes both hands. Cried salty tears about the rights of criminals. We have the power to eradicate crime altogether."

"Not to mention personal liberty," Salter couldn't resist adding. "Which would be eradicated at the exact same time."

Lehman stared at Salter. "That's pathetic."

"That's the U.S. Constitution."

"That's bullshit." Lehman grinned in a way that Salter did not like at all. "What is it you've done, anyway, Salter?"

"Done? I don't get what you mean."

"In your past. What are you hiding?"

"I wasn't aware I was hiding anything. If you'd like to continue on to the Criminal Justice Information Division—"

"In my experience," Lehman interrupted, "the only people who got traumatized about the Patriot Act were people who had something to hide. Something they didn't want uncovered. Those with a clean conscience were perfectly happy to allow the government to keep them safe from the terrorist threat."

"That's a self-serving, gross exaggeration."

"Which doesn't prevent it from being a fact. What do you think his secret is, Muldoon?" He gave his deputy director a wink. "Unpaid child support? Drunk driving? Perhaps some sexual incident. Dallying with prostitutes. Child porn on his computer."

"If he has a secret," Muldoon said dryly, "it's probably more like he stole a comic book from the local grocery when he was seven."

Salter pondered which of the two had insulted him more.

"Maybe," Lehman said, chuckling, "but I still think anyone so opposed to this badly needed amendment must have a dark secret."

"Wait a minute," Muldoon said, raising a perfectly sculpted index finger. "I'm not crazy about the amendment myself."

"Yes, but I'm assuming you're a sensible person who will eventually come around to the right way of thinking. Particularly if you like your job," he added pointedly. "Salter here will never come around. He'll be mumbling about constitutional rights as he watches the mushroom cloud rise."

"Doesn't really matter what I think, does it?" Salter asked. He knew he should ignore the man—not take the bait—and continue the tour, but Lehman was just so obnoxious, Salter found it impossible to overlook. "Your problem is the Senate."

Lehman smiled. "We're working on that."

"Yeah, I saw the press conference. If the best you could find in the Democratic party was the most junior senator in the entire legislative body, you're in trouble."

"To the contrary," Lehman said. "Seducing Mr. Kincaid was a brilliant stroke. My idea, of course."

Muldoon started to say something, then apparently thought better of it.

"Stupid kid doesn't know how popular he is. He's coming off two big wins, after the Glancy case and the Roush nomination. He'll rally popular support to the point where those senators will have no choice but to approve, regardless of their party affiliation. After that, getting three-fourths of the states will be a breeze." He paused. "They'll come around. And so will you two."

Salter did his best to mask his reaction but it was a struggle. "I will never think this amendment is a good idea. Not if the foreign troops were landing on our soil as we spoke. Never."

"The troops have already landed, Salter. But they're not wearing uniforms and they don't march in formation. They're holed up in little cells, making bombs and training snipers and taking flying lessons. Torturing the director of Homeland Security. And now that I hold the post myself, I don't want to see that happen again. Do you?"

Salter bit back the obvious response.

"Speaking of which," Muldoon said, breaking in, "did you read that report I sent you, Carl?"

"Which one, Nichole? You spit out more paper than the photocopier."

"The one about the woman. Believed to be a Saudi national. Witnesses say she took out two attackers at once without even trying hard."

"I don't care about muggers. Even when they attack people from the Middle East."

"Carl, think about it. We're talking about the Middle East, where half the countries still keep their women buried in beekeeper's uniforms and execute them for showing their faces. And yet this woman acts like she stepped out of a Jet Li movie. Doesn't that make you the least bit curious?"

"No," he said curtly. "It does not."

"Well, I'm going to organize a team to follow up—"

"No, Nichole, you will not."

This time, Salter was pleased to see a much more graphic reaction on Muldoon's face. He knew that although she was Number Two in the hierarchy and followed Lehman around like a lapdog, she was accustomed to having a great deal of authority and the ability to do what she thought needed to be done.

"Just a small team, Carl. Just to make sure."

"No. No team at all."

"Carl, this could be related to the attack on the president."

"It isn't."

"You don't know that."

"I know we have limited manpower, so we're not going to divert anyone to chase around some lady who got lucky with a mugger."

"But, Carl—"

"You heard me, Nichole. This discussion is now officially ended."

Muldoon stopped talking. But Salter could see she wasn't happy about it. He wondered if she would really take no for an answer, or just wait until the boss wasn't looking and do whatever she wanted. She seemed the type.

"We have to focus on finding out who the April nineteenth assassin was, and it wasn't some Saudi woman who took a kickboxing class. We need to focus on getting this amendment passed. God knows I wish we had it in place already. I'd have caught the killer a week ago. I'd have his whole damn cell by now."

"Then you would declare a national emergency," Salter asked, "if the amendment were in effect now?"

"Damn straight I would. Have you forgotten what happened, Salter? What we witnessed in horror from our rooftop vantage point? Did you enjoy watching all those people die? A little girl? The first lady of the United States? If that's not a national emergency, I don't know what the hell is."

"That's my main problem with the amendment," Salter said. "It leaves that decision up to . . . someone who might not be impartial."

"Like the FBI?" Lehman rolled his eyes.

"Every FBI special agent, myself included, has been through an intensive eighteen-week training course at Quantico. I don't know what the people at Homeland Security do. They're mostly patronage appointments, aren't they?"

"I think you've got a serious case of agency envy, Salter. Which is very closely related to another kind of envy you may have studied in psychology class. Now have you got anything else to show me?"

Salter steeled himself. He hadn't wanted this crappy liaison assignment, but he would do his duty.

"As I suggested before, let's move to the CJIS Division. It's the main FBI repository for law enforcement data—largest in the world, in fact. It incorporates the Uniform Crime Reporting Center, the National Crime Information Center, Integrated Automated Fingerprint Identification System, and the National Incident-Based Reporting System. State and local police all across the country tap into our databases when they need an assist. The CJIS complex is bigger than three football fields. They collect fingerprints, DNA, incident reports—"

"But they haven't figured out who tried to kill the president, have they?" Lehman tweaked.

"No," Salter said, leading them down the main corridor, not missing a beat. "Have you?"

22

THE OLD SENATE CAUCUS ROOM

*B*en had not been in this most elegant of all the assembly rooms
in the Senate complex since the confirmation hearings for Justice Roush. Hadn't missed it any, either. The room was beautiful,
but the ornate decor couldn't erase the stress and trauma that he
now associated with this room and probably always would.

Relax, he tried to tell himself. *Enjoy the ride. You're not defending anyone this time around. Not attempting anything difficult,
really. Just offering up some testimony. Lending support to a bill.
That's what senators do. Isn't it?*

The Old Senate Caucus Room had remained virtually un-
changed since the building was constructed almost two hundred
years ago. The white marble columns and the gold-leaf crown mold-
ing were reminiscent of Versailles. The high ceiling made the room
appear much larger than it actually was, particularly when viewed
on television. It made for an impressive display, which was why the

Senate used it almost any time they suspected a hearing might get significant media play.

Media play. The thought made Ben's stomach whirl like a butter churn. He hated media play. Off on the left side of the room, he saw the single television camera shared by all the networks that would record and transmit the committee hearings to anyone who might be able to tear themselves away from *The Price Is Right*. The blinking red light laughed at him and dared him to speak aloud. He hated being on television and he hated seeing himself on television even more. He could always spot a flaw, something he could have done better. He'd come a long way since his early days, but he was still no Clarence Darrow or William Jennings Bryan, and he never would be.

Media play. His hands got sweaty just from whispering the words to himself. And he was considering running for a full Senate term? Who was he kidding? At least when he'd been at the White House press conference he'd had the president's advisors to assist. Now he was on his own. Not even Christina was here. She hadn't spoken to him for days.

There had been protestors outside, mostly from the ACLU and other civil libertarian groups. The Capitol Police were doing their best to keep them under control, but they had shaken Ben as he passed by. Some even called him ugly names. Traitor. Fascist. The press was almost equally aggressive, shouting questions and shoving microphones in his face. He should be used to that by now. But in truth, ever since the Oklahoma City attack, he had found himself more jumpy and nervous, especially in a crowd. They might be relatively harmless political protestors exercising their First Amendment rights, but now, Ben's imagination saw every disapproving face as a potential assassin, heard every loud noise as a gunshot. It unnerved him—exactly what he did not need before testifying.

He remembered the September 2006 incident when a man crashed his car into a security barricade and ran into the Capitol Building with a loaded handgun. He had led the Capitol Police on a merry chase before they finally cornered him in the basement and took his gun—along with the crack cocaine in his pocket. Didn't matter what precautions anyone took. If a loony with a car and a gun could get in here, no place was safe. No place and no one. The next attacker could be lurking just—

"You aren't wearing the red."

Ben jumped a foot in the air when he abruptly heard a voice in his ear. He turned and saw Tracy Sobel leaning toward him. "What are you talking about?"

"I left a message on your machine. About your attire. Blue suit, red tie."

"I did wear a blue suit." He only had two, and they were both blue.

"But not the red tie. Our media consultants thought that the red tie was key to persuading the home audience."

"Perhaps we should focus on persuading the Senate Judiciary Committee. Otherwise it won't matter what the people think."

"It always matters what the people think," Sobel said, checking off items on her clipboard faster than Ben could read them. "That's why we spend so much time manipulating the people and telling them what to think."

"Well, let Director Lehman wear the red tie."

"No, he's supposed to wear brown. He's law enforcement. People want law enforcement to seem sturdy and competent—not warm. You, on the other hand, need to be warm."

"And that is because . . . ?"

"Let's just say you don't have a naturally effervescent personality. Shall we take a seat?"

Ben followed her to a pre-designated position on the front row of the gallery. "I happen to think I can . . . effervesce as well as anybody."

"Yes, just keep telling yourself that. Try not to stutter when you do it."

Ben took his seat. He noticed that Sobel's makeup was more pronounced than usual; he assumed that was because she knew she was about to be on television. Seemed even the president's chief of staff wanted to look good to the folks out in Televisionland. He'd heard rumors that she had ambitions that went higher than chief of staff. He was beginning to suspect they were correct.

A few minutes later, they were joined by Senator Jeffrey De-Mouy and Homeland Security Director Carl Lehman. DeMouy was the first to crush Ben's hand. "Good to see you again, Kincaid. Ready to sell this bill to the committee?"

"Ready as I'll ever be," Ben said, and he meant it. "I assume you'll go first."

"Actually, I'm not going at all."

"What?"

Sobel intervened. "The president was concerned about having both of his designated hitters appear before the committee."

"Then use *him*!"

Sobel smiled slightly. "No. Traditionally, the committee calls witnesses who have actual knowledge of the matter at hand. True, they are usually advocates, but the advocacy is based on some experience or education. And they usually aren't senators. Why should one senator have to listen to the opinion of another senator in committee? That's what they'll have to do when the bill goes to the floor."

"Then why—?"

Sobel held up her hand impatiently, as if to prevent him from asking a question to which she already knew the answer. "You're in an entirely different situation. For one thing, you only barely count as a senator."

"Thank you so very much."

"Moreover, your background is in criminal defense—the exact antithesis of law enforcement. You'll make a good contrast with Director Lehman. You sit on different sides of the courtroom and yet you both support this bill."

"But that part about experience and knowledge—"

Again she cut him off. "You were there on April nineteenth. You experienced the attack firsthand. Forgive me if this seems callous, but it's a fact—your close friend was critically injured. That gives you an enormous amount of credibility. No one's going to question your right to address the committee."

There it was, just as plainly as it could be put. In the world of politics, even the potential loss of a dear friend ultimately became nothing more than grist for the political mill.

"Got some good news," DeMouy said, grinning. "The House Rules Committee just voted in favor of the amendment. It will go to the floor of the House next week."

"Where it's certain to be adopted."

"That's what the pundits tell me." He gave Ben a pointed look. "Which means it's all down to the Senate. Where the president put us in charge."

That's just dandy, Ben thought. If he hadn't been nervous before (and he had been), he was certainly nervous now.

Sobel withdrew a stapled bundle of papers from a manila envelope and handed it to Ben. "Here are some remarks we had one of our top speechwriters prepare for you."

"What? I don't need a speech."

"Fear not—no one expects you to deliver it verbatim. Just look it over. After your statement, there will be questioning. You might see something in there you can use."

"Like what?"

She shrugged. "Who knows? A persuasive argument. A clever turn of phrase. A witty bon mot. You can never tell what you might need when the time comes. Best to be armed with everything that's available."

Ben tried to hand the bundle back to her. "I don't need anyone to tell me what to say."

"I'd give it a good look-see if I were you." Director Lehman leaned forward, catching Ben's eye. He was so tall, he towered over Ben. "Goodness knows I read mine. Several times. I was happy to get the help. Words don't come naturally to me like they do to you."

Hmm. Ben reconsidered. Perhaps it wouldn't hurt to look the script over just once. . . .

A few moments later, the committee hearing was called to order. The audience, mostly senators, staff, friends of senators, and a few carefully chosen members of the press, rose as the committee members filed into the room.

They took their seats, and the designated chairman for this hearing, Senator Byron Perkins, a Democrat from Arkansas, called the hearing to order. "A proposed witness list has been submitted and agreed upon by representatives of both parties. Do I hear a motion?"

Senator Bening, a Republican from Colorado, jumped in. "I move that the witness list be accepted as drafted, with the possibility of additional witnesses being added if the committee deems it desirable."

"We have a motion on the table," Perkins said. "Do I hear a second?"

He did. The motion passed unanimously. And the first witness was called: the newly confirmed Director of Homeland Security, Carl Lehman.

Sobel had suggested that Ben was the emotional choice for the witness stand, but as Lehman strode toward the table at the front of the room, the camera following his every step, Ben realized that it would be impossible for anyone watching him to forget why the country had a new director of Homeland Security—because the previous one had been tortured and killed, probably by the same forces that masterminded the April 19 attack on the president.

Lehman began with his opening remarks. "I may be new to Homeland Security," he explained, "but I've been a member of the law enforcement community almost all my life, first at the state and now at the federal level. I've worked with good men and women, hardworking dedicated souls. And we've done good work. Put away a lot of bad guys and, I like to think, made this country a little bit safer. But it's no surprise to anyone that we have constantly been hamstrung by lawyers trying to get clients off on technicalities. People using the Bill of Rights as a Get Out of Jail Free card for some of the most vile criminals who ever walked the face of the earth. The crime, the people, even the welfare of the nation, seem not to matter sometimes. If there is some way to get the accused off, no matter how certain his guilt, these lawyers will use it."

He turned, adjusting his gaze slightly. Although it made little difference to those on the dais, Ben realized this would have the effect of allowing him to look directly into the camera. He'd be making eye contact with the television audience.

"We now enter what I believe is the most dangerous time in the history of this great nation. Our enemies have a greater capacity for destruction than they did at any previous time. We cannot be lazy, we cannot be indecisive, and we cannot allow hypothetical principles to compromise our safety. That was the route Rome took, and you know the result. After hundreds of years of dominating the world, they fell to the barbarians, a people less civilized, less technologically advanced—but far more brutal. I don't want to see that happen to America."

Ben knew the fall of the Roman Empire was much too complex to pin on a single cause, but he had to admit this was an effective piece of rhetoric, one likely to score well with the home viewer.

"Extraordinary times call for extraordinary measures. That's all this amendment is about. In times of great need, we will give the law enforcement community the powers they need to maintain domestic tranquillity—just like the Constitution says. In a perfect world, the privileges found in the Bill of Rights would be absolutes and there would be no need for this bill—but we do not live in a perfect world. When the choice is between an abstract principle and the survival of this nation"—he paused, letting the words have their intended effect—"I choose survival. I hope the members of this committee feel the same. I strongly urge you to recommend that this amendment go to the floor for a vote by the full Senate, and I hope you will do so as soon as possible. No one can know how much time we have. Or how little."

A few senators asked Lehman questions, but they led only to reiterations of the position he had taken in his opening statement. His feelings were clear. There was no point in browbeating a sincere and intelligent witness. Ten minutes later he stepped down. The somber mood he had created permeated the room. The gallery was silent as he took his seat next to Ben.

Ben knew the lackluster questioning did not in any way mean that the committee was convinced—he was certain some of the Democrats still intended to oppose. That was what he was here for.

Was he sure he was doing the right thing? he asked himself for the millionth time. He had thought so when he agreed to do this. He still thought so. And yet, when he heard the director talk about the Bill of Rights as an implicit security threat, a cold shiver ran up his spine. He was talking about fundamental American civil liberties.

The philosophical cornerstone of the nation. The American invention that, slowly but surely, was in fact spreading across the world. Could he really be sure—?

One thing he could be sure about. He knew what Christina thought.

In the past, he had always relied on her instincts. Now, in the early days of their long-delayed marriage, he was directly opposing them. It didn't feel good.

And then he thought of Mike, lying in that hospital bed, barely breathing. He thought of the sorrow in his sister's voice as he spoke to her for the first time in years. He thought of the terror in the eyes of the people in Oklahoma City when the attack began. The mother holding her dead child. The bullet-ridden corpse of the first lady . . .

What would Mike want?

Did he really need to ask? Mike was law enforcement, a dedicated cop who spent half their time together griping about defense attorneys and the laws that made it so difficult to catch and convict criminals. He knew what Mike would want.

"Thank you, Director Lehman," Chairman Perkins said. "I think you've given us all something to think about." He glanced down at the itinerary on his desk. "And for our next witness . . . the chair calls Senator Benjamin Kincaid."

Tracy Sobel gently touched Ben's shoulder. "Are you ready?"

Ben drew in his breath, then slowly released it. "I'm ready."

23

225 BLEEKER STREET
WESTBURY, MARYLAND

"I—I can't breathe," she gasped, barely able to speak. "You're killing me!"

The man did not respond. His lips pressed together as he tightened his grip around her throat.

"You're—choking—" The color drained from her face. She tried to struggle, but it was useless. Her arms were fastened behind her, and he was directly on top of her. "Please—please—"

The man pressed his thumb against her trachea, cutting off the flow of air to her lungs.

She opened her mouth as if to speak, but the blockage of her air passage made it impossible. All that came out was a creaking noise, a whisper of what she was trying to say: ". . . strangling . . . me . . ."

He bore down on her with even greater force, watching as her eyes rolled back into her head. All the color drained from her face and she looked almost vampirish, like a body that might be found in the coroner's office under a sheet.

Their hips continued to rock back and forth together, two bodies acting with one motion, even as her eyelids fluttered and she cried out.

With one final burst of energy, she began thrusting her hips upward uncontrollably, moving what little she could, feeling her consciousness slowly fading as the pleasure became almost unbearably intense.

"Oh, God." Her voice was but the murmur of a whisper. "Oh, Godddddd . . ."

He pounded all the harder, faster, with a rhythmic insistence. She relinquished herself to it, letting her body melt into his, feeling the warm press of his hands on her throat.

"Oh, Godddddd . . ."

She kicked him, her secret signal to him that the time was now upon her. He accelerated one final time, thrusting against her with a growing urgency until he felt the arch of her back and the trembling of her body that told him that she had climaxed. A second later, he released her throat.

After it was all over, he untied her hands and she tumbled into his arms, coughing and gasping and crying all at once.

"Oh my God, Jason. That was . . . that was like nothing I've ever felt before."

"Good, baby. I'm glad."

"How—" she said breathlessly, still gulping for air. "How do you do it? Time and time again."

He pressed her head against his chest. "I know my lady."

"You do?"

"Oh, yes. My Belinda likes a bit of danger. A lot of danger. Parking garages where anyone might walk in. Spankings that you can't control and can't stop. Erotic asphyxiation."

"That felt so . . . intense."

"People feel the most powerful orgasms when they're on the brink of death. Asphyxiation stimulates sexual excitement. It's a scientific fact. That's why hanged men often die with a hard-on."

"How do you know these things?"

"Call it a hobby." He brushed his hand softly against her raven hair. "Are you going to be all right?"

"Oh, God yes. God. Yes."

He took her head in his hand and gently raised her chin. "You seem as if you have something on your mind. Any regrets?"

"The only thing on my mind is—how long before we can do it again?"

They lay in bed together, naked, Belinda drifting gently in and out of sleep. "My God," she murmured. "If the girls at Bryn Mawr could see me now."

"They'd probably want to join you for a ménage à trois."

She slapped him on the shoulder. "You are so naughty."

"And you love it."

"Yes," she said, rubbing her naked leg against his thigh. "I do."

"Don't start anything," Jason said, still staring at the papers in his lap.

"You like your work more than you like me."

"Obviously not. Since I'm not only not doing what my boss told me to do, but screwing his wife." He kissed the top of her head. "Give a guy fifteen minutes to recharge, okay?"

"Fifteen minutes? You're getting old."

"Compared to whom? Your husband?"

"Mmm. Good point. Speaking of whom—is there any chance he might make a surprise early trip home?"

"None. I set his schedule, remember? He'll be at Homeland Security all day."

"Doing what?"

"Don't ask me. It's very hush-hush. Even before the Oklahoma City attack, he was spending an inordinate amount of time up there. And now with this amendment in the air, they have even more to talk about."

She snuggled closer, glancing with blurry eyes at the papers he was reading. "Whatcha reading?"

"This is some fascinating research I found on the Internet."

"About the amendment?"

"About how to make ricin poison."

Her spine suddenly stiffened. "You were serious."

"Damn right I was serious. Do you know how easy this stuff is to concoct? You can buy the ingredients at the grocery store. The chemistry isn't that complex, either."

"And you learned this on the Internet?"

"Hey—it's not just for terrorists anymore."

They both laughed over that one.

"Jason," she said quietly, after the merriment faded. "I'm—I'm not sure I really want you to do this."

He put his papers aside and stared at her with an expression that indicated little patience for this conversation. "Well, there are two problems with that. First, you do want it—you just don't want the guilt attendant to admitting that you want it."

"That's not true."

"Of course it is. Are you seriously suggesting that you want to go back to a sexless, loveless life with that old codger? Living off the paltry allowance he gives you? No, you don't. And secondly—this is not something *I'm* going to do. It's something *we're* going to do."

"I—I wouldn't know how."

"It's simple enough. I'll mix up the ricin. You get it on your husband's mail and make sure he's the one who opens it."

"Isn't there a simpler way?"

"Of course there is. There are a million simpler ways to kill someone. But anytime a married person gets murdered, the police immediately suspect the spouse. And nothing personal, but I'm not sure that blue-blooded etiquette-school training prepared you for third-degree questioning by the D.C. cops. So we need to do it in a way that looks like something you couldn't possibly do, something that will be attributed to the same terrorists who took out Senator Hammond." He smiled. "Ricin-laced letters. It's a classic."

She stared at him long and hard. "You've really thought about this, haven't you?"

"Haven't *you*?"

"Well . . ."

"You haven't considered how nice it would be to have a young lover without worrying about your rich and powerful husband finding out? You haven't contemplated the pleasure of having all that money you'll inherit to yourself, of being able to spend it as you wish?"

"Won't you be out of a job?"

"Not unless I want to be. At least half a dozen of your hubby's colleagues have tried to steal me away. But I really don't plan to be a chief of staff all my life."

She placed her hand on his hairy chest. "You want to run for office, don't you?"

"Doesn't everyone in this town? And with your money—I'll be able to do it."

"You think you could win."

"I think I'll be invincible. I know the Senate better than anyone. Know all the right people. Know what I have to say and do to get the big contributions from the PACs and the lobbyists. And I'll have a really hot ex-senator's wife who's willing to do anything for me."

She pushed herself up on her elbows. "You presume a good deal! Maybe I don't want to play a part in this twisted scheme."

"Or maybe you do. Maybe you're just playing hard to get in the hopes that I'll go down on you."

"Jason!"

He laid his papers on the floor and rolled over. "Don't bother. I know what you want." He sighed. "Back to the salt mines."

"Jason!"

He dove under the covers and went to work.

"Jason. Jason, listen to me. I just don't know if . . ." But a second later he made contact and she lost whatever objection she had considered lodging. She liked the way he made her feel. She never got enough of it. She would do anything to make it continue, to feel him licking her and fondling her, making her head swim and her heart pound and her entire body feel like a woman's body is supposed to feel. She wanted it to continue. She wanted it to go on forever.

And for that, killing her revolting husband seemed a very small price to pay.

24

THE OLD SENATE CAUCUS ROOM

*T*he sergeant at arms met Ben halfway to the front table. Ben raised his right hand and laid the other on the Bible proffered. "Do you swear to tell the truth, the whole truth, and nothing but the truth, so help you God?"

"I do."

Chairman Perkins tapped his gavel. "Please take your seat, Senator Kincaid."

Ben pulled out the chair at the center table and tried not to think about the unblinking eye of the camera that he knew was now poised upon him, beaming his likeness to countless millions of televisions across the country, perhaps across the world. His knees were already wobbly and he knew it would not take much to give his whole body the shakes, something that would probably not make a great impression on the committee, much less the television audience.

Chairman Perkins cleared his throat. "I understand that you

have a few remarks you would like to make before we begin questioning, Senator."

"Yes, Mr. Chairman, I do." All of a sudden, Ben seriously wished he had kept the script Tracy Sobel had offered him. It was the usual political claptrap, rhetorical questions and stacked arguments and such, but at least he wouldn't have to think. Because right at the moment, he was having a hard time with the thinking.

"I have been asked to give my thoughts regarding the proposed Constitutional amendment this committee is considering." Sobel had asked him not to refer to it as the president's amendment out of respect to Congress, which has the constitutional authority to start the amendment process. "Let me begin by saying that, as a lawyer, I understand the gravity involved in any effort to amend the Constitution. Once done, it can only be undone by another amendment. No court can declare the law invalid; a law which is part of the Constitution is by definition constitutional. Therefore, this consideration is perhaps the most important of any proposed laws this body has the possibility of adopting."

Ben made the mistake of looking at the television camera; the red light was on and he knew what that meant. The world was watching. His mouth went dry. A cold clamminess spread across his entire body. He struggled to keep it together.

"We have amended this Constitution relatively few times since the Bill of Rights, and the most important of those have come about when there was a sense of great need, either just before, during, or after times of great crisis. I will suggest to you that this is another such time."

Good God, what was it Sobel wanted him to be sure to say? He couldn't remember. Oh—right. "It may seem strange to some of you that I, a criminal defense attorney, favor a bill that some see as an abridgement of the Bill of Rights. But if this amendment becomes part of the Constitution, then by definition, no rights have been abridged. The law has changed. Our laws, including the Bill of Rights and the way we interpret them, have changed repeatedly throughout the history of this nation. It would be strange indeed if now, after all this nation has been through, they did not change again. Who can deny that recent years have witnessed violence of a magnitude never before imagined outside of a war battleground? The first attack on the World Trade Center, the bombing of the Murrah Building, 9/11. And now this most recent horror. While the death toll does not approach that of the previous two tragedies, in many ways, the shock value was greater. In this instance, viewers all across the nation witnessed a blatant attempt to take out the head of our government—which came dangerously close to success. We lost our first lady, one of the most beloved women in American history. If for no other reason, in the memory of that dear lady, we must take action to see that nothing like that is ever repeated. To ensure that the people of this nation are as safe as it is possible to be in this modern world. That is why I urge each and every one of you to give the strongest consideration to lending your support to this proposal, and to allow it to leave the committee for a vote of the full Senate."

Ben resisted the temptation to add "Whew!"

As he scanned the faces of the senators on the committee, he saw very little indication of how any of them were disposed to vote. In fact, he saw little of anything. Had he put them to sleep?

Out of the corner of his eye, Ben saw Tracy Sobel, her arms folded across her chest, obviously unhappy. And he knew why. As far as they could tell from the unofficial polling that had taken place nonstop since the amendment had first been proposed, the committee appeared to be evenly divided. If there was to be any chance of this getting to the Senate floor, someone—several someones, perhaps—was going to have to change their minds. That was the job they had chosen Ben to do, because he had the potential to be emotional and dramatic. Instead, he had come across like a robot, carefully analyzing the pros and cons and coming up with a logical but unexciting conclusion.

If logic were enough to win the day, Ben's participation would not have been requested or required. They needed more. He hadn't delivered.

"Will you take questions, Senator Kincaid?"

Hell, no, he wanted to say, but he went with, "Of course."

Senator Scolieri from Ohio was the first to speak. "Senator, as a Republican, I'm getting a lot of mail from people who are concerned that this amendment represents an erosion of civil rights, and that once those rights are removed, we may never retrieve them. I'm curious what you, as a Democrat, would say in response."

"I would say that the Emergency Security Council, if it is ever convened, is a temporary measure."

"But how temporary? The amendment puts no limitations on how long an emergency state can be sustained."

"Realistically, Senator, I don't think there's any way it could. We can't predict the future. We have to give the Council the power it needs to get the job done."

"But what is the job?" asked Senator Keyes, a Texan Republican. Keyes had been chairman of the Judiciary Committee during the Roush confirmation, and Ben's archenemy throughout the entire proceeding. But now that they appeared to be on the same side, for all you could tell, he and Keyes were the closest of friends. What was that expression about politics and bedfellows? "Shouldn't there be some explanation of what constitutes an emergency situation? Otherwise, doesn't the Council have too much leeway?"

"I think any attempt to define what constitutes an emergency situation would either be so vague as to be pointless or so specific as to render the amendment ineffectual. Could the Founding Fathers have predicted that one day a foreign nation would be able to threaten us without leaving their own borders? Obviously not. Could they predict airplanes being used as weapons, or ricin powder in the mail, or contaminants capable of poisoning entire water supplies? No. And sadly, I am certain that the years to come will introduce new threats we couldn't begin to discuss or describe today. The amendment must remain open-ended so it will be capable of adapting to a changing world."

Ben glanced over his shoulder. Sobel seemed slightly more pleased. At least, he supposed, the question-and-answer session was more animated than his lame little speech had been. But he knew she wanted more. Moreover—he knew they needed more if they were going to get this amendment out of committee.

The time for the softball questions had passed, as the chairman shifted his gaze from the Republicans to the Democrats. How ironic—the hostile questioning would come from Ben's own party.

"I have a question." This came from Senator Lucy Largent, a

liberal Democrat from California. "Senator Kincaid, this amendment appears to me to put an enormous amount of power in the hands of the director of Homeland Security. Are we taking a terribly big risk here? Putting so much power in the hands of one person?"

"The Constitution already puts a great deal of power in the hands of one person. The President of the United States."

"But the president is elected by the people. The director of Homeland Security is appointed."

"By the president, who is elected by the people," Ben replied succinctly. "We all know that the president appoints unelected officers who wield great governmental power. His cabinet members. Federal judges."

"Even those officers can be recalled or impeached. I don't see any provision that would allow anyone to replace or impeach any member of this Emergency Security Council."

"The president always has the right to replace the people he appoints, other than federal judges. Quietly calling for the resignations of those who have displeased the Oval Office is a common facet of modern political life. If the president doesn't like the job being done by the directors of Homeland Security, the FBI, or the CIA, he can replace them."

"What if he calls for a resignation and the appointee refuses?"

"I think that is unlikely."

"I don't think we can know what someone might do if they're given power of this magnitude," Senator Largent said, obviously not placated.

"Would it be better if the amendment gave this power directly to the president, so that he or she could unilaterally decide to suspend civil rights—like Abraham Lincoln did during the Civil War?" Ben paused, letting them all ponder that for a moment. "I don't think so. We are much safer having a committee composed of the top law enforcement officials in the country making the critical decisions. The director of Homeland Security may be the chairman, but he or she is still only one member of the Council. I think this amendment has been structured so as to give the rights of the American people the maximum protection possible while still ensuring safety during a time of crisis."

"You've just explicated an implied prioritization that gives me great concern," said Senator Cole Stevens, a Democrat from Vermont. In Ben's experience, the man always talked more like a college professor than a politician. How he ever managed to get elected—three times—was beyond Ben's comprehension. "This amendment esentially says civil rights are swell, but security is more important."

"Frankly," Ben said, "I think you're right, and I have no problem with that, and I don't think the Founding Fathers would have, either. We all know that we will have no civil rights if we lose our freedom. Without liberty, there are no civil liberties."

"You're giving me slogans, not answers," Senator Stevens insisted.

"I disagree."

"I wasn't finished. You're giving me slogans, and to be perfectly honest, I'm shocked. Isn't your conscience bothering you at all?"

Ben did not respond.

"As far as I can tell, Mr. Kincaid, your whole career has been about defending the rights of the people, protecting the innocent, making sure no one is railroaded by the mighty machine we know as the American government. And now you come out in favor of this amendment which flies in the face of everything you've stood for your entire life. How can you *do* this?"

Ben remained silent, unsure what to say.

"I asked you a question, Senator Kincaid." His voice rose in volume. "In all good conscience, how can you do this?"

"If you'd been there on April nineteenth," Ben said, his voice trembling, "you'd want this amendment, too." He spoke barely louder than a whisper. In the back of the Caucus Room, people leaned forward, straining to hear. "If you had felt the . . . the . . . stark terror I experienced—that everyone there experienced—you'd want this amendment, too. I was embarrassed at how easily I succumbed to fear. I would've done anything to get out of there, anything. Thank God for the Secret Service and the other heroes of that day, because I was not one of them. I was a puddle—shaken to the core. I haven't had a decent night's sleep since—I don't know if I ever will again." He took a deep breath. "No one should be able to do that to another human being. No one."

He drew up his chin and started again, his voice gradually gaining strength. "Oklahoma City should be the safest city in the world. It's a modest metropolis buried deep in the heartland where folks still smile at strangers and give up their bus seats to people older than they are. And yet it has been hit twice—twice—by terrorism, first with the bombing of the Murrah Building, and now with this assault on the life of our commander in chief, purposefully staged at the site of the prior tragedy. I ask you—if Oklahoma City is not safe—what place is?"

Ben paused, wondering silently where this had come from. He had not planned it. He hadn't planned to be so emotional—or so honest. It just erupted out of him when he heard Senator Stevens's question.

"The April nineteenth assassin might have been gunning for the president," Ben continued, "but he got my best friend, Mike Morelli. Let me tell you something about Mike. He's a major, a top officer in the Tulsa homicide division. He has made his work his life. His work has benefited the community more times than I can count. If I live to be two hundred, I could not possibly equal his history of public service. But there's more to Mike—" His voice cracked. Ben swallowed, took another breath. "There's more to him than that. This is the man who sat by my bedside when I was sick and comatose for more than a week. This is the man who stayed up all night—on a work night no less—reciting poetry and singing the *Flintstones* song, trying to get my nephew to sleep. He has quite literally put his life on the line to save mine—and he did it again on April nineteenth."

Ben's head turned from side to side, as if he might somehow, somewhere, locate an answer he could not elucidate. "Mike Morelli is a hero. And that hero is at this moment lying near death on a hospital bed, his doctors unsure if his eyes will ever open again. That is not right." His voice swelled, both in strength and volume. "Mike Morelli deserves better. I would do anything—" And at that, Ben's voice broke down completely. Tears sprang unbidden to his eyes. Several moments passed before he could continue.

"I would do anything," Ben whispered, "to turn back time and prevent Mike from being injured. But of course, that's not possible.

I can't do that. But I can do everything in my power to make sure this does not happen to *your* best friend, Senator Stevens, or *yours*, Senator Largent, or anyone else's. To take all possible steps to make sure this never again happens to anyone. I'm not sure about logic or principles or constitutional law—but I am sure about this. This is the greatest of all nations, my friends. If we can prevent tragedies of this magnitude from happening—then we must."

Ben let several more moments pass, wiping his eyes dry. After he thought he had collected himself, he finished. "That's why I support this amendment, ladies and gentlemen. And that's why I hope you will do the same."

Silence blanketed the caucus room.

Less than an hour later, the committee recommended that the proposed amendment be presented to the full Senate as soon as possible, by unanimous vote.

25

NIGHT OWL HOTEL
WASHINGTON, D.C.

Fortunately, none of the bullets had lodged in Shohreh's body, so Loving was able to use his medic experience to clean and dress the wounds. Her arm was in a sling and her leg and the left side of her face were bandaged, but it was nothing she wouldn't recover from in a few weeks. He couldn't offer her anything for the pain, but she didn't seem to mind. She was a tough woman; he knew that already from the way he'd seen her fight in the cemetery. He'd offered to take her to a hospital, but she had refused.

Once she was resting properly, Loving returned to the cemetery to question the sniper who attacked her. Unfortunately, he was gone.

When at last she was well enough, he sat down on the edge of the bed to ask her some questions. She began questioning him before he had a chance.

"Where am I?" she asked, then immediately clutched the side of her face. Loving had bandaged the scrapes and gashes, but he knew they still hurt, especially when she talked.

"You're safe. I've brought people here before. I know the manager. And I trust him. Omar Khasban. Nice old Iranian guy."

She looked at him cautiously. "So you do not believe that all people of the Middle East are brutal killers?"

"I know better. Some of my best friends—"

"And you do not fear those of the Islamic faith?"

"The core teaching of the religion is love, ain't it? Teachin' people to be good to each other? Like pretty much every other religion I ever read about."

"You do not think we are all barbarians?"

"Stop me if I'm wrong, lady, but didn't I read that over half of all Muslims live under democratic governments?"

She continued to stare, obviously evaluating, being her usual cautious self. "You are very enlightened for one who seems so . . . simple."

Loving grinned from ear to ear. "Yeah, I get that a lot. Works well in my line of work."

"And that is—?"

"Private investigator. Work for Ben Kincaid, first when he was a lawyer, now when he's a senator. Either way, he manages to get into trouble pretty much constantly. Ben is working to pass this new amendment the president has proposed, and his wife hates it, and she's got this crazy idea that the Oklahoma City attack wasn't about terrorists at all."

Shohreh's voice grew quieter. "Indeed."

"Yeah. Christina's got some notion—I don't really understand it—but it's got somethin' to do with the first lady. Like maybe, she thinks Emily Blake was the target, not just fallout from the attack on the president."

"This . . . Christina . . . is a very unusual woman."

"You got that right. And you haven't even seen the way she dresses."

"Has she shared these ideas with the authorities?"

"I think she's tried, but no one's listenin'."

"Why were you looking for me?"

"Well, that's a long story."

"Condense it for me."

Loving laughed. She almost did too, but it made her face hurt too much. "The first lady died because of a change in procedure made by a Secret Service agent, Tom Gatwick, who was on the spot in Oklahoma City. I've reviewed the tape to see who he spoke to before, during, and after the attack."

"You saw me."

"Yes, I did. And so did the kajillions of law enforcement types who have been reviewing the same tape. The problem is—none of them knew who you were."

"But you figured it out."

Loving waved a hand in the air. "Aww, I got lucky."

"I very much doubt that."

"I happened to be visitin' my pal with the DCPD—Lieutenant Albertson. We've worked on some cases together in the past."

"You were partners."

Loving shrugged awkwardly. "More like . . . friendly antagonists. When he wasn't trying to arrest me, we exchanged information."

"America is a very strange country."

"You got that right. Anyway, I happened to be visitin' one day when I heard an eyewitness talk about the strangest thing. He'd seen this tiny little Middle Eastern woman walkin' down an alley not far from here. He saw three other men walk into the alley and thought she was about to be mugged. Bein' a resourceful citizen, he got out his cell and called 911. 'Cept, as it turned out, by the time he was off the phone, she'd already trounced two of the chumps and sent the third hidin' in the darkness. Said she was some kinda ninja fighter or somethin'."

A thin smile crossed Shohreh's face. "I have been trained in the art of the Muay Thai."

"Thai kickboxin'? I'm impressed."

"I'm impressed that you know what the Muay Thai is."

"I try to stay up with all the new ways people have of killin' each other. Pays off in my line of work."

"But this witness—it was dark—he had no camera."

"He had a cell phone camera with a flash. True, the picture pretty much sucks, but he also gave a description to a sketch artist, and between the picture and the sketch, the cops came up with somethin' that I thought looked a hell of a lot like the woman in the video. Uh, pardon my French."

"I speak French. That is not French."

"It's an expression. Uhm . . ." How to explain? "Never mind. So that's what put me on your trail."

"How did you find me?"

"I trolled the area where the fight broke out for days. Staked out the corners with video cameras. Paid people. Eventually got a line on your apartment. Watched this evenin' as you came out and followed you to the cemetery. And a good thing I did, too. Who was that creep?"

"An emissary of a man named General Yaseen Daraji. A man who very much wants me dead." She told Loving, in sketch form, of her troubled history—her life of privilege in Iraq before her family was killed, being forced to live with relatives, then being left with no one, forced to flee to Afghanistan, and eventually joining the terrorist cell organized by the General.

"And you think this Yaseen had somethin' to do with what happened in Oklahoma City?"

"I know that he did."

" 'Cause the Feebs are all busy with that other group."

"They are wrong."

"Then why hasn't this . . . General guy stepped forward to take credit for the killin'?"

"Because he does not want credit. He wants others to be blamed."

"What's the point of a terrorist attack if you don't take credit?"

"You law enforcement people are being played. Deliberately misled. I believe the General is acting on behalf of another."

"Who?"

"If I knew, I would tell you. But I do not."

"But you were there. In Oklahoma City."

"Because the General asked me to be there."

"Why?"

"He did not say."

"If you're not workin' with them—why go?"

"He promised he would grant me my freedom—sever all ties, end all grudges. I would be free of his cell forever. He would not try to kill me."

"I can see where that would be temptin'."

"Yes. I was so desperate for the peace he offered—I acted stupidly. I did as he asked. But it seems clear now, especially with what you have told me. I believe he may have been setting me up."

Loving prided himself on being brighter than most people thought, but he was still having trouble with all this. "Why would you think that?"

"That Secret Service agent—Gatwick, you say?—was not the first to approach me. The agents said they had received an anonymous tip that a woman fitting my description might be carrying a weapon."

"But you weren't."

"But I was supposed to. The General gave me one. I took it—but declined to bring it to the memorial service. I was . . . suspicious."

"Damn good thing you were."

"I did not want it to sully my person. The Qur'an teaches us to live in peace. I have sworn off all forms of violence."

Loving arched an eyebrow. "You were doin' pretty good back in that alley."

"Self-defense is another matter. The Qur'an allows all people to defend themselves. We do not have your Christian doctrine of . . . how do you say it? Turning the other cheek."

Loving nodded. "Easily the least observed principle in the whole Bible."

"It is against human nature. We were meant to survive, to fight. Peace does not come naturally."

"I think you may be wrong about that. But I can see where you might think it, given the company you've been keepin'. So why are you lookin' for this General now? Seems like the best thing you could do is stay away from him."

"I believe he was using me to draw attention away from his true accomplices. But now I know too much. I can tie him to Oklahoma City, among other crimes. He wants me dead."

Loving nodded. "I know people who can make you disappear. Give you a new identity. IDs and everythin'."

Shohreh laughed so hard, she clutched her bandages to ease the pain. "I have been that way before, thank you. The General is smart. A new identity will not stop him. But that is beside the point. I do not want to disappear. I want to seek out the General. And now I have lost my only lead."

Loving allowed himself a hint of a smile. "Maybe not. I think the man who tried to kill you back at the cemetery can help us."

"But—you said he had disappeared already when you returned."

"That's true. But I searched him before I left. And I found this address scrawled on a scrap of paper."

Shohreh snatched the paper away from him. "I know this house. I thought it was long since closed down. They must have reopened it. They must have needed it to deal with . . . an upsurge in business."

"Terrorism?"

"No. How they finance the terrorism."

"Oil?"

She looked at him, her eyes wide. "Will you help me? I must find the General. For Djamila's sake."

Loving's forehead creased. "Who's that?"

She suddenly grew distant. "A little girl. An innocent whose life was taken by the General and his cruel business."

"And that business is?"

Shohreh's eyes lowered. "Sex."

"You mean—you mean he makes his loot off . . . hookers?"

Shohreh shook her head sadly. "Children."

26

Agent Gatwick tried to stay in the shadows as he slowly made his way to the appointed rendezvous site. He hated this whole business. He hated meeting at night; he hated meeting in darkness. And he especially hated meeting in a parking garage. It was way too Deep Throat for his taste.

Why did they have to meet like this, anyway? The explanation he'd been given was that certain "enemy eyes" might be watching. To him, that was all the more reason not to meet in secret. Meet in their offices and close the door, for God's sake. Surely even the NSA couldn't eavesdrop in the Secret Service offices. And a meeting like that wouldn't attract any undue suspicion. This one surely would—if anyone found out about it.

He would just have to make damn sure no one found out about it.

"Psst!"

Gatwick whirled around. There, huddled behind a Land Rover,

was the director of Homeland Security, Carl Lehman. A huge over six-foot-tall black man wearing—swear to God—a trench coat.

Gatwick knew the man was his boss, but he still couldn't manage to keep his mouth shut. "I'm sorry, but don't you feel just a little bit—silly?"

Lehman frowned. "What's that supposed to mean?"

"The director of Homeland Security. Crouched in shadows."

"May I remind you what happened to the last director of Homeland Security?"

Okay, there the man had a point. "Do you have some reason to believe we're in danger?"

"Don't you get it?" Lehman slowly rose, careful to keep himself in the dark and out of view of the concealed video monitors. "I'm always in danger."

"But today—"

"I was on national television today. My face was beamed all over the globe. Every terrorist on earth knows what I look like."

Fine. Allow the man his paranoia. It seemed to boost his ego. "It wasn't a terrorist who asked to meet with you. It was me."

Lehman's eyes darted left, then right. "You can never be too careful." He paused, then added, "I think it's best we're not seen together, Tom. At least not until this amendment passes."

So that was it. "Why would us being seen together arouse suspicion?"

"You support the amendment."

"Along with virtually every other Secret Service agent."

"Yes," Lehman said slowly, "but there are . . . special circumstances in your case. You know it as well as I do."

A deep furrow creased Gatwick's brow. "Those special circumstances are exactly what we need to discuss. I've got Zimmer crawling all over my ass."

"Sounds unpleasant."

"He's certain he's uncovered some kind of conspiracy."

Lehman's left eyebrow rose. "Does he indeed."

"Yeah."

"What does he know?"

"Just enough to be irritating."

"What are the goals of this imagined conspiracy?"

"He has no clue. But he thinks I'm in on it. I'm not sure he doesn't think I'm in charge of it."

"How flattering for you."

"Not so much. He wants to blame me for the death of the first lady."

"Wasn't he shielding the first lady when she was killed?"

"Exactly!"

Lehman waved the air dismissively. "Guilt. He screwed up. Didn't take the bullet. So now his superego has to find a scapegoat, someone else to blame, some way to tell himself he was not at fault. I wouldn't worry about it."

"I have no choice but to worry about it!" Gatwick said, raising his voice. Lehman drew a finger across his lips, hushing him. "The man is not stupid. And he has a very big mouth. People listen to him." Gatwick folded his arms, suddenly very cold. "I think something is going to have to be done about him."

"Something . . . done about him? What exactly did you have in mind?"

"I don't know. You're the director of Homeland Security. You tell me."

"You want me to fire him?"

"At the very least."

"Are you saying—?"

"Look, do you understand how much I'm hanging out here? I made the changes to Domino Bravo—just like you told me. And the first lady got killed, along with more than a dozen other people."

"All I was doing was trying to fix one of my predecessor's poorly designed protocols."

"Zimmer doesn't know that. My ass is totally hanging out on this one."

"I will make sure your ass is covered," Lehman assured him. "Haven't I deflected all hint of blame thus far?"

"I don't know what you've done so far, but I'm worried. I don't want to become the scapegoat for a national tragedy. I need a comfort margin."

"You need a prescription for Xanax, sounds like to me."

Gatwick could feel his anger rising. Nothing was more irritating than the feeling that you weren't being taken seriously—especially when there was so much to be taken seriously. "It's not just me, Carl," he said pointedly. "Both our necks are sticking out here."

Lehman stiffened. "I haven't done anything I'm ashamed of."

"That's beside the point. If Zimmer talks enough about a conspiracy in the Secret Service—"

"—then absolutely no one will listen. There has never been a traitor in the Secret Service. Never."

"So I told him. But it didn't quell his suspicions. He's been watching media tapes of the incident, looking for clues to what really happened. He volunteered for the investigation just to get access to the files."

"You don't know that. He might be motivated by a sincere desire to catch the killers."

"Bullshit. He's after *me,* period. This morning he was trying to access my personnel files. Didn't have the security clearance, but I got a flash alert informing me of the attempt. So what are we going to do about it?"

Lehman smiled. Gatwick sensed he was trying to be reassuring, but somehow, when he was cowering in shadows and wearing that ridiculous trench coat, it just didn't come across. "What we have to do, Agent Gatwick, is make sure this amendment passes."

"I don't see how that gets Zimmer off my back."

"I do. Get this amendment passed and I'll be able to do anything I want."

"Didn't the amendment get out of committee?"

"Yes, but we don't know what will happen on the floor of the Senate. Unofficial polling shows those in favor and those against are about equal in number."

"Just get that Kincaid kid to cry again. The rest of the Senate is sure to fall into line."

"I'm a little worried about that young senator, actually."

"Why? Didn't he do exactly what you wanted him to do?"

"Yes, but he's conflicted."

"He told you this?"

"He didn't have to. I've been around a long time. You don't get far in law enforcement or politics if you can't read a man's face, and that man still has his doubts."

"Well, as long as he keeps them to himself . . ."

"Yes, but will he?" Lehman batted a finger against his lips. "A change of heart at the wrong moment could throw a monkey wrench into our plans. We need some sort of insurance. Some way to make sure he plays ball until the Senate approves this amendment."

Gatwick took a step backward. "Wait a minute, Carl—I don't need to be taking any more chances."

"You don't need to piss me off, either," Lehman said harshly. "Not if you like doing what you do and living like you live. And keeping your secrets secret."

Gatwick's nostrils flared. Lehman was using him. But what could he do about it? At this point, there was no turning back. "What is it you had in mind?"

"I'm willing to leave that to your discretion," Lehman said, his eyebrows dancing. "But you know, the man is a newlywed. . . ."

27

Ben sat in the front living room of the apartment—what Christina called her purple-and-pink paradise—and wondered where she was. First she slammed the door on him; then, last night, she didn't come home at all. That had happened before. She was one of the most industrious staffers in the Senate, and her constant socializing and gossiping and temperature-taking and all the other things that made her invaluable often kept her so late that she simply slept in the office. But it couldn't be a coincidence that she had managed to have absolutely nothing to do with him since he came out publicly in favor of the amendment. And now that it was out of committee and most of the pundits said it was due to his testimony—

Well, he wasn't surprised she wasn't here tonight.

But he wished to God she were.

Maybe if he took her on that honeymoon they never managed to have. Just as soon as the amendment got through the Senate, he could whisk her off to France. First class, maybe. He couldn't afford first class. Come to think of it, he couldn't afford to go to France at all. Weren't senators supposed to be rolling in dough? Where were all those under-the-table bribes and overseas junkets when you needed them? Maybe if he called a few lobbyists . . .

But he suspected Christina would not go for that.

Maybe if he used his newfound clout to get that Alaskan Wilderness Bill passed. Not that he actually had any clout, as far as he knew, but he should. He was doing a favor for the president. Shouldn't the president now do a favor for him? Might be a stretch—President Blake had been very vocal in his opposition to the bill for the last two years—but still, wouldn't that make Christina happy? She'd been fighting for that one since the day they arrived in Washington. Maybe if he got really tight with Senator De-Mouy . . .

But he suspected even that would not make Christina forget what he had done.

And for that matter, neither would a million-dollar contribution to her favorite charity, an autographed set of Red Dirt Rangers CDs, horseback riding with Prince Charles, a diamond-studded hair band, a silver-plated harmonica, the ability to warp the space-time continuum, or lunch with Madonna. And he didn't have any of those things, either.

Didn't matter. Wouldn't work.

Which made her angrier? he wondered. The fact that he supported a proposal she so adamantly opposed or the fact that he had done it without consulting her first? After all, he didn't have that much time to think about it. The president's chief of staff had told him to call before midnight, and midnight was only minutes away when he finally called, and if he had stopped to call Christina first, time might have run out and—

And these were all excuses. He hadn't called Christina first because he knew what her reaction would be. He chickened out.

Now he was paying the price. He just hoped the assessment wasn't permanent. He had longed to be with her for so long. To think that he had screwed it all up so quickly ate at him like a two-foot ulcer. Could she ever forgive him? Or was this marriage over before it had even begun?

The doorbell rang, thank God. He knew it wasn't Christina— she was hardly likely to ring the bell before entering her own apartment—but whoever it was, they would provide some distraction from his own morose musings.

He pushed himself out of the easy chair and opened the door.

His first thought was: I didn't know Victoria's Secret sold door-to-door.

She was a short woman, but what she had, she had in great amplitude. As he stood there trying to think of something intelligent to say, her overcoat dropped off her shoulders and fell to the floor, revealing the entire outfit, what there was of it. The corset was black; the frilly edges of the teddy were white. The cups beneath her breasts barely covered the nipple and the backside revealed more bottom than most hospital gowns.

She tossed her blond hair behind her head and smiled. "See anything you like, Senator?"

Ben swallowed. "I—I think you—you m-must have the wrong apartment."

"I don't think so. Pucker up, you handsome hunk of manhood."

She strode toward him with a determined and confident certainty. Ben held up his hands, but she brushed them away and threw herself at him. Before he knew what was happening, her lips were planted on his. A moment later, she leapt up into the air and wrapped her legs around him.

"I—really think there's—there's b-been some sort of mistake," Ben said, struggling to get his face free from hers.

"You know you want it, handsome."

"I'm—pretty sure I don't."

"Let me convince you." Ben felt her hand grabbing in a place where it should not be grabbing.

"Do—I know you?" Ben asked, pulling away.

And the instant his face emerged over her shoulder, the flash erupted in his eyes.

28

"Got it!" Jones said, as he ran into the office, practically colliding with Christina at the front desk.

"Do you indeed?" she answered, not looking up from her phone messages. Over the years, she had become accustomed to Jones's occasional bursts of irrational enthusiasm and had learned to restrain her expectations. "And what would that be?"

"Something you're going to want to see."

Christina laid down her papers, sighing. She knew she would never find out what he had until he felt she had given him the proper amount of attention. "All right, Jones. What've you got?"

"Oh, nothing much . . ."

"Jones," she said firmly, giving him the look. "Don't toy with me. What is it?"

Jones had also worked with Christina long enough to know that when she gave him the look, it was time to submit. "Just a little something you wanted from the Bethesda Coroner's Office."

Her eyes instantly widened. "Already?" She snatched the envelope out of his hands. "Freedom of Information Act requests usually take weeks. Sometimes months."

Jones laid a hand across his chest. "You're not the only one who has connections in this town, you know."

"Apparently not." She pulled the papers out of the envelope and began to read:

CORONER'S REPORT—EMILY BLAKE

Office of the Coroner-Medical Examiner   Case No. 1003-76
Capitol Boulevard, Washington, D.C.

Report of Investigation

Decedent: Emily Margaret Blake

Age: 42

Sex: Female

Race: White

Occupation: First Lady

Employed by: The White House

Type of Death: Apparent Natural_____ Violent__X__
At Work_____ Not at Work _____

Description: Height: 5' 6"   Weight: 131   Hair: Black   Eyes: Brown
Tattoos: One, left buttock   Scars: None identified
Other Identifying Features: Large birthmark in center of back
Rigor Mortis: None   Livor Mortis: Slight posterior

Narrative Summary:

Victim arrived dead via Air Force Two at approximately 12:42 local time. Preliminary examination revealed massive brain trauma apparently induced by a bullet to the head . . .

Christina blinked. "The first lady had a tattoo on her butt?"

Jones nodded. "It's true what they say. You never really know someone until they're dead."

Christina scanned the report. It was more than a little ghoulish, reading intimate details about a woman so beloved by her country—including Christina—after she was dead and buried. But there was a reason. Something was going on here, something more than just a stray bullet during a presidential assassination attempt. She intended to get to the bottom of it.

Christina continued scanning. Toxicology, tissue samples, blood screens, serology . . .

"Wait a minute," she said abruptly. "What's with the black bar?"

Jones peered over her shoulder. Sure enough, black bars covered the six lines that followed the topic heading SEROLOGY.

"It's been redacted," Jones said, stating the obvious. "Before the document was released."

"But why? Under the FOIA, government agencies are not authorized to redact any document unless there is a potential threat to national security."

"So the first lady's blood test poses a threat to national security? You think she had . . . some kind of disease?" He didn't mention any disease in particular, but he knew what they both were thinking.

"I don't see how that could possibly have been covered up."

"Loving thinks the government can cover anything up."

"Including the fact that President Blake is a Martian. I don't think that's it."

"But what, then? What could be so secret about her blood?"

"Serology isn't necessarily limited to blood analysis, in a coroner's report. It could cover any bodily fluids."

"I'm still not seeing the threat to national security."

Christina pondered a moment, batting a finger against her lips. "Seems rather improbable, doesn't it? And yet, there must be some reason this information was redacted. Perhaps because, whether it affected national security or not, someone just didn't want this information made public."

"Who would have the power to get this document altered just because he or she didn't want it made public?"

"There are only a few possibilities," Christina said. "None of them good."

"You think this is about the first lady, don't you? The whole thing."

Christina thought carefully before answering. "I don't know what it is. But I intend to find out."

Christina was still pondering the coroner's report when she heard a knock on the door of her private office.

Jones poked his head inside. "Someone here wants to see you."

"Are they from the coroner's office?"

"I don't think so. Suit-and-tie types."

"Shoes?"

"Very nice. Gucci, I think."

Christina frowned. "Lobbyists. Tell them I'm busy."

"I don't think you want to do that, Ms. McCall."

She looked up, startled by the voice emanating from somewhere behind Jones.

Jones drew himself up, obviously miffed. "I asked you to wait outside."

"What we have to tell Ms. McCall can't wait."

"If I tell you it can wait, then by God—"

"It's okay, Jones," Christina said, stepping out from behind her desk. At the same time, two men, both in identical black suits, entered. One glance at them was enough to give her the creeps. Unfortunately, they had also piqued her curiosity. She preferred to take the risk that she would regret talking with them to spending the rest of the day wondering what they wanted. "Come on in."

After they were in her office, she whispered to Jones, "Turn on Line X," then closed the door behind him.

She retook her position behind her desk, while the two men sat in the chairs on the opposite side. They looked impervious to standard intimidation techniques, but if nothing else, she received some comfort from the hierarchical arrangement, her safely behind the desk, them watching from over yonder.

"What can I do for you, gentlemen? Is this business or pleasure?"

The taller of the two, apparently the designated spokesman,

leaned forward, smiling a smile that Christina did not find warm or friendly. "We'd like to talk to you about the president's proposed constitutional amendment."

Christina remained calm. "That does seem to be the hot topic of the day."

"We're lobbyists . . . of a sort. For the amendment. We feel it is vitally important to the future of this nation that the amendment be passed."

"So some people think."

"We wanted to be sure we had your support."

Christina brushed her long strawberry blond hair behind her head. "Oh, my—this is embarrassing. You must think I'm the senator. But I'm not. I'm just a lowly chief of staff. I don't get to vote."

The tall man once again smiled the creepy smile. "I am aware that you're not a senator, Ms. McCall. But you're married to one."

"Guess I can't deny that."

"And there are many who feel you're the most influential voice in the senator's ear."

"That probably depends on what I'm saying."

"What most of my sources tell me you're saying at present is— you don't think the amendment is a very good idea."

"I'm afraid there is some truth in that. But I still don't get to vote. And Ben is very adamant about this amendment. You may have seen him on television. When the president made him his go-to boy for the Democratic Party. Or perhaps you heard him single-handedly sway the Senate subcommittee."

The tall man glanced at his silent partner. The partner reached inside his suit jacket, but the tall man held up a hand, stopping him. Not yet.

"We have been very pleased with Senator Kincaid's performance so far. That's why we want it to continue, until we get this law out of Congress and into the hands of the people."

"Do you have some reason to doubt his resolve?" Christina asked. "Because I certainly haven't seen any."

"There are those who consider him . . . unacceptably risky. A dangerous element that might turn at any moment. Especially if his newlywed wife starts putting pressure on him."

Christina couldn't resist arching an eyebrow. "And exactly what kind of pressure do you foresee me putting on him?"

The tall man smiled again. *Yuck.* "I'm sure you have your ways. Most women do."

"Look, this has been fun, in a not-really-fun sort of way, but I'm done playing. Just tell me what you want and then I can tell you to go to hell and we can all get on with our day."

The two men exchanged a look, one that took a good deal longer this time.

"Fine," the tall man said, steepling his fingers, "we'll play it your way. We want you to cease and desist putting any and all pressure on your husband to withdraw his support from this amendment. In fact, we'd take it as a personal show of good faith if you would lend your personal support to the amendment and tell him you're backing him all the way."

"Then all I can say," Christina said, biting back her emotions as much as was humanly possible, "is that you don't know me very well."

"Yes," the tall man replied, and his voice dripped with a sorrow that almost resembled something genuine. "I suspected that would be your response." He turned to his companion and nodded. A moment later, a small packet of photos emerged from his breast pocket.

He tossed them onto Christina's desk. "Don't get any wacky ideas about running off with them. We have copies, obviously. And the digital files from which they were printed."

Christina's eyes narrowed to tiny slits. "Is this something I'm supposed to look at?"

"I think that would be a really good idea."

Christina reached for the photos, silently dreading it, wondering what they might have caught her doing. She knew that she could be blunt, indiscreet, much too direct for this town. Had they somehow caught her doing something she shouldn't? Browbeating a senator's administrative assistant? Sneaking into closed meetings? Parking in a senator's parking spot?

She pulled the photos from the folder.

They weren't of her. They were of Ben! Ben with—

Her hands covered her face.

"I know this must hurt," the tall man said. "Particularly given that you're newlyweds. But Washington can be a stressful place to sustain a marriage. Temptation is everywhere. My sources tell me that the senator has spent many nights alone"—he paused when he heard the gasping sound from behind Christina's hand and saw her shoulders heaving—"and even the best of men might . . . do things he might not have done had he stayed in the bucolic safety of Oklahoma. This is the big city and—"

He stopped. He didn't like to hear a woman cry—who did? So he had not been listening closely. But it was impossible for him to avoid noticing the weird sound she was making. Those sharp intakes of breath. The heaving shoulders . . .

She wasn't crying. She was laughing!

Christina moved her hand from her mouth, her face convulsed with merriment. "Did—did you really think—?" She couldn't finish the sentence. She fell back into her chair, still giggling.

"I understand," the tall man said quietly. "It's a defense mechanism. You laugh so you don't cry."

"N-No," Christina said, quivering as she spoke, "I laugh so I don't kick you losers in the butt."

"Ms. McCall, perhaps you don't understand the gravity of the situation. Your husband, a member of the U.S. Senate, has been caught in flagrante delicto with a prostitute—"

"Oh, please."

"My understanding is that her name is Brandi Delight and that she is quite popular in some congressional circles and that the . . . action was hot and heavy when the photographer by chance happened by—"

"In the hallway!" Christina screamed, still rippling with laughter. "When he happened by in the hallway?"

"I heard . . . something about a hotel room . . ."

"Do you think I don't recognize the hallway outside my own apartment? What did you clowns do—throw her on top of him while he was getting the morning paper?"

"I assure you, the scene is just as it appears—"

"Well, it appears to me that poor Ben is stunned and desperate to get away from this floozy in the cheap Frederick's of Hollywood getup."

"I think I know a little more about this than you do—"

"No, sir, you don't. Not even close. Or you wouldn't be trying this stupid stunt." Christina rose to her feet, hovering over her desk. "Ben would never be with this woman. He wouldn't be interested in the first place, but even if he were, he wouldn't do it, because he loves me."

The tall man rolled his eyes. "Love is blind."

"No, you stupid ass, love is knowledge, especially when you've loved someone as long as I have Ben. I don't care what you do with your hidden photographers and Photoshop. I know damn well Ben wouldn't be with this woman, even if we're having a spat. So give it up already."

The tall man tugged at the lapels of his jacket. "If you don't take these photographs seriously, Ms. McCall, I can assure you the press will."

"What press? The *National Enquirer*? No legitimate paper will run these photos, because they'll know they're as faked as I know they are."

"There's always someone, somewhere . . ."

"Maybe so, but you're not going to go to any of those places, because if you do, I'll expose your little scheme for the nasty political blackmail that it is."

"No one will believe you."

"I think they will." Smiling a genuine smile, Christina patted the phone on her desk. "Because you see, for the entire duration of our conversation, I've had you on speakerphone. A very amped up, powerful, speakerphone. And our office manager has been recording every word you say. It's what we call Line X."

"I don't believe you."

"Believe it, fool. We come from the world of criminal justice, and some of the people there make you government twerps look like total amateurs. You take those photos anywhere near the press, and the recording goes with them."

"I still don't believe you."

Christina glanced at the phone. "Playback."

There was a sudden beep on the phone console, followed by the sound of the tall man's own voice. ". . . we'll play it your way. We want you to cease and desist putting any and all pressure on your husband to withdraw his support from this amendment . . ."

Both men rose to their feet, eyes wide. "What you have done, Ms. McCall, by recording our conversation without obtaining prior permission or giving notice, is a violation of the Federal Wiretapping Act."

"How ironic that you should suddenly be concerned about civil rights."

"I think it is incumbent upon us to confiscate this recording." Both men moved toward the door.

"Don't bother with the strongman tactics," Christina said, stopping them. "Jones isn't an idiot. He's already halfway to the Senate copy room, making duplicate recordings with about a hundred other assistants. So unless you're planning to take them all out, just chill and accept the fact that you've been beaten at your own nasty little game. And while we're at it, let me inform you that I know perfectly well you're not lobbyists. You're Secret Service."

The two men stopped in their tracks.

"For one thing," Christina continued, "your idiot partner is still wearing his Secret Service lapel pin. For another, you're packing a .357 SIG under your jacket, standard Secret Service issue. In fact—don't I recognize you? Weren't you in Oklahoma City on April nineteenth?"

"I think we'll be going now. I'll take the photos."

"No," Christina said, scooping them off her desk, "I don't think you will."

"We have copies."

"No doubt. But I want these to show Ben. So we can have a good chuckle over them in the years to come. I think maybe I'll file them with the wedding photos."

The tall man squinted. "You are one sick puppy."

"This from the man who was willing to destroy a new marriage to gain a political advantage. You're the scum of the earth, buddy, and don't try to tell yourself otherwise. Now get the hell out of my office!"

Christina watched with great pleasure as the two men did exactly that.

She settled back into her chair, allowing her blood pressure to return to normal, letting down the impervious facade she needed to keep those particular demons at bay.

Ben, Ben, Ben. What have you gotten yourself into this time?

But she already knew the answer to that question. And she knew something else as well.

As much as it made her stomach roil, as much as she hated to do it, she would have to support Ben. She would have to give him whatever help he needed, as long as he was determined to support this amendment. Otherwise, these sharks would eat him alive.

She hated this amendment. But there were worse things in the world than being needed by the man you loved.

29

Loving tightly gripped the steering wheel of his van. "I still can't believe it. Children?"

"Horrifying," Shohreh said softly. "But sadly true."

"In a third-world nation, maybe. But here?"

"The General's principal operations are still overseas. But he has gained a foothold here. The federal government gives such scrutiny to large sums of money transported from overseas banks since 9/11. He needs a domestic source of income."

"But—*children*?"

"You can see now, perhaps, why I am so determined to find him. And stop him. It is not only that he threatens my life. If the General is allowed to continue his revolting business—there is no telling how many lives could be destroyed. He is far from the first. He will not be the last. But usually, those who traffic in sex do not use their filthy profits to finance terrorism."

"That's just—sick," Loving said, banging his hands against the steering wheel and swerving around a broken-down car blocking the fast lane. Loving hated D.C. traffic. Interstate 66 was the worst, but tonight he'd managed to skirt through it without any of the usual tie-ups. He'd taken the Key Bridge exit and followed the road across the Potomac, turned right onto M Street, and in less time than usual found himself in Georgetown. Hard to believe anything so sleazy could exist in this swanky college town. Sure, in the past he'd found art thieves here, and also, come to think of it, vampires. As he passed through the main shopping meccas surrounding the intersection of Wisconsin Street, he was reminded of the mall where two trained killers tried to drill him full of holes. Okay, those had been bad moments in Georgetown. But this was something else again.

"And you think this address I found on the assassin might be— what did you call it? A stash house?"

"I'm almost certain of it," she replied. "I know it was used that way in the past. Once they have smuggled the young girls into the country, they must put them somewhere."

"Where do these girls come from?"

"Eastern Europe and the Middle East, usually. Countries in turmoil. Remember—until the 1990s, prostitution barely existed in Russia. Almost all women had legitimate jobs. But after communism collapsed, things changed. Poverty soared, as did unemployment. Many young women, some of them well-educated, even married, were forced to become prostitutes. And what of the children? In such a world as that, it became easy for these traffickers to lure or kidnap unprotected girls."

"How do they fly them in from the Middle East?"

"They bring them into the United States through Mexico."

"To become prostitutes."

"No," Shohreh said, her voice low. "Sex slaves."

"There's a difference?"

"The difference is huge. These children become prisoners. They don't speak the language. They have no money. They have no identification or travel papers. If they attempt to escape, they will be harshly beaten—perhaps even killed, to set an example to the others. They may be kept hungry, sleep deprived. Their mental state, probably never strong, begins to crumble. They can't think clearly. They don't know what to do—except follow instructions. They never earn any money. They are rented out for sex—sometimes ten times a day. They are sold cheap—the profit is made through volume. Perhaps fifty dollars for fifteen minutes of what you might call ordinary intercourse with most clothes still on. For a little more, clothes might be removed. Oral sex costs more. A hundred dollars might get a customer anything he wants."

"That's just . . . disgustin'."

"Occasionally they will be sold outright to pay a debt to another trafficker or a drug lord. But that is worse, not better."

"And you say this goes on a lot?"

"More often than you can imagine. No one knows the exact numbers. But the CIA says that approximately twenty thousand people are trafficked into the United States every year. Most people who have studied this horror think that at least half of those become sex slaves."

Loving could not conceal his outrage. "In Washington, D.C.? The nation's capital? Why doesn't the government do something about it?"

"They've made noises. But there's been no real action. The traffickers are too slick, too professional. They remain invisible. Your former President Bush called sex trafficking 'a special evil' and a multibillion-dollar 'underground of brutality and lonely fear.' He pushed for some sort of action from the UN. But nothing happened. He signed the Trafficking Victims Protection Act, which finally recognized that people trafficked against their will should not be treated as illegal aliens and made it illegal to traffic children for the purpose of sex. Violators can receive thirty-year sentences. But still the evil continues. It is too profitable to be eliminated so easily."

"And that girl you mentioned—Djamila. She got caught up in this?"

Shohreh's eyes darkened. "Yes."

Loving nodded, his gaze fixed on the road. "I'll do anythin' I can to help you."

She laid her hand gently on his shoulder. "I know you will."

"It's just around the corner. I still think we should call the cops."

"I assure you that would be a mistake. They would know. The General would escape. The children would be relocated or, if there was not enough time, killed. Their only hope is that we get to the General. Bring him to the authorities."

"Cut the head off the beast."

"Exactly."

"Okay, then. Let's go find the beast."

Loving stared at the house across the street, astonished.

"Are you sure we're in the right place?"

"I am. I remember it well."

Loving couldn't believe it. He had expected to end up in a wretched poverty-stricken neighborhood. Instead, he was in a perfectly ordinary, perfectly respectable middle-class enclave. There were children playing on the street. Bicycles and basketballs. The house itself was two stories, Victorian-style, with an arched gable and yellow trim. Everything about it belied what apparently took place within.

"How can they . . . conduct their business . . . without the neighbors noticin'?"

"Have you ever lived in a neighborhood such as this?"

"Well . . . no."

"These people do not socialize with their neighbors, for the most part. Perhaps once a year at the neighborhood block party. They may know the names of their immediate neighbors, they may wave to them as they pass by walking their dog, but little else. They know more about the celebrities on the cover of *People* magazine than they do about the people who live next door." She sighed. "Drug pushers have also learned the advantages of living in a respectable neighborhood. They are more invisible than they would be in a lower-rent district, and much less suspect."

Loving frowned. "We gonna find a lot of toughs in there? Protectin' the merchandise?"

"If we are lucky, there will be no men at all this time of day. The children are usually cared for by women."

"Women participate in this freak show?"

"I wish I could say this horror is solely the product of deranged and greedy men, but it is not so. Female accomplices become surrogate mothers to the children. They are better at gaining the children's trust. They are much more adept at managing them, handling them, making sure they do as expected. They deliver the warnings— and the beatings. They teach them how to . . . perform. How to act sultry, sexy, scared—whatever the customer wants. Usually scared, especially with the youngest girls." She inhaled deeply, as if purging herself from within. "The men may be the traffickers and controllers. And of course, the customers. But women operate the business on a day-to-day basis."

Loving felt as if he were about to hurl. *Focus on the mission,* he told himself, *and try not to think about what goes on inside.* "See that basement window? I'm goin' in."

"I will follow."

"No."

"I insist."

Loving held her back firmly. "You can't get through that window with an arm in a sling and a wounded leg."

"You might be surprised what I can—"

"Besides, you're my backup. If I don't come out in an hour or so, you can assume I screwed it up and the General has fled. Call Lieutenant Albertson at the DCPD."

Shohreh reluctantly nodded. "I will do as you say. But I do not like it."

Loving had no trouble getting inside the house. He slipped into the basement silently, without attracting attention from the neighbors.

The basement seemed perfectly ordinary. Tools, firewood, and lots of dust. Till he looked closer.

There were mattresses on the floor, more than a dozen, uncovered, filthy, putrid.

When he examined the nearest workbench, he found antibiotics, a large quantity of what he knew to be the infamous "morning-after" pill, as well as a stomach medication he knew could induce abortions.

Then he saw the girls, all huddled together in the far corner, staring at him. Some looked as if they were not even twelve; none appeared older than seventeen. Their faces were dirty, grimy. They smelled as if they had not bathed. Their clothes looked as if they had worn them for weeks. They stared back at him like freaks in a carnival show, their eyes unblinking, their minds barely comprehending.

One girl, a petite thing whose hair might be blond if it had been washed recently, stepped toward him. She had an air of comprehension about her, some small sense of resilience. Perhaps, he thought, her mind was not yet totally shattered. Perhaps that was why she acted as the leader.

"We've been expecting you," she said with a thick accent, obviously attempting some grotesque parody of grown-up hospitality. "Are you my next customer?"

"No," Loving said, his lips pressed tightly together. "I'm your last. We're gettin' outta here."

30

Ben hated these underground corridors. It wasn't just that they were narrow and cluttered to such a degree as to induce claustrophobia in the sanest of people, although there was that. It wasn't that he was reminded that many of the other senators had a private hideaway down here and he didn't. It was that he was reminded of the first time he came here, after a corpse was found in Senator Glancy's hideaway, the event that triggered Ben's involvement in Washington and ultimately led to his becoming a senator. He would never forget the first time he stepped in and saw all the blood and that poor woman upended on the sofa with her neck—

Never mind. He did not need to go there today. Eyes on the prize. He was looking for Senator DeMouy, using the best clues he had available. There were no maps of the hideaways: in fact, on the official maps of the building, they did not exist. They weren't even in the blueprints. But they were down here and they were highly cov-

eted. The only way to find someone was if you already knew where
his or her hideaway was. Or, as in this case, if you had a lead from
a well-placed person such as the senator's administrative assistant.

"You like Cajun?" she had asked, not waiting for an answer.
"Follow your nose."

Which Ben was trying to do, but he was feeling a little stuffy so
he was not altogether sure this was going to work. What could be
harder than finding someone who had come to a place that, after all,
was called a hideaway, used for the purpose of, well, hiding away.
When a senator like DeMouy wanted time alone, far from the prying eyes of reporters or the outstretched hand of the lobbying
army—but didn't have time to leave the building—he or she re-
treated to a hideaway, safely nestled in the subterranean basements
of the three Senate office buildings. After the first ricin poisoning,
many senators left their main offices but tried to conduct business
here, and they came in droves after Senator Hammond was killed.
Given the tumult currently under way upstairs, Ben should've
known to check the hideaways first; even the Senate majority leader
had to get away from the madding crowd on occasion. He probably
liked to kick back, listen to some zydeco, maybe eat some takeout—

And that was when the aroma hit him like a blunt instrument.
Had he been stuffed up before? Not anymore. He could feel his sinuses decongesting with every step.

He knocked on the door.

"Come on in!"

Ben was prepared for almost anything—he had found a corpse
in one of these rooms, after all, and he'd caught senators making out
with unauthorized personnel on more than one occasion—but nothing could have prepared him for this.

The leader of the Senate Republicans. Wearing a dirty apron.
Swinging a large ladle like a baton.

"Ben! Therese told me you were coming. You're just in time!"

Lucky me, Ben thought, as he slowly approached. The pungent
smell of Cajun cooking assaulted him. Although now that he
thought about it, he was somewhat hungry. When was the last time
he actually ate a meal?

"Are you a gumbo fan?" DeMouy asked, beaming. He dropped the ladle back into a huge pot on the stove and stirred.

"I'm . . . not sure I've ever had it."

"What do you folks eat in Oklahoma?"

"Um . . . hamburgers? Chicken-fried steak? Mashed potatoes and white gravy."

DeMouy gave him a long look. "Tell me you don't eat grits."

"Well . . . certainly not where I grew up."

DeMouy pulled out a chair. "Sit down, my boy. You are about to have the best culinary treat of your young lifetime."

Ben took the proffered seat. "And—you made this down here?"

"Absolutely. All by myself. Even chopped the okra. Five pounds' worth."

Ben grimaced. "You know . . . you can buy it already sliced. Frozen."

DeMouy looked as if he had just been forced to eat a bug. "That's not how my mama taught me to do it and that's not what I'm going to do. Might as well just buy a bowl at Chili's."

"That would probably save time, too."

"It's not about saving time, Kincaid. It's about creating some-thing wonderful." He smiled. " 'Sides, I like cooking. Relaxes me. Forces me to think about something other than this damned amend-ment. Filé?"

"Uhh . . ."

"Yes, of course you want filé. What's gumbo without filé?" He scooped a huge ladleful of gumbo into a bowl, sprinkled something green on top of it, and passed it to Ben.

Ben stared at the concoction. "Mind if I ask what it is?"

"I already told you, son. It's gumbo!"

"Yes, but . . . what's in it?"

DeMouy rattled off the ingredients like a cooking encyclopedia. "Okra, obviously, onions, celery, garlic, bell peppers, bay leaves, tomato sauce, shrimp, chicken broth, diced tomatoes, and rice."

"Is that it?"

"No." DeMouy winked. "But I can't give away the secret ingre-dients. My mama would kill me."

"Seven secret herbs and spices?"

"Salt and pepper." He waited a beat. "So, Kincaid . . . you planning to take a bite?"

"Oh—you wanted me to eat this."

"No, Ben, it only takes four hours to make. I was hoping you'd just use it to clear your sinuses."

Ben tentatively raised a spoonful, blew on it, then slowly drew it toward his mouth.

"Well?"

Ben swallowed. "Actually, it's pretty good."

"You're just saying that."

"No, I really—awk!" He clutched his throat. "Bit—" He gasped for breath. "Bit of an after bite, huh?"

DeMouy grinned. "That's the way we like it down South." He slapped Ben on the back. "My mama raised six sons, all by herself. She needed something to help keep them under control."

Ben shoveled in several more bites. It was growing on him. And he was breathing a lot more freely, too. "You really do enjoy cooking, don't you?"

"Have to admit it." He took the chair opposite Ben at the table. "Making meals is a lot more gratifying than making laws. A lot quicker, too."

"No doubt." Ben tried to time his remarks so as not to interrupt his devouring of the gumbo. "So, your AA told me you needed to see me desperately. I assume that wasn't just because you thought I looked underweight."

DeMouy chuckled. "Can't say that it was. We've got ourselves a problem."

"We do?"

" 'Fraid so. On this amendment."

Ben wiped the corners of his mouth. "Have the polls changed? Last I heard, it was a shoo-in in the House and the votes were about evenly divided in the Senate. All we need is a few more votes and we're golden."

"Yes, but that could be tricky."

"Why? Everyone in the country's talking about this amendment. It's on the top of everyone's agenda, whether they're in the Senate or chatting at the watercooler. All we need to do is fling some major oratory at it. As a trial lawyer, I found that if you reference God, Abraham Lincoln, and the United States of America often enough, you can win anything."

DeMouy laughed again. "That's probably true, son. But even the president can't force a bill to the Senate floor, and neither can we."

"But—the bill got out of committee—"

"Ben, have you ever heard of a legislative hold?"

"Legislative hold . . ." He took another bite, hoping to buy time while he decided whether to bluff or not.

"Don't feel bad if you haven't. It isn't something they teach in eighth-grade civics class. Some people refer to it as the Senate's dark secret."

Ben leaned forward. "Okay, now I'm interested."

"It all goes back to the ancient and somewhat labyrinthine parliamentary procedure that still by common agreement governs congressional practice. It's a cinch for any member to slow down or even stop the Senate's business by making an objection before the bill hits the floor. The press talk about how the Senate bickers and bewails the death of collegiality, but that's hogwash. Believe me, if there were no collegiality, we'd never get anything done. We wouldn't even have anything to talk about."

"I thought the Senate majority leader set the agenda."

"True, but he does it by unanimous consent agreements on what's going to be discussed and how long we're going to discuss it. He tries to find out if anyone's going to object before he takes a bill to the floor. He asks the party leaders in advance if anyone's going to object. Since any senator has the power to object, the majority leader postpones a bill until the objections can be resolved—or horse-traded out of existence."

"I don't see anyone being bold enough to put a hold on this amendment. It's much too high profile."

"Actually, I've gotten word of three different senators willing to do exactly that. And one of them is a Republican!"

"But all the polls show that the people favor this bill. I would think the political fallout for those making the objection—"

"And now you're going to see why this is called the Senate's dark secret. The secret reason so many bills favored by the public never get to the floor." He paused. "Legislative holds can be made anonymously. One senator can keep a bill off the floor indefinitely. There is zero accountability."

"But that's totally undemocratic."

"You're not the first to think so. But it still gets done all the time. Back in 1999, Tom Daschle and Trent Lott got together to broker a deal that would force all senators who put in a hold to be reported to the sponsor of the bill and have their name submitted in writing to the party leader. But the deal fell apart."

"And this occurs frequently?"

"Ohio's Howard Metzenbaum used to put a hold on every single tax bill that came through his door. It was so common the AAs started calling the holds 'Metzes,' as in, 'Don't waste your time, there's a Metz on that bill.' Sometimes the senators will use 'rolling holds.' "

"Dare I ask?"

"One senator places a hold on the bill, does some trading, gets what he wants, and then someone else puts a hold on it. If they team up, they can keep a bill off the floor for a long time. With three senators already ponying up to play this game—it could be a good while before this amendment is voted upon. And I think time is of the essence here, both for political and national security reasons."

"Certainly the president thinks so."

"The longer this drags out, the less chance there will be of passing it. And if the president's term ends—it's over."

Ben couldn't resist the thought flashing through his brain. *Maybe that would be best. Maybe we need more time for reflection. Maybe these three senators are the voices of courage, not obstruction.*

But he stopped himself. More thinking in that direction would only lead to madness. He had given his promise.

"So what are we going to do about it?"

"Well, the traditional approach would be to offer the three roadblocks something they want even more than they want to block that bill."

"I'm the most junior senator in Congress," Ben said wearily. "I don't have anything to give."

"Don't feel bad—even I don't have anything to give that they want more than they want to slow down this process. No, the only solution I can see is to out these guys. Go public. Let them feel the heat. Take responsibility for their actions."

"Didn't you say the holds were anonymous?"

"I sure did."

Ben's eyes narrowed. "Do you know who they are?"

"Wish that I did. But, no, I don't. Well, I have a hunch about the Republican. But as for the other two, I have no clue."

"Then how—?"

"But I understand," DeMouy continued, "that pretty little chief of staff of yours really gets around."

"Christina?"

"Yes, you remember. I believe you married her a while back." DeMouy grinned. "I know you two haven't been here that long, but apparently she really has a way with people. As well as a gift for sniffing out secrets."

"That she does."

"My secretary Therese has been with me twenty-one years, and she says she's never seen anything like that little firebrand of yours. So I was thinking—"

"You want Christina to find out who the three holdups are."

"Of course, you didn't hear me say that."

"Understood. If anyone could do it, it would be Christina. There's just one problem. She opposes the amendment."

DeMouy waved a hand in the air. "Yeah, I heard about that. So what?"

"So, she has been known to be somewhat . . . on the stubborn side. I could go back to my office now and ask, but she—"

"Office. Please. Ben." DeMouy looked at him sternly. "You are married to this woman, right?"

"Riiight."

"Don't ask her in the office. Ask her tonight."

"Tonight?"

DeMouy's voice dropped an octave. "In the bedroom."

"Why—?"

"You know." DeMouy jabbed his elbow into Ben's side. "After."

"After she's asleep? What would be the point?"

"Not after she's asleep. After"—more jabbing—"you know."

"I do? Oh. *Oh!*"

"Now you get the picture."

Well, he had a distant memory, anyway. "I really don't think—"

"Just give it a try, son. How do you think I captured the heart of that young little filly of mine? It's the way to go."

"It is?"

DeMouy nodded enthusiastically. "Might consider bringing home flowers, too." He smiled, then retook his ladle. "Now how about some more gumbo? You did pretty good with that first helping."

Why not? Ben thought, as he held out his bowl. He needed some time to think. Somehow, he suspected this project was going to require a lot more than a bouquet of roses.

31

*B*en tiptoed quietly into his apartment, flowers tickling his nose. It was dark inside and quiet—good. He must've beaten Christina home.

He flipped on the lights, then gently laid down the bouquet of roses, then the box of chocolates, then the Hallmark "Heartfelt" card ("Sometimes you have to stop thinking and follow your heart"), then the Hershey's Kisses. He had briefly considered getting her a puppy, but wasn't sure how it would fare in a small apartment with three cats.

He had practiced his speech about a thousand times, but he hadn't thought about where he wanted to be standing when he delivered it. So many questions! Perhaps leaning against the mantel of the fireplace, a pipe in one hand, the light of the fire illuminating his face in a mysterious yet attractive manner . . .

But the fireplace was a fake—you couldn't really burn wood in it, and he didn't smoke a pipe. Christina had thrown out his button-down sweaters.

Perhaps reclining on the sofa, supine, several shirt buttons un-buttoned. Or just in an undershirt. Or perhaps even—

Who was he kidding? He couldn't pull any of that off, even if he did think it would work, which he didn't.

And that was before he received the anonymously delivered manila envelope bearing the photos of him and—that woman. In the teddy. Whoever she was. Thank goodness Jones hadn't been around to receive the mail. Didn't matter who the envelope was addressed to. He would've opened it just because it was marked PRI-VATE and underlined twice. The pictures looked so . . . incriminat-ing. What would happen if Christina saw them? How could he prevent her from seeing them? If she did, it would all be over, that much was certain. He would never be able to talk his way out of that one.

He hadn't seen her in so long and missed her so much. Jones told him she was planning to go home tonight, so he had hoped that maybe, if he did everything right, there was still some small possibil-ity . . .

He picked up the picture of her he kept on the coffee table so he could see it wherever he was in the room. It was taken on their wed-ding day, on the steps of the Supreme Court building, just after the disastrous "you may kiss the bride" incident. He cringed just think-ing about it. What on earth had she ever seen in him? How could he think there was anything he could do to change her mind? Him, the loser who couldn't even manage to get her away for a honeymoon.

It was hopeless. Christina had every right to be ticked off at him and she wasn't going to stop being ticked off at him until—

"That you, handsome?"

Ben started. He rose to his feet. "Hello?" He paused another moment. "Christina? Is that you?"

She stepped slowly out of the bedroom wearing a shimmering blue full-length nightgown. "Who'd you think it might be? Your girlfriend in the black teddy?"

Jeez Louise. "Christina, you have to believe me. I don't know who she was. She just—appeared. I did not have . . . anything with that woman. I promise you that—"

"I know, Ben."

"Seriously, I never even—" He stopped short. "You know?"

"Of course I know."

"How could you possibly know?"

"Because I know you." She came closer. Standing before the window, he could drink in the entire lovely picture. The blue was perfectly matched to her eyes, just barely revealing the shoulders he loved so well. . . .

She saw the roses on the counter and picked them up. "These for anyone in particular?"

"Huh? Oh!" Ben snapped to attention. "Those are for you. I mean, obviously they're for you. Who else would they be for?"

"And the chocolates?"

"And the card. And the, um, Kisses."

"Mmm," she said, licking her lips. "No puppy?"

"Well, I didn't—" He halted himself again. "You really do know me, don't you?"

"Uh-huh. Like my nightie?"

Ben suddenly felt very hot under the collar. "Um, uh, yeahhhh . . ."

"I bought it for our honeymoon, but—"

"I am so sorry. I've told you—"

"Shhh." She placed a finger against his lips. "No need. It'll work tonight just as well."

"It will?"

She drew him very close to her. "It will." She leaned forward and kissed him on the neck.

"Uh, Christina," he said, trying very hard to think about . . . something other than the obvious.

"Mmm," she said, still kissing.

"All this stuff. The flowers and candy and . . ."

"Mmm." Her left hand was unbuttoning his shirt.

"I—I need your help."

"I know."

"There—there are three senators who have put a—a legislative hold on—"

"Dawkins, Stringer, and Reneau."

"You already know?"

"Yup."

"How?"

She lifted her face from his chest only for a moment. "Ben, darling. Haven't you noticed? I'm the best." She resumed kissing.

Ben tried to keep his mind on the current political crisis, but it was becoming increasingly impossible. "Do you—d-do you think there's any way we can get those names out? Like, um . . ."

"A front page article in *The Washington Post*?"

"Uhh . . . that would work."

He could feel her smile against his chest. "Be sure to read the paper tomorrow morning then."

"Christina." He stopped her, taking her head between his hands, and gazed into her lovely face. "Does this mean you've changed your mind about the amendment?"

"No, you dodo. It means I love you. Now are you going to take me to bed or am I going to have to get out the handcuffs?"

As it turned out, the cuffs were not required.

32

DEPARTMENT OF HOMELAND SECURITY
NEBRASKA AVENUE NAVAL COMPLEX
WASHINGTON, D.C.

Agent Zimmer couldn't help but wonder why Director Lehman would be calling a press conference today. Didn't they all have enough to do without pandering to the press? He knew that every available agent, everyone who wasn't actively engaged in protecting a member of the president or vice-president's staff, was investigating the April 19 attack. And Lehman had been unofficially but no less determinedly campaigning for the passage of the president's proposed amendment.

There had been rumors swirling through the building the past few days, rumors that someone somewhere in Homeland Security had uncovered something big. Maybe that was the reason for the conference? Zimmer only hoped that were true. It would be a great coup for the department, not to mention a great morale builder, if the turning point in the case arrived not from the FBI, with their vastly greater law enforcement facilities, or from the NSA/CIA, with their vastly greater data collecting abilities—but from the humble old Secret Service. That would make him very happy.

And it would give him an excuse to worry less about Agent Gatwick. Ever since their confrontation a few days before, Gatwick had studiously avoided him. But Zimmer knew he had been talking. Stirring up trouble. Probably trying to get him fired. Maybe he imagined it, but he thought Director Lehman had been chillier toward him, too. Zimmer still hadn't reported his suspicions to his superiors—he just didn't have anything sufficiently concrete to report. But he was worried that his silence might have allowed a conspiracy to grow, or allowed Gatwick more time to cover it up. . . .

At any rate, if Lehman was calling everyone together to announce that the case was solved, he would have a lot less to worry about.

Lehman had gathered the press on the steps outside the Naval Complex, the standard blue podium poised between Lehman, a few close advisors, and scores of journalists. The only person up there from Homeland Security that he recognized was Nichole Muldoon. Everyone in the department knew Muldoon, and it wasn't simply because she was beautiful. Her rise in the department had been astonishing. Countless male colleagues had been passed over, including several who had been repeatedly decorated for bravery. Naturally rumors flew about who she knew or who she was doing as the left-behind grappled for some explanation for her success other than the obvious—that she was a very talented, hardworking Secret Service agent. Zimmer had never had much to do with her, but he tended to think the hostility he knew many had for her had more to do with sexism and male insecurity than anything else.

Lehman approached the microphone and addressed the crowd. "Thank you for coming. I'll try to be brief. I'm sure most of you are aware that the Secret Service has been actively involved in the ongoing investigation of the April nineteenth attempt to assassinate President Blake. That attack led to a certain constitutional amendment now being considered in Congress, and I, like most people in the law enforcement community, have been an active proponent of that measure. Some critics have suggested that since the amendment directly concerns the Department of Homeland Security, and the director in particular, perhaps these two positions create a conflict of interest. Well, ladies and gentlemen, today I have gathered you together so that I can answer my critics."

He paused briefly, his eyes unblinking, then continued. "You're right."

In the brief moment of silence, Zimmer thought he heard the sound of collective surprise.

"Now, don't misunderstand me. I'm not suggesting that anything untoward or inappropriate has occurred. To the contrary, I know that there has in fact been no inappropriate activity and that those Secret Service agents who have worked on this case have done so with all their heart for totally selfless reasons—because of their great devotion to this nation. But in perilous times such as these, it is important that the people of the United States have complete confidence in their government officials. Even if there is no basis for suspicion, we must strive to eliminate the suspicions."

Lehman turned slightly, adjusting his gaze. "It is for this reason that I am hereby declaring that the agents of the Secret Service will no longer be involved in the domestic investigation of the April nineteenth attack."

Heads turned. The crowd murmured. No one had been expecting this. It seemed crazy—especially when rumors were flying that someone in the department had made a breakthrough.

"It is clear to most people involved that this attack was unprovoked and in all likelihood executed by foreign powers. Therefore, this falls squarely within the province of the CIA and the NSA, or perhaps the FBI, given their current increased involvement with counterterrorism. Of course, Homeland Security will continue to coordinate with these agencies and advise on how best to protect our people. But the involvement of the Secret Service is hereby at an end."

Hands flew into the air. Zimmer couldn't tell whether Lehman had actually chosen a journalist or if one of them had simply spoken first.

"Don't most law enforcement officials think the more people we have working on this investigation the better?" a woman asked.

"No, ma'am. That is exactly what we don't think. And as I'm sure you realize, I didn't make this decision without first consulting with the president and the heads of the various agencies. What we feel is that everyone should be doing what they specialize in doing, what they're trained to do. The Secret Service exists to protect our leading officials. And so we will."

"How much does this have to do with the amendment?" a voice shouted from the rear. Zimmer wasn't sure, but he thought the bespectacled elderly gentleman was with the *Post*.

"I'm not sure what you mean."

"If this amendment passes, the director of Homeland Security becomes the chairman of the Emergency Security Council, with not only the power to declare a state of national emergency but to suspend certain constitutional rights. If it happened today—that would be you."

"And don't I know it," Lehman said, drawing a small chuckle from some of the reporters. "You're right—that is a consideration. Since the bill concerns me and my future job description, I think it's best that I stay out of the political process, not to mention any investigation that might directly affect that process."

Zimmer felt a tug on his shoulder. His first reaction was to ignore it—he was much more interested in the press conference. Then the tugging became more insistent.

He whirled. "Would you please—?"

His eyes widened. It was Deputy Director Nichole Muldoon. "Let's talk," she said succinctly.

Wait a minute—hadn't he seen her on television? She must've left the conference while Lehman spoke. Zimmer wasn't even sure why he did it, but he followed her through a side exit into a secure conference room.

Why wasn't she standing behind her man at the podium? He hadn't seen her leave any more than he'd heard her creep up behind him.

She shut the door and locked it. "So. What do you think of that?"

"I'm . . . surprised."

"You're not the only one. I was surprised, and I'm the deputy director. I didn't think he could go to the bathroom without running it by me first." She frowned. "Turns out he can."

"I can't believe we're out of the investigation."

"Neither can I. Especially since—" She paused, eyeing Zimmer carefully. "Since I have some reason to believe that someone may have discovered something. Something important."

"Then why wouldn't he say so? Why would he shut down the whole operation?"

"I don't know. It makes no sense."

"And more to the point—why are you talking to *me* about this?"

She smiled, a thick-lipped smile Zimmer found much more attractive than comfortable. "Do you mind talking with me?"

"No, but—we hardly know each other."

"True, but I hear through the grapevine that you've done some investigating of your own."

"Where'd you hear that?"

"Doesn't matter. You've successfully gotten Agent Gatwick into a tizzy."

"I have?"

"You have. And I'm not the only one who's enjoying seeing him spin around in circles trying to deflect unspoken rumors. I'll tell you this, though—I know he met with Director Lehman very recently. Secretly. I'm pretty sure he wanted Lehman to protect him from you. And then—poof! Lehman takes us out of the investigation."

"Are you suggesting—?"

"I don't know what I'm suggesting. I just think it's strange. Very strange." She came even closer. She had a musky scent about her, like a strong aftershave lotion, something he wouldn't have thought he'd like on a woman. As it turned out, he did. "Tell me, Zimmer—can you get in to see the president?"

"*What?*"

"You heard me. Even I can't get in to see the president—especially not without Lehman knowing and getting a full report on everything that was said. But you might."

"What makes you think so?"

"You've been protecting him—how long?"

"Since he took office."

"You're friends?"

"I wouldn't go anywhere near describing us as friends. I make it a point not to develop personal relationships with—"

"But you're friendly."

Zimmer tilted his head. "I suppose. Or we were. Remember—I was protecting his wife when she was killed. We haven't talked since."

"All the more reason to ask for a meeting. So you can express your remorse and regret. He'll like that. You can both cry on each other's shoulder." She paused, then looked him directly in the eyes. "Then you can tell him what you know about Gatwick."

"And Lehman?"

"Mention to the president Gatwick has met with Lehman. Tell him about the changes made to Domino Bravo. The president may not be a rocket scientist, but he can add. He can draw his own conclusions, once he has the facts."

"I don't know. . . ."

"Zimmer—Max. If someone in our department has learned something about what happened on April nineteenth, I for one do not want to see that get buried. Do you?"

"Of course not."

"Then ask for a meeting."

Zimmer thought for a moment. "I will see him tomorrow. It would be an easy chance to mention that I'd like to chat with him in private sometime."

"That's the spirit. Do it." She paused, placing her hand on his shoulder. "Then let me know what happens. I know this will be uncomfortable for you, Max. But if our bosses do know something they're not telling, we have an obligation to make sure it comes out. An obligation to Emily Blake. And everyone else who died on April nineteenth."

33

Christina sailed through the office doors as if floating on a cushion of air.

Jones took one look at her and frowned. "Damnation."

The moderate swearing did not dampen her spirits in the least. "Some problem, Jones?"

"Well . . . I guess you couldn't exactly call it a problem," he said, twiddling with his cell phone earpiece. "Good news, actually. I was just looking forward to having the pleasure of using it to bring you out of the state of grump in which you have been residing for the past oh-so-many days."

"I have not been grumpy."

"You have. But it's academic. I can see that the grump has left the premises. What happened?"

"Nothing happened."

"Oh, right."

"Well, Ben and I were both home last night. For the first time in a long time."

Jones's left eye twitched. "Do I want to hear this?"

"We just spent a quiet evening at home." She paused. A lascivious grin came unbidden to her face. "Well, actually, he wasn't all that quiet."

"No," Jones said, averting his eyes. "I do not want to hear this."

"This morning was pretty excellent, too. Come to think of it, I wasn't all that quiet this morning."

"Earth to Christina. Administrative assistant does not want to hear about this."

"Oh, you know you love it."

"I'm absolutely certain I don't."

"So what's this hot news you have?" she asked, deftly changing the subject.

"You'll never guess."

"The legislative holds on the constitutional amendment have been lifted."

His expression could not have gone flatter quicker had he been hit in the face with a frying pan. "Who told?"

"No one. But it was inevitable."

"Excuse me. No one in this entire building saw this coming. How could it have been inevitable?"

She winked. "You should read the morning papers, Jones. All kinds of interesting stuff in there."

Still smiling, she sashayed down the corridor and into Ben's office.

"Hey, lover boy."

He jumped to his feet, hushing her at the same time. "Christina, what have I always told you?"

"That I'm the best lover you've ever had?"

"Other than that."

"That my sheer unadulterated beauty makes you tremble."

"Keep trying."

"No PDA in the workplace."

"That's the one I had in mind."

She leaned across his desk. "I'll try to contain myself." And then, without a bit of warning, she planted one right on his lips. "But with a pistol like you, it'll take some doing."

"Christina—" But before he could protest further, she was smooching again and he seemed to lose his enthusiasm for resistance.

Jones appeared in the doorway. "Boss, you got a memo from—"

Ben and Christina abruptly jumped apart. Jones slapped his forehead.

"Jiminy Christmas, I hate this!"

"Jones, relax. . . ."

"Why did you two have to get married? Why couldn't you just go on smoldering with unspoken passion? I liked that much better!"

"Jones—" Ben said, but it was too late. He was gone.

Ben turned his attention back to Christina. "You see what happens when we break the rule?"

"Oh, honestly, Ben. What would Jones do if he didn't have something to complain about? He'd be miserable."

Ben flopped back into his desk chair. "Did you come in here for a reason? Other than . . ." He waved his hand aimlessly in the air. "to break our rule."

"I certainly did." With a flourish, Christina pulled a small stapled report out of a file folder tucked beneath her arms and dropped it in front of him.

Ben scanned the cover. CORONER'S REPORT. "Ugh. Why on earth would I want to read— Ohmigosh. Ohmigosh! Do you know what this is?"

"Well, duh."

"This—this is the report on Emily Blake." His voice dropped to a whisper. "The first lady."

"Yes, thank you for that clarification."

"How did you get this?"

Christina shrugged. "The Freedom of Information Act. Augmented somewhat by the coroner's secretary, who was persuaded to unlock her file cabinet and go on a coffee break at an opportune moment."

Ben looked at her sternly. "Did this inducement involve cash?"

"No, just good gossip. What do you think I am, some sort of crook?"

"Well, I have known you to flout the rules on occasion."

She gave him a look that was indescribable, then pointed to a section on the third page of the report. "Check this out. When I first got the report through the FOIA, this part had been redacted."

Ben quickly scanned the five lines that followed the section heading SEROLOGY. A few moments later, his face began to flush.

"Pretty hot stuff, huh?"

Ben placed a finger under his collar. "I don't really see that it's . . . I mean . . . she did meet her husband at the airport, after all. And we know they hadn't seen each other for several days. I hardly think it's unusual, even for the First Couple . . ."

Christina rolled her eyes. "You're not reading carefully enough, ADD boy. Try again."

Ben perused the passage again, this time more slowly.

"Oh," he said, followed a few minutes later by an even lower-pitched "Oh." Which finally culminated in an "Ohhhhh."

"Now you can see why the passage was redacted, right?"

Ben cleared his throat. "I can—can—certainly see why someone might want it kept quiet."

"Someone like the President of the United States?" Christina smiled. "Ben—you've got to ask him about this."

"Are you kidding? I can't ask the President of the United States about—about—this."

"Ben, you have to."

"I most certainly do not."

"Ben, it could be important to figuring out what really happened on April nineteenth."

"How could this possibly relate—?"

"Just ask him about it. You two are buddies now, right? He made you his point man on this puppy. Fine. He wants your support, he should be willing to assuage any doubts you have about it."

"What makes you think I have doubts?"

"Ben, you dither back and forth about which toothbrush to use in the morning. But I don't care if you have doubts or you don't. I want to hear the president's explanation."

"I don't know. . . ."

"Ben," Christina said, giving him her most direct in-your-face look. "Heaven knows I wouldn't want to seem pushy. But you owe me. I got those legislative holds lifted, even though I think this stupid amendment is dangerous and un-American. Now it's your turn to do one for me."

Ben struggled to argue with her logic, but as usual, it was unassailable. "Does it have to be the President of the United States?"

"Ben, the fact that it is the President of the United States may be the key to understanding what really happened." Her voice dropped a notch. "To understanding why Mike is lying comatose in a hospital bed. So do this for me, Ben." She paused. "And for him."

34

President Blake stared out the window at the rolling back lawn behind the White House. Thank God for Teddy Roosevelt. Before him, the area where Blake now stood had been covered by gardens and greenhouses. Teddy was the one who decided he needed a retreat from his wife and boatloads of children and pets and nieces and nephews. He'd had the West Wing constructed to give himself a private retreat where he could actually get some work done. Taft enlarged it, and every president since had worked here, in this office, gazing out at this magnificent view.

When was the last time he took a moment to go outside and enjoy that lovely expanse of green? Probably not since that damned Easter Egg Roll, easily the stupidest of all the annual presidential duties. He'd rather free some idiotic Thanksgiving turkey every day than have to do that Easter egg hunt. Of course, when the cameras were rolling, he loved all the adorable orphans and inner-city youths who were rounded up each year to chase after those inedible eggs.

But if it were up to him, he would've canceled the event a long time ago.

Emily had loved Easter, and she had taken particular joy in the egg roll. That's the kind of person she was.

God, he missed her. He missed her so much. And the pain of separation wasn't eased any by his lingering feelings of remorse.

There she was, staring back at him from the photograph on his desk, the slightly naughty smile, the beautiful brown eyes. *What happened?* she seemed to be asking. *What went wrong?*

He only wished he knew.

There was a knock on the northeast door. "Come in."

Tracy Sobel entered the office, as brisk and efficient as ever. "Time for your first visitor, sir."

Right, he thought, mentally running his calendar through his brain. He had two private confabs coming up, both relating to April 19, and neither likely to be pleasant. "Who's on first?"

"I think it would be best to start with your Secret Service agent. He should be easier to handle."

"And Kincaid?"

"At the helipad." Sobel paused, thinking a moment before continuing. "Just don't be fooled by the milquetoast mannerisms, the stammer, the awkward shyness. He's smart."

"So I've noticed. Speaking of which—I see that the legislative holds have been lifted."

Sobel smiled slightly. "So you do read my memos after all."

"Not to mention *The Washington Post.* Who leaked the names?"

"I'm not positive—but I think it was your boy Kincaid. Or someone on his staff."

"And who organized the holds in the first place?"

"I assume it was the new Senate minority leader."

"He says not."

"Well, then I don't know. I haven't heard anything."

"And that in and of itself is unusual enough to set my brain spinning." He continued staring directly into her eyes. "It wasn't, by any chance . . . you, was it, Tracy?"

She appeared shocked. "Me? Sir—I'm your chief of staff."

"Yes. But I also know you personally oppose this amendment."

"We've been over this ground before, sir. Regardless of what I may personally feel, I would not obstruct a piece of legislation you yourself proposed."

"No, you'd get someone else to do it. Like three senators who could prevent it from getting to the Senate floor indefinitely."

"Sir, I assure you I did nothing of the kind. I have never been anything but loyal to you. Don't you trust me?"

President Blake leaned back in his chair and stretched. "I hope this won't shock you, Tracy, but I didn't get this office by trusting people. Trust is for losers. You win by eliminating trust from the equation. By leaving people no choice but to do what you want them to do."

"Then you don't believe me."

Blake laid his hands flat on his desk. "If you tell me you had nothing to do with it, then I have no choice but to accept that."

Sobel took the tiniest step closer. "Sir, I had absolutely nothing to do with those legislative holds."

"Good. I'm glad." He rearranged some papers on his desk. "Would you please send in Agent Zimmer?"

"Of course, sir," she said, but something about the way she said it told him that this wasn't over yet. Which was fine. If she did it, let her worry. If she didn't do it . . .

Well, it probably still wouldn't hurt for her to be a trifle on edge. Worry was a healthy thing. And he didn't like anyone who worked for him to be too brisk and efficient. Made him a little crazy.

"Thank you for seeing me, Mr. President," Agent Zimmer said as they shook hands. "I truly appreciate it."

"Least I can do," Blake replied, as if a private conference with the president were the most common thing in the world. "After all you've done for me."

"I guess I should get right to it—"

"Let me stop you before you even start, Max," the president said, snatching a piece of paper from his desktop. "I've seen your letter of resignation. And my answer is: No way in hell."

"Sir, I had valid reasons—"

"I don't care. I need you."

"The Service has hundreds of capable agents—"

"I want you."

Zimmer paused, unsure what to say next. The thought most dominant in his brain was: *This man's wife died while I was protecting her.* And yet he did not seem to bear Zimmer the least malice, didn't assign the least blame. He was being so generous, it bordered on the inhuman.

"Sir, there's more to my offer of resignation than you might imagine. What I have to tell you concerns other members of the Secret Service. I think it might be best if I removed myself from the departmental equation. Eliminated the possibility of any personal or professional motivations."

"Well, I'll tell you what, Max. You tell me what you came here to say. Then I'll decide whether you need to resign or not."

"Sir—"

"Max, you know I don't have to accept any letter of resignation unless I want to. So that's the best offer you're going to get. Might as well start talking."

Zimmer paused, trying to think how best to broach the subject. He had practiced this speech, practiced the whole meeting a dozen times. But now he couldn't remember a word of what he had planned to say. "Sir, it concerns Special Agent Gatwick. He used to protect—"

"I know who he is, Max," the president said abruptly. Was he imagining it, Zimmer wondered, or had the president stiffened slightly the moment he spoke Gatwick's name? "Please continue."

"On April nineteenth, Agent Gatwick made changes to the standard agency protocol. He altered the security strategy in a way that turned out to . . . not be a good idea."

"I know all this, Max. What's your point?" His eyebrows knitted together. "Surely you're not suggesting that Gatwick anticipated the attack. That he knew what was about to happen?"

"I—I just don't know, sir."

"Have you reported your thoughts to your superior?"

"Yes. And Director Lehman not only did nothing—he met with Agent Gatwick privately, at a clandestine meeting. And then he took the Secret Service out of the investigation, which also strikes me as very suspicious."

"What is it you want, Max?"

"I think there should be a complete investigation of Agent Gatwick's actions, what he did, what impact it had, and who knew about it. And I believe that Agent Gatwick should be relieved from active service pending the outcome of the investigation."

"That's out of the question."

The president had responded without a moment's hesitation. What was going on here?

"Sir, if there is any chance that Gatwick had inappropriate knowledge, he needs to be taken out of play until we determine if he continues to pose a threat to national security."

"Sorry, no. Can't be done."

"But—"

The president turned, walking away from him. Zimmer could no longer see his face. "I can't do it, Max."

"Surely you can see—"

"You're not listening to me. I can't do it."

"With all due respect, sir, you're the leader of the free world. You can do pretty much anything you want."

"Okay, then, I *won't*. I won't do this. I will not allow the first lady's name to become . . . besmirched."

What?

"Emily was a fine woman, Max. No matter what. She was first-rate, right down the line. I won't take any action that might create suspicions. Tarnish her memory."

My God, Zimmer thought, *is he saying what I think he's saying?* Zimmer had hassled Gatwick at times, thought maybe there had been some inappropriate flirtation, but he had never really believed that—

Was it possible all those rumors were true?

"Mr. President, the whole sudden decision to withdraw from the investigation—"

"Yes?"

"Well, I don't understand it."

"Frankly, Max, you don't have to understand it. Your job description is to protect, not to understand. But you can rest assured that Director Lehman did the right thing for the right reason, and with my full support. In fact, if I recall correctly, I suggested it."

"Sir—"

"I think this conversation has gone about as long as it needs to go. Your resignation is not accepted. So get back to work." He paused, then added, "And concentrate on your job, not any more idle suspicions that might crop up in your brain."

"But, sir—"

"This is your commander in chief speaking to you, Special Agent Zimmer. Have I made my instructions perfectly clear?"

Zimmer stood at attention and gave him a small salute. "Yes, sir."

"Good. You may leave by the southwest door. Ask Gina for a cookie. The kitchen baked them fresh this morning. Best snicker-doodles in the whole damn free world."

35

"Thank you for agreeing to meet me here, Ben," President Blake said as they rode the elevator up to the helipad. "I know you're busy, and this can't have been convenient."

"I'm grateful for the meeting," Ben replied, wondering just how high the elevator could go. There were no floor markings. He imagined that, like Willy Wonka's glass elevator, it might shoot through the ceiling at any moment. "But . . . I do think it would be best if we had some privacy."

"We'll have privacy up here," Blake assured him as the elevator bell announced their arrival. "And even if other people were in the vicinity, they wouldn't be able to hear a word we were saying."

The doors opened and Ben was immediately assaulted by a sudden burst of noise that was almost deafening, not to mention what felt like hurricane-force winds.

"I know it seems overpowering at first," the president said, "but believe me, you get used to it."

Ben doubted he ever would, and he also questioned whether he could possibly discuss the delicate matters he had in mind here. Had Blake done this to him deliberately? Could he know what Ben wanted to ask? Ben didn't see how it was possible, but the circumstances still seemed suspect.

"There she is," the president said, gesturing across the helipad. "The president's personal helicopter. Marine One. You're probably wondering—why is a vehicle that travels through the air called Marine One? Well, once upon a time, it was the property of the U.S. Marines. So your next question is: Since it isn't anymore, why don't they change the name? And the answer to that one is: I have no idea."

Shielding his eyes from the almost overpowering gusts of wind, Ben gazed across the helipad. He had once ridden in the copter Mike co-owned with some other police officers, but he hadn't enjoyed it, never hoped to do it again, and still didn't know anything about them. "Why are there three?"

"Anytime I fly, two other outwardly identical copters fly with me. Decoys. Reduces the chance of a successful strike by a surface-to-air missile."

"Three-to-one? Still unpleasant odds."

"Yup. I tried to get the Senate to approve a convoy of ten, but you misers were too cheap." Blake walked Ben closer to the elegant machines. The engines were already started, thus creating the thunderous noise Ben had heard when he stepped off the elevator. "Beautiful, aren't they? Sikorsky VH-60Ns. Travel at one hundred fifty knots. Can get you anywhere you want to go in no time at all. Not as luxurious as Air Force One, of course. But damn fast." He waved to people Ben couldn't see somewhere overhead. "Snipers. Don't worry—they're on my side. And they knew you were coming." He opened the door to a nearby equipment shed. They stepped inside and Blake closed the door behind them.

"There. That's a little better." He glanced at his watch. "Okay, Ben, you have exactly ten minutes before I take off for a secret meeting at an off-site Pentagon installation. What can I do for you?"

Ben knew there was no way to broach this subject gently, so he took a deep drink of air and plunged right in. "Mr. President, in the course of my own . . . private investigation into the tragedy of April nineteenth, I obtained a copy of your wife's autopsy report."

"What? Why?"

Ben continued, hoping that if he moved fast enough, there would be no time for outrage. "The first copy we obtained had been redacted, even though the information eliminated could not possibly pose any threat to national security. Who would have the clout—and the motivation—to get something like that done? The obvious answer, of course, was you."

"Are you saying—?" Blake did a double take. "What the hell are you saying?"

"The redacted material I later learned revealed—let me apologize in advance, sir. I know this is exceedingly indelicate, but there's no way to say it except to say it." Ben took another deep breath; his eyelids fluttered. He felt as if he might faint at any moment. "At the time of your wife's death, her vagina contained sperm cells."

Blake gaped at him wordlessly. "What—the—hell—" His nostrils flared. "What business is that of yours?"

"Well, sir, it does raise some questions."

"About what, you little farm country cluck? Emily and I had been apart for a week. We had a little private time on Air Force One before we drove into Oklahoma City. Why is this any of your business?"

"There's a problem, sir."

"You have a problem with me making love to my late wife, who by the way I loved very deeply?"

Ben's mouth felt dry as stale bread. "No, sir, of course not. But you see—the coroner ran DNA tests. Your wife was carrying sperm—from two different donors." He felt his knees wobbling, but he plowed forward. "She'd been with two different men. Within the previous eight hours."

President Blake's eyes were steely gray. He forced Ben back against the wall of the shed. "What is this about, Kincaid? What are you trying to do to me?"

"The only thing I'm trying to do is . . . understand."

"What's to understand, you little pissant? There was nothing— nothing—" His voice broke, and all at once his face crumbled like the walls of Jericho. "Emily was having an affair." His voice cracked. "It had been going on for nearly six months. I knew, of course, but I never—never said anything to her about it. I—" He shook his head. Tears sprang to his eyes. "I kept hoping she'd come to me herself. I—I knew we'd been . . . growing apart. This job—it keeps you so damn busy. Spend all your time worrying about the fate of the world. It's easy to forget about—about your wife. Until it's too late."

Ben stared at the floor, unable to make eye contact. "Do you—know who it was?"

President Blake nodded. "The leader of her Secret Service team. Gatwick. You probably met him in Oklahoma City."

"I'm sure that was . . . very difficult for you."

"You don't know the half of it. First, there's the shame. The knowledge that you drove the woman you love into the arms of another man. The knowledge that—you failed as a husband. But the problems are even greater when you're the president. Something like this—well, it creates a vulnerability. The possibility of blackmail."

"Someone was blackmailing you? The president?"

"All I'm saying is, it was a concern. Suddenly I found myself in a position where I couldn't say no. Anything he wanted—well, how could I deny him anything, knowing what would happen to me if he went to the press? He could bring down this entire administration, just at the time when America needs to be strongest."

"Sir, you told me before that this amendment originated with Homeland Security. Is that why you're proposing it? Because you have no choice?"

"I never said that," Blake said, suddenly stiffening. "I believe in this amendment one hundred and ten percent. We need it to keep our people safe. It's vital to the security of this great nation."

"But even if that's true, you don't have any choice but to support it, do you?"

"I don't know what you're talking about, Kincaid. I want this thing passed—as quickly as possible."

"Who was the man, sir? Who was he? Was it—?"

"And let me tell you something else, Kincaid. My chief of staff tells me you're a lot smarter than you act. I hope to God that's true and that you'll be able to accept this piece of advice. Don't cross Homeland Security. Don't cross anyone behind this amendment. Their eyes are everywhere. Their ears are everywhere."

"What does that mean?"

President Blake wiped his eyes, then checked his watch again. "I have to catch a copter, Ben. Let me just reiterate: I want this amendment to pass. I'm counting on your support." He leaned closer, making sure he had Ben's attention before he finished. "And you need to be careful, Ben. Very careful."

36

U.S. SENATE, RUSSELL BUILDING,
OFFICE S-201-R
WASHINGTON, D.C.

Jason Simic was careful not to tiptoe. That would be too telling. He didn't really think there was any chance of him being spotted. But in any case, he didn't want to appear to be in stealth mode. He wanted to seem to be what he always seemed to be: the hardest-working most effective chief of staff in the building, tireless, charming, productive. Every senator wanted him, but he was attached to Senator DeMouy.

And his wife.

That, however, was about to change.

He smiled at Effie when he entered the office. DeMouy's faithful secretary of many years liked him almost as much as she did her boss, and he knew it.

"Boss still at work?" she asked. She had been working a crossword puzzle, a sure sign of just how late it was. She didn't get many spare moments in the course of the day. Certainly not enough to finish a puzzle in *The New York Times*.

"Still dining with his wife. Those lovebirds might be gone all night at this rate."

"Really?" He knew Effie had been around long enough to know the score, most specifically that DeMouy and his wife were anything but lovebirds. But he was planting seeds. "In the Senate cafeteria?"

"Love knows no boundaries. I don't know what's going on with those two, but something really seems to have rekindled. I think maybe the death of Senator Hammond made her realize just how lucky she is—and how fragile life can be."

"It would be nice to think something positive came out of that monstrous act." Effie glanced at her watch. "Do you think—?"

"He specifically told me to tell you to go home."

A relieved smile crossed her face. "And you?"

"The same."

"But you're not going, are you?"

Jason smiled a winning, toothsome smile. "For once, I am, actually. I just need another five minutes in my office. The amendment, you know."

Effie shook her head as she collected her coat and purse. "You're a hardworking boy, Jason, and I admire that. But when are you going to get a life?"

"I have a life. Here, in the Senate."

"Then let me be more specific. When are you going to get a girl?"

"I don't have time for romance, not now. Wouldn't be fair to get someone else involved in this crazy life of mine."

"All that remark tells me is that you haven't met the right girl. I know a sweet young lady at my church—"

"Effie, stop."

"Sings like an angel. Makes a fabulous artichoke dip for all the church functions."

"Effie, you're worse than my mother."

"It's only because we care so much about you, Jason. And sometimes those blue bloods out on the Sound aren't as good at matchmaking as an old busybody like me."

Jason tried not to laugh out loud as he watched the old biddy leave the office. Blue bloods indeed. Everyone always assumed he came from money. It was the way he talked, the way he dressed, the way he carried himself. No one seemed to get that it had nothing to do with the way he was raised. It was all either learned or earned. He had a good ear. He'd learned how to talk Massachusetts better than a Kennedy. He'd learned how to dress snappier than politicians who had private wardrobe consultants. He still didn't have much money, but he had learned how to spend what he had in the right way to produce maximum good impression for minimal investment. He was very directed, very determined. He always got what he wanted, eventually.

Witness the case in point.

He had been fascinated by politics since he was a young boy. On election nights, his parents would let him stay up late to watch the returns roll in. He was in college on the fateful night the Bush–Gore race came down to a handful of votes in Florida. He never slept, not for forty-eight hours. After that, he knew what he wanted to do with his life. He started ingratiating himself with local politicians, working in their campaigns for free, running errands, fetching coffee, making photocopies. Eventually he moved up to more important tasks and, in time, developed a reputation for himself.

After two years of low-level gophering, he heard that Senator DeMouy was looking for a new chief of staff. He wasn't from DeMouy's state, he didn't know the man, he didn't have the qualifications, age, or experience for the job—and he didn't let that stop him. He didn't just apply for the job; he orchestrated a blitzkrieg. He sent tapes, papers, videos, strategy plans. He knew DeMouy was planning a reelection bid so he learned everything there was to know about the man's state, his traditional constituency, and what he could do to increase it. When it was time for his interview, he had more than just a résumé—he had a battle plan. DeMouy was suitably impressed. Said he'd never seen anything like it in all his years in the Senate. Of course Jason got the job.

But that was just a start. Was he content with a chief of staff position? No. It was just a stepping-stone. A benchmark on the way to something greater, something much more important. He wasn't satisfied with the corner office down the hall. He wanted the big office. Senator DeMouy's office.

And maybe, just maybe, he wouldn't even stop there.

There were many things he could accomplish by hard work, schmoozing, exchanging favors, displaying exemplary resourcefulness. But there was one thing all the smarts in the world couldn't give him: money. Big money, the kind you would need to run a federal campaign. That had been a stopper for him, the one puzzlement he couldn't resolve.

Until he met Belinda DeMouy.

In retrospect, it was amazing he didn't meet her sooner, but he had been busy impressing her husband and for the most part the husband didn't seem to have all that much to do with her. That should've been his first clue. When he did meet her, he was able to size her up in a single glance: lovely, lonely, frustrated, isolated. Trapped in an empty life that had no meaning. Days filled with obligations and teas and meetings and charity events and a lot of other crap that she cared nothing about. Her ice princess act didn't fool him. He knew there was a very sexual woman locked up in there, desperate to get out. All he had to do was find the key.

As it turned out, it wasn't hard.

He couldn't know how bad her love life was, how impotent her older husband had proved, how he papered over his sexual failings with a slavish dedication to his work. Give the woman an orgasm, indulge her perverted little danger fantasies, and Jason found she would do anything for him. Anything at all. And in truth, it was DeMouy's own fault. His failings and his absences made their affair more than possible. It made it easy. His stupidity had made him a cuckold.

And it was about to make him dead.

Then Jason would have everything he needed.

His cell phone beeped, just once. He glanced at it—Belinda. That was the signal.

Jason slowly withdrew the envelope marked PHOTOS from his briefcase and deposited it on the desk where DeMouy would be sure to see it. Then he left the office and started down the corridor to office 212-D. Because something had occurred to him these past few days, something he had not even shared with Belinda. The death of Senator DeMouy by identical means as Senator Hammond was sure to confuse and mislead, but it was still possible the police might figure it out. He couldn't be sure he had matched the previous crime in every possible respect.

There needed to be two deaths, both by the same means. That would clearly tie all the murders together and make them seem undeniably the work of a terrorist advancing some twisted political goal. The obvious reason to target Senator DeMouy was because he was one of the leading advocates for the proposed constitutional amendment.

So the other victim should be Senator DeMouy's partner, the other leader in the fight to get this amendment through the Senate.

It would all be so obvious. The police might not even bother to question Senator DeMouy's loving wife.

Jason couldn't help but smile as he walked down the corridor. He had considered everything, every possible contingency, worked it all out to perfection.

Guess what, Senator Kincaid? he thought as he walked briskly down the marble stairway.

You've got mail.

37

U.S. Senate, Russell Building,
Office S-201-R
Washington, D.C.

Senator DeMouy entered his office with a big smile on his face. He'd had his doubts when the president wanted to make Kincaid his Democratic point man for the amendment drive, and he hadn't hesitated to express his misgivings, either. Oh, Kincaid seemed amiable enough, but he was a novice, had no power coalition, had no one who owed him favors, and seemed . . . a bit on the weak side. Not the charged particle you need to ram something like this through Congress quickly. Admittedly, the list of Democrats who might be persuaded to take the job was slim—but surely they could do better than Kincaid?

The president had assured him that he had given the matter careful consideration and dismissed DeMouy's concerns with a blithe nonchalance that he found baffling at the time. Now he had a little more perspective on the matter. The president evidently knew something he did not—that Kincaid had a powerhouse chief of staff. She was a novice, too, but it didn't matter. She was everything that

Kincaid was not. Where he was merely smart, she was savvy. Where he was prudent, she was bold. Where he was gentle, she was pushy. And where he was . . . well, perhaps the kindest way to put it would be . . . undistinguished in appearance—she was a firecracker.

The reporter at the *Post* was naturally refusing to identify his source, but DeMouy had a few sources of his own, and all the evidence was pointing toward Kincaid's little firecracker. The plan he had outlined over gumbo had worked—and then some. Good grief—in all the years he'd had to put up with legislative holds, why hadn't anyone thought of this before? Of course he knew the answer. Even if the thought had occurred, no senator would do it or authorize their staff to do it. It would be considered an unpardonable breach of congressional ethics. But Christina McCall was not a senator, and DeMouy rather suspected she had not asked for permission before she acted. She saw a solution to the problem and she went for it. In this case, her newcomer status could aid her immeasurably. He could already hear her voice: *Oh my goodness—you can't do that? I had no idea. . . .*

Life was good, at least on the professional level, with the promise of great things to come. Back home . . . well, he preferred not to think about it. This dinner tonight had just confirmed for him what a farce his marriage had become. Did Belinda seriously think he didn't know? Not that he really cared that much what she did, but his constituents would, and he was up for reelection soon. He couldn't take risks of that magnitude.

As he entered his office he saw a stack of mail on his desk. That was unusual: Effie usually opened it all. But Jason had suggested he let her go home and he'd agreed. Well, it could probably wait—

A long, cream-colored envelope with blue lettering caught his eye.

PHOTOS, it said in block lettering across the front. There were no stamps.

Who would be sending him photographs? He couldn't think of anything he was expecting, any recent photo shoots or campaign pics or—

Wait, what was he thinking? This could be from the Cajun Cooking Fest last month in New Orleans. He'd only taken second place with his gumbo—the gold was taken by a jambalaya that he thought was markedly undistinguished—but that was just as well. It was probably best for publicity purposes if he appeared competent and versatile, and female constituents would love the fact that he could cook, but if he actually won, that might create resentment. Perhaps even the suggestion of a fix. No, second place was best, and if they got a pic of him in a messy apron tasting the gumbo, that would be great for a campaign ad to run in a daytime TV spot. Maybe during *Oprah*.

Still, it would be smarter to wait for Effie to come in. She knew about the rubber gloves and all the other stuff you were supposed to do these days when you opened the mail. It seemed stupid, but it wouldn't hurt him to wait just a—

His cell phone rang. Those things were such damned annoyances.

He glanced at the cover and saw that it was his wife, Belinda, calling. That was unusual. "Belinda?"

A female voice crackled on the other end of the line. "Thanks for dinner, lover boy."

"It was my pleasure."

"I've been hoping we could become . . . closer. I'd like to think this is perhaps the beginning of a new era for us."

"You would? Well, maybe it could be."

"I sent you a gift. In an envelope. On Effie's desk." She was breathing heavily, practically purring into the receiver. "Photos."

"Oh, that was you."

"They're photos of me."

"Of you? Doing what?"

She giggled, the naughtiest laugh he ever recalled hearing in his life. "See for yourself. I think you'll like them."

"Give me a hint."

She laughed again, a deep, lusty laugh. "Let's just say that once you see those photos, I think you'll be able to throw away those little blue pills that don't seem to work well anyway. But this will. *Ciao*, baby."

DeMouy suddenly realized he was breathing deep and fast. *My God, maybe she's right.*

He couldn't restrain himself. He picked up the envelope, slid his finger under the flap, and ripped it open.

A cloud of white powder rose into the air and swirled around his face. Senator DeMouy immediately knew he had made a horrible mistake.

He dropped the envelope as if it were on fire, but it was too late. He ran to the bathroom and splashed cold water on his face and into his nostrils. He snorted it in and down his throat. What had Jimmy Claire told him to do during the security briefing? He could hardly remember. Oh, yes—don't open the mail. Not much help now. Or if you do, use protection. He had to get to the infirmary. Maybe there was an antidote or some kind of treatment.

He whirled around much too quickly. All at once he realized that he was dizzy, that the bathroom was swirling up and down like a roller coaster, which was really inconvenient because he was having a hard enough time concentrating without having the room gyrate.

His eyes began to bleed.

He tried to brace himself against the white porcelain sink, but his hand slipped and he went tumbling downward.

His chin bashed into the hard rim of the sink, jarring him into near insensibility. His mouth began to bleed. He felt chilled; then all his muscles started to spasm uncontrollably.

The poison had taken its hold. He couldn't move. There was no one else in the office. And he knew ricin killed very quickly. There was no hope. . . .

Wait! He heard footsteps out in the corridor. He knew those footsteps. Spike heels moving with determination and alacrity. That was his Belinda.

Through blurred vision, he saw his wife's face appear in the haze above him. "Belinda," he said, barely whispering. "Is it you?"

"Oh yeah. It's me all right."

"Help . . . me."

"I'll be happy to help." He didn't see her leg move, but a moment later he felt the impact of the toe of her pump driving itself between his legs. "Help you into oblivion."

The pain was excruciating. Unconsciousness was creeping upon him. He couldn't stop shaking. But he knew if he closed his eyes now, he would never open them again.

"But—how—?"

"That's easy to explain." Another face appeared in the haze above him. It was Jason! Jason Simic, his chief of staff. "She did it with my help." His voice descended into a snarl. "You didn't appreciate what you had, you ancient asshole. So now you're going to lose her. And everything else. Putz."

Belinda started to kick him again, but Simic stopped her. "Cool it, sweetheart. Fun as it might be—we don't want to leave a mark. This has to look like an anonymous, long-distance ricin poisoning."

A wave of darkness crested before his eyes, and hard as he tried to fight it, his eyes fluttered closed, just as he had predicted, never to open again.

"Is he dead?" Belinda asked.

Jason used the time-honored two-fingers-against-the-carotid for confirmation. "Very."

"Shouldn't we leave?"

"For now. You can discover the body, but not till I'm long gone. Give it at least half an hour. It will seem more credible if you don't find him immediately."

"*We did it,*" she whispered, staring down at the motionless body of her husband. "We really did it."

"You had doubts?"

"I don't know. Somehow, it didn't seem real—until now. Watching him die. That was . . ."

"Disturbing? Traumatic?"

She placed her hands behind his neck and curled herself up against him. "Hot."

He jabbed his hand between her legs. "Oh yeah?"

"Ohhhhh yeahhhhh."

"Enjoy it, Danger Girl. This is one experience you won't be having again any time soon."

"God, I want you. I want you inside me."

"That can be arranged. Just stay clear of the poison." Less than a minute later, their clothes were in a heap on the floor and Jason was on top of her, caressing her breasts and licking the side of her face.

"Oh my God, Jason. Oh my God. I'm going to come."

"Wait for me, darling."

"I can't. I can't. I—" She looked to the side and saw her husband's dead face, his eyes open and staring at her lifelessly, uncomprehendingly.

"I had fantasies about you being forced to watch," she said breathlessly, as if her husband could actually hear. "I only hope that you're somewhere in hell now, seeing the show."

"I'm ready," Jason whispered, pounding furiously.

"Oh, God, Jason. Oh yes. Oh, Godddddd . . ."

In the aftermath, an intern at the other end of the corridor would remember hearing her scream and the police would assume it was triggered by the shock of discovering her husband's dead body. Only the two of them would know it was a scream of ecstasy, as Belinda DeMouy experienced the most powerful, most intense, and most satisfying orgasm of her entire life.

38

UNDISCLOSED LOCATION IN GEORGETOWN

Standing in the darkness of the basement, Loving reached toward the young girl's shoulder. She involuntarily flinched; then, as if reminding herself what she was taught to do, she relaxed.

Loving could understand what must be racing through what was left of her brain. Very well. They could talk without touching. It would be better that way. She might actually trust him.

"Is anyone else here?" Loving asked in hushed tones. He had spotted the wooden staircase that led to the ground level of the house. The door at the top was open. "Any other grown-ups?"

"Miss Magda went to the grocery for food. She said if we were good, she might bring us candy." The girl paused, her face expressionless. "But she always says that. And we're never good enough."

"What's your name?"

The girl hesitated. "They call me Angela. But that isn't my real name." She spoke English with a pronounced accent—Russian,

Loving thought, but he was really no judge. Under the circumstances, he was amazed she could speak at all.

"What's your real name?"

Another long pause, and then she answered, "I don't remember."

"Do you like Angela?"

"I guess."

"Then that's what I'll call you. I like it, 'cause it sounds like Angel. You're a little angel."

She didn't smile. But Loving liked to think her face brightened.

"How long have you been here?" he asked, scanning the room full of girls.

"We didn't come together. I've only been here a few weeks. That's why I'm in charge." Normally, that would seem like the exact opposite of the way any hierarchy would work. *Unless,* Loving imagined, *you assume that life as an illegally trafficked sex slave is so hard that it puts the children on a one-way track to a permanent vegetative state.*

"Do you know a girl named Djamila?"

Angela thought for a moment. "I don't think so. But they make everyone change their names."

Of course they did. The bastards. "Do you know a man they call the General?"

Angela's back immediately stiffened. "Do you work with the General?"

"No," he said hastily. "I do not. But I'm tryin' to find him."

"If you want a session, you should talk to Miss Magda."

"I do not want a session," Loving said, gritting his teeth. "But I want the General. Very very badly."

"He will probably come tonight to collect the money. He usually does."

"Do you ever get any of the money?"

She looked at him as if he had taken leave of his senses. "We are not allowed to carry money. If we had money, bad men would try to hurt us."

Ah. Wouldn't want you to be exposed to bad men. "Do they ever let you outta this stinkin' basement?"

Again, she looked at him as if he just didn't comprehend. "We like it in the basement."

"You do?"

"We are safe in the basement. When the door opens—we must work."

Now he was beginning to understand.

"At first, I liked it when the door opened and they called me by my new name. I would get a bath, maybe even a new dress." She looked down at the tattered pinafore she was wearing. "But that was a long time ago."

As her head lowered, Loving noticed a bruise on the back of her neck. He gently lifted her hair and took a closer look. More bruises. Gently, making sure she understood he meant no harm to her, he rolled back the left sleeve of her dress.

What he saw there made him sick to his stomach.

"How long before Miss Magda comes back?"

"I don't know."

"Damn." Loving stood, glanced at the stairs and the door, then at the window through which he had entered. "Look, gather your friends and anything they need. We're gettin' outta here."

"I thought you wanted the General."

"I did. But now I think it's more important that I remove you and your friends. So gather up all—"

"What's going on here?"

Loving turned, swearing under his breath. A large brunette woman in a plain frock stood at the top of the stairs. *Damn, damn, damn!*

"Can I help you?"

She spoke with a thick Russian accent, but she was not nearly as old as he expected. Miss Magda had saved herself from a life of sexual slavery, he guessed, by going into business with the slavers.

"Uhhh . . . you Miss Magda?" Loving asked, trying to pull himself together as quickly as possible.

"I am. May I ask why you are here? In the basement?" Loving noticed that as soon as Magda entered, Angela slunk back into the shadows.

He grinned sloppily, doing his best to look like the sort of scum who might actually come here for a "session." "Uhhh, sorry—I rang the bell but no one answered so I came on in. I'm here to do a little business. I understood you had some goods of particularly high quality."

"I'm sure we can produce something you will find . . . pleasing," she said. "May I ask how you came to know of our services?"

There was only one name he could produce. "I'm a friend of the General. Name's Loving."

"I don't think I've heard him mention you."

Keep treading water, he told himself, *till you figure a way out of here.* "Well, I guess we're more business associates than friends, tell the truth. I handle his, uh, Southwest distribution."

"Ah, so he succeeded in cracking the Mayor's territory."

"Oh yeah. Piece of cake. You know the General."

"Indeed I do. And . . . if you have your own outlets, why do you need to come here?"

Didn't matter what excuse he came up with. She wouldn't have asked if she weren't already suspicious. He had no way of knowing what it was, but something he said hadn't washed. "I'm in Washington on business. You can imagine. And while I was here . . . well, it's a long ways to home."

"I understand entirely. Did you see anything that might be of interest?"

He cleared his throat. This whole charade was making him sick to his stomach. But he had to keep it going. At least until he could make a break for it. "Well, Angela and I hit it off."

"An excellent selection. I'll set that up for you immediately."

"Great."

"As soon as I take care of my scheduled customer. Emil?"

Loving felt his gorge rising. Would he really have to sit here and watch some pervert pick a child to his liking, someone sufficiently scared enough to bloat his male ego?

Emil entered the doorway.

It was the assassin. The man he had clocked back in the cemetery.

No wonder the son of a bitch had this address in his pocket. He was a customer. Probably took his assassin's fee out in trade.

For a moment, Loving held out hope that the man might not recognize him. No such luck. Then he hoped that he might be able to get past him, if he moved fast enough.

Emil pulled a large gun with a protruding silencer out of his overcoat pocket.

Loving grimaced. This just wasn't going to be his day.

He scanned the room quickly. There was no way he could get back out the window, much less up those stairs, without getting drilled. As far as he could see, he had only one chance.

He buried himself amidst the children.

Emil sneered. "Do you seek to protect yourself by hiding with little girls?"

I'll do whatever the hell it takes to keep myself alive, Loving thought. He wondered if Shohreh had seen this man come in. Surely she would have recognized him. Even though it had not been an hour, perhaps she would call the police. He hoped.

Emil walked slowly down the stairs, his gun pointed. "Do you think it would bother me to kill a child? Or even many?"

"I don't know if it would bother you," Loving said, keeping himself covered. "But I think it would piss the hell out of the General to lose such hard-to-get merchandise."

"About that, you may be right. Fortunately, that is not a situation I will have to confront."

"Don't kid yourself, creep. I ain't comin' outta here. And my friend has already called the police. They should be here any minute."

"I think not," Emil said. "But in any case, Magda, prepare to evacuate the house."

"Right." She glared at Loving. "Damn you. Do you know how much trouble it is to pack up and move this operation?"

Sorry to be so inconvenient, Loving mused. "You're not takin' these kids anywhere."

"Oh, I am rather certain that I am."

"No way in hell I'm budgin'. Your only chance is to blow this joint before the police get here, or you're lookin' at thirty years under the Federal Protection Act."

"Ah, such bravado. So you think you are going to save these poor helpless waifs?"

"That's exactly what I'm gonna do."

"But what if they don't want to be saved? Have you considered that?"

"You must be jokin'."

Emil smiled, then nodded. "Angela."

"Huh?" And that expression of confusion was the last syllable Loving managed to utter before he received a crushing blow to the back of his head.

He tumbled to the cement floor, feeling as if his brains had been scrambled. Through distorted vision, he managed to see Angela standing beside him. Holding a baseball bat. Just as expressionless as ever.

Emil relieved her of the bat.

"Thank you, my dear. You will be rewarded later. Perhaps even some candy." He glared at Loving, helpless on the floor. "And you too will be rewarded, my courageous and so terribly stupid friend. In the manner that you deserve."

Loving held up his hands, but there was nothing he could do to stop the blow. He saw the baseball bat careening downward, once more making a line drive toward his skull.

And a moment later, he saw nothing at all.

39

U.S. CAPITOL READING ROOM

There were few places in the Capitol more incongruously named than the Senate Reading Room, Christina mused, since no one ever went there to read. By all rights, it should have gone the way of the Senate Library, another large room no one ever seemed to visit. In this case, however, some energetic majority leader had seen fit to convert the Reading Room into the Viewing Room, with theater seating and a large projection screen. In addition to getting about five hundred cable channels, it had a closed-circuit link to the floors of the House and the Senate. It seemed to Christina that if someone really wanted to know what was happening on the floor of the Senate, they would just walk across the hall and look. Unless, perhaps, a senator did not wish to be spotted by his fellow senators. Or the folks at home watching on C-SPAN.

All day today, the screen had been following the House

floor debate on the proposed constitutional amendment. Christina and Jones and several others had been watching for hours. It was a long shot, but if the House rejected the amendment, any Senate vote would become irrelevant. She and Ben could put this behind them and move on to something more important, like the Alaskan Wilderness Bill or the antipoverty bill. Or their honeymoon.

But it was not to be. "Blast," Christina muttered under her breath, halfway through the voting.

"Don't give up yet," Jones whispered. "There are still several congressmen who haven't voted."

"Not enough. This monster has passed the House. And last night's polls show popular support is greater than ever. And you know what that means."

"Bye-bye civil rights?"

Christina pursed her lips. "It means it all comes down to what happens in the Senate. If the bill passes—it'll be law in a matter of months." She paused, shaking her head. "And our Ben is leading the charge."

"Well, that should be a comfort. It's not as if Ben has a reputation as a Senate power broker."

"Jones, how long have you known Ben?"

"Almost as long as you."

"And has Ben ever had a reputation as a power . . . anything?" She sighed. "And yet, he usually manages to get the job done. He finds a way."

Jones looked at her gravely. "And you think he'll do that again. For the amendment."

Her voice was quiet. "I know he will."

She was about to say more when she heard a commotion outside the back door of the Reading Room. "What on—?"

She didn't need to watch the rest of the vote anyway. It was like watching the last third of the *Titanic* sink beneath the waves—she knew how it was going to end.

Outside, dozens of people raced down the central corridor, mostly Capitol Police. One of the officers nearly knocked Christina to the floor. She took a step back into the relative safety of the doorway.

"What's going on?"

She tried to ask questions, but the police officers raced by her without even acknowledging that she had spoken. Off to the right, she saw Jimmy Claire, the Senate Information officer, sprinting double-time.

Him, she could handle. At least he didn't carry a gun.

She ran toward him and grabbed an arm. "Jimmy!"

Held fast by her grip, he slingshotted back and nearly barreled into her.

"What's happening?"

His eyes were wide and wild. "Haven't you heard the news?"

She took a guess. "The House approved the proposed amendment."

"No. Senator DeMouy has been murdered."

"*What?*"

"He was found a few minutes ago. He'd been dead for a while." Jimmy paused to catch his breath. "Looks like another case of ricin poisoning via mail."

Her hand instinctively covered her mouth. "Oh my God. How could that happen? You said that all the security measures had been tripled. How could—?"

"That's what we have to figure out. Please, I need to—"

"But why would anyone want to kill Senator DeMouy?"

"Hell if I know. They already killed the minority leader. Maybe the majority leader was next in line. Or maybe it has something to do with the amendment."

Christina felt a cold chill race up her spine. "What do you mean?"

"Figure it out, Christina. The amendment will beef up anti-terrorist laws. Maybe this terrorist doesn't want the laws beefed up."

"So he's taking out the leading proponents of—" She froze in midsentence. "Oh my God. Oh my God."

She raced toward the electronic tram that would carry her

back to the Russell Building while simultaneously dialing her cell phone.

"Pick up, damn it. Pick up!"

No one answered.

"Ben!" She sprinted toward the downward staircase that led to the subterranean passageway. "For God's sake, Ben—don't open the mail!"

40

Ben found the office empty. How often did that happen? At first, it seemed rather refreshing. Then, inevitably, insecurity and neurosis tainted the peaceful picture. Did everyone know something he didn't? Was there someplace he was supposed to be?

What the heck. He'd been working like a dog for days. If he missed one briefing on some issue somewhere, it wouldn't be the end of the world. He already had some meetings with Senator DeMouy on the amendment that he couldn't get out of, wheeling and dealing to get the remaining votes they needed to assure passage. He wanted to make sure he got home in time tonight. Christina told him she'd been shopping at Victoria's Secret during her lunch hour.

Yes, he definitely wanted to get home tonight.

He noticed a stack of mail on his desk. Was he imagining it, or was Jones getting lazier on a daily basis? Pretty soon he'd have to answer his own phone. Of course, back in Tulsa, he'd always answered his own phone. But now that he was an important D.C.

senator—well, that just wouldn't do anymore. Besides, when people called a senator they always seemed to want something. He supposed when people called a lawyer, they usually wanted something, too. But at least they expected to pay for it.

He reached for the mail—then stopped. No, the mail, too, would only bring him more work. He could let that slide for now. He opened his briefcase and pulled out his notes from the last meeting and began to read.

A few moments later, he felt his cell phone ringing. He flipped it open.

"Hello?"

There was no caller ID. And there was so much static on the line he could barely make out the voice, except he could tell it was female, and he thought he heard his wife's name.

"Christina, is that you?"

More static. "Sweetie, I can't hear you. Are you somewhere near? I can go meet you."

If anything, the static intensified. He could pick out only a few words here and there. ". . . open the mail . . . don't let Jones . . . surprise . . ."

"What? Are you saying you want me to open the mail?"

". . . don't let Jones . . ."

This was impossible. Why would she not want Jones to—?

Oh, wait. His birthday was coming up, wasn't it? Must be a present, or the receipt for something she ordered, something like that. Another perk of marriage. She remembered birthdays; he always forgot birthdays, even his own. Now she could shop for both of them.

"Christina, tell me which envelope," he shouted, trying to be heard over the static.

There was a clicking sound; then the line went dead.

Well, hell's bells. What was he going to do now?

He picked up the stack of mail, but one envelope immediately caught his eye. It was long, oversize, and cream-colored, with blue lettering. No stamp, which meant it must have come from somewhere within the building. Handwritten on the front was the word: PHOTOS.

He just hoped they were photos of Jones. Last time someone mailed him photos featuring himself . . . well, he preferred not to think about it. He was very fortunate Christina had been understanding—once. He didn't care to push his luck.

Seemed like as good a place to start as any. As soon as he was ready, he slid one finger under the flap. The envelope opened easily, and Ben detected a faint odor emanating from the package. . . .

Part Three

In Order to Form a More Perfect Union

41

Undisclosed location in Georgetown

The room was so dark, it was difficult to tell if he was awake or still dreaming in fitful sleep. His head felt as if it were made of lead, and a blacksmith was hammering away, battering the metal into another shape. Slowly he tried to stretch one muscle after the next, but he found he could barely move at all. Something was restricting him; all he could do was lift his head, and even that caused an enormous amount of pain, so he abandoned the effort.

Someone else had the courtesy to do it for him.

Loving felt the hand grip his chin roughly, as he might grab a tomato he was planning to squash.

"Are you awake?" someone in the darkness growled, in a thick Eurotrash accent.

Loving considered answering, but it seemed like too much effort, too likely to hurt.

Unfortunately, the man holding his face began to shake it, and that hurt even worse. "I said, are you awake?"

Loving's throat felt dry and creaky, like a gate hinge in serious need of oil. "Gettin' . . . there."

"You Americans. You think you are so tough. You will conquer the world. And then, a few little blows to the head and you are gone for days."

Days? Had it really been days? Good God—what had happened to him? Where was he?

"Pretty sure . . . two blows . . ."

"Yes, and then you tumbled like the proverbial sack of potatoes. We had much more fun with you after you could no longer resist."

It was Emil, gloating like the pervert pig he was. Loving wondered just exactly what they had done to him. He'd been in some tough scrapes before, but he'd never felt this bad, this . . . hurt. He thought his body was cut and bruised all over. He wasn't wearing any clothes, or perhaps they were so torn there wasn't enough left to matter, he couldn't be sure. He seemed to be tied to a chair, his arms stretched behind him, his ankles tied to the chair legs. There was not the slightest give in any extremity. Duct tape, probably. There was no chance that he might escape.

"You thought you would be the great rescuer, no? You, the all-powerful American, the cavalry, come to save the day, just as you ride in all over the world to force your will on people who do not wish it." He leaned in close to Loving's face. "Did it ever occur to you that perhaps not everyone wishes to be saved by you? Or did that thought only arise when you saw the young girl bringing the baseball bat to your head?"

"You . . . brainwashed her."

"You are a fool." He slapped Loving harshly across the face. "If it were up to me, I would have killed you long ago. But the General thinks you might have some information, something I doubt very much. You are just a stupid American who has blundered where he does not belong. But this is not my decision to make."

Loving heard the blip that told him a cell phone was being activated.

"He is awake."

The cell phone snapped shut.

"Prepare yourself, American. Angela told me you sought a meeting with the General. Your wish is about to be granted. You will not enjoy it."

All at once, the light flashed on from an overhead fluorescent hanging fixture. Loving winced and closed his eyes—he had not realized they were open. Even with his eyes closed, the light seemed blinding.

When he finally managed to open his eyes a crack, the General was standing directly before him.

The first thing Loving couldn't help but notice was that the man was short, almost little-person short. It was hard to judge when he stood so close, but Loving suspected that he was not even five feet tall. And yet he stood erect, with military bearing, in some sort of uniform, his hands behind his back, a billy club clutched between them.

Napoleonic complex, big-time.

"This is the General, Mr. Loving."

Loving's head twitched.

"Oh yes, we know who you are."

Loving grunted. "Flattered."

Almost the instant he spoke, the General whipped his right arm around and clubbed Loving on the side of the neck. He wanted to cry out at the sudden blow, but he was determined to not give the bastard the satisfaction.

"You will speak when you are spoken to, and only when you are spoken to. You will answer all questions. If you do not, you will be punished. Severely."

What, Loving wondered, *you gonna lock me up in one of your safe houses and sell my sexual favors for fifty bucks a pop?* But he decided it probably wouldn't be prudent to say that.

The General hovered over him, his club poised. "Why did you break into my house?"

Despite the sad shape his brains were in, Loving tried to determine his best course of action. His natural inclination was to be a smart aleck, but again, he sensed that might not be the best way to handle a would-be Hitler like the General. He remembered reading somewhere—possibly in an issue of *Maxim*—that the first rule of surviving a torture interrogation was to answer the questions without conveying any information of value.

"I was lookin' for you," Loving said, his voice hoarse and gravelly. He still couldn't focus; the room seemed to be swirling around him.

"And why did you look for me? Why do you even know that I exist?"

"Hey, you're famous. In certain circles."

"Who told you about me? Who gave you the address to my house?"

"Your pal, Emil."

Emil stepped into the light. "It isn't true, General. I would never tell him anything. I did not even speak to him."

"Your ace assassin kept the address in his pants," Loving sneered.

The club swung again, this time bashing against the side of Loving's head.

"I did not ask you a question," the General intoned. "You will only speak when I ask you a question."

Loving's head was swimming. He was still tap dancing on the edge of consciousness. "You hit me with that damn thing again . . . I won't be able to answer anythin'."

The General laughed, loud and obnoxiously. "You think you have been hurt? You do not know the meaning of what it is to be hurt! We can hurt you so badly, you will never recover. We can make it go on for days!"

Even if he were a pip-squeak, Loving didn't doubt the General could deliver on his threat. He'd noticed that people were always more effective when they were doing something they enjoyed.

The General grabbed Loving by the hair and pulled his head backward as far as it would go. "Tell me what you know about my business! And who have you told?"

"I know everything. I've told everyone!"

"Have you told the senator?"

Despite the numbness creeping through his body, Loving felt a cold chill race down his spine. "What senator?"

"Your boss, Mr. Loving. The one who thinks he can get anything he wants by invoking God, Abraham Lincoln, and the United States of America!"

"What would you know about it?"

"I know far more about the Senate than you can imagine. How do you think I've managed to stay clear of government interference for so long?" He jerked Loving's head back again. "Tell me what I want to know! Who have you told about my business?"

Loving closed his eyes, bracing himself for what he knew would follow. He didn't want to do it. But he had no choice. If he knew Loving was connected to Ben, he couldn't even dance around the truth. Couldn't even give the man a hint. "Are you in business? You look like some kinda military officer. Thought you worked at the Pentagon, maybe."

The General threw his head forward in disgust. He raised his club into the air, then stopped himself. "No," he growled through clenched teeth. "That is not nearly enough for such as you." He turned. "Emil. Bring me the instrument."

Loving didn't like the sound of that at all.

A moment later, the General stood before him again, holding a long cylindrical black wand. Being from the Southwest, unfortunately, Loving knew that wasn't made for doing magic tricks. It was an electric cattle prod.

"You'll tell me what I want to know," the General said, doing his best to maintain an even tone. "You'll tell me now."

"I already told you. I don't know nothin'. There's nothin' to tell."

The General touched the cattle prod to Loving's exposed gut. Thousands of volts of electricity shot through his body, cauterizing open wounds. He could prevent himself from crying out, but he couldn't stop his body from wrenching back and forth, heaving, twisting like a snake in a vise.

"Tell me," the General said quietly.

"I don't have any answers for you," Loving said, when he had regained the power of speech.

This time, the General placed the prod against his left nipple. The electricity radiated through his soft tissue. He lurched forward, as much as possible while strapped to the chair. He began spasming uncontrollably, his body jerking one way then the other. The juice flooded his brain, confusing him, making it difficult to think, difficult to do anything except experience the intense agony from which there was no escape.

"How long do you wish this to go on, American? Answer!"

Loving wasn't even sure he could speak, but he was certain there was nothing he could say that would appease this sadistic bastard, not without putting others in immediate danger.

"Don't . . . know . . . nothin'," he managed, with great effort. "Told . . . no one."

The General placed the cattle prod against his genitals.

He couldn't help himself. This time he screamed. Screamed so loudly, the sound was deafening to himself. His body twisted with such intensity that for a moment he thought he might actually wrench himself loose, but of course that was a delusion, a wishful thought. The screaming and the crying continued as his body spasmed uncontrollably. The General jabbed him with the prod again and again and again until finally, blissfully, he was enveloped in darkness once more.

42

U.S. SENATE, RUSSELL BUILDING
WASHINGTON, D.C.

Christina raced down the corridor, fighting the traffic that flowed in both directions, forward and backward, all around her. By now, word of the poisoning had spread across the building. Everyone was in a panic. The Capitol Police were trying to maintain some semblance of order, but the numbers overwhelmed them. Rumors were flying of other suspicious mail, other poisonings. Truth or panic? There was no way for her to know.

She had been calling Ben continuously the entire time she had been running toward their office. He had not answered. Despite the fact that she had finally managed to teach the man to keep that thing in his pocket at all times, he had not answered.

Which left only two possible explanations. Either he didn't want to. Or he couldn't.

What possible reason could he have for not taking a call from her now? There simply wasn't any.

Only the latter possibility remained.

She raced up the steps to the second floor, taking them two at a time. "Ben!" she shouted, well before she was close enough that he could hear. She couldn't help herself. Some of the other people racing down the corridors stared at her as if she were insane. She didn't care about that, either. All she cared about was her sweet husband, her sweet stupid husband who was just naïve enough to open a deadly envelope given the proper incentive.

My God—why had she left him alone? Why didn't she see this coming? The President of the United States had told him he could be in danger—wasn't that warning enough? How could she have been so blind? She almost slammed into the Capitol Police officer posted outside the door.

"Sorry, ma'am. You can't go in there."

"I work in there!"

"Sorry, ma'am. The office has been quarantined."

"Quarantined? Why?"

The officer took a deep breath. "There's been another ricin poisoning."

Christina's eyes widened with despair. "Oh my God. Ben!" She pushed forward.

The police officer gently but firmly held her back. "Ma'am."

"Oh my God. I'm too late! He's—he's—Ben!"

"You calling me?"

She whirled around. "You're alive!"

"Thank you, Princess Obvious."

She slugged him on the shoulder. "You idiot! I was afraid you were—" She stopped herself. "I was afraid you'd opened the mail."

"I did. But I wore rubber gloves and a mask like the security people told us to do. What do you think I am, some sort of idiot?"

"You—you—"

"Good thing, too, 'cause there was something weird about one of those envelopes. That's why I called the Capitol cops."

"Which envelope?"

"The big one. The one you told me to open."

"The one I—what?"

"The one you told me to open. Before Jones saw it. When you called."

She stared at him, her mouth gaping. "What are you talking about? I didn't tell you to open anything."

Ben's eyebrows moved closer together. "That wasn't you?"

"Besides which—I've been trying to contact you and not getting any answer."

"But I definitely got a call."

"Give me your cell." Ben passed it across to her. She pushed a few buttons. "Yes, you've definitely had a call, but not from my phone." She pushed several more buttons faster than Ben could follow. "Let me give you another news flash, handsome. This isn't your cell phone."

"What?"

"Someone switched out on you. Looks like your phone, but it isn't. Has a different number. That's why they were able to call you—and I wasn't." She looked up. "Have you been keeping this phone in your pocket like I told you to do?"

Ben squirmed. "Usually."

"Usually?"

"Well . . . sometimes I leave it in my briefcase."

"And you leave your briefcase lying around all the time."

"Not all the time."

"At meetings?"

"Well . . ."

She pounded her forehead. "Anyone with access to this building could've switched phones on you."

"But who would want to?"

Christina looked at him with cold dark eyes. "Whoever wanted you to open that envelope filled with ricin. The same person who killed Senator DeMouy."

Ben's eyes widened like balloons. "When did this happen?"

She wiped a hand across her brow. "My God—the President of the United States warned that you might be in danger. He didn't know the half of it." She paused, her mind racing. "Or did he?"

"Christina—what are you talking about?"

"I'm talking about the fact that someone just tried to kill you, Ben."

"But—why?"

"The same reason they killed Senator DeMouy."

"Which is?"

Christina slowly wrapped her arm around his shoulders and hugged him tight. "Because he was leading the drive to toughen the nation's antiterrorism capabilities via a proposed constitutional amendment. An amendment someone apparently does not want to become law." She looked at him grimly. "Even if it means killing the key players supporting the amendment."

43

When Jason Simic came through the back door under the cover of darkness, Belinda was waiting for him. She was decked out in black—a padded push-up bra and a skintight mesh catsuit with a zipper at the crotch for convenience.

She wrapped her arms around his neck and pressed up close against him.

He dropped his briefcase. "My God, Belinda, can't you wait till I get the door shut?"

She pulled away, obviously put out. "I remember when you couldn't wait until I got my bra unsnapped."

He walked to the nearest bay window and closed the drapes. "It's different now. I probably shouldn't even be here. I assume a short visit is okay—I am your late husband's chief of staff, after all. It's only natural that we would have much to talk about. But a lengthy visit might arouse suspicion."

"Your body arouses me, big boy."

"Stop!" He lifted her hands and removed them from his body. "Tell me what happened with the police."

"They don't have a clue. It's just as you said it would be. They're totally off track. Asked if Jeff had received any threats from known terrorists, that sort of thing. Didn't show the slightest sign of suspicion that I was involved."

Which they wouldn't, Jason knew, even if they had suspicions. But still, it was a good sign.

"Did they talk to you?" she asked.

"Oh yeah. I had no information about any threats against his life. But I have been concerned about the safety protocols at the Senate. Three senators dead, a fourth almost killed. It's frightening. I told them I was considering getting out of politics."

"That's bull."

"Yes, it is. But they don't know that. And they never will."

She took his hand and walked him to the sofa. "Jason—you didn't tell me you were going after Senator Kincaid, too."

"There was no point. I didn't need you to play lovey-dovey with Kincaid. No one would connect you with that crime."

"But since there were two attacks—both against the leaders of the pro-amendment faction—the police seem convinced this was politically motivated."

"Yes, I am brilliant. You're welcome."

"How did you do it?"

"Easy. I switched cell phones on him while he was conferencing with DeMouy about the amendment. Then I planted the envelope. Then I made a call at the last minute to make sure he went for the envelope. Used my falsetto and a static inducer to mask my voice. Pity he survived—but it doesn't really matter. The diversion was the important thing, and the police now seem entirely diverted. Because, as I may have mentioned, I am brilliant."

"Yes, you are. But a little scary, too."

"Oh, but you like that, don't you?" He leaned in close till she could feel his hot breath on her face. "The danger. The rough edges. Makes you all wet, doesn't it?"

"Jason . . . stop."

"Whatever you say, darling. I'll wait till you want it," he added, because he could see from her dilated pupils and heaving breasts that she already did very much want it.

"I can't believe we got away with it," she said, her voice becoming softer and more breathless.

"It isn't over yet," he reminded her. "But we do appear to be in the clear."

"How long do you think it will be before we can . . . you know. Go public."

"I'm not sure what you mean."

"About us. How long until we can stop hiding?"

"Soon, baby. Soon," he said, although he knew that would be insane. He needed her money, yes, but he now realized that marrying his murdered boss's widow would be too risky by half. Just plain stupid. And he was anything but stupid.

But he decided to keep those thoughts to himself. At least until he had the money.

"You do want to marry me, don't you, Jason? You want to be with me?"

"Of course I do."

"I'm not just a . . . a plaything for you?"

"Of course not."

"When will we be together? When?"

Time for a distraction. He pressed her down on the sofa and clamped a hand over her gauzy breast. "We're going to be together in about one minute. Two at the outside."

"No, I mean—"

"Strip for me."

"What?"

"You heard me. Strip. Slowly."

"If—that's what you want." She began fumbling with the strap of her adroitly designed brassiere.

"That's what I want. I want to feel your breasts pressing up against me. I want to stroke them. I want to taste them. I want to put them in my mouth and feel your nipples getting hard."

"Oh, Godddddd . . ."

"Then I want you to go down on me. Then I'll go down on you. And then I'm going to screw you in a way you've never been screwed before."

"You—you are?"

"I'm going to pound you like a hammer and suck you till you can't stand it anymore, but I'm going to keep on doing it anyway, until you cry out and squeal and beg me to stop but I won't stop, and you'll come again and again and again."

"Oh, God, Jason. Oh, Godddddd—"

"Then I'm going to take you from behind. Right here on the sofa."

"Take me, Jason. I want you so much! Take me now!"

And he would. Whatever it took to keep her happy, and contented, and quiet.

Until he didn't need her anymore.

Then he would give her something altogether different.

44

*B*en had been quiet all the way down Memorial Drive, from the Lincoln Memorial, across the Potomac, and through the portico that capped the main entrance to the cemetery. It seemed appropriate, not only because this was a somber occasion, but also because he felt chastened and subdued by the fact that another public servant had fallen to this never-ending wave of terrorism. Not to mention the knowledge that he was almost the next victim.

As the driver approached the destination, Ben marveled at the stoic majesty of this most famous of cemeteries. The green hills were lined with row after row of what appeared at a distance to be identical white grave markers stretching off into infinity. They passed the Tomb of the Unknown Soldier and, shortly after that, the Eternal Flame that marked JFK's burial site. Ben had not even been born when JFK was slain, but that president's legacy of hope and vision still had a special meaning for him.

Arlington was a military cemetery, but as Ben knew from his

morning briefing, there were a few exceptions, a few special individuals of national import who had been buried here even though they were not military casualties or even veterans. Pierre Charles L'Enfant, the architect who laid the design for Washington, D.C., was buried here. Four Supreme Court justices, Thurgood Marshall, William O. Douglas, Potter Stewart, and Harry Blackmun, were buried here. Two Capitol Police officers, John Gibson and Jacob Chestnut, who died in the line of duty, were interred at Arlington. And the ashes of Marie Teresa Rios Versace, author of *The Fifteenth Pelican*, which became the basis for *The Flying Nun* television show, were scattered here. Ben wasn't entirely sure how that one fit in, but it must've seemed like a good idea at the time.

More recently, Arlington had served as a final resting place for many people who died as a result of terrorist attacks. Julian and Jay Bartley, killed in an attack on the U.S. Embassy in Nairobi. Dana Falkenberg, killed in the 9/11 attack on the Pentagon. Michael Hammer, murdered by guerrilla fighters in El Salvador. The Secret Service agents who died in the attack on April 19 shared a tomb, not even fully completed yet. Senator Hammond had been buried here. And now the government and his family jointly had decided that Senator DeMouy should be buried at Arlington.

As Ben stepped out of the car, he saw a wide array of people had come to pay their respects. President Blake was here; he was scheduled to deliver the primary eulogy. Even though he would not specifically refer to the proposed constitutional amendment, his presence at the funeral of yet another victim of terrorism was sure to make a statement. He stood at the head of the grave site with his chief of staff, Tracy Sobel, and the senator's widow, Belinda DeMouy. Ben also spotted Homeland Security Director Carl Lehman with his deputy director Nichole Muldoon.

Ben walked slowly to the head of the gravesite. He knew the Secret Service would want time to identify and clear him before he got anywhere near the president. He approached the grieving widow and introduced himself.

Belinda DeMouy was dressed in a solid black dress. Despite the veil over her face, Ben could see that her young face was streaked and red from crying.

"Let me offer my most sincere condolences," Ben said, pressing her hand between both of his. "I'd only known and worked with your husband for a short while, but I could see he was a great man with a good heart." Ben smiled a little. "Even if he was a Republican."

"He was a good man," she repeated softly. Her watery eyes looked as if they might spill over at any moment. "And a good husband. He cared about people. Genuinely cared about them."

"I could tell that."

"And then to have him taken away so suddenly and in such—such a horrible way." Belinda's hand shot up beneath her veil, covering her eyes.

"I'm so sorry," Ben said. "This is a tragedy. Tragedy on tragedy."

"But—but at least you were spared," she said, still holding Ben's hand. "I take some comfort in knowing that the murderer didn't get everything he wanted. That someone will carry on my Jeff's work."

"I was just lucky," Ben replied softly. "I happened to remember to use the gloves."

"Thank God. Your envelope was laced with the poison, wasn't it?"

"It was. As I said, I was very lucky. If there's anything I can do for you, Mrs. DeMouy, now or at any other time, please let me know."

"Thank you. I—I would like to know, from time to time, if it's not too much trouble—"

"It isn't."

"I'd like to know how the work on the amendment is progressing. It was Jeff's final crusade, and—well, I just want to know it's in good hands. I want it to be remembered as part of Jeff's lifetime of service."

"I'm sure it will be." There were others waiting to speak to her. Ben released her hand and sidled down what had become an informal reception line.

Tracy Sobel was the next person he greeted. "I'm glad you and the president could be here today."

"So am I," Sobel replied. Ben noted that her face was remarkably free of sorrow. "Do you realize that all the major networks are going to interrupt their programming to carry the president's eulogy?"

"That's . . . lovely."

"Are you kidding? That's goddamn fantastic. The president could hold a prime time address and not be guaranteed The Big Three. This is a coup of major proportions."

Ben felt his irritation growing. He tried to contain it. "I'm . . . sure the president has no intention of exploiting this national tragedy."

"Of course not. That's my job." She leaned closer to Ben and whispered, "This will be a major victory for proponents of the amendment."

"I'm sure you're happy about that."

Did Ben imagine it, or did Sobel stiffen slightly? "The president will be happy. And that's my job. Keeping the president happy."

After the minister in charge read the religious service, several others were given an opportunity to speak. Senator Scolieri, who had known DeMouy since they were Senate pages together forty years ago, told several amusing anecdotes of their youthful antics. Senator Bening of Colorado talked about DeMouy's legislative legacy. Bening's chief of staff, Joe Conrad, spoke of his great and abiding love for DeMouy and his lovely young wife, Belinda. They heard from a few friends and relatives outside the world of politics. Then, finally, it was time for the president to speak.

"I know this is a time of sadness for those who knew Jeff De-Mouy, and even for those who did not. This is a time of sadness for all Americans, all peoples around the globe who believe in the right to work without the fear of terrorism. I had the privilege of working with Jeff on many occasions. Sometimes we agreed, sometimes we didn't. But I always valued his opinion. He was one of the special few you could count on in a crisis. He would do the difficult tasks even when his plate was already full. He would take the unpopular chores, regardless of the consequences, when he knew it was the right thing to do. He was a great American, and so it is appropriate that his final resting place be here, where he can spend the rest of eternity surrounded by the best and the brightest America has ever known."

President Blake made what Ben now recognized as the familiar shift from Camera A to Camera B, then continued.

"Some people have asked me what I think Senator DeMouy's legacy will be. The simple truth is—I don't know. But I can tell you what I hope it will be. I hope he will be remembered as the last great American who fell at the hands of terrorists. I hope that we as a nation will not allow his death to be meaningless, but rather, will see it as a turning point in the way we think. I hope that this will be the moment when we rise up as one nation and say: No more. We will not allow the lives of our leaders, friends, innocent citizens, and even children to be taken in the pursuit of someone else's political agenda. We Americans have always been strong, and now we will be even stronger. We will fight the good fight, as the Good Book tells us to do. We will take whatever actions are necessary to make sure that Senator DeMouy has not died in vain."

Very well said, Ben thought. He came about as close to campaigning for the amendment without specifically mentioning it as was humanly possible. A stratagem employed by numerous successful leaders throughout the history of the world.

After the president concluded, Ben felt a tapping on his shoulder. He turned and saw a man he recognized. Even if he wasn't wearing the standard sunglasses and suit, he knew this man was a Secret Service agent. Agent . . .

"Zimmer," the young man said. "We spoke at . . . well, you know. On April nineteenth. In Oklahoma City."

"I remember," Ben said quietly.

"Could I possibly have a minute of your time?" Zimmer asked. "It's important."

"Of course." The crowd was dispersing anyway. Ben followed Agent Zimmer to a quiet nook a few hundred feet to the north.

"What's this about?" Ben asked.

"It's about April nineteenth," Zimmer replied. "And it's about a colleague of mine. Special Agent Gatwick. You know him?"

"I met him on April nineteenth," Ben answered. And he remembered what the president had told him about Agent Gatwick as well. About Gatwick and the late first lady.

"Do you realize what he did?"

Ben hesitated. He was surprised that the word was out, but he supposed that inflammatory secrets of this nature were hard to keep under wraps. "I've been told."

"By whom?"

"I'm not sure I should say."

Zimmer eyed him carefully. "Are we talking about the same thing? Because what I'm talking about—I think there are only two people on earth who know, other than Gatwick himself."

"You're talking about . . . the affair."

"No. I'm talking about Gatwick's actions on April nineteenth. Regarding the first lady."

With whom, if Ben understood the autopsy report correctly, he'd had sex less than eight hours before. "What did he do?"

"He altered the protocol. On his own self-assumed authority."

Ben's forehead creased. "I'm not really following. . . ."

"Gatwick moved the first lady from where she should have been to where she was when the shooting started. On the other side of the raised platform. By you."

"Yes, I remember that."

"As a result, I was the only Secret Service agent anywhere near her. There should have been five agents in the immediate vicinity, but instead, there was only one. Me." His voice choked a bit. "And I couldn't save her."

Ben reached out to him. "You couldn't possibly have saved her alone. The bullets came too fast. I remember." He touched the still swollen scar on his cheek. "It's a miracle I made it out. And I'm hardly the target the first lady was."

"Yes, but the president made it off the stage, didn't he? Because he was where the agents were. And if Emily Blake had been beside him, as she should have been, I believe she would be alive today."

"So . . . are you saying that Agent Gatwick acted erroneously? Incompetently?"

Zimmer stared directly into Ben's eyes. "At the very least."

"Surely you're not suggesting—"

"All I know is that his actions allowed a tragedy to occur that has shocked the nation right out of its senses."

Ben blinked. "Don't you support the amendment?"

"No, I don't."

"I thought the whole law enforcement community—"

"You were wrong. We shouldn't be rushing around trying to rewrite the Constitution. We should be trying to find out what really happened."

"You sound like my chief of staff. But you know the government is investigating."

"I'm not. The Secret Service was taken out of the loop."

"There were reasons—"

"There are always reasons, Senator Kincaid. Or excuses. But at some point, when there are too many excuses and not enough rational thought, you have to sit up and wonder—what the hell is going on? What's really happening here?" His voice dropped to barely a whisper. "Before it's too late."

45

Loving had no idea how many times they had repeated the cycle. They tortured him until he passed out. Then they used buckets of ice-cold water and drugs to revive him, and then they tortured him again. He had lost all sense of time, all sense of purpose. He could barely think. All he could do was feel the pain. He had hoped that eventually he would become numb to the hurting, but unfortunately, with each new iteration, his body felt weaker, his resistance lower, his power to tolerate this agony diminished. He had no idea how much longer he could last. But he knew it would not be forever.

He would like to think he was being strong to protect his friends—Ben, Shohreh—but at this time, he wasn't sure he was capable of any such self-sacrifice. The only thing that kept him in the game was the certain knowledge that if he did tell the General what he wanted to know, the sadist would surely kill him.

Unfortunately, death was beginning to seem very attractive.

For the last several sessions, Loving had gone into total lock-down mode, not saying a word. He had taken the "elusive answer" routine as far as he could possibly take it. There were no more satisfactory answers, and wisecracks were clearly not appreciated, so he just remained silent—other than the constant screaming like a woman that embarrassed him so. But he couldn't help himself. Even though his work had always put him in the line of danger, he'd never experienced an ordeal like this, nothing so prolonged or intense or . . . skilled. Never.

At one point, he tried playing dead. He thought he did it well—an Oscar-caliber performance. But the General was not fooled. Physical abuse tended to be stimulating, especially as long as they stayed away from the head and the genitals, and there was plenty of pain that could be inflicted without entering either of those regions. When Loving continued to play dead, the General kicked him and spat on him and eventually injected him with something. Epinephrine, perhaps? Or strychnine, for all he knew. At any rate, playing possum was no solution.

He had also hoped that if he held out long enough, the General would become bored, or would realize that all his efforts would never produce the information he wanted. Unfortunately, the General was a narcissistic little sadist who enjoyed what he was doing and was supremely confident that he would be successful. He would never stop, not till he had what he wanted. Loving would just have to bear it. Hold out until he couldn't hold out any longer. Or until they killed him in the process.

"You want to blame me. But this is your own doing," the General said, as he artfully drew a line of blood down Loving's exposed back with a knife. Loving writhed in agony with each touch. "You invaded my house, my business. You tried to steal my girls."

Loving knew he should remain quiet, but he couldn't help himself. "You're just makin' excuses. You're lovin' every minute of this."

"In fact, I am not. I have many other duties that require my attention. But I can make no decisions until I know to what extent you have jeopardized my operation."

"That's a load of bull, you psycho."

The General's eyes narrowed. "Psycho. You dare accuse me of that, of enjoying this? Did we invade your country, you stupid American? Did we destroy your way of life? You complain of what I do to you, but it is nothing compared to the torture you self-righteous Americans inflicted at Abu Ghraib and Gitmo Bay."

"That was war."

"And what is this? Do you think my cell was organized just to provide for the needs of those with special sexual interests?"

"I thought you used your sex shop to finance your terrorism," Loving said, biting back the pain. "But now I wonder if I didn't get it backward. Maybe the terrorism is the excuse you use to conduct a sick business that gets your rocks off."

The General touched the cattle prod to Loving's face, just below his right eye. All at once, Loving's eyesight short-circuited. The world went black. He screamed.

"I do what I do at the behest of others," the General said softly. "With their full support and cooperation. But perhaps you already knew that. All the more reason I must know what you know."

Loving was blind, but he wasn't about to admit it. "No."

"Do you know the shooter? The man at Oklahoma City?"

"I'm guessin' it was Emil."

"You would be wrong. It was Emil's brother. A most loyal man."

"Why isn't he here for the fun? You must not like him as much."

"Mikhail is preparing for the next assault. The one that will plunge your pathetic country into chaos. The execution that I have guaranteed will be completed."

Guaranteed? Loving wondered, through his fogged and pain-muddled brain. *To whom?* He said he worked at the behest of others. Did that mean the General was not at the top of the food chain?

"How much do you know about my associates?"

"I've said all I'm gonna say."

The General chuckled. "I doubt it."

Even without seeing it, Loving could sense the prod coming closer to him.

"I tell ya, I'm done."

"It will go easier on you if you talk."

Loving hesitated. "You mean you'll let me go if I tell you what you wanna hear?"

"No. But it will go easier on you. I will kill you quickly."

Loving pretended that wasn't tempting and kept his mouth shut.

"I do admire your resilience. You have behaved honorably. You have shown considerably more fortitude than did your former director of Homeland Security. But there comes a time for all things to pass. This is it. You must tell me what I want to know or I will take more than your eyesight. I will take your manhood. Permanently. I will take your fingers, one by one. I will cut off your feet. I will burn you. But I will not let you die. I will never let you die, even when you beg me for it. I will simply whittle away at you, piece by piece, until you have told me what I want to know."

"If I ever get loose," Loving said in low tones, "you are a dead man."

"This I do not doubt," the General said. "But alas—you will never get loose. Emil? Please assist me. Open the captive's mouth."

The assassin stepped forward and grabbed Loving's head by the hair. With the other hand, he forced Loving's jaw open. Loving tried to resist, but he was too weak.

Slowly, the cattle prod made its way toward his mouth. When at last it was inside, the General activated it.

There was no way Loving could describe what he experienced. It was as if he had been turned inside out, electrocuted from within. He couldn't even scream with the damn thing gagging him. And the General did not relent. He did not remove the prod, even as the cold electricity burned Loving's tongue and loosened his teeth. When at last oblivion did come, he was glad. Even though he knew it was only a temporary respite, he was glad for this one small mercy.

46

Director Lehman stared out the window of his limousine, his eyes hidden by dark black sunglasses.

"Zimmer's talking to Kincaid," he announced.

If he had expected this revelation to provoke a dramatic response, he was sorely disappointed. Silence prevailed in the backseat.

"Did you hear what I said?"

"I heard," Nichole Muldoon said. "And as your deputy director let me say this: Who cares?"

"Kincaid's the president's point man on the amendment. The main man, now that DeMouy's gone."

"And again I say: Who cares?"

"Zimmer's obviously trying to pollute the stream. Screw up the passage of the amendment."

"You don't know that," she replied. She opened the side cabinet, checking to see if the brandy snifter was filled. It wasn't. "They

could be talking about anything. Zimmer could be expressing his regrets that Kincaid lost his close comrade."

"No way. Zimmer's against the amendment."

"Is that a crime now?" Muldoon asked, arching a perfectly
plucked eyebrow.

"No, but it should be." Lehman continued staring as the limo
pulled away from the gravesite. "Damn. I hate having this thing left
in the hands of that cluck from Oklahoma. DeMouy, I trusted. I've
worked with him for a long time. I knew him well."

"I knew him pretty well myself," Muldoon replied. "But that
doesn't mean Kincaid can't get the job done. Look what he accomplished at the subcommittee hearing."

"Yeah, but that sob sister stuff won't work twice. The opposition will be ready for it. He'll have to connect with their brains and
their pollsters, not just their guilt."

"Well, maybe DeMouy taught him a few tricks before he kicked
off," Muldoon said dryly. "He certainly had lots of them."

Lehman slowly removed his shades. "You know, Nichole—I'm
not entirely sure you're taking this matter as seriously as you
should."

"You mean, as seriously as you want me to."

"I mean, I'm your boss and I want this damn thing passed."

"Really? At the press conference you said it was important that
you remain out of the advocacy process."

He gave her a withering look. "This isn't some damn press conference trumped up to appease the president. This is me, the boss,
talking to you, the underling. And me, the boss, is sick of feeling
that you're not pitching for the right team."

"Carl, you know I've always done my job well. Better than anyone else you've ever worked with. But you can't force me to support
a law that I don't, that I think is an extremely dangerous, bad idea."

"How can you say that? Did you not see the expression on the
face of DeMouy's poor grieving widow? How long are you willing
to let the terrorists walk all over us?"

Muldoon unbuttoned the top of her blouse and fanned herself.
"Is the air conditioner on? Are you as hot as I am?"

"Don't even think about trying that sexpot crap. That might

work on some pansy-ass FBI guy like Joel Salter, but it will not work on me. Answer the question. How long are you willing to let the terrorists take potshots at our senators?"

"Actually," she said, ignoring the suggestion regarding her sexuality, "I'm not convinced this had anything to do with terrorists. Or political advocacy of any sort."

"What are you talking about? What else could it be?"

"There are a million things it could be. And I see no evidence that it's terrorists. That's just a conclusion everyone is jumping to. A conclusion that is very convenient for your cause, I might add."

Lehman gave her a look that could chill Hades. "Muldoon—I am getting very concerned here."

"Does that mean you want me to undo another button?"

"No. It means I can't work with someone who opposes my directives."

"I have never opposed your directives. I have always done everything you wanted done, with great efficiency and effectiveness. That's why I'm the deputy director."

"A fact that could change very quickly."

Now Muldoon was the one conveying the harsh look. "You can't fire me because I don't share your political views."

"No, I would have to come up with some other excuse. But I can fire you. And I will. If you don't stay quiet and stay out of the way." His voice dropped. "I don't like obstacles."

"I would never do anything that stupid. I'm a career girl, you know. Career comes before politics. Or anything else."

Lehman gave her a long look, then sighed. "Yes, that part I believe. Just remember—I will not tolerate obstacles. I want no trouble—not from you or Special Agent Zimmer." His eyes narrowed. "Or Senator Benjamin Kincaid. I want you to keep a very close watch on him and report anything that might indicate he's not the staunchest advocate this amendment could have. Because if I get any sense he's wavering—he will have to be dealt with. Immediately."

"Dealt with?" Muldoon asked.

"You heard me. And you know what I mean." He paused. "I

can think of a lot of approaches more direct than incriminating photos or a poison envelope."

At the opposite end of the cemetery, a newly minted Cadillac
One was motoring the President of the United States back to the
White House. But the president was not traveling alone.

Special Agent Gatwick had often ridden in Cadillac One, usually when it was transporting the late first lady. Sitting in the front
passenger seat, riding shotgun—literally—watching in all directions
for any possible threats. But today was different. This was the first
time he had ever ridden in the back of the car with the president. At
the president's request.

"Thank you for joining me, Tom. Is it all right if I call you
Tom?"

"Whatever you like, Mr. President." Gatwick was nervous, and
not just because he was riding in an unaccustomed seat.

"Something to drink?" The president opened a side cabinet and
withdrew a brandy snifter. It was full. "I'm having one. Just a little
one. It's early yet."

"Nothing for me, sir. Thank you," Gatwick replied, although he
would dearly love a drink right now. Anything to settle his nerves.

The president poured a drink, then downed it in a single gulp.
"Excellent. Imported, you know. Perhaps I can manage one more.
Sure you won't have anything? You seem a little . . . on edge. Might
help."

"I'm sure." Was it Gatwick's fevered imagination, he wondered,
or was Blake deliberately playing with him? Either way, it was giving him a serious case of the creeps.

"I thought the two of us should meet," the president said,
stretching expansively across the car seat. "I mean, I know we've
run into each other on occasion, when you were on duty. But I
thought we should have a chance just to . . . talk. In private."

"Why is that, Mr. President?"

Blake looked at him as one might look at a small child whose attempts at dissembling are so pathetic as to draw a smile. "Tom, let's
not play games. I know. What's more—I think you know I know."

Gatwick looked at his knees and said nothing.

"Emily was a wonderful woman, wasn't she?"

Gatwick remained silent.

"Wonderful, indeed. So full of energy. So warmhearted. So . . . loyal."

The president paused, but Gatwick didn't take the bait.

"Tom," the president said, as casually as if he were ordering ice cream, "why were you fucking my wife?"

"Mr. President, I never meant—"

"Oh, please spare me the excuses. We're both grown-ups. So was Emily. These things don't happen by accident. They happen because the participants want them to happen." He stopped for a moment, as if realizing that by interrupting his companion he had stifled the conversation. "Did she give a reason? Or was she just . . . overwhelmed by your masculine good looks? Because frankly, I've been watching you for a long time, and I'm considerably less than overwhelmed. If she'd taken a shot at Brad Pitt—well, who wouldn't? But you?" Blake shrugged. "It's kind of insulting, really."

Gatwick spoke quietly. "She said she was lonely. That you were always busy."

Blake nodded slowly. "Yes. That's what I imagined she would say."

"And she said that you were having . . . problems. In the bedroom."

"Well, she hardly needed to add that." He stared out the window, watching the landmarks of Memorial Drive pass by. "It's hard being the leader of the free world."

"I would imagine so."

"So many people depend on you. So much rests upon your shoulders. It should hardly be surprising if a man suffering under that kind of stress occasionally has . . . issues."

"Of course."

"Don't patronize me. You took advantage of the situation to put cuckold horns on my head. You're a sorry son of a bitch."

"As you say, sir."

"And I want your resignation."

Gatwick's head rose. "What?"

"You heard me. I'm your boss, remember?"

"Carl Lehman is—"

"I'm the commander in chief, Tom."

"I'm not in the military."

"If I want you out—you're out."

"I won't resign."

"I'm not giving you a choice."

Gatwick drew in his breath. "You have no direct authority over me."

"You're not listening to me, Tom. I'm the president. Your job is to protect the executive branch. How long do you think you'll last if I don't want you around? I don't even need a pretext. I know for a fact that some people in your own office think your protocol changes on April nineteenth resulted in the death of my wife. All I have to do is make a phone call."

Gatwick's lips tightened. "You can't fire me."

"I would prefer it if you resigned. It would look better."

"Then let me put it differently. You don't want to."

The president slowly drew himself in. "Do I understand this correctly? Are you threatening me?"

"Weren't you just threatening me?"

"I was managing my branch of the government. That's my job."

"Well, I like my job, too. And I intend to keep it."

"If Carl Lehman knew what you've done—"

Gatwick cut him off with a laugh. It seemed he had no choice but to be an enemy of the president. Very well, then. In for a penny, in for a pound. "You won't rat me out. If I lose my job, I go public."

"You think that will help you get reemployed?"

"I think that's a revelation you don't want in the public forum. It could ruin you."

"Like hell. I've done nothing wrong."

"If the truth came out about your late wife's hanky-panky, it would, first, make you look like a weak-kneed loser, and second, make your late wife considerably less sympathetic in the public eye. You're counting on that sympathy to get your amendment passed. And probably to get yourself reelected."

"Public opinion is already wildly in my favor. On both counts."

"Because you're a bereaved husband who lost a wife who had a huge approval rating. If it turns out you're a—what was your word?—*cuckold,* and she was a tramp—"

"You son of a bitch."

"I didn't start this, Mr. President. But I'm not going to sit around and let you walk all over me. If you hadn't been such a crappy husband, it wouldn't have occurred in the first place."

"You twisted sick—"

"Maybe I am partly to blame, and maybe she is. Maybe no one is. But I won't let you take my job from me. Especially not now."

"Why not now?"

"Never mind. This is a critical time for both of us. We want to continue to get our jobs done." He looked the president straight in the eye. "So you leave me alone and let me get my work done, Mr. President. And I'll leave you alone and let you do yours."

47

U.S. SENATE CHAMBER

Ben spent ten minutes just getting past all the protestors outside the entrance to the main Senate building. The Capitol Police were doing an admirable job of managing the huge and boisterous, and in some cases downright angry, crowd. Several years back, the Capitol Police were almost a joke, once referred to as the least qualified security team in the country, mostly staffed based upon political patronage rather than qualifications. That changed with 9/11. In this era of suicide bombers and maniacs crashing into the building, the Senate took its security very seriously. The Capitol Police were well trained, highly organized, and double the numbers of a decade before. Metal detectors, a host of surveillance cameras, and many other security measures had been implemented. Most times, Ben thought of them as a hassle, hoops to be leaped through to get to his office. Today, he was glad they were here.

Despite all that had happened in the interim, the polarized forces making themselves heard outside the Capitol Building had not changed much since the time of the subcommittee hearings. Civil libertarian groups still opposed the amendment, although Ben noticed now their placards and chants put more emphasis on the need for calm deliberation and sober second thoughts, with less emphasis on the potential threat to freedom. There were as many if not more people forcefully advocating the adoption of the amendment; Ben knew many of them had been privately bused in by PACs beholden to the president's party. They went about as far as they could possibly go to suggest that this amendment was needed to stop the "slaughter" of American citizens. Many held placards bearing an enlargement of what by now had become a famous, almost iconic photograph—the mother in Oklahoma City holding her dead little girl in her arms.

As they passed by, Christina whispered into Ben's ear. "Makes you proud to be on their team, doesn't it, Ben?"

"It's not the people who matter. It's the cause."

"I'm just saying that any cause that has to resort to such . . . dynamic means of persuasion . . ."

"The placards aren't for me. They're for the television audience. They may not work for us, but they'll go a long way with the rank-and-file, pork rind–eating American."

"Somehow, I never envisioned you siding with the pork rind–eating American. Do you even know what pork rinds are?"

"I said, stop already."

"I've never seen them in our apartment. And I'm pretty sure they don't sell them in Nichols Hills."

"Christina—*stop*!"

Ben was glad when they finally passed the pillared Capitol crypt, the vice-presidential marble busts in the spectator gallery, the historic Ohio clock in the hall outside the chamber, and through the large gilded doors. As he expected, the chamber was flooded with people and awash with activity. It was a marbleized fishbowl, a microcosm of government in action. Pages were running everywhere in the ubiquitous white shirt and black slacks uniforms they had worn for ages, even before young women were allowed to be pages. They scurried across the chamber floor like ants in an ant farm, delivering notes and messages back and forth between senators as alliances were considered and offers proposed. Normally, they would distribute copies of the legislation on the day's agenda and the calendar, but today there was only one matter that would be discussed and everyone already had a copy. They also maintained the relics of the Senate's earlier era: they kept the spittoons out of the walkways and made sure the snuff boxes were full, even though Ben had never once seen any senator actually take snuff the entire time he had been in Washington.

The parliamentarian and her assistant stood at the ready in the rear of the chamber, both clutching their copies of Robert's Rules of Order. If this debate went like most that were considered of great import, or were likely to be televised, they would be busy. The clerk of the Senate and the sergeant at arms were chatting; although the sergeant's functions were largely ceremonial, with this many people in a single room, who knew what might happen? The galleries were already filled to capacity, and Ben knew twice as many people had been denied seating. Usually, the gallery at best was half filled with tourists—it was harder to get a ticket in the post-9/11 era—but today it was filled with lobbyists, senate staffers, spouses, and others with a serious interest in the day's debate.

The press well was equally full, and was perhaps the only incongruous element, the only section of the chamber that was significantly different from what Ben might have seen in 1820. By agreement, a single camera—the C-SPAN camera—would provide its feed to all other networks that wanted it. Ben suspected the major networks would be monitoring ratings very carefully. So long as people were watching, they would preempt regular daytime programming, but as soon as the audience waned, it was back to *All My Children*. Newspaper reporters were armed with notepads and tape recorders. Ben also spotted the current CBS anchorwoman; presumably she was going to provide live updates from outside the chamber.

The floor of the chamber was dotted with various groups of senators exchanging the amiable chatter that Ben had learned could often contain significant hidden depths. The favor swaps that were necessary to get anything passed were often described in the vaguest friendliest terms; clerks and staff members would later hammer out the details. In this case, the proposed amendment would actually require a two-thirds majority, much stiffer than the usual fifty-one votes needed to make a law. No one was sure whether it could command that much support.

"Shouldn't you be out there . . . talking to someone?"

As if she had appeared by magic, Ben found Tracy Sobel just beside him.

"Did you have someone in mind?"

"I could make some suggestions. You are supposed to be the president's man on the spot. You should be trying to convert votes."

"I thought that was the purpose of the debate."

"Oh, please." Sobel rolled her eyes. "As if anyone listens to that, other than the obsessive-compulsives who watch C-SPAN all day long. You need to make some deals. Offer up some pork barrel."

"I don't have any pork barrel to offer."

"You're in tight with the president. You should be able to get anything you want passed. At least," she added ruefully, "anything that only requires a simple majority."

"I'm handling the debate. My chief of staff handles the wheeling and dealing."

"And she's done an admirable job. Women are always better at getting to what really matters. Men excel more at the stuff that's just for show." Sobel drilled a finger into the soft part of his shoulder. "Don't let us down. Get this thing passed."

"I intend to."

"Good. I'll be watching."

Ben supposed, as he watched her walk briskly to some other senator she could harass, that she didn't really mean that as a threat. But being a person who had recently received a poisoned envelope, he found her exit remark more than a little creepy.

Ben took his desk at the rear of his party's side. Thanks to the recent deaths and subsequent gubernatorial appointments—hastily made so every state would be fully represented in this important debate—Ben was no longer the junior Democratic senator. The senator replacing Robert Hammond now had that honor. Ben had barely met the new Oklahoma senator—Jerome Collins, a black doctor who had served in the state senate—but he was a Republican sitting in the low-ranked desk on the opposite side, and had made it public even before he was appointed that he supported the amendment.

Out of the corner of his eye, Ben saw the sergeant at arms clear a path. He did not announce the arrival of the vice-president, as he did the president on his rare visits, but he did ensure that the man and his security detail could enter unmolested. The vice-president was also the president of the Senate. He didn't attend all that much, but he was sure to be there today to manage the debate. Since a two-thirds majority was required to pass the amendment, his tie-breaking power probably would not be of any use. Erwin Matthews, the vice-president, had already announced that he would retire rather than run for reelection with the president, so he was in effect a lame duck. This could well be his last important duty, and the one best remembered. Ben could only wonder what effect that would have on his performance.

Ben watched as Vice-President Matthews banged his gavel and called the Senate into session. "Reverend Maplewaite, would you please deliver the invocation?"

The chaplain-of-the-day was appointed by the senators on a rotating basis. Normally, the chaplain delivered the prayer to a near-empty room, since only those senators who had to be present would be present on a typical day; the rest would wait in their offices until they heard the twice-ringing bell that told them of a quorum call or vote. Today's chaplain, however, would not only get to deliver his invocation to the full Senate but to a large television audience as well.

"Blessed Father, as we embark upon this new era in the history of this country, let us remember the words of guidance you have given us to measure our actions and temper our impulses. Let us be inspired by . . ."

Like most chaplains, Reverend Maplewaite kept his prayer largely nondenominational, but it was still a prayer. Schoolchildren couldn't pray, but the Senate could, every day. Despite the obvious implications regarding the First Amendment requirement of separation of church and state, every session of the Senate had opened with a prayer, and Ben suspected that every session would continue to open with a prayer for a long while into the future. It might be unconstitutional, but the only parties with standing to challenge it would be the senators themselves, and what senator wanted to go on record as opposing a daily invocation?

After the prayer ended, Senator Keyes rose to his feet. "Mr. President," he said grandly, obviously aware that he was on television, "may I suggest the presence of a quorum?"

"You may, Senator."

"Mr. President, I request that by unanimous consent the quorum call and all related proceedings be dispensed with."

Another senator seconded. The vice-president called a voice vote and it passed, no surprise. As far as Ben could see, there was not an empty desk in the chamber.

Senator Bening, another Republican, rose. Ben knew that these plum on-camera appearances had been assigned by agreement beforehand. The vice-president was a Republican and he could choose to recognize whomever he wanted.

"Mr. President, I would request that by unanimous consent the reading of the journal of yesterday's proceedings be dispensed with."

This measure passed with equal ease. Ben had never seen a day when the journal was actually read. There would be no reason to oppose this antiquated parliamentary technicality, except perhaps to delay, and no one was going to do that with so many eyes watching.

Finally, Senator Scolieri addressed the chair. "Mr. President, I move that the Senate proceed without delay to the consideration of the pending business, Calendar Number 1873, Senate bill 1451, a bill to amend the Constitution of these United States."

The recommendation was accepted.

The debate began.

Ben could not help but sense the crackling electricity in the air. He was feeling nervous himself, and he had no intention of speaking until much later in the debate. Perhaps because of the anticipated television audience, perhaps because both proponents and opponents recognized that this was an important piece of legislation, all words were being chosen carefully. Moreover, the barbed remarks and innuendos normally flung at opposition forces were at an all-time low. There was no shuffling of papers or clinking of water glasses; everyone was paying rapt attention to what was being said. Pages were delivering messages like rapid-fire machine guns, but they did it quietly. A few senators were scowling, but most maintained their best expressions, well aware that the camera could skirt to them unannounced at any moment.

"The senator from Colorado," the vice-president recognized, and Senator Bening once again rose.

"Thank you, Mr. President." Bening tugged at his vest, straightening it, then tugged at the gold watch chain that dangled from his vest pocket. "I think everyone present is aware that I support this amendment with the greatest possible enthusiasm. But it is possible that you do not understand exactly why I lend it my support. I would like to take this time to explain my reasoning."

Ben wondered just how long his time would be. Due to the importance of the matter at hand, all time limits had been removed. Moreover, it was anticipated that virtually ever senator would want to speak, if only to make sure there was some footage to be shown in their home states on the evening newscasts. Those two factors alone ensured that the debate would be a lengthy one, taking several days to complete, regardless of how much civility prevailed.

"Of course I've considered the practical aspects, the need to change with the times, to protect our borders, to keep this nation safe from our enemies. I've talked to the people in my home state, in the big city of Denver and small towns like Durango and Silverton, and I hear the same thing over and over again: Tell us our government will do whatever it can to keep us safe, to make sure that a horror like 9/11 or April nineteenth never happens again. I know what the people want. And it's my duty as a senator to give it to them. I want all Americans to go to sleep at night feeling safe. I want them to be able to tuck their children in at nights and tell them that there are no monsters lurking under their beds, that they will be secure until the morning's light."

Ben could see Christina glaring at him from her seat in the rear of the floor. He didn't need a message to know what she was thinking. This was more of what politicians had been working on the American people for too long. The politics of fear. Persuasion through terror.

"Even here in our nation's capital, all the experts I've talked to, from the Pentagon on down, favor this amendment. Certainly everyone in law enforcement does. And so does the leader of this nation, President Blake. I think I take nothing away from this august body when I remind you all that the president himself started this ball rolling, that this is his initiative and given his recent tragic loss—understandably so. Make no mistake—he is a wartime president. It may be an undeclared war, but it is a very real war just the same: the war against terror, the war against violent means to political ends. We are at war, and he is the commander in chief. He is the decider, the man who has to make the choices essential to keeping this nation safe. It is our patriotic duty—the duty of all Americans— to support this bill, in order to form a more perfect union."

Hardly a few seconds had passed before a page delivered a folded written message to Ben. He opened it.

SO WHAT DOES THAT MAKE ME, A COMMUNIST? IS EVERY-ONE WHO OPPOSES THE AMENDMENT A COMMUNIST? ARE THERE 205 COMMUNISTS IN THE STATE DEPARTMENT?

Ben didn't need a signature to know who had written the note.

"Mr. President!" Several senators rose at once. The vice-president scanned the assemblage.

"Mr. President," Bening said, "I have not yielded the floor."

"I realize that," Vice-President Matthews said. "I hope you also realize that many senators want to speak today."

"I would not think that I would have to instruct the president of the Senate on the rules of Senate procedure."

Matthews looked down with narrowed eyes. "I would not suggest the senator from Colorado take it upon himself to instruct the president of the Senate on anything. I would suggest, however, that this might be a very good time for the senator from Colorado to yield the floor."

Ouch. Ben winced, feeling Senator Bening's pain.

Bening's eyes roamed the senate floor till they lighted on a friendly face on his side of the aisle. "I will yield to the junior senator from Montana."

Ben nodded. Another Republican, natch.

"Very well. The floor recognizes Senator Potter."

Potter rose. He was one of the younger senators, tall, dark-haired, athletic. Despite still being in his first term, he had made a splash during the recent Supreme Court nomination. During the process, Ben had learned that, among other things, the man had a conscience and was capable of crossing party lines to do what he thought was right. Even if they disagreed on an issue, Ben had to admire that.

"I want to thank the senator from Colorado for his courtesy," Potter began, "and I want to thank the vice-president for his. I know the job of orchestrating a senate debate is no small chore, especially when passions are as enflamed as they seem to be regarding the matters now at hand. I want to commend the president of the Senate for the firm hand but good heart he has shown today."

Ben wanted to barf, and he was quite certain Christina was already doing so. Simple courtesy to one of the top men in your party was one thing, but this blatant sycophancy seemed over the top, even on a day when the cameras were rolling.

"I want each member of the Senate gathered here today to look into his or her heart and ask themselves the question: What is the real issue before us? Because I think we all know, whether we favor this amendment or we don't, that there is more being debated, more pending before us, than the simple matter of a proposed constitutional amendment. I would suggest, ladies and gentlemen, that we are discussing nothing less than the future of this nation."

He turned slowly, Ben suspected, so the single camera could capture his youthful good looks from the best angle.

"When this nation was still new, some of the earliest Congresses had to determine what course would be taken to defend the country from her enemies. Armies, navies, spies, alliances, moneylending— these were the types of issues our Founding Fathers had to consider when determining how to keep this nation safe. They did not have to deal with ricin poisoning, or snipers, or bombs capable of destroying entire cities. But if they had"—here, he extended his hand in the patented Clintonesque thumb and forefinger gesture that was not quite pointing, because pointing was too in-your-face—"I feel certain that they would have met the challenge. And just as they did not hesitate to draft the Constitution in such a manner as to keep all Americans safe, so they would not have hesitated to amend it when it was necessary in a technologically advanced society to ensure that those selfsame Americans would remain safe."

There was some stirring in the gallery, some whispering on the floor. These were not new arguments, but Potter was delivering them with vigor and persuasive charm. Ben could imagine what the whispering was about. He would not be surprised if Potter's name were floated as a possible running mate to replace Vice-President Matthews. Perhaps, in four more years, he might be ready for a presidential run himself.

"I am particularly moved by Senator Bening's reminder that we are a nation at war, at war against the insidious enemies of freedom that use terrorism to gain an unholy advantage. We all know that special measures have to be taken in wartime, and this amendment is in total conformity with that tradition. But I will remind the Senate that any emergency state declared pursuant to this amendment is a temporary condition enacted only so long as it is absolutely necessary to keep this nation secure. I think most Americans will agree that this is a rather small price to pay to ensure that the fundamental liberty of this nation is maintained. A vote for this bill is a vote for a free America—the kind of America we want our children to grow up in, a landscape unscarred by the destruction and pain of terror."

Presumably in the effort to maintain some semblance of fairness, the vice-president next recognized a Democratic senator, Byron Perkins of Arkansas.

Perkins was angry, or perhaps more accurately, Ben mused, had decided that the angry young man image was one that might score well on television.

"First of all, I want to say that I am disheartened and dismayed by the blatant attempts of the distinguished senators from Colorado and Montana to ramrod this amendment through the Senate by evoking fear rather than intelligence. They deplore the fear-inducing tactics of terrorists, but are effectively trying to instill terror themselves. Their approach may be less violent, but it is in spirit identical to that practiced by the maniacs and sadists behind April nineteenth."

At least a dozen senators rose, most from the other side of the aisle. "Mr. President!"

The vice-president looked down. "Will the senator from Arkansas yield?"

"I will not!" Perkins replied. "I have barely begun."

"Then would the good senator from Arkansas at least care to observe the standard rules of decorum and courtesy that have been honored by this legislative body since it began?" This came from the elderly senator from New Hampshire, Emerson Thomas. He had not been recognized by the chair, but he was so old no one was likely to slap him down.

Perkins was not cowed. "I am offended by the suggestion that I have done anything inappropriate, or even out of conformity with the standard procedure of Senate debate."

"In the Senate, sir," Thomas cackled, "we can disagree without being disagreeable."

The vice-president intervened. "Gentlemen, let me say that I think we are very likely going to be discussing this matter for some time. Passions are high and fevers are hot. This is a controversial matter, so regardless of what you think might be the standard procedure of the Senate, I would like to ask every senator to make an extra effort to maintain civility and respect for one another at all times. Please refrain from invective and personal attacks. We don't always have to agree with each other—but we do have to live with each other." He took a breath, and with what appeared to be some regret, added, "Senator Perkins, you may continue."

He did. "I agree with the chair's remarks," he said, although, Ben thought, you couldn't tell it from what he was saying before. "But I will not yield and I will not be silenced by the climate of fear being created by those who support this bill. I am sure that if we were not already on Red Alert, they would have put us there today. . . ."

Ben was distracted by another page silently dropping a note onto his desk as she passed by. He opened it.

He was invited to a nearby conference room by the leader of the opposition to the proposed amendment.

According to the note, he wanted to make a deal.

48

The problem with having a torrid passionate affair with a danger addict, Jason mused, as he staggered off the side of the bed, disoriented and practically limping, was that eventually you would run out of ways to simulate danger. Eventually she would want the real thing. She would need the real thing to get off. And even though Jason was happy enough to send Belinda into multi-orgasmic paradise to the best of his ability, this was not a time when he was willing to court real danger.

Tonight's sexcapade had been successful, but he had gone about as far with her as it was possible to go without leaving a mark. Belinda was still being interviewed by reporters and police officers. He couldn't afford to do anything that would create suspicion. He shouldn't be here at all, really, but given a choice between taking that risk and finding out what would happen if Belinda didn't get her sexual jollies, he had decided a surreptitious romp in the hay was the best course. Her suggestions that they "do it in the road" or some similar public place, however, just weren't going to happen.

She was insatiable. He knew she would be back in an hour or so, ready to go at it again. The woman must be part rabbit, for God's sake. He'd heard of women reaching a sexual awakening, but this was ridiculous. How was he going to keep the excitement level at the fever pitch she needed to get off? He was running out of ideas.

He decided to comb through the garage. Some sort of bizarre garden apparatus might be just the thing to stimulate that oh-so-familiar squeal of passion. . . .

Rakes, hoes, snow shovels? No, somehow he just couldn't see it. Trowels, shovels, spades—ugh. This place was a pit. Obviously, Belinda never came out here. Not that he blamed her. He had never been much for home gardening. Why waste life doing something you could pay a grateful teenager to do for you?

The garden hose. What would he do with it? Tie her up with it? Splash her down with it? Both at the same time?

Underneath a workbench, he found a metal lockbox about the size of a nineteen-inch television. What would the late senator have done with that? The dust told him that it had been untouched for days, so he knew it was nothing Belinda used regularly. Curiosity overcame him. What was the big secret?

There was no way he could open the lock, but it was looped through a fairly thin piece of plastic. Maybe he could sever the whole thing off the box and not have to worry about the lock.

It took a while, but a combination of wire cutters and a very strong wrench enabled him to pry open the box at last.

There were no tools inside. For the most part, it was papers. And photographs. The papers were largely in English, but some were photocopies of documents written in another language.

He picked up one stack of photos. All at once, his jaw dropped. They were obviously surveillance photos, and he knew who the primary subject was, too. How could he not?

Oh my God, Jason thought, his hand to his mouth. How could he ever have guessed—

He pushed himself to his feet, staggering, unsure what to do next.

What had they done? he wondered, as he slammed the lockbox shut.

Good God—what had they done?

49

UNDISCLOSED LOCATION IN GEORGETOWN

The first thing Loving realized, when he regained consciousness, was that his blindness was only temporary. For that he was grateful. But since he was still tied to the chair, and it could only be a matter of moments before the General returned, how long could he expect that to last?

The second thing he realized was that there was a tugging at the tape strapping him to the chair. Someone was cutting him loose.

"Please do not move," the voice behind him said. "The door is open. The General could return at any moment."

"Shohreh!" Loving whispered under his breath.

"Do not move. It is hard to cut your bonds with one arm still in a sling."

"How did you find me?"

"I have been here for some time," she said, still working. He could feel his bonds slowly loosening. "I was waiting for an opportunity to slip inside. This is the first chance they have given me to be alone with you. I was able to persuade Miss Magda to provide a list of all properties held by the General. After giving her a taste of what would happen if she did not." She paused. "I am . . . sorry for what you have had to endure on my account."

"Never mind that. Did you call the police?"

"No."

"What? I told you to call Lieutenant Albertson at—"

"I thought it best that we handle this ourselves."

Loving wanted to argue, but his brain was too muddled, and at the moment, the one thought that was uppermost on his mind was getting out of there before his torturers returned. "How's it comin'?"

"Almost there." Loving felt a final thrust from behind the chair. "Done. You are free."

Loving started to rise. His muscles ached from being bound so long, making it difficult to move. He was cut in about a thousand places and—he suddenly realized—naked. He searched the room for something he could use to cover himself.

"Stop!" she hissed. "They're coming back. Make it seem as though you are still bound."

Loving heard the approaching footsteps on the other side of the doorway. Even though his instinct was to bolt, he returned to the chair he had come to hate so much. Shohreh hid somewhere in the back behind a table.

The General was smiling as he entered. "Ah, you are awake. Perhaps you have had some more thoughts about whether you would like to talk to me?"

Loving quickly sized up the situation. He could burst forth and tackle the General, but Emil was right behind him, holding his gun. There was no way Loving could get to him before a bullet stopped him cold. It would be a suicide run.

"Maybe I'm ready to talk. Whaddaya wanna know?"

The General eyed him suspiciously. He was probably caving too quickly after resisting so long. Unfortunately, it wouldn't take long for the General to realize that he was no longer tied to the chair. Especially if he started again with the cattle prod.

"What do you know about my operation?"

"Which? The kiddie sex or the kiddie terrorism?"

The General pursed his lips. "Whichever brought you to me."

While Loving considered his answer, he saw Shohreh emerging from the shadows. Somehow, she had made her way to the front of the room, near the door. She seemed able to move without making the slightest sound. She was inching toward Emil, as if she thought she might attack him from behind. Seemed foolhardy to him, when Emil had a gun and she had an arm in a sling. But there was no way he could stop her without exposing them both. The best he could do was buy her some time.

"I was lookin' for the terrorists behind Oklahoma City."

"And you think that was my group?"

"I think you played a part. But your operation is much too po-dunk to have done it alone. You needed help. Inside information."

"And where do you think I obtained this information?"

In fact, Loving had an idea, but he wasn't going to tell him that. "I dunno. I was tryin' to find out when I lucked into your little sex slave house. And that's really all I know."

"And who have you told about this?"

"No one. I never had a chance." Shohreh was very close now, just behind Emil. He had to hand it to her—she knew how to move quietly. "Didn't report in to the senator, didn't call the police. No one knows."

The General folded his hands. "I believe you. Now then. Was that so hard? If you had only told me this sooner you could have spared yourself much misery."

"Yeah. But now you're gonna kill me."

"True. But that was an inevitability the moment you entered my house. The pain you have experienced here was not. Emil?"

Loving watched as Emil raised his weapon and carefully pointed it at Loving's face. He knew he couldn't escape.

Shohreh, if you are going to do something, this would be a good time. . . .

He had expected that at best she might try to wrestle the gun away from him, giving Loving time to get into the fight. Instead, she seemed to fly forward, lifting off one knee and switching to the other in midair, kicking the gun out of his hands.

The General whirled around and started toward her. That was

Loving's cue. He burst out of the chair that had held him so long. His entire body ached, but he put that out of his mind so he could do what he needed to do. What he wanted to do. He grabbed the General in a neck hold, twisting his head sideways. The General tried to resist, but Loving had him in a lock.

Emil stopped, unsure whether to save the General or fight Shohreh.

Loving looked up at her. "Can you keep Emil busy for a moment or two?"

"Quite easily."

"Good. I'd like a moment alone with the General."

"Do not be foolish," Emil said, holding his hands between him and Shohreh. "I have talked to Mikhail. I know you are trained in the art of Muay Thai. That will not help you. I have fought the most skilled—"

He didn't get any further. Shohreh silenced him with a swift kick to the jaw.

Loving almost smiled. And this was the woman he'd told to wait outside so she didn't get hurt. *Sheesh.*

Loving held the General's head tightly between his hands. He forced the little man backward, towering over him, pushing him against a wall. He bashed his head back hard.

The General's eyes seemed to roll about in his head. He was obviously more accustomed to dishing out pain than taking it.

"Do you remember what I said?" Loving growled, leaning into the man's face. "What I said I'd do if I ever got loose."

"Yes," the General said. His left eye was twitching. "But I do not believe it. I do not think you are a killer."

Loving could feel the damaged teeth in his sore mouth clenching tightly together. "You—hurt me. You took away my dignity. I—thought I could take anything, but"—his hands pressed tighter together against the man's head—"I think you deserve to die."

The General seemed to deflate, to grow smaller right before Loving's eyes.

"Go ahead, American. You come from a nation of murderers. What's another death to you?"

"You cut me! You hit me with that prod again and again."

Loving gasped for air. "You've ruined the lives of countless children. You should be destroyed. For the sake of humanity."

"Then do it!" the General shouted. "Do it!"

Loving took a step back, slowly bringing his respiration under control. "But you're right, damn it. I'm not a killer. And I won't become one for a sick bastard like you." With a single powerful thrust, Loving slammed the General's head against the wall again. His knees gave. He crumbled to the floor.

Turning, Loving saw that Shohreh had thoroughly dispatched Emil—and recovered his gun.

She was pointing it right at him.

"Hey now—what's this about?"

"Move away," Shohreh said evenly.

"Move? But—" Loving glanced at the General's crumpled body. He was barely conscious. "Wait a minute. What are you thinkin'?"

"The same thing you just said. He deserves to die."

"Yeah, but that doesn't mean—"

"Move away!"

"Shohreh!"

"I don't want to hurt you, Loving. You have done so much for me!" Her voice lowered. "But I will, if I have to. To get to him. Now move away."

"And if I don't?"

"Then I will be forced to kill you."

No wonder she wouldn't call the police. One look into her eyes told Loving she meant what she said. Reluctantly, he stepped aside.

Shohreh crept down beside the addled General. She took his collar in one hand and pressed the gun against his face. "Do you know who I am?" she shouted.

The General's eyelids fluttered. "Little Djamila."

Loving did a double take. "What? *You're* Djamila?"

Shohreh's eyes became glassy, as if focused on some distant point. "That was my birth name. Back in Iraq. Before the war. After my parents were killed, I was lost, alone. I tried to survive, but the chaos was too great. I—" Her fingers tightened around the General's throat. "This man said he would protect me. Care for me."

"I did!" the General protested. "I fed you, clothed you. Without me, you might have died."

"I did die. You killed me. Djamila died a thousand times over at the hands of your filthy customers!" Tears sprang unbidden to her eyes. "When I was too old to be of service to his clients anymore," she told Loving, "he allowed me to join his cell of assassins. Finally I found the strength to leave him, but even then he lured me back to Oklahoma City. After that last betrayal, I knew there could never be peace for me. Not so long as he remained alive."

"Shohreh," Loving said, inching closer. "Think about this. You don't want to be a murderer."

Her eyes were cold black dots. "I do."

"Then you'll be no better than him."

"I would never do the things he has done to me. And hundreds of other children."

If he could just get close enough to get that gun away . . . "Shohreh, you're making a mistake."

"Perhaps, but there is no choice." She pulled back the hammer. "This is for Djamila."

"No!" Loving sprang forward, but he was much too late. The bullet burst into the General's face point-blank. The wall was splattered with blood and brains.

Shohreh stepped away, dripping. "I will go with you," she said, handing Loving the gun. "To the police. Whatever you think should be done."

Loving took the gun and carefully emptied it. "You know that you'll go to prison. Maybe for the rest of your life."

Shohreh nodded slowly. Then, at last, her eyes turned back to the dead and motionless figure of the man who had tormented her for so long. "It was worth it."

50

SENATE CONFERENCE ROOM-D12

Ben couldn't help feeling guilty about leaving the Senate chamber in the midst of the heated debate, but the truth was, it was likely to go on for days, and the flaming oratory taking place was not going to persuade anyone of anything, nor was it intended to do so. The senators were taking advantage of the television coverage to explain themselves and to shore up their support with their key constituencies. Viewed from that perspective, the speeches were little more than free political ads, and on those rare occasions when Ben was able to watch television, he habitually skipped the commercials.

One political truth had become apparent to him in his short time in Washington: If there was any persuasion occurring among senators, it did not take place on the Senate floor. It happened in the proverbial smoke-filled rooms, where private deals were done. Any persuasion came not as a result of flaming oratory but pursuant to standard quid pro quo; you give me something I want and I'll give you something you want. And we both go home happy. A little.

The conference room to which the folded note had directed him was not filled with smoke, but he knew the principle was the same. Smoking was supposedly forbidden in the Senate complex now, although Ben knew that in reality it occurred fairly frequently behind closed doors. He hoped his visitors didn't indulge; he still couldn't be around cigarette smoke for more than a minute without gagging.

A few minutes later, the door opened and Senator Dawkins entered, trailed by the new minority whip, Senator Pollitt of Pennsylvania. They took a seat on the opposite side of the conference room table.

"Here we are again, Ben," Dawkins said, smiling faintly. Dawkins had been on the Senate Judiciary Committee when Ben represented Judge Roush during his Supreme Court confirmation hearings. Dawkins had been bitterly opposed to Roush's nomination. To say that there was no love lost between the two was an understatement in the extreme. Ben wondered if the lingering tension between them was the reason he had been chosen by the powers that be for this meeting.

"Our fearless leader couldn't make it," Dawkins explained. "He's going to be speaking soon. Doesn't want to miss his turn. He gave me full authority to deal."

"That's swell," Ben said cheerily. "Shouldn't we get the new majority leader in here?"

"Why bother? Everyone knows you're the one in charge on this bill, even if you are supposedly a Democrat. You're the president's hand-picked playmate."

"I wouldn't put it quite like that."

"The truth hurts, huh? And to think people were concerned that you would prove too liberal for the modern Democratic party."

"I follow my conscience, not my party. The president and I just happen to agree on this proposal."

"Right. You're a man of conscience." He gave Pollitt a knowing look. "Hard to imagine anything that could be more trouble in Washington than a man of conscience."

Ben had heard this trite line of reasoning so many times, it was hard to resist the urge to drum his fingers. "I assume you're authorized to make some sort of deal?"

"Well, now, that's very direct, isn't it? No monkeying around for you."

"I have a busy schedule."

"Ah. As opposed to the rest of us slackers." He gave his companion the nod. "Read him the formal proposal, Dan."

Pollitt looked down at his notes. "We're willing to trade SB-4582 and SB-4888 for the proposed amendment."

Dawkins's eyebrows danced. "What do you think, Ben?"

"I think I have no idea what you're talking about."

"We're offering to support the amendment in exchange for your withdrawal of support on two other matters. That would include the support of any senators who have made pledges to you with regard to those bills."

"And I'm supposed to recognize the bills by their numbers?"

"Most of us do." He paused a moment. "But you rely rather heavily upon your chief of staff, don't you? Let me spell it out for you." Dawkins leaned forward, laying his hands flat on the tabletop. "We'll throw our support behind your amendment—a guaranteed twelve votes you don't have yet—in exchange for your dropping these two other bills."

"I can't believe your magic twelve will go against public opinion on such a high-profile issue. Every poll has shown that a majority of the general public wants this bill."

"That may be so, but the twelve senators I have in mind come from very liberal jurisdictions. They aren't going to suffer any damage from failing to support a Republican president's initiative that appears to abridge civil rights."

"The amendment only creates a temporary—"

"Yes, yes, I've already heard your song and dance, thank you. Note the use of the word 'appears.' The point is, they are free to vote as they like. You now have an opportunity to determine what they're going to like."

Ben sighed wearily. He hated politics. And he didn't mean that in a general, abstract way, either. He hated politics. "What two bills do I have to kill? Don't make it the Alaskan Wilderness Bill. My wife has been working on that for months. My support is nonnegotiable."

"We're aware of that." Dawkins nodded at Pollitt.

Pollitt cleared his throat. "We want you and yours to drop your support for the antipoverty bill and the education initiative."

Ben's eyes fairly bulged. "Are you kidding? Those are the two most important bills pending, other than the amendment."

"We're aware of that, too."

"I've been an outspoken proponent of both. Christina has been working the floor to accumulate pledges of support for both."

"Still aware."

"Are you saying you don't favor education and favor starvation?"

"These are difficult, changing times. It might've been different when Senator Hammond was still minority leader—he knew how to assemble an alliance and collect pledges and get things passed. But we don't have him now. We have an all-new slate of leaders with much less experience, little political capital, and no one owing them anything. We don't know that we could get those bills passed. And even if we could, the simple fact is, Ben—we can't afford all three."

"I don't follow."

"We can't afford it. Not politically or financially."

"I don't think the expenses relating to the amendment are all that great—"

"But the expenses relating to the war on poverty are enormous. We finally managed to scale back welfare not that long ago and to restore some sense to the budget. This looks too much like a reversal."

"Tell that to the people in the South who can't feed their children."

"I wouldn't bother. They don't vote."

"They're still Americans."

"Thank you for that helpful clarification." He sighed wearily. "The truth is, we can't represent all four hundred million Americans. It's not shameful to suggest that our primary efforts should be devoted to those who actually contribute to the nation's betterment."

Ben could see this was going nowhere. "I thought the goal of having more people contribute was the reason we want to improve the American education system. Oh, wait—you want to kill that bill, too."

"Throwing money at schools isn't going to make anything better."

"Why don't we try it and find out?"

"Because we can't afford it. And this bill looks too much like No Child Left Behind—a Republican effort, if you'll recall. And one that resulted in little discernible improvement in the American education system."

"So we should just abandon the schools? No! We should try again."

"Ben, there are a lot of things out there I'd like to fix, but the reality is, even if we knew how—which we don't—we can't afford to do everything at once. We are still carrying the debt of the Iraq War and are likely to be doing so for a good long time. Given our financial limitations, it's better to abandon what we can't afford or can't guarantee we can pass. Better to have one successful initiative and two that don't come to a vote than three initiatives that fail, which is what we're looking at right now."

"That's a cold viewpoint."

"Every senator has to learn to prioritize. Comes with the job. You will, too, in time. Unfortunately, right now you've somehow managed to acquire a measure of power that far outstrips your senatorial experience, so I'm having to explain these fundamental principles I would never have to explain to a more seasoned senator."

"If this is supposed to win me over, it isn't working."

"Look, Ben, in the subcommittee hearing, you said this proposed amendment is the most important matter before us as a nation. Did you believe that, or were you just foaming at the mouth for the television cameras?"

Ben did his best to suppress his irritation. "I meant it."

"Fine. So prioritize. Make a deal. Guarantee the passage of this amendment by forfeiting two other probably unpassable bills."

Put that way, Ben had to admit that what he said made a certain amount of sense. He hated this business of trading one law for another—it wasn't the way government was supposed to work. But he also knew that without those twelve votes Dawkins controlled, he would never get this amendment out of the Senate.

"What do you say, Ben? Do we have a deal?"

"I . . . I don't know," Ben hedged. "I need some time to think about it."

"We don't have time, Ben. This thing will come up for a vote in a few days. We have to give our people their walking orders."

"I don't care. This is important. I want a chance to think. Talk it over with Christina."

"Who's wearing the senatorial pants in this family, Ben? You or your wife?"

Ben tried not to let such an obvious ploy get to him—but it was hard. "There's nothing wrong with seeking the opinion of people you trust. Only an idiot thinks he's so smart he can't benefit from input from others."

"Ben—are you having doubts about this constitutional amendment?"

Ben felt his question like a stabbing pain in his gut. Had he betrayed himself with a word, a facial expression? Why would he ask that?

"I . . . don't have any doubts. I'm behind this bill one hundred and ten percent."

"Then do what you need to do to ensure its passage."

"I told you already. I want more time."

"Can I at least tell the twelve that you're tentatively accepting the offer? They need to know how they're going to vote. Just in case someone asks. Or their turn to speak comes up."

"I already told you—"

"Come on, Ben—give the poor boys something."

"I . . . guess . . . if you made it clear my acceptance was tentative . . ."

"Good!" Dawkins slammed his hand on the table. "That's what I wanted to hear. I'll talk to all the people in charge. They'll be very glad to hear that you've made the right decision."

"But—I haven't—"

"You're doing the right thing, Ben. I promise. You are. I mean, personally, I don't care that much for the amendment. But the people want it, and sometimes you can tell when a law's time has come. The new majority leader is giving me a nice piece of pork barrel for my home state. It's worth it."

"You mean—you don't even—"

"So bottom line, everyone gets what they want. Or what they need. This is a win-win scenario, Ben. It really is." He rose and shook Ben's hand vigorously, then ran to the door, Pollitt following close behind.

When the door was opened, Ben saw Christina in the corridor outside. She saw him, too.

"Ben—there you are! I didn't know what happened to you."

"I, uh, had to take a meeting. I—"

"Never mind. You can tell me later. I just got a message from the hospital about Mike."

Ben felt a hollow sensation in the center of his chest. "And?"

"He's awake, Ben. And stable. He's going to make it."

Ben felt such a rush of emotion he could barely speak. "Really?"

Christina hugged him tightly. "It's true. And Ben—he's asking for you."

"Really?"

"Yeah. I've already booked you a flight. Jones will take you to the airport."

"But—the debate—"

"Will go on for days. It'll survive without you for a little while." She gripped his shoulders tightly. "Ben—Mike wants to see you."

He didn't hesitate a moment longer. "I'm on my way."

51

The top figures in the entire domestic security force were sitting together under one roof in the Oval Office, a gathering that would normally violate emergency procedure protocols. In this instance, however, President Blake felt it was necessary. As a compromise to the concerns about a "catastrophic event," he allowed the FBI director to send Joel Salter in his stead. On the two facing sofas were Homeland Security Director Carl Lehman and his assistant Nichole Muldoon, and two selected members of his Secret Service detail, Max Zimmer and Tom Gatwick.

They did not sit on the same sofa.

President Blake leaned against the front of his desk, which had the effect of locating him at the apex of the pyramid, its vertical walls formed by the two sofas and the four men and one woman located upon them.

"I have to do it," the president said. "It's nonnegotiable."

"It's suicide, is what it is," Salter said. He was as nervous and twitchy as ever, the president noted, and being seated next to Nichole Muldoon seemed to be causing him some considerable trauma. "The FBI votes no."

"This is not subject to a vote," the president said firmly. "I'm going to do it. I've called you here so you can figure out how you're going to keep me safe."

"I don't understand why this appearance is so essential."

"You don't have to understand. It's not your job."

"All my sources tell me the amendment will get through Congress and then be readily approved by the states. This is unnecessary. It's like you're daring the original killers—who I might remind you are still at large—to try again."

"I said, this is nonnegotiable."

"I mean, if your strategy is to get this amendment passed by martyring yourself, I could understand that. But I think it's a poor strategy."

The president almost smiled. Maybe Salter had more spunk than he realized. "Carl. Your thoughts?"

"Well, we're not nearly as skittish as the FBI, but what else is new?"

Salter was seething now. *Good. Let him redirect his anger at someone else.*

"Which is not to say we think it's a good idea," Lehman continued. "But if you're determined to do it, we'll keep you safe."

"But we'd still prefer you didn't do it," Muldoon interjected hastily. Did she always dress like that? the president wondered. He could see why she had come so far so fast. "Better safe than sorry."

"Pardon my subordinate," Lehman said, stimulating the irked ire of Muldoon. "We wouldn't presume to tell the president what he should or should not do."

"I'm glad to hear that," President Blake said. He was enjoying this exchange. It had been a good idea, despite what his advisors thought, to gather all these people together at once. Sped things up considerably. And he also gained substantial insight into the players by watching them interact with one another. "Have you prepared any plans?"

"My boys have," Lehman replied. "Tom?"

"Wait," the president interjected. "These two? Zimmer and Gatwick?"

"They're the senior members of your security detail, Mr. President."

Gatwick sat on the sofa, silently reminding the president how he had resisted the suggestion that he resign. *What the hell. I'll be working double-time to prove myself now.* "Are you two going to be able to work together?"

After a moment's hesitation, they both simultaneously said, "Yes, sir."

"Seriously. I know what's been going down between you two. And I know you were both on duty on April nineteenth. Are you going to be able to do this job?"

"Absolutely," Gatwick said, evidencing not the slightest trace of doubt, much less disdain for his colleague. "We've taken the liberty of drawing up a full-scale security plan. Would you like to hear about it?"

"Of course."

"We call this Domino Charlie. It's a variation on Domino Bravo—but we think we've improved the old protocol in many respects. Our security team will arrive in Baltimore long before you get there to plan and make sure you're secure. We've chosen a site with no rooftop access that could be used by snipers. We're going to put you in a thirty-one-car motorcade. That will include local police escorts, a car for your personal physician, a communications van, a disguised ambulance, and a SWAT truck bearing a full-scale counterassault team. Just let them try to start shooting like they did in Oklahoma City. First second these guys hear a gunshot, the shooter will be a dead man."

"How can you be sure of that?" Salter asked, obviously skeptical.

"The communications array will be scanning the area constantly. Its sensors are trained to immediately track any gunshot to its source. We'll radio the information to the SWAT team, who will be equipped with long-range laser-tracking rifles. Plus the men are all crack shots. Like I said, even assuming a killer could somehow penetrate our defense perimeter, which is impossible, a shooter could get off one shot at best. Then he's dead. Period."

"Well, I like the sound of that," the president said dryly.

"We will have three Cadillacs just like yours. The decoys will carry additional Secret Service agents to the site. Yours will also be full of agents, so the three will be indistinguishable to potential snipers. All roads from the airport to the speaking site will be cleared and sealed off, well in advance of your arrival."

"How many men are involved in this operation?" Muldoon asked, an eyebrow raised.

"Enough," Gatwick said curtly. Apparently Muldoon didn't scare him, the president noted, and he knew he didn't have to take any grief from a deputy director. "Max, why don't you tell the president what happens when he arrives?"

"Sure." Zimmer scooted forward on the sofa. He was doing his best to make it appear that there were no conflicts between him and his fellow agent. But they both knew better, didn't they? "Once The Beast arrives at the speaking site, it will park at a predetermined location that has completely unblocked exit points. In fact, we have secured three such points, and the decision as to which one you will actually park at will not be made until minutes before your arrival, so even if—" He broke off. "Just in case."

Nice one. But the president knew well what he meant to say. So even if there is a security leak, and even if it turns out to be from within the Secret Service, no one can reveal the debarkation point much in advance—because it simply will not have been chosen yet.

"You will enter stage left and leave the same way. More than a dozen agents will be discreetly deployed but nonetheless able to reach you in under two seconds. Your physician will also be close by. The podium you speak from—the Blue Goose—is both bulletproof and bomb resistant. Countersnipers will be concealed in the nearby treetops. The kill zone—pardon the expression, sir—will be scrupulously covered at all times. The crowd will be searched and forced to pass through metal detectors. Psych experts will scan the crowd using closed-circuit monitors, watching for any indicators of possible trouble. Aberrant or suspicious behavior. Faces will be scanned and run through the FBI database." He took a deep breath. "Let me assure you, Mr. President, that we are taking every possible precaution and then some. There will not be a repeat of April nineteenth. It simply will not be possible."

The president nodded. "How will you secure the receiving line?"

Zimmer and Gatwick exchanged a glance. "No receiving line, sir."

"What? I've got to shake some hands. It's what I do."

"Not this time, sir."

"If I left it to you people, I'd never shake anyone's hand."

"True enough, sir. But on this occasion, so soon after the previous attack, and with the nation feeling vulnerable—it's out of the question."

The president frowned. "I don't like it." Pause. "But I suppose I can live with it."

He could immediately see the relief on the Secret Service faces. He knew they wouldn't allow it, but he wanted them to sweat a little, just the same. Wouldn't do for the Secret Service to get the idea they could tell the president what to do. Even though they pretty much could.

"Let me just say again," Salter interjected, "that I find this whole plan unduly risky. Doesn't matter what these people do. There's always a chance that a determined killer might slip through the cracks."

"Now you're just being paranoid," Lehman said, shaking his head. "Get a testosterone injection already."

"This isn't about showing who can be the cockiest badass in the federal government," Salter said. "It's about protecting the President of the United States. Sir, I ask you again. Please. Don't do this."

"For once, I actually agree with Agent Salter," Muldoon said. "Perhaps this would be best postponed to a calmer time."

"Not an option," the president replied. "My advisors don't share your confidence regarding the passage of this amendment in the Senate. I have to get out there and stump. Stir up enough public support that those congressional toadies can't say no to me. Understand? So work together, people, and make it safe. We're going to do this. Let's make sure we do it right."

He hoped he had been firm enough. He knew they thought this was a crazy, dangerous scheme. Didn't matter. He had to do it. He saw everything so much more clearly now. This would be his legacy, what he would be remembered for. The Emily Amendment, that's what future generations would call it. It would become his greatest achievement and his wife's living memorial.

Emily would like that. Wouldn't she?

Maybe he had failed her on April 19, maybe he had failed her even before that as a husband, but now, finally, he could give her what she deserved. And if that meant taking a few risks—

So be it. Emily had never been afraid to take risks, even some that broke his heart. But she was fearless. He would follow her example. He would get this amendment passed. And God help anyone who tried to stand in his way.

52

"Mike!"

Ben rushed into the hospital room, still dragging his carry-on luggage. Kate Baxter was seated beyond the bed, close at hand. Mike was awake—awake and sitting upright, looking healthier than he had since the shooting incident, and sturdier—and seriously pissed.

"My God! It's good to see you. I was so afraid—" Ben rushed forward, arms extended for a hug.

Mike held up his hands. "Please. No chick-flick moments."

Ben pulled back, grinning. "I'm glad to see the concussion had no effect on your prickly personality."

"You might be surprised. Look who's here, Kate," he added. "It's our distinguished senator."

"I guess he needs your vote," Baxter said wryly.

"Well, he ain't gonna get it."

Ben took a tentative step closer. "I came as soon as I heard you were awake. How do you feel?"

"Terrible. But not bad for a guy who got thrown twelve feet by a car bomb. This IV is pumping something yummy into my bloodstream, and that helps. How are you doing?"

Ben's head tilted to one side. "I—feel fine."

"No, I was inquiring more as to the state of your mental health."

"I . . . don't think I quite follow you."

Mike looked at him levelly. "What I'm trying to ask in the nicest possible way is: Have you totally lost your goddamn mind?"

Ben felt as if a shock wave had slammed him up against the wall. "Mike . . . I know you're probably a little loopy from the pain medication—"

"I'm not remotely loopy, thank you very much, but you're acting like a crazy person, and you're not even on any medication, as far as I know. Or am I wrong?"

Ben walked to the side of the hospital bed, trying not to show his disappointment. He had been waiting and praying for so long for the moment when he might speak to Mike again. This was a far cry from what he had expected.

"Kate," Mike said abruptly, "would you mind stepping outside for a moment?"

She tucked in her chin. "Oh, I was good enough company when you were unconscious, but now that you're awake and there's another guy around you're throwing me over?"

"I'm not throwing you over. I am, however, preparing to use language unfit for a lady's ears."

"What, you're going to recite poetry?"

Mike almost smiled. "Yeah, lots of it. Possibly even some Shakespeare. You should flee."

"No need to say more. I'm a-fleeing." She stepped past Ben and excused herself.

"Now, then," Mike said, fixing his gaze on Ben with piercing eyes, "perhaps you'd like to explain yourself."

"I don't know what you mean."

"Don't play games with me, Ben. I've talked to Christina. She tells me you're supporting this cockamamy constitutional amendment. In fact, she tells me you're leading the crusade."

"Well . . . yes."

"In fact, she tells me that you caved on an education bill and a bill that might feed starving children in exchange for the passage of this amendment."

"I'm considering it."

"You're considering ignorance and starvation in order to get this fascist wet dream written into the Constitution?"

Ben felt floored. "I—I thought you'd support it, too."

"Excuse me? You thought *I'd* support it?" He stared at Ben incredulously. "Like maybe while I was sleeping I entered an alternate universe and joined the Nazi party?"

"No, but you are a member of the law enforcement community—"

"Which is exactly what equips me to know just how much trouble this law could be. I see every day what can happen when law enforcement has too much power. When the proper checks and balances are not in place. Good God, Ben—you've seen the same thing in the courtroom. What were you thinking?"

Ben pressed his fingers against his forehead. He was confused and disoriented and finding it difficult to speak coherently. "I thought you would approve—"

"After all we've been through together? Ben—have you forgotten what happened in the Kindergarten Killer case once the Feds came to town? Have you forgotten how a tiny cadre of corrupt cops managed to get you tossed into the slammer and accused of murder? And that was under the *current* legal system. Imagine what might happen if this law were passed. The Feds declare an emergency state and suddenly anyone in the FBI or Homeland Security can do anything they want to any American without any possibility of legal review. It's outrageous. It goes against everything the Constitution stands for."

"Well, we have to do something. The terrorists killed the first lady. And three senators. They tried to kill me."

"Or someone did, anyway."

"What's that supposed to mean?"

"It means I've spent most of my time since I woke up reading about this case, and I am unconvinced that there's any link between the death of Senator Hammond and the attacks on Senator DeMouy and you."

"They were all ricin poisonings."

"So what? Ricin is easy to concoct from easily obtained items. Spend ten minutes on the Internet researching it and you can make some, too. That's no justification for this crazy new law. For repealing our basic civil liberties."

"Only on a temporary basis."

"You hope!" Mike tossed back. "But you don't really know, do you? Because once this security council has declared a state of emergency, they can do anything they want. For as long as they want."

"If you assume that every law will be abused, you'll never pass anything."

"When it comes to law enforcement types getting more power, you shouldn't pass anything. You're playing with fire. What were you thinking, Ben?"

He hesitated, still unsure what to say, still stunned by Mike's reaction. "I was thinking that . . . given what happened to you—"

"Stop right there. Don't lay the blame for this pitiful exercise in poor judgment at my feet. I don't want this law. And if you'd thought clearly about it for one moment, you'd have realized that."

"Mike—you were almost killed!"

"And that means I want to repeal the Constitution? I can promise you, I don't."

"April nineteenth was a tragedy. We have to make sure it doesn't happen again."

"I agree. And the way we do that is by taking extra precautions. Working every possible security detail. Maybe even beefing up law enforcement—meaning their resources, not their powers. But you don't make people safe by giving up their most basic rights. What good is being safe if we have no freedom?"

"Most people approved of the Patriot Act—"

"Because 9/11 was so shocking most people couldn't think straight. And Congress was afraid to go up against the president.

Make no mistake, Ben—the current president is manipulating public opinion in exactly the same way, trying to push this through before everyone shakes off their stupidity and realizes what a truly bad idea it is."

"Mike—" Ben wanted to reach out, but he didn't know how. "When I saw you in this hospital bed, not moving, not waking, because you took the time to shove my sorry butt out the door before you saved your own, I—" He shook his head. "I don't know. I had to do something."

"I get that, Ben. I truly do. You thought I was headed for 'the undiscovered country' and you wanted to do something about it."

"I wasn't sure . . . what to do."

"Right. 'And the native hue of resolution is sicklied o'er with the pale cast of thought.'"

"I had to do *something*."

"You want to do me and my colleagues a favor, pass a bill that gets us the money and equipment we need to do our job right and pay public servants in the manner that they deserve. Expand our capabilities—not our power."

"I—I don't know what to say."

"Then don't say anything—to me. Get back on the damn plane and tell the president that he can take his amendment and shove it—"

The phone rang, interrupting him.

"Perhaps that's the president now." Mike picked up the phone. "Close, but no." He held out the receiver. "It's for you. Loving."

"Loving! He hasn't checked in for days." Ben snatched the phone. "Loving? Where are you? What's happening. Why—?"

Ben's voice fell silent. For the better part of the next minute, he just listened.

"Who have I told what? What's that got to do with anything?" Ben didn't begin to comprehend, but he thought a moment and answered the question.

"You're kidding! I don't believe it." Another pause. "Are you sure? My God, that changes everything. And—"

Another pause, this time even longer.

"Loving, are you certain? Because this is very important. The president is making a public appearance tomorrow in Baltimore to drum up support for the amendment. He—"

Ben's eyes widened. "You've got to find out. Get over there as soon as possible. Then call me back." Ben disconnected the line and began dialing again.

"What is it?" Mike asked, his eyebrows knitted. "What's going on?"

"Something . . . very . . . bad," Ben whispered as he dialed the phone.

"Come on. You can give me more than that."

Ben glanced up as he waited for the receiver on the other end to pick up. "If Loving's intelligence is right—and let's face it, it usually is—the April nineteenth killer is a lot closer than we ever imagined. And about to strike again."

53

Jason got out of bed when he heard the noise in the garage. He knew it was probably nothing, but given what he had found out there himself—and had no opportunity to get rid of—he was understandably a little paranoid.

When he entered the garage wearing nothing but a bathrobe, he was startled to find a huge burly man reading through the documents he had discovered. The strongbox was lying on the floor, wide open.

Jason turned to run, but the man grabbed him and threw him on the ground. "I won't hurt you. Just don't get in my way."

Jason stared at him, uncomprehending. "Who the hell are you? What's going on?"

"Name's Loving. I'm conductin' a search."

"Don't you need a warrant or something?"

"I'm not a cop."

"Then you're trespassing."

"Sue me. I think the nutcases behind Oklahoma City are gonna try somethin' else. I wanna stop them." He gave Jason a closer look. "You the chief of staff?"

"Who wants to know? Look, if you don't leave immediately, I'll—"

Loving grabbed him by the neck. "Let me make this short and sweet. I've been tortured, hit, cut, threatened, had an electric cattle prod rattlin' my teeth. You are not gonna intimidate me. I've already found the goods. So why don't you do yourself a favor and tell me what's goin' on?"

"I don't know what you're talking about. Why are you here?"

"Because while I was bein' tortured I found out the man I thought was the head of a terrorist operation had help. On the inside."

"And who was that?"

"I didn't know at first. Then the General started hintin' about his connections to the Senate. Then he quoted one of my boss's favorite jokes, somethin' about God and Abraham Lincoln and the United States of America. I've heard Ben say it before, but I didn't figure he'd said it to this punk sex trafficker. So I called Ben and asked him if he'd repeated it to anyone in the Senate. Guess what? He had. One person. Your boss, the late Senator DeMouy."

"Are you saying—?"

"You know what I'm sayin'. Your boss was the inside man. All this crap proves it." Loving pointed at everything he had found hidden in the garage strongbox—the photos and the papers, the ones that weren't in Arabic. Detailed plans. Names and addresses. Constant references to Homeland Security. The Secret Service. Oklahoma City.

"Oh my God," Jason gasped. "I found this stuff but I never imagined—" He stared off into space, eyes wide. "All those meetings Senator DeMouy took at Homeland Security for undisclosed purposes. Late-night meetings. His calm after the attack on Oklahoma City. His staunch advocacy of the proposed constitutional amendment . . ."

When he heard the noise at the door, Jason almost jumped a foot into the air.

"Jason? Why did you get out of bed? Why are you out here in the cold?"

Belinda was wearing only her panties, standing at the door. When she saw Loving, she covered herself with her hands. "Who the hell are you? What are you doing in my garage?"

"Gettin' the skinny on your late husband."

She stared at the papers and photos on the workbench. "I've never seen any of this before."

"And for a damn good reason."

She took an old tattered towel off a shelf and wrapped it around herself. "I'm tired and I don't know what you're talking about and I think I should call the police."

"Be my guest. I've got what I needed. You've probably heard that the terrorists who attacked in Oklahoma City had an accomplice. An inside man?"

"Y-yes?"

"Well, guess what—you were married to him."

Her mouth opened, then moved wordlessly. "That's—not possible."

"Yup. Your old man was a terrorist sympathizer. Makin' a hell of a lot of money at it, too." He paused. "And in case you're wonderin', I also found the stuff you used to make your homegrown ricin."

Jason and Belinda exchanged a glance. Jason cleared his throat. "I—I don't know what you're talking about."

"Save it for someone who might buy it." Loving threw down the papers and swore under his breath. "Isn't life sweet? All this time I've spent lookin' for this guy. The guy every cop in the United States has been searching for?" Loving smiled sadly. "You killed him."

54

"*. . . a*nd so, good citizens of Baltimore, I will speak to you with the same words my mother gave me many years ago when I was facing the darkest moment of my political career: Extraordinary times call for extraordinary measures. Can any-one doubt that we live in extraordinary times? I think not. I am reminded each and every day, when the Pentagon gives me its briefing on current events, when science and technology seem to reinvent the world every few years. Or when I gaze at the picture I keep on my desk, or the one by my bedside, of my dear lamented Emily, the first lady of this great nation. Emily always wanted the United States to be a strong, secure place to live. And so I urge you—"

Agent Gatwick was talking into his sleeve again. "All clear on the western front?"

"Roger that," Zimmer said, wondering how long it would be before they communicated with little lapel pins, like on *Star Trek*. People at the airport held extended conversations with those little clips on their ears. Why was the Secret Service still talking into their sleeves? "The Scarecrow is safe."

Gatwick grinned a little. After Oklahoma City, Blake needed a new code name, but this one was considerably more accurate than most. He liked it. Just as long as no one started calling him Dorothy. "SWAT teams in position?"

"Ready to go on your order."

"Excellent." Gatwick paced along the rim of the stage, just below where the president was speaking. Even though they were largely invisible, he knew there were agents and soldiers and government snipers all over the arena. Fort Knox couldn't be more secure. "Harold still watching the cameras?"

"Like they were showing *One Life to Live*."

"That's my boy."

"I think I'm going to amble through the crowd. Keep an eye out for anything suspect."

"Works for me. Check in every five or so."

"Will do. Tom—"

"Yeah?"

"We really are going to be okay here, right?"

"We've done everything there is to do."

"You're not exactly answering my question."

"Do your job, Max." His eyes scanned the horizon, the innumerable throng packed into one small place to hear the president speak. "We've done everything there is to do."

"I think we're fine," Nichole Muldoon said, peering through her binoculars. Homeland Security had barricaded a large observation box at the highest point of the amphitheater. They could see almost every nook and cranny of the arena from here, and most of the places they couldn't see directly were covered by closed-circuit cameras. "I mean, how could anyone get past all the security we've got here? Even if an assassin could get in—and I don't think anyone could get in here with a slingshot, much less a rifle—he couldn't get off a shot before our SWAT team converged."

"I hope you're right," Director Lehman said, his lips frozen in a perpetual frown.

"I told the president I was against this."

"And did he listen? No. Too damn worried about his amendment. Damn—I want the thing to pass too, but I don't want anyone to die for it."

"I know you don't, Carl. No one does."

He pressed his fists against each other. "I'm good at this job, Nichole. You know I am."

"I know you are."

"I can protect a president against almost anything. Except his own stupidity."

"Carl, please try to relax. Your pacing is making my skin crawl." She placed a hand gently on his shoulder. "You've done everything it's possible to do. The sniper couldn't possibly get in here. And he'd have to be insane to try."

"Yes," Lehman said, slowly blowing air through his teeth. "Unfortunately—he probably is."

". . . that in generations to come, this historic legislation will be remembered as Emily's Amendment and that she will be remembered as not only a wife but as a patriot, someone who made the ultimate sacrifice to remind us what we always have been and always shall be—strong. Fearless. Ready to face whatever challenge this world throws at us. Therefore, speaking to you as your president, I urge you—call your congresspersons. Call your neighbors. Call everyone you know and tell them that America will be strong again—and you want to be a part of it. Tell them that—"

In the days following the attack, it would be remarked upon repeatedly how fortunate it was that the Blue Goose was bulletproof, because if it had not been, the president would be dead. Despite the enormous security precautions and the literally hundreds of people standing ready to protect him, the president would have been shot and killed but for the protective maze of translucent TelePrompTer screens and a bulletproof podium.

Barely a nanosecond after the shot rang out, eight Secret Service agents piled on top of President Blake. The audience screamed. The outdoor amphitheater, filled to capacity with spectators arranged in concentric circles of seats radiating away from the stage, left little room for maneuvering. Pushing and shoving commenced immediately as panicked spectators desperately tried to get out of the line of fire.

More shots rang out. Amid all the confusion, a horde of dark-jacketed agents moved swiftly through the amphitheater. Another wave of fire blanketed the stage, bringing the first victim to his knees.

"Not again!" the president cried, but his words were smothered beneath the weight of the agents shielding him, trying to pull him upright so they could move him to safety. "Dear God in heaven—not again!"

On the stage, Agent Tom Gatwick left his colleagues once a secure defensive perimeter had been formed around the president. Even though he knew this could make him a target, he was determined to convey as much information as possible from his key vantage point.

"I think he's in the second balustrade, stage right," Gatwick murmured into his sleeve.

"Roger that."

"Either of those turrets could make a suitable sniper's nest. I thought we posted guards."

"Must assume he took them out somehow. Commandeered their weapon."

Which meant it was possible they had lost even more lives. Gatwick didn't allow himself to dwell on the thought. He had to keep his head clear. They might not be able to prevent attacks like this, especially when the president was being so bullheaded. But they could at least make sure that this time they caught the bastard. Or killed him. Personally, Gatwick hoped for the latter.

This one was for Emily. Not the plastic Barbie doll her husband was trying to turn her into up on that stage. The real, vital, flesh-and-blood woman he had come to care so much for. And miss so desperately.

"Dick? Deploy the SWAT teams."

"Already moving into position."

From the stage, Gatwick saw the wave of black fatigues infiltrating the amphitheater. Good. All they needed was to get a bead on the target. Those guys never missed.

"Tom, I'm moving in."

"Zimmer, is that you?"

"Roger. I'm leaving my post. Heading for the balustrade."

"Negative. I repeat, negative. Do not move."

"I'm practically there."

"Zimmer, listen to me. The SWAT team is on their way. Let them take him out."

"They might not arrive in time. This guy knows how to disappear."

"Zimmer—!"

"Look, Tom, last time you changed the protocol. This time, I'm changing it."

"This is completely different!"

"Not to me. We're both trying to do the same thing—make sure this son of a bitch doesn't take any more lives."

"Zimmer—!"

"I'll update you at the first opportunity."

"*Zimmer!*"

Too late. Radio communication was silent.

Stupid kid—what was he trying to prove? But Gatwick already knew the answer to that question. The first lady had been killed while he protected her. Or perhaps he just wanted to prove that the Secret Service was still able to protect the president—and anyone else in their ambit. Zimmer wasn't a hero and he certainly wasn't a martyr. He was doing his job. It was still a mistake—there was no excuse for ignoring protocol or direct orders—but Gatwick couldn't help admiring him a little, just the same.

"Dick, tell your men to watch out for Zimmer. He's making a play for the sniper. He'll get there before they do."

"Understood, Tom. But if he gets in the line of sight—"

"I know. Just—tell them to do their best."

"Roger that."

The instant he stopped talking, Gatwick heard another gunshot. But this one didn't come anywhere near the stage. This bullet ricocheted somewhere off to the right. Near the balustrade.

The sniper had found a new target.

Gatwick just hoped to God it wasn't Special Agent Zimmer.

Zimmer crept up the stairs. Logically, the place to build a sniper's nest would be at the top. But there was nothing typical about this killer so it was best to be careful. One step at a time . . .

He heard a sound and froze. It was a miracle he could hear anything. With the screaming down below, the frenzied rush of the panicked crowd, the buzzing in his communicator that he was pointedly ignoring, there was a blanket of white noise muffling ambient sound and rattling his brain. But he had always had good hearing. He could distinguish all that background clatter from this last sound, something that was coming from somewhere much closer to him.

Just around the bend at the top of the stairs. Barely five feet away.

The sniper could be waiting for him. Zimmer would be entirely vulnerable as he rounded the corner.

He took another tiny step closer. What should he do? The whole point in coming up here was to grab the killer before he had a chance to pull another miraculous escape. He couldn't do that by taking baby steps all the way to the top.

At the same time, he had no desire to die. He admired heroes who had given their lives, but he wasn't ready to join their ranks.

If he didn't want to die, why the hell was he making this suicide plunge?

Easy to answer. Because he had sworn to serve and protect.

Because the Secret Service's reputation had been seriously tarnished by the last attack. He was ready for a little payback, and more important, he was ready to show the world that his department still had what it took.

He was doing it for Emily Blake.

This time they were bringing home the bad guy.

Zimmer stepped closer to the bend in the stairs. Then ever so carefully and silently, he took one more step and prepared to pivot around the bend. . . .

"Turn around!" Nichole Muldoon shouted.

Behind her, Director Lehman frowned. That was as expressive, certainly as visibly worried, as he got. Over the years he'd managed to develop a perfect poker face. Worked well in his line of work.

But he was plenty concerned.

"Can you see him?" Lehman asked.

"I can see his thermal image," Muldoon replied, peering through what might appear to the untrained eye to be a pair of binoculars. She was stationed at the highest point of the amphitheater, where Homeland Security had built its watch post so it could keep an eye on all the proceedings. The suspected sniper's nest was below her and to the right. "And another thermal image creeping up behind him."

"I thought the sniper was at the top."

"So does Zimmer. But if we know anything, it's that this guy knows how to move."

"Maybe it's one of the counterassault team members. SWAT."

"No. I'd pick up their beacon."

"Damn!" Lehman pounded the glass panel that separated them from the rest of the amphitheater. "And you tried calling him?"

"He's turned off his radio. Probably so the killer won't hear him coming."

"This is unacceptable." Lehman's fists clenched. "I'm going in."

Muldoon grabbed his arm. "You can't do that."

Lehman shrugged free. "Watch me."

"You're not a field agent."

"I was." He marched toward an elevator at the side of the room.

"But you're not anymore. You're the director of Homeland Security. You're fifty-three years old! You don't go running into dangerous situations."

"This time, I do. I'm not letting any more of our men be killed."

"Carl, listen to me. I'll call the SWAT leader—"

"I can get there first. This elevator will take me to the base of the stairs. If I run, maybe I can get to the killer before he gets to Agent Zimmer."

"Carl, no. You're too important to this department."

"Sorry, Nichole. I'm doing this."

Muldoon prepared to spew out more commands and invective, but the elevator doors closed between them. A moment later, Lehman was on his way to the balustrade.

Zimmer rounded the corner, gun poised in both hands, ready to shoot anything that moved.

There was nothing there. Nothing and no one. Not even a sign that anyone had ever been there.

Zimmer slowly released his breath. Had Gatwick been wrong? It seemed unlikely. But there was no one here. And no apparent means of egress . . .

Wait a minute. He took a step closer. There was a hatch in the floor.

He pulled the short hank of rope and lifted the lid. There was a ladder beneath, and as near as Zimmer could tell, the ladder went down at least two flights to the base of the staircase.

If the killer climbed down this ladder, he could easily join the crowd and make his escape. Or he could . . .

Zimmer whirled around.

The dark-skinned face leered at him, grinning in an exaggerated, grotesque manner, like a cat that has finally caught its elusive mouse.

"Surprise," the man said, and a second later, the butt of a high-powered rifle slammed into Zimmer's face.

Zimmer hit the floor immediately. The assailant had knocked a tooth out, bloodied his mouth, and dropped him to the ground, all with one unexpected blow.

So, Zimmer thought, his face to the concrete, *it comes down to this.* All that training. All that experience. So he could be taken out with one blow by a terrorist. He wasn't a hero. He was a loser.

Zimmer felt a boot in his gut, then he felt it again, then again. Consciousness was wavering.

"I wish I had more time to play with you," the man said in what sounded like a Russian accent. His face was alarmingly happy. "I enjoyed playing with your former leader. That went on for hours. But I do not have the time now. I must simply kill you and move on."

He flipped the rifle around and pressed the business end to Zimmer's neck. "Farewell, American pig. I will laugh as—"

He didn't get to finish his sentence. All at once, he lurched forward, face first. His rifle flew across the stairwell.

Through blurred eyes, Zimmer saw his boss, Carl Lehman, standing behind, fists clenched. *I must be hallucinating,* he thought.

"Don't bother getting up," Lehman said. He drew his handgun and pointed it. "The SWAT team is on its way. You can't escape. Don't make this—"

Like a flash of lightning, the assassin leaped forward and wrapped himself around Lehman's legs, knocking him sideways. Lehman fired, but the bullet went wide of its mark. He fired again just as his considerable bulk hit the concrete. The fall knocked the weapon out of his hands.

"Stupid old man," the killer snarled. "Are you so feeble you don't realize this is what I wanted all along? To kill another director of Homeland Security!" He crawled over Lehman, then brought a fist down hard on his face, flattening his nose. Blood spurted everywhere, including into the killer's face. He hit Lehman again. The blows rained down, fast and hard, pummeling Lehman's face. Lehman tried to resist, but he didn't have the strength. He was a punching bag, a tired old punching bag being terminated, and there was nothing he could do to stop it.

The assassin adjusted his aim to Lehman's solar plexus. Lehman felt as if his lungs were exploding. He couldn't catch a breath. He doubled over, trying to protect himself, but it was no use.

The next volley of blows went to the groin. Then the man rose and began kicking, shattering Lehman's knee with a single blow. The pain was excruciating. And just when Lehman thought he couldn't possibly bear any more, he felt the nose of his own handgun pressed against his neck.

"Your predecessor fought harder. He was much your superior. It took hours before he talked. In ten minutes, you would tell me everything you know. But I don't have ten minutes."

He pulled back the hammer. Lehman closed his eyes.

He heard the shattering report of a gun.

And then Lehman was shocked to find he could open his eyes. It took a moment for the thought to register: *I'm still alive!*

The assassin was crumpled on the concrete. Behind him, wobbling on his knees, was Agent Zimmer—holding the dead man's assault rifle.

"On your knees," Zimmer barked. The killer was wounded, but far from dead. "Hands behind your head."

The killer did not immediately respond. He seemed confused—perhaps dazed by the fall.

Down the stairwell, Zimmer detected the sound of many heavy footsteps.

"Hear that?" Zimmer barked. "That's the SWAT team coming to have their way with you. My advice is that you tell us everything we want to know, and then there's a chance, just a chance that one day, far in the future, you might possibly—" He broke off. *"No!"*

The sniper's hand had darted to his pants pocket, then a second later, to his mouth.

Zimmer rushed forward, but the killer rolled away before he could grab him. His body had become limp, as if someone had removed his spine. White foam spewed out of his mouth.

"Damn!" he shouted. "He's taken poison. Medic!"

Zimmer was vaguely aware that the SWAT team emerged and filled the space behind Director Lehman. The crisis had passed.

What a fool he'd been. He was never meant to be a hero. And he'd screwed it up. But fortunately, Lehman gave him the chance he needed to recover himself and finish the job.

The danger was over. The bad guy had been caught. The president was safe. The Secret Service had redeemed itself. He had redeemed himself. And somehow, he'd managed to remain alive.

That was good enough. For today, anyway.

55

U.S. SENATE CHAMBER

"... hat so long as we are a free nation, we have the right to retain and defend our freedom by any means that the people choose. We have heard the people; they have spoken. They have asked for this amendment. We do not, therefore, take anything away from the American public, but only give them what they want to protect what they already have. And to ensure that the heartrending outbursts of violence this nation has witnessed in recent days can never be repeated."

Ben rushed into the Senate chamber just as Senator Grayson finished his oratory. As he had arranged via text messages from the vice-president's assistant and the parliamentarian, Ben would be the next speaker, and the final speaker before the vote. The previous three speakers had all been in favor of the amendment, creating an oratorical roller-coaster ride that they planned to culminate with the words of the president's chosen advocate—Senator Ben Kincaid of Oklahoma.

"Thank you, Senator Grayson." The vice-president scanned his notes, as if there were any doubt in his mind about what was to happen next. "For our final speaker, the chair recognizes the senior senator from the state of Oklahoma."

Ben rose from the desk he had only recently arrived at and slowly walked toward the center of the chamber. "Thank you, Mr. President. I thank you for your evenhanded orchestration of this pivotal debate, and for the rare privilege of being the last to address this august assemblage of the finest elected officials this country has to offer."

And that concluded the sucking-up portion of his address. Not necessary, he knew, but it couldn't hurt. It remained to be seen whether, when Ben finished, he would still have any friends in this august assemblage.

"I have listened with great interest to all the opinions that have been expressed regarding this amendment. Even during my absence, I stayed in contact with television and summary reports from my chief of staff. There seem to be common themes emerging. Whether pro or con, virtually every speaker has referenced the tragedy of April nineteenth, or the murder of Senators Hammond and De-Mouy. This is not surprising. One of my good friends, Mike Morelli—who was almost killed on April nineteenth—recently reminded me that in the wake of 9/11, the powers-that-be repeatedly referred to that tragedy in the ensuing days to obtain passage of legislation or to secure reelection. In the wake of 9/11, we passed the Patriot Act, a measure that always stood on shaky constitutional ground and probably would not have survived had it come before the Supreme Court. But that wasn't enough. Illegal activities became rampant, including a multiyear program of domestic eavesdropping conducted by the NSA on orders from the White House, and a clearly unconstitutional policy of opening private mail without a warrant. Prisoners were detained indefinitely without being charged or given access to a lawyer. Torture techniques were condoned. All illegal, yet in those panicked years following 9/11, it happened. It seems that even now, there is no tragedy so great that someone will not exploit it for political advantage.

"There was much confusion about who was behind 9/11. We went to war against a nation we were told was involved—but in fact may have had little or no connection to the tragedy. Similarly, there has been much confusion about who was behind April nineteenth. No one was sure exactly who did it or why it was done, but we were all certain it was an act of terrorism and consequently, dire measures needed to be taken to prevent such terrorism in the future. Except—"

Ben let the mid-sentence pause linger, giving everyone a chance to wonder what exactly he was going to say next.

"Except," he repeated, "the massacre of April nineteenth did not originate with a foreign power. We now know it was orchestrated by the late Senator DeMouy, using cash-hungry sex traffickers as accomplices, in a cynical if not demented attempt to set himself up for a run at the presidency, using the tragedy as a platform to gain national exposure. What's more, we now know that Senator DeMouy's subsequent death had nothing to do with terrorists. To the contrary, in perhaps the ultimate moment of irony, this callous killer was himself murdered by his wife and his chief of staff—lovers trying to eliminate an unwanted spouse. What once seemed so large turns out to be very small indeed. The motivation that the president and others have given us for this sweeping change in the American way of life turns out to be misplaced. The real threat was within our borders all along."

Ben detected a stirring from the Republican side of the aisle. Even though he had not yet stated his position, those who were paying attention had begun to sense that this speech was not going where they expected.

"What can we learn from this? Does this prove that America will never face danger from terrorists? Obviously not. Can we say that America will never have any use for increased abilities to gather intelligence and prevent crime? No. But regardless of whether this legislation is desirable, we almost rushed into it to deter a threat that did not actually exist. You can discern the pattern as easily as I can—decisions made in haste, decisions made in the aftermath of tragedy, decisions based upon fear, are rarely sound ones. If we are to say farewell to fundamental American liberties this nation has enjoyed since its founding, perhaps that is a decision that should be made pursuant to cold, logical deliberation—based upon reason, not fear."

There were many perplexed expressions on both sides of the aisle. The secret was out now. He might as well declare himself.

"As you may have already surmised, I no longer favor passage of this bill. I announce this with considerable heaviness of heart. I know the president and others have counted on my support, but that is support that I can no longer give in good conscience. Even though I tried to deny it at the time, the fact is, I was swayed—misled, perhaps—by the horrible injuries suffered by my friend. He sacrificed himself for me, for his president, and I was desperate to ensure that a tragedy of that enormity could not happen again. I was willing to give up even more than our civil liberties—I almost traded my support of two measures that this country sorely needs to be strong, not militarily or defensively, but to ensure that this remains a land of opportunity for one and all."

As soon as Ben paused, Senator Keyes shot to his feet, obviously angry. "Will the senator from Oklahoma yield the floor?"

"I will not," Ben said firmly. "But I will promise that I won't talk much longer."

Keyes fumed. "Surely this turncoat doesn't think he has the right to monopolize the floor."

Ben smiled. "This turncoat believes he has the right to speak, and further believes that his entire talk will take considerably less than the hour and ten minutes that Senator Keyes spoke yesterday, so I don't really see that he has any grounds to complain."

Keyes persisted. "Will the senator yield for a question?"

"No, but I will pose this question to you, Senator Keyes. What are you so afraid of?"

Ben took a breath, paused, turned, then continued, before Keyes was tempted to answer his rhetorical question.

"What I think you and others are afraid of, Senator, is not foreign mercenaries or political demagogues, but the American people. Because people are inherently unpredictable—especially when they are free. They cannot be readily controlled. And that's what this bill is, ultimately. An attempt to gain more control over the rank-and-file citizen. That's understandable. If this episode has taught us anything, it's that we must always remain vigilant. Not just against terrorists—but against ourselves. We ourselves pose the only real threat to American democracy.

"I have changed my mind, or perhaps more accurately, returned to what I always deep down knew was right, honored the voice in my head that was trying to tell me I was making a mistake. I just wouldn't listen. I was working against instinct, against my heart, because I hoped to honor my dear friend. Today I plan to honor Mike by voting against this amendment that he, a prominent law enforcement officer, despises. And I hope that each and every one of you finds someone you can honor by ensuring that no matter what the future holds for them, they will never be stripped of their fundamental rights.

"I hope each of you will examine your own reasons for supporting this bill. If you are convinced this is the direction the nation should take—so be it. But if you are voting based upon fear, or panic, or to retain popularity or party favor—please don't. These are perilous times, unique in our national history. The greatest danger we face is not terrorists, but the thudding impact of unexamined certainty. Doubt is healthy. Doubt is evidence of thought. We no longer can afford knee-jerk reactions or politicians toeing the party line to comply with some parodistic idea of party dogma. Do we seriously believe that only Democrats care about the environment, poverty, and education? Or that only Republicans want America to have thriving businesses, a strong economy, and low taxes? Of course not. If there is one great truth that has emerged from this sordid incident, it's this: We are in this together. We stand or fall as one. We exist as a nation—or not at all."

Ben slowly returned to his desk, laid his hands flat upon it, then turned to deliver his final words.

His voice dropped to a whisper. "This is the United States of America, ladies and gentlemen. The United States of America." He paused, letting the full impact of his words sink in. "We stand for something. And God willing, we always shall."

It started slowly at first, just two hands pressed together on the far Democratic side of the floor. Then that clap found a partner somewhere on the opposite side. And before Ben knew it, the entire floor seemed to be applauding. He heard cheering from the press pit. Senators rose to their feet, one after the other. The gallery swayed with the impact of stomped feet, hooting and hollering. Even those Ben knew would still vote for the amendment were awarding him their respect.

He turned and, in the far rear of the chamber, saw Christina beaming at him. Which meant more to him than all the other accolades combined.

Five full minutes passed before the vice-president managed to restore order in the Senate chamber.

"Senators, we will now vote on the pending matter of Senate Bill 1451. The yeas and nays have been ordered. The clerk will call the name of each senator in alphabetical order. Respond with 'yes' if you favor passage of the bill, 'no' if you do not favor passage. The bill must obtain two-thirds of the votes cast in order to pass."

The clerk began, a solemn tone to his voice. "Mr. Abernathy . . ."

Abernathy, a third-term Democrat from Maine, rose to his feet. "Yes," he said firmly.

"Mr. Anderson?"

"Never."

"Mrs. Atkins?"

"I vote yes."

"Mr. Baum . . ."

56

Ben gazed, partly amused, partly dumbfounded, at the festive decor that had graced his office while he was out. Banners and crepe paper chains festooned the walls. Streamers dripped from the ceiling. A champagne station stood where there was normally a sofa. There were snacks of all kinds, healthy and not, and the guests included not only senators and their spouses but virtually everyone Ben could think of who had any connection to the proposed amendment—who was still speaking to him.

As always, Christina did excellent work.

"Impressive," Ben said as he admired the redecorated office. "But this is a party. Shouldn't it be a funeral?"

Christina arched an eyebrow. "How do you figure?"

"The amendment died."

"Yes, but the country survived."

Ben was impressed by the wide array of visitors Christina had ensnared—not only a dozen members of the Senate, but people from the House, the Secret Service, Homeland Security, the FBI, the NSA—and a lot of people Ben couldn't place because he had no idea who they were.

"What did you do?" Ben asked. "Promise them my vote?"

"I'm not sure how many people that would bring in," Christina said evenly, "but the free champagne worked wonders. Truth is, after the ordeal of these past few weeks, I think most everyone was looking for a place to blow off steam. Some people, of course, have families and spouses to handle that sort of thing. The rest are here."

"Any chance the president will be dropping by?"

Christina squirmed. "Well, under the circumstances . . . I think it's unlikely."

"You tried, didn't you?"

She grinned sheepishly. "His secretary indicated that he wasn't taking your calls. Ever."

Ben sighed. "Well. That's politics. Is Loving here?"

Christina shook her head. "I forced him to go to the hospital. Against his will, natch. He acts as if he's fine. But I think his . . . experiences with the General really shook him up."

"Are his wounds healing?"

"Yes. I was actually more concerned about . . . his mental state. He went through a lot. Sounded horrible—and I'm betting he didn't tell me everything."

"He'll bounce back. He always does."

Christina's eyes lowered. "I hope so," she said quietly.

Ben had thought he was staying well on the sidelines, out of the general view, but that didn't prevent the new minority leader, Nancy Caldwell, from tracking him down.

"Ben, please—don't tease me any longer."

As Ben gazed at the attractive blond senator from Vermont, he was very aware of Christina's eyes bearing down on him. "I'm not sure what you mean."

"I'm talking about this protracted dithering about whether you're going to run for reelection. Surely now you realize that you have no choice."

The heat radiating from Christina's eyes intensified. "Oh, I'm fairly sure I have a choice."

"No, you don't. Ben, we need you. We only have a hairsbreadth plurality. We can't afford to give a seat away."

"You don't know that I would win. I think I'd be a terrible campaigner. I know I'd hate it."

"I'm not sure you'd have to do anything. Your approval ratings are off the charts. The folks back home seem to think you're some sort of hero—and I'm not just talking about Oklahoma, either."

"People have short memories."

"True enough. But look what you've managed to do in a short period of time. You're one of our party's top leaders."

"Oh, hardly that."

"You've led two major political initiatives."

"Yes, and both times on the side of the Republicans."

"Which proves you're a centrist. Very good campaign fodder."

"And the proposed amendment failed."

"Because you wanted it to."

"I don't think I'm the only person in the Senate who was having doubts. Many were probably looking for a good excuse to change their minds. And I gave it to them."

"Put it any way you like—you turned the tide." She stepped closer. "Seriously, Ben—we need you. The party needs you. The country needs you. But if you're not going to run, we should start grooming an alternative. When can I expect an answer?"

Ben glanced at Christina. "You'll know something . . . just as soon as I do."

Caldwell nodded, then quickly ducked close to Christina's ear. She whispered, but not so softly that Ben couldn't hear, "Spouses sometimes have a little influence. Talk him into it. He could make a real difference."

Christina smiled. "No promises. But we'll talk about it."

Caldwell drifted toward the champagne. A few minutes later, Ben spotted Secret Service Agent Max Zimmer entering with Deputy Director Nichole Muldoon.

"The hero of the Baltimore affair," Ben noted quietly. "Are they dating?"

"Haven't heard," Christina replied.

Which Ben assumed meant they were not. "Just as well. She's technically his boss, isn't she?"

"Technically. Of course, Lehman runs the show. Now that he's out of the hospital."

The two approached Ben, smiling. Zimmer's face was still bruised a dark purple in several places. Collateral damage from stopping an assassin, Ben assumed.

"Senator Kincaid," Zimmer said, nodding. "I want to congratulate you on that fine speech you made in the Senate."

"Were you there?"

"No, but they've been playing it over and over again on all the cable news stations. Practically a repeating loop. You're getting tons of publicity, all of it good."

"Well . . ."

"I for one am glad the amendment is dead and buried."

"That goes for me, too," Muldoon echoed. "So congratulations."

"I think I should be congratulating you, Max," Ben replied. "You saved the day in Baltimore."

"We did our jobs. We were ready for him."

Muldoon explained, "When we realized we couldn't talk the president out of this foolhardy appearance, we decided to use it to flush out the killer. We left a path open for him—then closed it up behind him as soon as he went into action." She paused. "That man was just as smart as he was deadly. He always seemed to be one step ahead of us. Always knew what we were doing before we did. Always had a contingency. Like that little trick with the hidden floor panel."

"I didn't, obviously," Zimmer said, chuckling. "If Deputy Director Muldoon hadn't been watching, and Director Lehman hadn't intervened, I'd be so much oatmeal." He looked at her with an expression that Ben thought expressed more than mere thanks. "Thank God you two were there."

"I'd like to echo that sentiment, if I may."

Ben turned and saw FBI Agent Joel Salter approaching.

Muldoon arched an eyebrow. "Now this is a surprise."

"No doubt, given the sulky, petulant way I've been acting ever since I got the Homeland Security liaison detail."

"Oh, you exaggerate."

"No, I've been petty and small and stupid. To be honest—you intimidate me, Nichole. More than just a little."

She pressed a hand against her ample bosom. "Who, me?"

"Yeah, you. I may be stupid—but I'm not blind. In Baltimore, you showed me what you really are—a hero. If you don't mind, I'd like to shake your hand."

"I would be honored," Muldoon said, extending hers.

"The honor is mine."

Something was bothering Ben as he observed this moment of reconciliation. Something that he had heard since he left the Senate chamber, or seen, or—

Something. But he couldn't place it. He'd had this sensation before: the nagging feeling that there was something he was missing, something on the tip of his brain that he just hadn't processed yet. It was irritating, not only because it reminded him how slow-witted he could be, but because he knew he would obsess over it for hours on end until—

Until he remembered.

"Oh my God," he said sotto voce. "Oh no."

Christina laid a hand on his arm. "What is it?"

Ben's face went white. "I think I've made a terrible mistake. I think we all have."

"Ben, what are you talking about?"

Without explanation, Ben moved toward the door. "Thanks for the party, Chris—but I've got to get out of here."

Christina dogged his heels. "To go where?"

"To have a little talk with the director of Homeland Security."

"I'm not sure he'll see you."

"I don't plan to give him any choice. He's got some serious explaining to do."

"Ben, the amendment controversy is over. It's dead and buried."

"This has nothing to do with the amendment." He threw on his jacket. "This has to do with murder."

"Ben, what's going on?"

"No time to explain." He kissed her on the cheek, then raced out the door.

"Ben, don't you dare run off without telling me—"

But before she could even finish the threat, he was across the hallway and down the stairs.

"Damn," she muttered under her breath. She walked angrily back to the party. "I hate it when he does that."

57

DEPARTMENT OF HOMELAND SECURITY
OFFICE OF THE DIRECTOR
WASHINGTON, D.C.

"Thank you for seeing me," Ben said as he entered Carl Lehman's office. "I appreciate it. I . . . wasn't sure what to expect."

Lehman stood and shook his hand. His face was bandaged and bruised, but mostly functional. "I'm not one to hold grudges, son. The amendment is dead. Time to move on."

"That . . . wasn't exactly what I meant."

"Oh?" He pointed to a nearby chair. "Please take a seat."

"Thanks, but I'd rather stand, if you don't mind. I think better on my feet." Which was true, he had learned over the years. And right now, he really needed to be able to think.

"What's the problem?"

"My problem is . . ." Ben took a deep breath. "I saw your assistant, Nichole Muldoon, a little while ago."

"Why is that a problem? She give you one of those patented I-can-see-through-your-clothes looks of hers?"

"No. But she said something. She reminded me how much inside information the sniper seemed to have, during both attacks. Even if you assume he tortured some information out of your predecessor, he was still uncommonly knowledgeable about Secret Service procedures. Who would be doing what and when. Where the security detail would be stationed. How to find the sniper nest he eliminated. How to plan an escape route. We've always said he needed inside information."

"He was working with Senator DeMouy."

"And I'm sure that was helpful, but in the end, I don't think the assistance of a politician would cut it. He had access to information he could only have gotten from someone working in or with the Secret Service. That's the only way he could have gotten as far as he did."

Lehman leaned slowly forward. "What are you saying?"

Ben began to pace. "I've always been troubled by the suggestion that Senator DeMouy masterminded the attacks. Did he really have the know-how? Would his co-conspirators have continued with the plan after his death? Doesn't make any sense. And to imagine that he did all this just to position himself for the White House? Troubling."

Lehman batted his lips with his index finger. "I'll admit, I've had difficulty with that part of it myself. But I assumed there was more to it that we hadn't uncovered yet."

"Did you?" Ben asked, staring at him intently. "Did you really?"

"What's that supposed to mean?"

This was where it was likely to get sticky. In Ben's experience, people rarely liked being accused of murder. Especially if they were guilty.

"If this wasn't about stacking the deck at the next presidential election, what was it about? Wanton violence? Seems too well planned. Regime change? Nah. Grudge against Emily Blake? I considered that, especially when I learned what everyone else in Washington apparently already knew, that she was having an affair. But I couldn't believe anyone would arrange a major assassination attempt and kill all those people just to eliminate the first lady. The person who orchestrated the attacks in Oklahoma City and Baltimore was seriously trying to stir up terror—to make the American people feel weak and poorly defended. Vulnerable."

Lehman was squinting, as if his difficulty understanding translated into difficulty seeing. "Who would want to do that?"

"Isn't it obvious?"

"No, it isn't."

"The only person who would benefit from instilling terror—is someone who really wanted that constitutional amendment to pass."

If Ben were hoping for a big reaction, or perhaps a confession, he was disappointed. "Nah," Lehman said succinctly.

"Excuse me?"

Lehman shrugged. "Doesn't make any sense. Don't you remember? The president didn't propose the amendment until after Oklahoma City."

"That doesn't mean someone couldn't have already dreamed it up. And staged Oklahoma City to get it on the agenda and to ensure its passage."

"But who would do such a thing?"

"Who benefits most?" Ben said. He stopped pacing and hovered over Lehman's desk. "I would say the person who becomes the chair of the Emergency Council. The person who leads the small committee that has the ability to give and take fundamental human rights as they unilaterally see fit." Ben paused. "And that would be the director of Homeland Security. You."

Lehman went bug-eyed. "Are you kidding? Me?"

"What's so incredible? You have the experience, the knowledge. The inside information."

"I've been a devoted public servant for more than three decades. I've given my entire life to law enforcement."

"And no doubt have been frustrated by what you perceived as law enforcement's inadequate powers."

"That's absurd."

"Is it?" Ben leaned closer. "I'm remembering something the president told me. After April nineteenth, he was obviously in a state of shock from having lost his wife in such a violent manner. He was very subject to influence. Malleable. An easy target for someone with a private agenda. And he told me that the idea for the proposed amendment had actually come—from you."

Lehman raised his head. "That's true. . . ."

"This whole thing has been an insane power grab concocted in your sick mind to—"

". . . but the idea didn't originate with me."

Ben stopped short. "It didn't?"

"No. It was suggested to me." He drew himself up. "And I think I can prove it."

58

DEPARTMENT OF HOMELAND SECURITY
WASHINGTON, D.C.

Ben was pleased to see she was already in the computer room. That would make this ever so much simpler.

"Deputy Director Muldoon?"

She turned and greeted him. Her blouse was unbuttoned at least two buttons below what Ben might've expected from a deputy director, but he was not one to criticize. "Please call me Nichole, Senator. I got your message. How can I help you?"

Ben glanced over his shoulder before answering. "Nichole, what I'm about to tell you is extremely confidential. Can I trust you to keep this to yourself?"

She nodded. "The Department of Homeland Security is subject to congressional supervision. If a distinguished member of the Senate gives me an instruction, I'm honor bound to take it, unless it conflicts with other duties."

"This won't," Ben replied. "Far from it. Nichole, you know that for some time many people have suspected the Oklahoma City as-sassins had inside information. I have reason to believe that infor-mation came from this department." He took another deep breath. "From Director Lehman."

"What?"

"You heard me. Even when he was deputy director, before Mar-shall was killed, he was one of the few people with the access and in-formation to pull this off."

"I don't believe it."

"Think. Whose idea was it in the first place?"

"President Blake's?"

"No. Blake got the idea from Lehman."

Muldoon's eyes fairly bulged. "Have you told him about your suspicions?"

"I just confronted him, yes. Problem is, he says the idea didn't originate with him. He says he just took credit for it, but it origi-nated with someone else in the department."

"Who?"

"He claims he doesn't recall. That it came in an in-house e-mail."

"And you believe that?"

Ben smiled thinly. "It doesn't matter what I believe. It's easy enough to prove or disprove. If there was an e-mail, it can be traced. We just need to get into the building's Internet server and search all Lehman's e-mail. As you probably know, even if a mes-sage is deleted from a computer, it remains on the server until it is erased."

"And you contacted me—?"

"Because Lehman told me that you oversee the in-house com-puter network. And I certainly can't ask him to do it." He took a step forward. "I need your help. Can you find that e-mail? If it ex-ists?"

"Of course," she answered. "It isn't hard. I'll get my tech staff on it immediately. I doubt if it exists—but if it does, we'll find it, and then we'll figure out who sent it."

"Nichole, I need this as soon as possible."

"Understood. It should be locatable employing some obvious and unique search terms. We'll crack open the server and get right back to you." She glanced at her watch. "Want to meet me again in an hour?"

"That would be great. I'll be in the second-floor interrogation room waiting for you." He paused. "Thank you for your help. If Lehman has been orchestrating this conspiracy, there's no way of knowing what he might plan next. Too many people have already died."

"Agreed. I'll get right on it."

"Thank you," Ben said, barely above a whisper. "The future of this entire nation may depend on you."

Fifty minutes later, Nichole Muldoon walked briskly into the second-floor interrogation room.

"Bad news," she said, before Ben had a chance to ask. "Or good news, depending upon your current operating theory. There's no e-mail."

Ben rose to his feet. "You're certain?"

"I've got the best people in the business. They checked and double-checked. It was an easy search to run. We scanned for references to a constitutional amendment prior to the presidential press conference when Blake announced it. Nothing."

"Lehman didn't get an e-mail giving him the idea?"

"I'm certain he didn't. We ran several searches. Even if it was initially proposed in some form other than an amendment, we would have found it. It just isn't there." She glanced at the door, as if paranoid that someone might be listening. "Does this mean it really was Lehman's idea? Why would he lie about that?" Her hand flew to her mouth. "Oh my God. Unless he really is guilty. Unless he is the mastermind behind the assassination attempts." She almost fell into the nearest chair. "It was him!"

Ben glanced across at her calmly. "No."

It took a moment for his response to register. "I . . . don't understand."

"It wasn't Lehman."

"But I thought you said—"

"I might have misled you a bit, Nichole. Sorry about that. But then—you flat-out lied to me, didn't you?"

"I—don't follow—"

"You didn't call in any tech help—because you didn't need it and you didn't want any witnesses. And you didn't invade the Internet server so you could find the e-mail. You did it so you could delete it."

"Have you lost your mind?"

"I don't think so," Ben said, slowly moving toward her end of the table. "Although there are some who might disagree."

"I'm telling you, the e-mail isn't there. Search for yourself."

"Oh, I don't doubt that it's gone now. But it was very much present two hours ago when Carl Lehman and I opened up the server and searched for it. Wanna see a copy?"

Muldoon blinked rapidly several times. "You set me up!"

"Yes, and so successfully, too. Maybe I have a future in politics after all."

She looked at him sternly. "I don't know what game you're playing, but I don't know anything about any e-mail."

"Please, Nichole—don't waste your breath. I have a copy. And we've traced it back to your desktop computer."

"Someone else must've done it while I was out of my office."

"We figured you'd claim that, which is why I set up this little charade. If you knew nothing about the e-mail and weren't responsible for sending it to Lehman, why did you delete it? And we can prove that you deleted it. By comparing mirrors of the server before you opened it and after. That constitutional amendment was your idea—your power grab. You were the brains behind the attacks in Oklahoma City and Baltimore."

"You're insane."

"No, I'm right, and we both know it. So why don't you stop playing games? It's just us two in here, after all."

"You're wearing a wire."

"I'm not."

Which didn't stop her from patting him down, quite thoroughly. If Ben weren't a married man, he might've enjoyed it.

"All right," Muldoon said, an expression on her face that Ben wasn't sure about. Was it supposed to be flirtatious? Alluring? Or threatening? He finally decided it was all of the above. "Let's just pretend for a moment that I masterminded those attacks. How did I do it?"

"Oh, I think it would be easy enough for someone as deeply entrenched in the world of crime as you are. Someone so knowledgeable about terrorist cells, who they are, what they can do. It wouldn't be hard for you to find some half-baked, broken-down, wannabe, sex-trading terrorist cell with a decent sharpshooter and torturer. Nor would it be hard to bend them to your will, not with your ability to float departmental funds to them, or to threaten them with prosecution, or to erase their records, or to arrange for them to be granted citizenship. I'll bet they were putty in your hands."

"Such a clever idea. But why would I want to do such a thing?"

"To get your amendment passed," Ben answered. "Oklahoma City was to get it on the national agenda. Baltimore was to make sure it passed—and to get rid of Lehman, so you would become the natural choice to take his place. You set him up—baited him into a foolish attempt to save Agent Zimmer's life, then probably radioed your accomplice and told him Lehman was coming. That part of your plan fell through, thanks to Agent Zimmer's enormous resourcefulness, but no matter. There would undoubtedly be other opportunities to knock Lehman off."

"And I did all this to get an amendment passed?" she asked quizzically, eyebrows darting.

"It is your brainchild, after all. You let Lehman, then the president, take credit for it. All the better—deflect suspicion from yourself. Attract no attention, while quietly making yourself the most powerful person in the world."

"Oh, please."

"It's a fact. The president may be the leader of the free world now, but as soon as the Emergency Security Council declares a state of emergency, they become much more powerful. They obtain the right to remove basic American rights and privileges. The president can't do that. Neither can anyone else. Sure, you've got a committee, but there are only six people on it, and you've demonstrated repeatedly that you are very skilled at manipulating others. Especially men. And most or all of the other committee members were likely to be men. You'd smile that smile and unbutton your blouse and they'd give you whatever you wanted. You'd control law enforcement, plus you would no longer be bound by any constitutional restrictions. You, pure and simple, would be the most important, most powerful person in the nation. You could do anything you wanted to do."

"But only as long as the emergency state continued."

"And I have no doubt you could keep it going for a very long time, if not forever, by issuing Orange Alerts or alleging that someone has weapons of mass destruction, or staging an assassination attempt—whatever it took. You're a clever woman. You'd find a way."

She stared at him, her eyes growing gray. "Maybe the country would be better off."

"Tell it to the people who died in Oklahoma City. Or Director Marshall or Senator Hammond. You must've been stunned when your henchman Senator DeMouy was murdered by his wife and her lover. But as always, you rose to the occasion. You realized that it helped you. You had no motive to kill him. All the murder did was silence a possible leak. You obviously didn't care how many people died—just so your precious amendment passed." He paused, then looked directly into her eyes. "Was your need for power so great that people had to die for it?"

Her nostrils flared. Her rosy face began to pale with anger. "You're so pious. So self-righteous. Of course, you wanted the amendment too, before you lost your nerve and killed it. But now you want me to take the blame for trying to make this nation stronger."

"You mean, for trying to make yourself stronger."

"No, I don't! Have you read anything about Rome?"

"I've heard this lame analogy before."

"It's a fact, Kincaid—America is dying. Can you seriously doubt it? Look around you. Crime everywhere. People getting dumber, not smarter. More violent, not more enlightened. More selfish. More desperate to be constantly entertained. And we face threats of a magnitude such as this nation has never seen before. Make no mistake—the barbarian hordes are banging at our gates. One well-placed coordinated attack could bring this nation to its knees—and they have the money and the determination to do it. What chance do we have? Namby-pamby do-gooders like you aren't going to save us. The only hope we have rests with people willing to fight for our freedom. People willing to take whatever steps are necessary to ensure our safety."

"By eliminating every constitutional right we have."

"If necessary, yes!" Muldoon said indignantly. "Good God, what business do we have monkeying around with search and seizure laws when the barbarians have nuclear weapons? Do you think they care about constitutional rights? Hell, no. They use them against us! They count on them to handicap us. They depend on our inability to arrest without cause or to search without a warrant or to restrict their speech or their ability to assemble. They think we're weak-willed fools. And they're right. What would you rather have— freedom of speech or freedom to live with some terrorist regime threatening to kill you at any moment?"

"You killed fourteen people. I'm betting you planted the bomb on the presidential limo while it was still at the airport." He paused. "The bomb that almost killed my best friend."

"How many died on 9/11, huh? How many others have died in terrorist attacks all around the world? Are we just going to sit on our butts and take this? Or are we going to do something about it?" She was breathing rapidly, heaving. "Well, damn me if you will, but I tried to do something about it. I refuse to play prisoner to those bastards."

"Except," Ben said, "your amendment would've made us all prisoners. Just a different kind. Instead of being caged by terrorists, we'd be caged by ourselves. By our own government."

"Isn't that better?"

"I prefer to remain free."

"At what cost?"

"Look—if you really wanted power, if you wanted to take on the terrorists, why didn't you run for political office? Maybe even the presidency?"

"That might work for an ass like Blake, but I could never be elected."

"I've been telling people for weeks now that I could never be elected. But the truth is—you just don't know."

"I do know. I'm unelectable. I'm pretty, smart, sexy, single, and female. No man would ever vote for me. They might all want to screw me, but they won't vote for me. If I want power—if I want to be in a position to save this nation from itself—I have to go about it another way."

"By killing innocent people."

Her jaw tightened. She stepped toward him, her eyes on fire. "You know, I've had about as much of your indignant twaddle as I'm going to take, you—"

"If you're about to threaten me, don't."

"You think I won't hurt you because you're a senator?"

"I'm quite certain you would. But you can't."

"I don't need to kill a pip-squeak like you. That e-mail doesn't prove anything. And as you may have noticed, my enemies have a habit of disappearing. Just when you least expect it. Maybe when you're walking to work, or strolling in the park, or out on a picnic with that pretty new wife of yours. Maybe I'll take her out, too. Two birds with one stone."

This time, Ben's jaw clenched.

"I know lots of people," she continued. "Dangerous people. I can take you out anytime I want. And if you breathe a word of this conversation to anyone, I'll deny it. I'll deny we even spoke."

"I'm afraid that ship has sailed."

"What do you mean?"

"Agent Zimmer will back me up."

"Zimmer?" She laughed right in Ben's face. "Zimmer is so desperate to get in my pants, he'd do anything for me."

"That may have changed."

"What's that supposed to mean?"

Ben tilted his head backward. "He's watching. On the other side of the one-way mirror."

Her face froze as solid as a stone.

"Why did you think I asked to meet you in the interrogation room? Honestly, for someone who thinks she's so smart and sexy—well, I suppose you are fairly sexy. Speaking objectively, of course. I'm not really turned on by cold-blooded killers."

She turned toward the mirror. "You're bluffing."

"No, I'm not. I've been in the courtroom enough to know that the e-mail probably isn't enough to get a conviction, so I decided to try for a confession."

"But—this room isn't wired for sound. I wouldn't have spoken if there was any chance you were recording."

"I don't have to record." Ben smiled. "Agent Zimmer reads lips."

"You son of a—" Her hand darted inside her jacket.

"Please don't bother pulling your weapon. These walls are bulletproof. You can't get Zimmer. And I doubt if you want to execute me with him watching."

"You—you—"

Ben heard the pounding of footsteps. "Sounds as if the troops are coming. I guess that means Zimmer and Lehman think they have enough." Ben observed her shocked expression. "You know what the saddest thing about all this is? I think you genuinely believe you were doing what's right for the country. You're crazy and delusional, but in your mind, you think you're a patriot."

"Last w-week," she stuttered, "you were a patriot favoring the amendment, too."

"Which only goes to show how easy it is to lose perspective. To self-delude. But I was lucky. I have friends, people who care about me, people I can talk to. Even after I lost myself, they helped me find my way back. But you were all alone, isolated, stewing in your sick, scheming, monomaniacal, psychotic mind. And you went too far. Much too far."

The door opened and a stream of armed agents rushed in. One

grabbed Muldoon's wrists and cuffed her; another began reading her Miranda rights.

"You went over the edge. You hurt people. Killed people. But the saddest thing is—you didn't do it because you didn't care." Ben started for the door. "You did it because you cared too much."

59

ARLINGTON NATIONAL CEMETERY
WASHINGTON, D.C.

Ben and Christina strolled through the cemetery after leaving the funeral for the Secret Service agent killed in Baltimore. More civilian graves in Arlington, more death arising from this national crisis. A crisis that was finally over. He just hoped that he—and everyone else in this town—had learned something from it. But how could you know? How could you ever be sure?

On their way out, they stopped at the Eternal Flame. As many times as he had been here, it still gave him a catch in his throat. He remembered little John-John—he, too, now gone—saluting his father's casket. Kennedy had so much promise, promise tragically cut short before it was realized. So many men had come to this town to change the world. And all too often their dreams did not become reality. The world was not changed. Or the changes were not for the better.

Ben was still staring at the flame as Christina curled up beside him and snuggled against his arm. "You know how you can tell the Union graves from the Confederate graves?"

Ben blinked, breaking out of his reverie. "No idea."

"The Confederate grave markers are pointed at the top."

"Why?"

"So those damned Yankees won't sit on them."

Ben smiled, then squinted. A tall, shimmering figure in black was making its way up the path he had just traveled. "Am I wrong, or is that Nancy Caldwell approaching in the distance?"

"She wants an answer, Ben. You've stalled her too long. She needs to know who the Democratic candidate for Oklahoma's senatorial seat is going to be."

"Political office," Ben mused. "Power. The chance to change the nation. Maybe the world. That's what brought this crisis down upon us, ultimately. And so much death."

"Very philosophical. But I think she just wants to know if you're going to run."

Ben turned to face her. "I am going to run . . ." He smiled again, then hugged Christina tightly. "Away."

"Excuse me?"

"I'm going to run away with a beautiful woman."

Christina arched an eyebrow. "Anyone I know?"

"Definitely." He reached inside his jacket. "Two tickets to Paris. Two weeks of a too-long-delayed honeymoon. What do you think?"

"I think you can't afford it."

"But we're going anyway."

"Seriously?"

He nodded.

"You're really finally taking me to France?"

Still nodding.

"I can't be positive," Christina said, "but I'm pretty sure this is one of the first signs of the Apocalypse."

"If you're going to be that way about it, the tickets are refundable."

"Don't you dare." She snuggled closer. "My hero." A moment later, she added, "But you're going to have to give Caldwell an answer. Soon."

"All the more reason we should take a long, restful vacation."

"Why is that?"

He looked deeply into her eyes. "Because when we get back, darling—we're running for reelection."

About the Author

WILLIAM BERNHARDT is the author of many novels, including *Primary Justice, Murder One, Criminal Intent, Death Row, Hate Crime, Dark Eye, Capitol Murder,* and *Capitol Threat.* He has twice won the Oklahoma Book Award for Best Fiction, and also received the H. Louise Cobb Distinguished Author Award "in recognition of an outstanding body of work in which we understand ourselves and American society at large." A former trial attorney, Bernhardt has received several awards for his public service. He lives in Tulsa with his three children, and readers can e-mail him at wb@williambernhardt.com or visit his website at www.williambernhardt.com.

ABOUT THE TYPE

This book was set in Sabon, a typeface designed by
the well-known German typographer Jan Tschichold (1902–74). Sabon's design is based upon the
original letter forms of Claude Garamond and was
created specifically to be used for three sources:
foundry type for hand composition, Linotype, and
Monotype. Tschichold named his typeface for the
famous Frankfurt typefounder Jacques Sabon,
who died in 1580.